DON'T LOOK NOW

"With plenty of possible suspects, Burton's latest will appeal to readers who want light romance and heavy suspense."

—Library Journal

BURN YOU TWICE

"Burton does a good job balancing gentle romance with high-tension suspense."

—Publishers Weekly

"Scorching action. The twists and turns keep the reader on the edge of their seat as they will not want to put the novel down."

—Crimespree Magazine

HIDE AND SEEK

"Burton delivers an irresistible, tension-filled plot with plenty of twists . . . Lovers of romantic thrillers won't be disappointed."

—Publishers Weekly

CUT AND RUN

"Burton can always be counted on for her smart heroines and tightly woven plots."

—For the Love of Books

"Must-read romantic suspense . . . Burton is a bona fide suspense superstar. And her books may be peppered with enough twists and turns to give you whiplash, but the simmering romance she builds makes for such a compelling, well-rounded story."

—USA Today's Happy Ever After

THE LIES I TOLD

THE LIES I TOLD

MARY BURTON

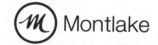 Montlake

Text copyright © 2022 by Mary Burton

Published by Montlake, Seattle

www.apub.com

Amazon, the Amazon logo, and Montlake are trademarks of Amazon.com, Inc., or its affiliates.

ISBN-13: 9781542032636
ISBN-10: 1542032636

Cover design by Caroline Teagle Johnson

Printed in the United States of America

Truth is the ultimate power.

When the truth comes around,

all the lies have to run and hide.

—*Ice Cube*

1

Him

The dead were always watching. And they did speak to us, though we rarely noticed.

Normally, the dead didn't bother me, but the night was cold, dark, and raining, and I was anxious as I gripped a coiled art show flyer and got out of my car. A light drizzle fell, and an uneasiness had piggy-backed onto my bones with the cold. I was tempted to go home and ignore you. Sane men don't chase the dead.

But when it comes to you, I'm not reasonable—never have been. So I returned to J.J.'s Pub, a corner, brick building with tall display windows and crimson-red front doors. Inside the vestibule, I unrolled the handbill, coiled tighter than a clock spring, and confirmed that I'd not lost my mind. You were still staring, smiling.

Your red hair swooped around your shoulders like a curtain and framed a face as pale as ivory. Once you had reminded me of an

Irish sprite, plucked straight out of Dublin, but now I saw you were Persephone, back from the underworld.

Your gaze held me, reached out, and the longer I studied the ironic humor swimming in those sapphire eyes, the more I remembered our intimate history and shared losses.

A rational mind wouldn't be lured by the dead or revisit a dangerous past. *Turn, leave, and slam the door shut on yesterday.*

But this pull between us transcends life and death. And this time I was not going to repeat old mistakes. The past doesn't have to equal the future. Eyes forward.

I pushed through the bar's doors, chased in by cold air that lingered at my heels, and shook off raindrops dripping from my jacket. The sounds of piped jazz horns mingled with warmth, laughter, and the smells of beer and french fries. I wasn't here for the art, food, ambience, or company. Just for you. I needed to see if you were really you. Honestly, I hoped you weren't, that it was a mistake. I'd spent too many years imagining your face, your smile, the way your eyes closed forever so long ago. I was afraid seeing a knockoff version would only taint my memories. I hoped whoever you were, you'd be ugly, fat, and easy to forget.

The bar was divided into two sections: the main room filled with round café tables and then, off to the side, a sort of annex. There was no one in the main room, but the smaller room held at least a dozen people, and laughter and conversation drifted from it.

J.J.'s Pub's back room, the gallery tonight, was certainly not Met worthy. A lesser artist might have turned down the space and waited for a better opportunity. But not you. You wanted the world to see the images that rattled in your mind and haunted me.

Outside the room was a sign that read EXHIBIT. Your picture was not on it. Disappointed, I wondered whether the dead were playing tricks with me again. They'd done this so often that I usually recognized their trickery. I should have just left, but I was still too curious. *Please be old and gray.* The young and youthful version of you was enshrined in my memory, and I wanted to keep it that way.

A sane man . . .

I brushed the last of the raindrops off my coat and moved toward the room. The space was small, with a low ceiling pitted with pot lights spilling pools of light onto a black-and-white tiled floor. There were no small tables in this space, and the chairs rimmed one wall. This setup gave any visitor a clear view of two dozen black-and-white pictures hanging on the walls, ghosted by the faint impressions of artwork that had hung here before.

On a round table by the door was another flyer, featuring several more images from your show. A makeshift catalog of sorts. The photos were moody, and the shades of gray captured the jagged rocks of the James River. A fast current splashed ragged, jutting boulders, and the combined effect suggested trouble and violence.

The last memory I held of you was on that rocky shoreline, and it still warmed me. You were laughing, a bit drunk, wild eyed, and begging me to kiss you. I still dream of pressing your body against the warm hood of my car on that cold day. Your body was so responsive, eager, desperate almost.

A laugh rose above the din of conversation, and it jerked me back to now. I looked over, and I saw you standing with your back to the wall as you talked to two men. Your smile was as bright as I remembered. Your hair remained a tumble of red curls, and a hint of freckles still sprinkled your nose. A black V-neck blouse dipped between full breasts and skimmed a flat belly before vanishing into faded jeans hugging narrow hips.

I stared, wondering whether you were real. The dead are clever and can play with a man's mind. They don't care about feelings or the living's need to get on with their lives. It's jealousy, I suppose: they can't live, so neither can you.

But as you moved among the living, it was clear they all saw you. They talked to you, laughed, smiled. You weren't a figment of my imagination. You were very real. Perfect.

Tightness clutched my chest. I felt suddenly both thrilled and sorry I had come. My grainy memories, replayed too often, were now faded and lackluster. Suddenly they wouldn't do anymore. Seeing you in the flesh had made them obsolete.

I'd never expected to see you again, beyond dreams and fantasies. And yet here you were, flesh and blood, twenty feet away. My system heated as my thoughts raced and collided. An overload was coming. Never a good thing. I pivoted toward the door.

Outside, I looked at the grainy image of your face. I'd thought I had never forgotten one detail about you. But now I saw time had degraded my memory. Dorothy in *The Wizard of Oz* had jumped from black and white to Technicolor.

2

MARISA

"Happy birthday to us, Clare." The Stockton twins had hit the big three-oh. The last thirty years had been rough for me, and it was a minor miracle I was here. But it was bittersweet: I wasn't the twin who'd been murdered thirteen years ago.

Perhaps that was why our older sister, Brit, believed celebrating our thirtieth birthday in style was imperative. Another decade bit the dust. We, or at least I, had officially grown up.

Despite several noes from me about a party, Brit had indicated that she'd already invited our high school friends, ordered our favorite cake, and chosen blue balloons—our favorite. No clowns, she swore with a smile. (We never liked clowns.) It would be fun, she said. Good to celebrate this milestone.

When Brit's talking points didn't sway me, she reminded me, as any good sister would, "You're lucky to be alive."

The comment cut deep and robbed me of a response.

"We were all worried about you after the accident in January," she said. "Refusing is basically selfish."

Selfish was a word Brit had aimed my way a lot over the years: I spent too much time squandering a life you never had. The truth pissed me off, and she knew it. I said yes to the party.

The party was being held at J.J.'s Pub, which was within walking distance of my apartment. J.J.'s Pub was a somebody-might-know-your-name kind of place that served killer fries and tall, cold brews. It was also owned by Jack Dutton, my high school drug buddy. We were both clean now, but back in the day . . .

My sister's choice of venues was strategic. Not only was she tossing her high school boyfriend Jack some business, but she knew I'd always show up for J.J.'s Pub fries, even on birthdays that felt like a loss, not a win.

The restaurant's dim light created sharp shadows, brightened only by soft pot lights and flickering table candles. The music was classic jazz piano and horns. Hard to believe I'd had an art show here two months ago. Felt like a lifetime now.

I walked up to the bar and ordered two shots of tequila. The bar was full tonight. Not a surprise on a Friday that was one of the first warmish evenings Richmond had seen this year.

The bartender, Chip, wore a light-blue collared shirt, khakis, and an eager grin. He was a prep who looked like he had driven too far east on I-64 and missed all the suburban exits.

Chip set up the shot glasses and filled each with a generous pour. He had flair—there was more than met the eye to the Boy Scout who had clearly heard about my birthday ritual. I settled on a barstool, knowing I'd have to make my way to the banquet room soon or Brit would hunt me down.

I glanced around at customers who were as prone to wearing suits and ties as they were torn jeans and graphic T-shirts. That was typical of Richmond's Manchester district, located on the south side of the James

River, across from the city's financial district. Most of the residents were drawn by the district's artistic urban vibe and river views.

The bar's door opened and slammed hard.

Panic. It rushed me from out of nowhere, seizing my muscles and constricting my chest in tight strips of invisible rope. I pressed my foot on the bar's footrest, as if pushing against my car's accelerator, ratcheting an imaginary speedometer's needle to nearly fifty miles an hour, a dangerous speed on the city's narrow side streets.

Lights reflecting in the mirror behind the bar conjured headlights in my Jeep's rearview mirror. The memory was hard to grab, but I knew my fogged brain, fragmented by adrenaline, registered that I was being chased. *He's going to kill me. I need to get away. Get help.*

A man sat on the barstool near mine. New Guy glanced in my direction and unsettled my nerves more. I hadn't hit the bars in a year, and I was out of practice. My first instinct was to simply retreat to the banquet room, but that would mean facing the buzz saw of birthday streamers and balloons.

New Guy cleared his throat, and I felt his unwavering attention. I wasn't normally jittery, but I'd been in a single-car accident in January. Crashed my Jeep into a utility pole. I didn't remember the accident or the days around it. A few days here or there shouldn't have mattered in the big picture, but those lost memories felt as if they mattered a great deal. My sister said I'd been taking drugs. I didn't believe I was, but with no memories, I couldn't prove it.

My heartbeat kicked up as my palms grew damp—a fight-or-flight response triggered by the car accident. Pride kept me on the stool. I turned toward New Guy.

Broad shoulders filled out a gray brewery T-shirt, and he wore faded but clean jeans and scuffed hiking boots that didn't jibe with winter-pale skin likely earned during hours behind a computer screen. He had a lean build, an angled face, deep-set eyes feathered with creases at the corners, and fading blond strands streaking chestnut hair. All suggested he loved the outdoors but paid the light bill with an office job that kept him really busy. Individually his features weren't memorable or even attractive, but as a whole, they had an appeal. The *Fifty Shades* version of Jamie Dornan.

He nodded to the untouched drinks. "Waiting for someone?"

The twin glasses sat side by side, close but not touching. "No. It's a bit of a birthday tradition."

He looked at me, clearly trying to decode my overcoat, jeans, black V-neck sweater, Doc Martens, and shorn auburn hair. I tucked a phantom curl behind my ear, wondering whether this new short hairstyle was as attractive as Brit kept insisting.

"Your birthday?" he asked.

"The big three-oh today," I said.

"Happy birthday."

"Thank you."

"Are you going to drink them?" He looked curious, like a man who enjoyed puzzles.

I glanced at the clear liquid. "No."

A brow arched. "That tradition, too?"

"It is." Or it had been for the last 365 days—I'd earned my one-year AA token at a meeting. And because I was now sober, I could keep the truth locked away.

He held out his hand. "Alan Bernard."

A collection of silver bracelets covering tiny white scars jangled on my wrist as I accepted his hand. His palm was faintly calloused, and his grip was strong. "Marisa Stockton."

"Do I know you?" His grasp and stare lingered, as if searching for the puzzle's corner piece.

The worn pickup line would have rolled off my back two months ago. Now it unsettled me. Since the car accident, my memory had been sketchy, like a video uploaded on spotty Wi-Fi. Missed words, frozen screens, blurred images dispersed among the coherent and clear. "Your name isn't familiar."

"Neither is yours," he admitted as he released my hand. "It's your face."

I smiled uneasily. "Maybe I have one of those faces."

He leaned forward a fraction, as if to share a secret. Hints of a cigarette and the warm spring air outside clung to him. "No, yours would be hard to forget."

The jazz piano blended with clinking glasses and conversations. My talent for small talk had never been great, and now it was rusty to the point of dilapidated. "It's been good to meet you, Alan."

"I'm going to be a regular here. Beer's good and beats an empty apartment."

"Food's also decent. Burger and fries are great."

"Care to join me?" He was not quick to accept a no.

"There's a birthday party in the back room, and if I don't show, I'll have a very unhappy sister hunting me down."

He didn't look particularly rushed. "Do you live around here, Marisa?" My name rang with a familiarity, as if we'd known each other for years.

"A few blocks."

"Me too. Maybe I'll see you again."

"Maybe."

As I rose, he glanced toward the shot glasses, mulling over their pristine status.

"They're yours if you want them," I said.

He held up his beer. "I'm never one to challenge tradition."

"How do you know offering the drinks to a stranger isn't part of the routine?"

"Somehow I don't think it is."

"Have a good one, Alan." Sliding my purse strap onto my shoulder, I touched him briefly on the forearm. The touch was spontaneous but reminded me of just how long it had been since I'd had human contact beyond an EMT shoving an IV in my arm or a surgeon cracking open my skull. Curling my fingers into a loose fist, I left him and the untouched drinks and made my way to the banquet room's open double doors. Above the entrance was a silver Mylar banner that read **HAPPY BIRTHDAY!**

"Let the fun begin."

3

MARISA

Friday, March 11, 2022
8:00 p.m.

I had one birthday wish—no, two. Maybe three. Wish #1: Clare was alive. Wish #2: if Clare couldn't be brought back from the dead, her killer was caught. And last and certainly least, wish #3: booze didn't haunt all my waking hours.

But seeing as wishes didn't come true, no matter how many candles I blew out, I didn't bother. I crossed the bar to the private banquet space and stepped inside.

I normally wasn't early; in fact, I'd flaked a few too many times during the last decade, and Brit wasn't here now because she was expecting me to be late. No doubt the time she'd given me was earlier than what she gave the guests. My new self-improvement mantra—"early is better"—would never be tested enough for my sister.

"Can I help you?" A waiter entered from a side door carrying a tray of glasses.

I removed my overcoat, still coolish from the ten-minute walk from my apartment in fifty-degree weather. "My sister made reservations for dinner. Her name is Brittany Stockton."

"Ah yes, you're here for the birthday party." He pointed at me. "Didn't you have an art show here in January?"

"That's me."

"I'm Mike. I worked that event."

Already a lifetime separated me from January. "Great. Thanks for helping out that night."

"It was fun."

I searched for hints that Mike and I'd met before, but I found no traces of the encounter. Maybe I simply didn't notice him in January. Brit told me my art show had been a hive of activity. But my exhibit, like Mike's shift, had fallen into a ten-day window that I now called the Black Hole.

"I'm also the birthday girl."

"Ah!" Mike said, smiling. "Happy birthday."

Brit, like our mother, loved birthdays when we were kids and marked each with a big party. How many times had she destroyed our mother's kitchen baking cakes for her planned parties? How many paper hats and chains had she made as a kid?

A round table surrounded by six chairs dominated the small room. Each place setting had a decorative birthday hat that appeared to be inspired by *The Wizard of Oz* and represented one of the story's main characters: Dorothy, Glinda the Good Witch, the Cowardly Lion, the Scarecrow, the Tin Man, and the Wizard.

"Do you feel any older?" Mike joked as he positioned a glass at each of the six place settings.

It was a birthday party for a six-year-old. Typical Brit. She never articulated it with words, but she missed the days when Mommy and Clare were alive, and the Stocktons could pass for normal.

My mouth twitched as I imagined Brit scouring Pinterest and Etsy pages. "This year I'm feeling my age."

His gaze skittered over my body quickly. "You've cut your hair since you were here last."

My long red hair had been a casualty of the head injury and surgery, and I still missed the weight on my shoulders and the ease of a quick ponytail. Without my signature mane, I didn't get noticed as much, but in my pre-sobriety days, I'd grabbed a lifetime's worth of attention, and the way I saw it, the new style served a greater karmic purpose.

Glasses rattled, and I caught myself conjuring a replay of my greatest mistakes. Clearing my throat, I drew in a deep breath. I hung my coat on a peg as Mike pulled out a chair facing the door. I sat in front of the Dorothy hat, which was centered on the plate, doing my best to feel special but already dreading Brit's plans. Any sign of a clown or a male stripper, and I was outa there.

Moistening my lips, I searched the menu, noticing it had changed. Subtle modifications. Prices, a few additional appetizers, and more desserts. I studied the pasta offerings, wondering what I'd liked best. Hard to say, these days. My taste buds had been MIA since the accident, another lingering souvenir of the head trauma. Maybe I'd stick with the crunchy fries.

Brit stepped into the small room, wearing a leather jacket and a navy jumper that flared above her ankles, skimmed her narrow waist, and rose to a halter top that hugged full breasts. Straight dyed blond hair skimmed her shoulders, highlighting an angled face, red lips, and bold smoky eyes.

The effect was very attractive. In fact, as I rose, I noticed my sister had lost a couple of pounds. Perhaps rumors of the new boyfriend were legit. Brit held a square box wrapped in silver paper and adorned with an ice-blue bow. No clowns yet, thank God.

My sister looked a little frustrated, which had been her signature expression since she was a kid. Put upon. Doing the best, given the limited resources.

"I was supposed to be here first," Brit said.

After moving around the table, I hugged her and drew in the familiar scent of Chanel perfume and hair spray. "You look terrific. Losing weight?"

Brit stifled a grin. "Think so?"

"I know so."

"Thanks. That's the best news I've heard all day."

Brit captured a short red strand of my hair between manicured fingers. "Very stylish. Very edgy."

"That's me, edgy."

"Are you sleeping well?" Brit asked. "You look tired."

"I'm great." I refused to sound annoyed. Brit had self-identified as a mother hen since our mother died. I shouldn't have blamed her. She didn't want the role. "What's in the box?"

She grinned. "That's for later, when everyone gets here."

"Everyone. I see the six hats. *Wizard of Oz?*"

"It was your favorite movie when you were little."

Was it? But I'd watched millions of movies when I was a kid. I still did. "Okay."

"You promised me free rein over the party. No questions asked."

"You're right." I grinned. "But I wouldn't say no to a hint."

A teasing smile proved she loved keeping secrets. "I won't give you one."

"Please." A little begging always put her in a good mood.

"Not one." Brit took off her jacket. "Don't look like you're facing a firing squad, M. It'll be fun."

"You're right." Attitude was everything.

"Wait no longer." A familiar deep voice resonated behind me, and when I turned, I found a smile.

I was a little surprised Brit had invited him. "Kurt Markman."

He'd dated our sister, Clare, in high school. They'd been crazy about each other; had volatile, exciting arguments; and maybe broken a law or two. When Clare's body was found, the cops and press focused a great deal of attention on Kurt initially. He had been Clare's boyfriend, and when the medical examiner swabbed Clare's cervix, they found his DNA. No vaginal bruising, no marks on her body beyond the discoloration on her neck. Witnesses noted Kurt and Clare had had a heated fight at the New Year's Eve party where she'd last been seen. Some said she'd stormed off. Others said he'd left her. Armed with scattered bits of truth, many media commentators had run stories—beginning with "that in all likelihood" or "a source suggested"—that Kurt had tracked Clare down and killed her.

The media and police pressure had gotten so bad that Kurt had fled Richmond to finish up high school in North Carolina. When he returned nearly a year later, his father was days away from dying of ALS. He'd lost a year with his father, and by then most had forgotten Clare's name except for the occasional reporter drumming up an anniversary piece. One year. Five years. Ten. Thirteen was too odd a number for a story, but maybe fifteen would work.

Kurt's six-foot-one running back's frame had filled out with muscle in the last dozen years, and the ink-black, collar-length hair that once swept recklessly over his forehead was cut short and silvering very slightly. His jaw was still strong, and the nose broken in a fight continued to add interest to a too-perfect face. Black blazer, white button-down shirt, faded jeans, and boots that he'd worn in high school. Gray-green eyes bore down on me.

Grinning, he drew me into an embrace that smelled of Old Spice aftershave, the brand he'd once mocked because his father wore it. "You look terrific, Marisa."

How had Brit convinced him to come to this party? We were hardly a blast from the past he wanted to remember.

As he wrapped me in his arms, my chest tightened, and my heart kicked up a beat. But I held steady and drew back slowly, as if I were fine. It wouldn't do to ruin this party that Brit clearly had taken a great deal of time to plan. "You're a terrific surprise, Kurt. It's been way too long."

He regarded my hair. "Thirteen years."

"A life," I said.

"I've been tracking your bridal-photography business, MIS Images," he said. "Doing pretty well."

"It's growing slow and steady."

"Better than that. Your photography has been in a few national online trade publications. You make the average wedding portrait look artistic and different."

I was a frustrated artist with a screwed-up personal life, but I knew how to work hard (even hungover or buzzed), and I had an eye for commercial images. However, showing my real art always felt awkward and exposed, so I'd put my energy into the paying work. I'd somehow established a quirky vibe that was now popular. "It pays the light bill."

"Whenever I'm in the market for a wedding photographer, you're my girl," Kurt said.

"There a lady in the wings?" I asked.

"Not yet."

Brit had said something once about him being divorced. I glanced to his left hand. Empty with no trace of a ring tan. "Can't rush greatness."

He grinned. "That's what I keep telling my mother." He turned to Brit, hugged her, but the embrace was tentative—chaste, as if Brit were an older, distant aunt. In reality she was only a year older than Kurt.

"I'm glad you made it," Brit said.

"Wouldn't miss it," he said. "Been too long."

"The bar is running an open tab," Brit said. "What can I get you, Kurt?"

"Craft beer."

"You got it. Soda for you, M?"

"Perfect."

Brit hurried out of the room, leaving a scented trail behind. The silence settled. The only thing Kurt and I had in common now was Clare's murder. We both had gone through the wringer after her death. The devastating news, the cops asking endless questions, the media attention, and then the friends who stopped calling.

"You're drinking soda?" he asked. "That a joke?"

"No punch line. Sober for one year now," I said.

"Wow. How's that been?"

"Not too bad." Lying was a birthday-girl privilege.

Brit entered with a tray sporting a beer bottle, a canned soda, and a misty glass of white wine. She doled out drinks and held up her wineglass. "This will be the first of many toasts tonight, but happy birthday, Marisa."

Kurt grinned as he drank from his beer bottle, clearly relieved for something to do. He looked around the room at the dark wood paneling, flickering sconces, and vintage bar signs now draped in pink and white streamers with balloons dangling from the ends. "Brit, you've outdone yourself. The room looks terrific."

Mama Brit beamed. "Thanks, Kurt."

"There's no place like home," he quipped.

"Exactly." In high school, Brit had a crush on Kurt, and there had always been a snap of attraction in her eyes when she'd looked at him. Then she'd left for college, and he'd started dating Clare.

"What's on the menu?" Kurt asked.

"We're having Marisa's favorite," she said. "Barbecue, rolls, creamed corn, and coleslaw. A little out of season but can't argue with a favorite."

I popped the top on my soda and drank. The menu offering wasn't my favorite, but Clare's. Like the tequila, Clare had loved a good barbecue. I'd always reached for pizza or fries when I had the choice. This wasn't the first time that Brit had confused Clare and me. When Clare was alive, it had happened all the time. Other than our fashion choices, there was no way to tell us apart if we were far away or it was dark. If Brit had been close, she might have noted Clare's eyes were slightly more almond shaped than mine. When we were newborns, our mother had written our initials in Sharpie on our heels.

This menu mix-up was par for the course. In fact, it felt right to have Clare's favorite meal tonight. We'd always shared our birthday with each other, so today should be no different.

"And the cake?" Kurt asked.

"Chocolate on chocolate," Brit said.

She'd gotten the cake right. So the rest didn't matter. "Perfect."

"Tell me about your wedding-photography business," Kurt said. "Never saw you chasing that dream."

Clare had been the artist when we were growing up. She'd loved to draw, filled dozens of sketchbooks, and even dabbled with photography. "Fell into it like I have most things. Became obsessed with taking pictures of Richmond: Main Street Station, the old tobacco warehouses, Hollywood Cemetery. When I realized I could make money doing this, I went full time."

"Feast-or-famine kind of business."

"The second part of this year is looking like a feast," I said.

"I heard you had an art show back in January."

"It was a small event."

"Still, a show is a show. Where does all the commercial work leave your art?" Kurt asked.

He had always been a good listener, keying in on whatever I was saying. He made me feel like an individual, and not one-half of MC, the nickname Brit had given her twin sisters. "Making it work."

"Marisa is underselling her January show," Brit offered. "It went well. She sold a couple of pieces."

"One piece," I corrected. "But who's counting?"

"One more than I've ever sold," Kurt said. "I'd like to see them sometime."

I sipped my soda, savoring the bubbles. After booze and the accident, the new loves of my life were carbonation and crunch.

"All right, you two, time to put on a hat," Brit said. "M, you're Dorothy, of course. And, Kurt, you're the Tin Man."

Kurt waggled his eyebrows, as he'd done in high school when Brit went all Mom Squad. "If I only had a heart."

I studied the blue velvet hat and Dorothy's stunned face and wondered how many thirty-year-olds celebrated their birthdays sober at a *Wizard of Oz*–themed party? I settled the hat on my head, angled it a fraction, and then fished out my phone. Holding it up, I mugged for the camera, snapped, and posted. It was not vanity, but business. The more posts I put up, the higher the impressions my photography business received. Customers like to see you as real, accessible, and fun.

Clare's laugh rang in my ears. "You look ridiculous, you know? Times when it pays to be dead."

Hearing Clare's voice was comforting. It'd been a while since my sister had piped up, and it was nice to know my former partner in crime was riding shotgun tonight.

Brit chose the Glinda the Good Witch hat and settled it on her head. Perfect fit.

I smiled at her, reminding myself again that when our mother died suddenly (suicide, overdose), Brit had been fifteen, and Clare and I had just turned twelve. Our dad had needed the help, and firstborn Brit had stepped into the role. She was so good at it, no one had ever asked if she liked it. And when Clare died, Brit was devastated. She compensated by throwing herself into her college and then law school studies. To this day, she never sat still.

Kurt settled the Tin Man's silver hat on his head. "How do I look?"

"A perfect fit," I said.

"Tin Man needed oil, and I'm in asphalt, an oil-based product."

"Are you still with your dad's asphalt business?" I asked. "In high school you said you'd rather die first."

"It's a good gig," he said. "The pay is great, and we all have to grow up eventually."

"So I hear."

A flurry of laughter echoed outside the banquet room, and when we turned, a petite brunette stepped into the room, carrying a gift bag covered in clowns. My dislike of clowns had always been well known, and the bag choice was meant to be a joke. Ha ha.

"Jo-Jo," I said. Jo-Jo, the bestie to team MC, had hosted the New Year's Eve party where Clare had been last seen. Once the cops and media learned her parents hadn't been at home during the party, there was enough fallout to drive them from Richmond.

Jo-Jo had married Brit's high school boyfriend, Jack, two years ago. It had been a surprising combination. The bad boy married the cheerleader, but after thirteen years, the old labels shouldn't have mattered as much. Jo-Jo and Jack now had the house in the suburbs, and odds were, they'd have a kid on the way within the year.

I didn't see Jo-Jo that much anymore, and I had to wonder why she'd accepted Brit's invitation. The last time I'd seen her had been at a wedding last November. She and Jack had been guests, and I'd been working. I'd been sober about eight months but still wasn't broadcasting it—after too many misfires, I didn't want to jinx things. Jo-Jo, remembering the high school version of me, kept sneaking me vodka shots. Finally, after dumping three shots in a potted ficus, I'd told her I was now sober. That had earned me an eye roll and a "just this once." Girls like her, who can shut off the drinking like a water tap, don't really get girls like me, who can drink until our livers fail.

Jo-Jo wrapped her arms around me. "I was so worried about you," she whispered. "I wanted to see you in the hospital. But was cut off at the pass."

I had asked Brit to keep everyone away. No one needed to see my newly shorn hair, pale skin, and confused expression. Not my best Instagram moment. "I wouldn't have remembered it anyway."

"Brit said you don't recall the accident."

I shrugged, refusing to let ten lost days bother me. "Just as well. Who wants to remember a car accident?"

Jo-Jo grinned. "Right. Who wants to remember?"

"Jo-Jo." Brit likes to draw out the *O*.

"Time to get your hat," I warned.

"Right. On to the business of this party." She turned and her grin widened. "Brit, can I be whoever I want to be?"

Brit, her white witch hat cocked, handed Jo-Jo the Scarecrow hat, complete with straw. "I've chosen all the hats. Keeping everyone out of their comfort zone."

"Why am I the Scarecrow?" Jo-Jo grimaced as she settled the hat on her head.

"Doesn't really matter, does it?" Brit said. "Hats are meant to be conversation starters."

"I'd rather not be remembered as brainless," Jo-Jo said.

"Think of yourself as the good loyal one. Kurt's certainly not made of tin and has a heart," I said. "And I'm no Dorothy."

Brit's smile faded. "It's all in fun."

"I know," I said quickly, seeing the tension rising in my sister. She never handled mutiny well. "Fun, right?"

"Exactly," she said.

Jo-Jo waved to Kurt. They hugged briefly, and that counted for something. During the police investigation, Jo-Jo had told the detective that she'd seen Kurt and Clare fighting before she'd vanished. "Hey, Kurt."

"You look good, Jo-Jo," he said.

"Thanks, Kurt."

Our next arrival was a man I didn't recognize. He was tall, good looking, and kept his dark hair cut short. He wore khakis and a button-down shirt, and his slightly doughy frame was not quite fat but certainly not fit. I pegged him as one of the financiers who worked in the city across the river. There were enough of those types around here because of our proximity to the city. The Banker Boys, as I called them, always looked a bit like fish out of water in this industrial area.

Brit hurried over to him and kissed him on the lips. He leaned into her and pressed his hand to the base of her spine. Okay, he wasn't here for me.

Tucking her arm around his, Brit brought him over. "David, I'd like you to meet my sister, Marisa."

"Nice to meet you, Marisa," David said as he handed me a bottle of wine. "Happy birthday."

I accepted the bottle and guessed that he and Brit hadn't been dating long. My older sister was always good about telling people that her baby sister was in AA. Still sober after one year. Fighting the good fight.

"Thanks, David," I said. No point making a fuss. In fact, it was nice passing as a real person instead of someone to tiptoe around.

"Oh, that's sweet." Brit usually pointed out errors, but she didn't this time. Definitely in the honeymoon stage of their relationship, when they each still laughed at the other's jokes, didn't wear their favorite sweats around the house all the time, and smiled even when annoyed.

"I like the hat," David said to me.

"Just you wait," I teased. "There's a hat on the table with your name on it."

"It's a silly party game." Brit was worried now. She clearly didn't want her new man to see her as mothering. Too soon for that. "If you don't want to wear one, you don't have to."

"I don't mind," he said easily. "Who am I to be tonight?"

"I was thinking the Wizard," she said.

"Perfect. I've always fancied myself a bit of a magician. Have I showed you my sleight-of-hand trick?"

Brit's nose wrinkled with a smile as she reached for the purple-and-silver spiraled hat. "No. And you're a sport."

To David's credit, he settled the hat on his head, raising his chin. "I think it suits."

"We're still missing the Lion," I said.

"Jack is the Lion." Like Jo-Jo and Kurt, Jack had known MC since high school. "Jo-Jo, where's your husband?"

"He said he would try to make it," she said. "He's working at the other restaurant, but he will try to stop by." Jack owned this bar, one across the river, and another opening soon in Church Hill.

"He warned me he might be late," Brit said.

Brit took another round of drink orders, and then she made sure all her guests had a glass in hand. Outside, rain started a quick pit-a-pat on the metal roof and rapidly accelerated to bombardment.

My world stilled as the roar of water mimicked a revving car engine. Heart beating faster, for an instant I could feel my fingers gripping a steering wheel as my foot pressed the accelerator. The car was moving fast, and controlling it was difficult. A sharp right and then the utility pole.

Shattering glass rained over me as the impact rocketed blinding pain through my body and head. A jackhammer on steroids, it cracked bone and smashed brain matter. The lights flickered in my world, and then they went out. The terror and fear faded, leaving a warm blanket of nothingness enveloping me. As I drifted in the darkness, the pain lessened, and I knew Death had come for me again.

I'd nearly followed Death the last time. She was so tempting, sweet, and kind as she pulled me toward a current that swirled downward. (Not surprising my journey wasn't upward or heavenly.)

A hand brushed the side of my face, and fingers pressed against my neck in search of a pulse. Was my heart beating?

"Marisa."

The masculine voice was jagged with fear and did not belong to Death. I tried to grab hold, use the voice to climb out of the maelstrom. Despite Death's promise of serenity, it wasn't my time.

"Why did you do it?" The man's name danced out of reach, as an arm brushed across my chest. I sensed someone pawing, groping for something. And then: *"I'm sorry. I'm so sorry."*

I'd had this "memory" before, but I still wasn't sure whether it was an actual recollection or one planted by the police's retelling of the facts. Memories are dangerous, I'd been told. They aren't permanent and can be influenced by new circumstances and incoming facts.

"Where did you go?" Jo-Jo asked.

I blinked. "Nowhere. Listening to the rain. It's really coming down out there."

Jo-Jo rolled her eyes. "And to think I blow-dried my hair tonight. I wanted to look fabulous for you, but it'll be ruined by the time I get home. Hoping Jack could see it. Shame to waste the effort."

"I'm sorry I won't see him in the Lion's hat. That's an Instagram moment."

"Can you imagine Jack in that?" She sipped her wine spritzer. "He's changed a lot since high school. No longer the life of the party but a hardworking stiff. Plans to own a real estate empire one day."

In high school, Jack had made his money selling drugs. He'd started with pot and graduated to cocaine and prescription pills by his senior year. Brit and Jack were the same age, but she'd been a year ahead in school. (Flunked kindergarten, he always joked, but rumor had it he'd done time in juvie.) They started fading when she left for college, and after Clare died, she broke it off. He understood, and they'd stayed good friends. Two years after he dropped out of high school, he was arrested for drug trafficking. He'd done three years in state prison but, once freed, turned his life around. A success story by any measure.

Brit clapped her hands. "Come on, kids, time to sit down."

"What's with the barbecue? That was Clare's fave," Jo-Jo said.

Hearing my sister's name was a bit of a jolt. No one ever said her name anymore. Death had taken my sister, but time was slowly erasing every trace of evidence that she'd walked this earth. Clare's first death had been quick, but this second one was agonizingly slow. Maybe that was why Brit had invited old friends who'd known Clare. She wanted to keep our sister alive as well. It was the only reason that made sense to me.

"I love barbecue, too," I said. The goal was not to stir the pot with Brit. She reveled in her maternal role, and I wasn't keen on taking that away from her. She'd been a lifesaver these last couple of months.

Brit looked at me, and I saw the wheels turning. She'd realized her mistake but recovered. "Can't forget Clare."

Both Brit and I had found ways to cope after our mother's death and then Clare's. She shifted her grief into her career, becoming addicted to hard work that numbed her mind. Me? The classic substance abuser.

"I can still picture Clare and Marisa by the river in their cutoff jeans, halter tops, and cowboy boots," Brit said. "Clare's boots were powder blue, and Marisa's were black."

"I always struggled with who was who," Jo-Jo said.

I remembered the day we'd bought those boots. It was the summer before she died. We'd both had the flu and for the first time in weeks felt really good. We'd dressed up and headed to our favorite spot on the river. I'd gotten wasted, and Clare had hooked up with Kurt for the first time.

"The school got their names backward in the senior yearbook," Kurt said.

It might have been funny if the yearbook hadn't been issued after Clare died. When I opened the book and saw my face with her name, I laughed so hard I cried. So fucking ironic. Even to the end, no one got us straight.

"I had another trick to tell you apart besides the boots," Jo-Jo confessed.

"The eyes," Kurt said. "M's stare is more intense."

"True," Jo-Jo conceded. "But I had another method. When Marisa is nervous, she curls her hair around her finger."

I ran a hand over my short hair, then caught myself. Maybe nerves explained why I'd been craving a cigarette all night. But I'd tossed that nervous habit along with the booze.

Jo-Jo brushed a lock of hair back from her eyes. "When this rain lets up, we'll sneak into the alley and have a smoke."

"First the party," Brit said.

I'd known Jo-Jo for more than seventeen years. There'd been a time when we'd been almost as close as I'd been to Clare. My sister and I had shared everything with Jo-Jo until we turned sixteen and learned she liked to gossip.

To Jo-Jo's credit, she'd sensed I hadn't told the full story of that New Year's Eve night, but surprisingly she'd never outed me—even after the cops charged her parents with serving minors. After Clare, Jo-Jo's family moved away, and I found myself on one side of a canyon and the rest of the world on the other. Without Clare and Jo-Jo, my partners in crime, I was lost. I should've embraced the real help Brit and Dad forced on me, but I didn't feel like I deserved to be saved. The booze helped me worry less about being lonely.

And when I finally sobered up, I realized that I'd never really known any of my friends or family. They were all strangers to me now.

4

Brit

Friday, March 11, 2022
9:00 p.m.

The group gathered around the table chatted fairly easily, and the sky above had finally stopped dumping water. I'd been back and forth about having the party for days, worrying about the weather, the guests who were having trouble making time for the party, and of course Marisa. In the end, I'd asked David to attend as my backup (he'd agreed imme- diately—*love him*), strong-armed a guest or two, and decided we'd beat the weather. No Jack, but maybe that was for the best tonight.

All the trouble seemed to be worth it. Even Marisa was pretend- ing to have a good time. She wasn't, of course. She was never really happy, never really had been, but she'd been more subdued since the car accident.

I still had nightmares about the late-night call from the police, the rush to the emergency room, and the endless waiting for the surgeon to tell me whether my sole surviving family member would live.

My sympathy for Marisa had waned seconds after the double doors to the emergency's waiting room opened and the surgeon, still wearing his scrubs, came to speak to me. I'd learned Marisa would be fine, that the swelling on her brain had been reduced, and she'd be her old self eventually. But I'd also discovered that my supposedly sober sister likely had drugs in her system. Tests might not pick them up after so many hours, but the paramedics who'd brought her here thought she was high. What other reason would she have for going more than forty miles an hour through a small city neighborhood south of the Church Hill district? Jesus.

Marisa had sworn she'd been sober for a year. She'd dutifully attended her meetings, collected her chips, and been building a real life. And then just like that, she'd screwed up. But that was the way it went with alcoholics, wasn't it?

The counselors had said missteps were a constant and present danger and families needed to help the addict. I had done my share of hoisting my baby sister back up on the wagon, and I was officially tired of it. But I rallied and rode to the rescue again.

And yet here I sat in this damn birthday party, wearing a Good Witch hat, pretending that everything was all right. Which it was, essentially. But Marisa's shit always hung over our heads, the proverbial sword of Damocles clinging by a thread. My little lost Dorothy.

A hand rubbed over my thigh, and I turned toward David. He was staring at me, clearly sensing that stress brewed behind my smile. He could read me so well.

"I can see into your mind, you know?" he said.

That smile. It always got me. "Can you?"

"I can. And just for the record, this is a great party," he whispered. "Terrific job."

A warmth spread through me as I gazed at him. We'd known each other for just a couple of months, but there was a connection I'd never shared with anyone else. "Thank you."

He winked, reached for his beer. "Your sister looks happy."

I stared across the round table at Marisa in deep conversation with Kurt. She was wearing the new camera strap he'd given her. It should have been Clare sitting next to him. "She does."

I'd been at a loss as to how to handle the party. Celebrating Marisa's birth reminded everyone that there had been another sister, Clare, who'd died at age sixteen. God, thirteen years since that runner had found Clare's body by the river. Thirteen years of Marisa spiraling and struggling. Thirteen years of dealing with my own guilt and loss. Clare and Marisa had been identical twins, bonded before birth, but Clare had been *my* sister, too. That fact got lost more often than not.

The guests looked as if they were enjoying the barbecue, based on the nearly empty collection of plates. The drinks had been refilled a few times, and even the hats had sparked comments and laughter—as any icebreaker should. Dispersed among the torn wrapping paper were the vintage Leica camera I'd given Marisa for her collection and a canvas camera bag filled with disposable cameras from Jo-Jo and Jack.

Marisa raised her soda glass to her lips as she nodded at something Jo-Jo was saying. Those two plus Clare had been three peas in a pod. They'd gotten into more than their share of trouble. Daddy had had to clean up a few of their messes, but the twins had known how to humor him and soothe his temper. I'd seen right through them. God, if I'd pulled half the shit they had, Daddy would have tossed me out on my fanny. When he finally gave me clearance to crack the whip, I'd been less forgiving. And yet nothing I came up with sidelined them for long.

Even the car accident hadn't really slowed Marisa down. That signature red hair was gone, but if anything, the shorter haircut made her look more attractive. Her clear eyes, cheekbones, and pale skin now all popped, and it was hard to admit how striking she was. Kurt certainly was enjoying the show. I'd even caught David stealing a few glimpses, though he'd had the decency to look chagrined when our eyes met.

The waiter came into our room, cleared the plates, and refreshed our drinks. Next on tap was the cake (topped with ruby slippers), after which I could safely put this birthday to bed.

"Do you have an early day tomorrow?" David asked me.

"Since it's Saturday, I opted to take it off." I was a lawyer, operated my own firm, and working weekends was standard. If business kept on, I'd add a paralegal and perhaps an associate next year. "I knew this was going to be a late night."

"So you won't be in a rush to get to bed early?" he asked softly.

Warmth spread over my face. We'd been lovers for six weeks now and were still in the can't-keep-hands-off-each-other phase. I shifted in my seat, already anxious to cut the cake and leave. "No. No rush at all."

"Good."

The flicker of candles on a chocolate cake on a cart appeared in the doorway. Four waiters had gathered, and they began to sing "Happy Birthday." At first Marisa didn't look up, seemed almost mutinous. But as the others at the table started to sing and clap, she found a smile and watched as the waiter set down the round cake with thirty-one candles. (The extra was for luck.) As the song wound down, Marisa drew in a breath, closed her eyes, and blew on the flames, which she extinguished immediately.

Over the smoking candles of the cake, Marisa met my gaze. "Thanks, Brit. This was really nice."

"It's chocolate cake. *Your* favorite." I knew for a fact that I'd gotten the cake flavor right. I'd always baked two cakes on Clare and Marisa's birthday. Red velvet for Clare and chocolate for Marisa.

"I never could resist it."

The waiter carried the cake to a side table, where he set the slippers aside and sliced it into generous portions.

"I wanted tonight to be all about your favorites," I said. I might have gotten the barbecue wrong, but Marisa had eaten a generous portion, so it wasn't exactly a miss.

"You spoil me," Marisa said. "Clare would've been thrilled by all this."

The smiles dimmed at the mention of Clare's name. Jo-Jo of course had brought her up, but I wished Marisa could have waited until it was just the two of us. Clare needed to be remembered, but there were times when I wanted to forget the damage our sister's death had caused. It wasn't selfish to want a few hours of normal, was it?

Marisa raised her glass. "Here's to Clare."

Kurt cleared his throat as he lifted his beer bottle. "Does anyone remember her laugh? No matter where I was, when I heard that laugh, I always smiled."

Jo-Jo gulped her wine. "And who else could talk her way out of a speeding ticket or ace the SATs? We all loved her."

I moistened my lips as the waiter placed a plate in front of each guest.

Marisa nodded, dropped her gaze. She jabbed her fork into the cake. "Thanks again, Brit."

My counselor had warned me that Marisa might experience moments that could trigger her drinking again. I had considered ignoring this day altogether but then decided to take the bull by the horns. Clare was dead. And Marisa and I had to deal with that fact every day for the rest of our lives. End of story. I didn't need to drink or to do drugs to dull that reality. But then I was the practical one. The one people called when they needed help or money. For a good time, the calls had always been for Marisa and Clare.

A collection of clown balloons appeared in the doorway. Everyone turned, and nervous laughter rippled over the room. The balloons lowered, revealing Jack's grinning face. He still was a good-looking man; in fact, thirteen years had added just the right amount of crow's-feet around his eyes and toughened his frame. The tattoos on his arms enhanced his bad-boy mystique, which even now was attractive.

Jack released the balloons into the room, barely noticing how they'd floated to the ceiling as he leaned down and kissed Marisa on the cheek. "Happy birthday, kid."

"I thought you were working," Marisa said.

"I am. Will be again soon but had to stop by." His hand lingered on Marisa's shoulder as he kissed Jo-Jo on the lips, shook Kurt's hand, and then glanced up to me. His grin reminded me of a host welcoming a patron walking into his restaurant. Nothing special. Very vanilla. Seemed it should have been more.

We'd dated in high school, but that had been a long time ago, and we'd both clearly moved on. Still, I wanted him to remember I'd been there for him like few would have. My steadfast loyalty had, in the end, been the ruin of us. I knew all his early secrets, and he'd finally admitted every time he looked at me, he remembered what he'd done wrong. His fuckups had become my fault. And still to this day, when he screwed up, he came to me for legal advice.

"Hey, Jack," I said brightly. "Thanks for getting this room for us."

"Only the best for the Stockton girls," he said.

Jack met David's gaze, held and studied it. His jaw pulsed. "I'm Jack. I own this place and another across town."

"David Welbourne. Brit's other half. Great place you got here."

"You two dating?" Jack asked.

"We are," I said, hoping it made him a tiny bit jealous.

"Congratulations." Jack laid his hands on Marisa's shoulders. "You guys need anything? What can I get for you?"

"We're all set," I said brightly. "Why don't you join us for cake? There's a hat waiting here for you."

His laugh was easy, quick, and slightly menacing, meaning if I pressed, it wouldn't end politely. "I wish I could. Jo-Jo, save some cake for me."

She smiled, her cheeks warming a little. "Sure."

"As always, great job, Brit."

He kissed his wife one last time, squeezed Marisa's shoulders, and stepped back. "I've work out front but just wanted to duck my head in. Sorry I can't stay. Enjoy the balloons, M."

"It's not a party until you put your hat on," Marisa teased.

"The hat's redundant," he said, stepping back as he surveyed the Lion hat. "We all know I'm a big scaredy-cat."

Jo-Jo scoffed. "You're anything but. But Brit did nail Marisa's hat. Dorothy. The dreamer. Lost."

I raised my glass. Leave it to Jo-Jo to say something inappropriate. "There's no correlation."

Kurt laughed. "I'd rather be a dreamer than heartless or brainless."

Marisa touched her hat, adjusting it, likely wondering whether she'd been somehow set up to look like the fool. Since my sister was a kid, she could be paranoid, always feeling like someone was trying to hurt her, likely a hangover from prior drug use, or maybe even the cause of it. Either way, since Clare had died, Marisa's paranoia had increased a hundredfold.

"What did I say?" Jo-Jo asked. "I thought that was the point. To poke fun at ourselves. *The Wizard of Oz* was Marisa's favorite movie."

Marisa's grin widened, but it was too bright. "Clare loved it most. I was a *Sound of Music* girl." That was right. A family escaping tyranny had struck a chord with her.

"Each time I read it to my students, I think of MC," Jo-Jo said.

"Give it a rest, Jo-Jo," Jack said softly. "Eat your cake."

It wasn't the first time the twins had been mixed up. Still, after thirteen years, it must sting a little.

"Marisa, you're one of a kind," I said.

She smiled. "Thanks."

"Happy birthday, again." Jack kissed her on the cheek and, as he turned to leave, glanced toward David and me.

Few would have considered Jack's eyes cold in that instant, but I knew him well enough to see the ice churning behind those baby blues.

5

MARISA

I was grateful when the party finally ended. I'd been ready to walk home, the remnants of my cake and the fondant ruby slippers secured in their original box, and the collection of presents neatly packed in a large paper bag that proved Brit was always two steps ahead. Kurt had insisted on walking me home.

"It was a nice party," he said. "Brit tried hard."

"Yes. She always does."

The box of cake in hand, I approached my building's locked entrance. I punched in the security code.

"She's still as uptight as I remember," he said.

"It's hard for her," I said, needing to defend. "She had Mom and Dad all to herself for three years, and then Clare and I showed up and basically sucked the oxygen out of the family."

"That's not true."

The lock clicked, and I opened it. He followed me inside and then down a hallway toward a lone elevator. Before the accident, I took the stairs, but it had been a long day, and my reserves were waning. I didn't want to stop and catch my breath in front of Kurt. Inside the car, I pressed five. The doors closed, and we slowly rose. When the doors opened, I said, "The pony express has arrived."

"I've aged five years," he quipped.

On my floor, we stepped off, and I walked to the lone door on the left. There were only two apartments on this floor. The other had been empty several months, but judging by a stack of broken-down, rain-soaked boxes by the door, it looked like I might have a new neighbor. Wrangling keys, I opened my door and flipped on the light, and Kurt followed me inside.

My apartment was the top half of a warehouse. Each of the five floors had two large apartments, creating ten units in all. Three years ago, when I'd first looked at the space, I'd immediately liked its massive square footage, large windows, and reasonable rent. It provided me the space to set up a photo studio in the front half, a small darkroom in a closet, and in the back a galley-style kitchen, my bedroom, and a bath. I used partitions to sequester the rear section when clients visited.

My photography studio was outfitted with a gray backdrop and several vintage settees I'd found at thrift stores to accommodate clients who requested a portrait or the occasional headshot.

The best part of the space was the large window that overlooked the James River and the city of Richmond on the north side. I'd angled my couch toward the window and often sat watching the sunrise. Sleep and I didn't always get along, so I'd seen my share of breaking dawns.

I set my cake on the concrete kitchen counter, then slid off my coat and tossed it on a chair. "Sorry, nothing to offer you to drink other than coffee, water, or seltzer."

Kurt set the presents down beside the cake. "I've had enough beer and coffee. Don't need anything," he said.

He was still very attractive, and it was impossible not to feel the allure. I'd not been with a man since I'd sobered up and was now very aware of that fact. Or maybe this unexpected pull was rooted in his connection to Clare. Maybe on our birthday, I wanted to feel linked to my sister.

In Clare's last days, she had said sex with Kurt had always been hot, frenetic, full of teenage groping and more hormones than sense. More often than not, it was over before it really began. Still, she'd always been left briefly warmed by a fleeting satisfaction that never lasted.

I wanted to feel that gratification now, even if it lasted only hours or minutes.

His gaze caught mine, heated, and I didn't look away. I moistened my lips. He was savvy enough to read the cues, and I wondered whether my come-hither look mirrored Clare's.

He came around the counter and cupped my face in his hands. "I love your eyes. They've always tempted me."

My eyes. So like Clare's. I stood still, knowing sex would burn off the sizzling nerves that hadn't gone away after the candles were blown out. I'd coped with these anxieties for several years with drugs and booze. But with those off the table, the sharp edges of my worries cut deeper.

He tilted his head down and kissed me on the lips, as if he'd once been familiar with my body. I leaned into him but kept my hands at my sides. My blood pulsed. His lips tasted of malt and sensuous energy. The bands twisting inside me eased a fraction, and I was on the verge of telling him he could do whatever he wanted to me.

"You taste good," he said as he rubbed my jaw with his thumb. When he kissed me again, his right hand slid up under my shirt, cupped my breast, and teased the nipple. Desire exploded, and I hissed in a breath.

As I teetered closer to letting go, I suddenly imagined Clare standing behind me, watching, more curious than annoyed. *"Seriously? That's the best you can do?"*

I ignored the voice and concentrated on his lips, that hand squeezing and fondling. *Let me just have this moment.*

"*He's going to disappoint you,*" Clare said. "*Nothing is ever as advertised.*"

I stiffened, drew in a breath.

"What's wrong?" He gripped a handful of my shirt, keeping my body anchored close to his. "You used to like that," he said.

You. "Clare did. Not me."

His grip on my shirt eased, and I stepped back, pulling the fabric from his slackened grip. He stabbed long fingers through his hair. "That's not what I meant."

"Did you mean me or Clare?"

"Don't turn that comment into a thing," he said softly. "*We're* here, and we're doing just fine."

But it wasn't just us. It never would be. Picturing Clare standing behind me, I took another step back. "Were we? Are we both looking for a way to bring her back to life for a little while?"

"You're overthinking this." Frustration leaked from the words.

"I don't think so."

"Clare would want you to get on with your life."

If he thought he'd said the magic words, he was wrong. "I'm not going to do this."

"Why not? *Marisa*, I know it's us in this room."

"No, it's not just us. She's here, too."

"That doesn't sound rational." Nervous laughter rumbled, but the need still lingered in his gaze, and I doubted he cared whether I was reasonable.

"It's not a day to be rational," I said.

"I'm not looking for Clare," he said.

I shook my head and moved farther out of his reach. "No. But I am. I've been searching for her for thirteen years."

"What's to search for? She's dead, not missing." His too-rational tone cracked the veneer, exposing my fragility. Maybe I was a little unstable. "I miss Clare, too," he added.

I closed my eyes. If I were still drinking, we'd have already been in bed naked. "We need to honor that feeling and try not to cover it up with sex."

He slid his hand into his pocket, a muscle in his jaw pulsing. "You're not being fair."

"Maybe not. But it is what it is." The platitude rumbled out on a sigh.

"Okay. I get it."

I wasn't sure he did understand. I thought he was horny and wondering whether this could still be salvaged. "I'm sorry. I can't."

I thought for a moment he'd reach out to me, but he stilled, finally nodding. "Nothing to be sorry about. Can't catch lightning in a bottle, right?"

"Something like that."

"I'd like to see you sometime soon," he said. "I'd hate for thirteen years to go by before we see each other again."

"Why did you come to my party?"

The desire melted from his gaze, leaving him more clear eyed. "We were friends once. Time to let the past go, I guess."

"Have you been able to do that?"

"I'm working on it."

"I'm not sure I ever will," I said.

He studied my face, searching for hints of the desire I'd felt just moments ago. He found none. "Guess that's my cue to leave."

"Right."

As he turned, he spotted a collection of framed black-and-white photos that I'd taken last fall. They were the ones I'd exhibited in my art show in January, right before the car accident. Odd, but I still didn't remember the show or bringing these pictures home and rehanging them.

Kurt studied the images closely. "You took these?"

"Yes. Sometimes I really do identify as an artist," I joked.

A smile quirked his lips. "Don't let what Jo-Jo said get to you. It's good to be a dreamer. She can be a moron and always found a way to take a swipe at you."

"That's not true."

"It's me you're talking to. I know Jo-Jo."

"She's evolved."

He chuckled as he leaned closer to an image of an old tree's twisted branches dangling over the high waters of the James River. "I know this location."

"We hung out on the rocks when we were in high school."

He swallowed, his Adam's apple bobbing. "It's also not far from where Clare was found."

"Yes." I'd stayed away from this place for years, and then last fall, I'd been pulled to the river rocks. I'd stood for hours, staring at the rushing waters, trying to conjure the secrets I knew were buried under the troubled surface.

When I returned to the site the next time, I had my camera and began shooting. After I developed the images in my makeshift darkroom, I stared at them, willing myself to see something that had escaped everyone thirteen years ago. *Tell me who killed Clare and left her body on the banks of the James River.* But no matter how many images I took, how long I stared, I saw nothing, heard nothing.

"Why're you chasing this now?" Kurt asked. "The cops crawled over every square inch of that land, hounded us all for months, and the press damn near ate me alive. Reopening this won't help anyone."

"Maybe these photos are my way of dealing with the shit that drove me to drink." I added a half smile, as if it would make me sound a little more reasonable.

"Have the cops been around lately?" Kurt asked.

"No. But I'm going to check in with Detective Richards tomorrow. He's supposed to retire soon."

"I can't believe he's still on the job. He seemed ancient when he talked to us."

"He was fifty-one at the time. He's sixty-five now." To Richards's credit, he'd initiated something new in the case every six or seven months to keep it from being classified as cold. Once he was gone, the files would still be at the station, maybe assigned to a new cop, but everything Richards carried in his head—the leads, theories, subconscious connections—would leave with him.

"He was rude," Kurt said. "He said terrible things to you."

"He was overworked and under a lot of pressure to solve the case. Since then he's never said no to me when I call and ask to stop by his office."

"When's the last time you saw him?"

"About eighteen months ago."

"He'll see you on a Saturday?" He reached for my hand.

I angled away from his outstretched fingers and walked to the door. "I have an appointment."

"Do you really think opening this wound will help you?"

No one wanted to remember how Clare had died. It was an uncomfortable truth that everyone assumed time would fix or heal. "It's not about me."

"Maybe let sleeping dogs lie."

"They aren't sleeping or lying. They're howling."

He exhaled. "I want you to be happy."

"I'll be happy when I find out what happened to Clare." I drew in a breath. "I'm tired, Kurt." That was true. Surging desire had cooled, and I felt drained. "I've an early shoot in the morning, and it's time you leave."

"Hey, I didn't mean to put up a barrier between us. I care about you."

"I get it. I do. I'm just exhausted."

He studied me a long moment and then nodded. "I'm glad I came."

"Me too."

His body angled as if he might lean in and try to kiss me. (Can't blame a guy for trying, right?) But he seemed to reconsider, nodded, and opened the door. He stepped onto the elevator, and I carefully closed and locked my door, standing still and listening to the elevator open and then the building's entrance close. I glanced out my window and watched Kurt disappear into the night.

Folding my arms over my chest, I walked to the black-and-white images on the wall. I stared, remembering the exact days and times I'd snapped each. With each shot I'd been chasing the light, hoping the next picture would whisper a secret the river held. It knew who had killed Clare. But it wasn't talking.

6

BRIT

I punched in the security code to Marisa's apartment building and walked to the elevator. Initially, while Marisa had been in surgery to relieve the pressure on her brain, I'd thought caring for her could be endless, so I'd had her keys copied and gotten the security code from the building manager. Braced for the worst, I had been ready to step up.

Turned out my sister was far more resilient than the doctors had initially thought, and she'd awoken. The only residual effects of the accident had been a mild form of amnesia, shorter hair, and wrecked taste buds. Marisa couldn't remember the ten days leading up to the accident, the crash, or why drugs had been found in her system. I decided to back off, considering how bad it could've been.

I'd searched every inch of Marisa's apartment after I talked to the surgeon and learned the paramedics suspected drug use. I'd been so pissed but not really surprised to hear about the drugs. All these days, weeks, and months of Marisa claiming to be sober had been a lie.

I had found not a drop of booze or any kind of drug. That didn't mean Marisa wasn't guilty. It just meant I'd not found the evidence. She was very intelligent, and addicts can be sneaky.

I stepped off the elevator, drawing in a breath and shoving aside the anger. It didn't do anyone, especially me, any good to dwell on the negative. *Positive thoughts, Brit. Positive thoughts.*

As I fumbled with my keys, I glanced to the other apartment on this floor and saw an assortment of moving boxes stacked outside. Marisa had a new neighbor. Good. At least she wasn't up here all alone. Why didn't she tell me . . . ?

Positive thoughts, Brit.

I shoved the key in the lock and opened the door. After flipping on a light, I moved to the kitchen. I dug two cleanish mugs from the cabinet and rinsed each out. Marisa could sleep through anything but freshly brewed coffee. When I heard feet hit the ground in the back bedroom, I smiled, rewashed a couple of plates, and set them beside a bag of bagels.

Reaching for the birthday bag, I pulled out the presents. I set out the Leica, the camera strap, and the bag filled with disposable cameras. All thoughtful gifts. I walked to a shelf near the window and set the Leica next to a dozen other cameras she'd collected. As I turned, I spotted a small red point-and-shoot camera. Daddy had given the camera to Marisa and a pink one to Clare when they turned sixteen. Marisa had all but worn hers out, but Clare had been more selective with her digital pictures, shooting only when her subject wasn't looking. Annoying but cute.

I folded up the bag and tossed the wrapping before I poured myself a cup, which I was sipping when Marisa appeared dressed in an oversize T-shirt that skimmed her knees. She was gripping her phone in one hand and a metal flashlight in the other.

"Good morning," I said.

"I thought I had a break-in."

"You know I have a key."

"I'd forgotten."

I filled another cup. "How's your memory?"

"Good except for the missing chunk." She set her phone and flashlight on the counter, took a sip, then grabbed milk from the refrigerator. She splashed enough in her mug to lighten it two shades.

"Have you seen the neurologist lately? I remember a follow-up appointment Wednesday."

Marisa raised her gaze. Sipped coffee. "I rescheduled it for Thursday morning. Too much work for the first of the week, and I like morning appointments better."

"You rescheduled? You can't do that. This is your brain we're talking about."

"It's one extra day, the last scan was clear, and this visit wasn't critical. The doctor said as much at my last appointment. So you can stop."

Drawing in a breath. "Stop what?"

Marisa grinned. "Mothering."

The smile caught me off guard, not because Marisa smiled so little (which was true) but because I remembered Clare, the bright, happy twin. When they were born, our mother placed both babies in my three-year-old lap. Clare had cooed, whereas Marisa had cried. Marisa had never been one to cuddle or play, but she was serious and introspective. When the twins had been small, Clare had done all the talking, and Marisa had been content to let her younger twin communicate for them both.

And when that detective had told us they'd found Clare's body after four days of searching, my father and I had turned to Marisa. Without makeup or her typical goth attire, she looked so much like Clare, and for an instant I thought the cops had made a mistake. Then Marisa spoke, her raspy voice shattering the illusion. She saw the disappointment mirrored on Daddy's and my faces. We'd both tried to cover, but Marisa had read our expressions.

It wasn't Marisa's fault that Clare was more vibrant, playful, and compliant. She always brightened up a room with her smile, and she always let the doctor examine her when she was sick, and she'd always taken her medicine. Marisa had fought Mommy and later me every step of the way on everything. M was who she was, and that had never been quite enough for me.

"It was good to see everyone," Marisa said. "Why'd you invite that group?"

"I thought it would be fun to go down memory lane."

"You hate memory lane." She dusted the everything seeds from her bagel onto her napkin.

"It wasn't my birthday. It was yours."

"Right. Well, thank you for the effort. It was nice."

I picked up my purse and walked to the framed black-and-white pictures. Each time I'd come into the apartment while Marisa was in the hospital, I'd stopped and stared at them. Moody and distant, like Marisa. And they whispered a message that always taunted me. "You should have another show." I turned, found Marisa cupping her mug in both hands, staring at the images. "Not still stressing about the missed ten days, are you?"

"Maybe a little."

"Why?"

"They hold secrets. And you know how I hate secrets." Marisa's light tone barely skim coated over the frustration fracturing the words.

"There are no secrets. There was your art show. You had three prewedding planning appointments the week leading up. And then a wedding the Saturday right after. The accident was the following Friday evening. There was nothing to miss but work."

"I sold one of my prints that week. To whom, I don't know."

"There was no entry in your Venmo account."

"It was a cash deal."

I walked to the door, opened it. "Call me if you need anything."

"Will do."

"Dinner with David and me soon?"

"Of course."

I stepped into the hallway, and as Marisa closed the door, I said, "See the doctor. Take more pictures. Lock the door."

The door closed, followed by a click, the twist of a dead bolt, and the scrape of a chain. "Satisfied?" Marisa said.

"Yes."

But I wasn't. Not even close.

7

MARISA

Saturday, March 12, 2022
10:00 a.m.

Today's wedding was going to be relatively simple. It was a courthouse elopement. Neither wanted any pregame photos, just the two of them rushing down the courthouse steps and then driving off in his vintage red Corvette.

I swallowed the last of my coffee and hurried to the shower. Out barely a minute later, I towel dried my hair. As much as I missed my long locks, I didn't miss the drying time. And shorter hair made me look different enough that I wasn't always seeing Clare staring back in the mirror. Maybe I wouldn't be in such a rush to grow it back out.

I dressed in my "uniform": black slacks, a turtleneck, and boots. I checked my cameras, which I'd charged yesterday before the party, and double-checked my bags for extra battery packs, tripods, and all the bells and whistles.

Grabbing my purse and keys, I stepped into the hallway and pulled the door shut. As I turned to go down the stairs, I spotted the growing pile of empty boxes gathered by the other apartment door. For several months, I'd had this floor all to myself, and I liked climbing the stairs knowing it was all mine.

As if my thoughts had set off an alarm bell, the door opened, and a tall man backed out of the apartment, dragging a big box filled with trash. When he turned, I stopped short, recognizing the outdoorsman / office-work guy from J.J.'s Pub last night. Alan.

Alan's smile telegraphed that he also remembered me. "Two tequilas."

"Guinness beer. You're the new guy on the floor?"

"I am. You live here?"

"For the last three years. I was beginning to think the landlord was never going to rent the space. Well, welcome to the neighborhood, Alan." Name recall was a must in wedding work. "If you need anything, I'm steps away."

"How about you show me where the dumpster is?"

"Sure. Walk out with me."

He lifted the boxes. "Lead the way."

I moved steadily down the stairs, holding the railing with one hand and my bag strap in the other. Alan's steady steps followed close behind me as I reached the door out to the first-floor lobby. Holding it open, I let him pass before opening the front door. I walked around the side of the brick building and down the alley, now littered with an old mattress, beer cans, and weeds that reached up between the cracks in asphalt still glistening from last night's rain.

"There's an alcove up ahead on the right. The dumpster is there."

Alan's gaze followed my outstretched hand. "I should've walked a little farther when I was looking for it."

A cold morning breeze blew down the alley, ruffling the folds of my jacket and traveling up my spine. "It's an easy mistake to make. Must go. Work."

"On a Saturday?"

"Wedding photographer."

That prompted a smile. "Be careful out there."

8

Him

NOW
Saturday, March 12, 2022
10:15 a.m.

I followed you from your apartment to the courthouse. You were still taking an Uber. Made sense at first after the accident. Gun-shy. Head injury. But it'd been two months, and you still hadn't bought a car or driven. That was not like you. You were an independent soul. That was one of the things that drew me to you.

As I parked in front of the courthouse, I watched your long legs climb the tall stairs with deliberate care. You were moving better, steadier on your feet, and walked with your old confidence. Your coat flapped open, no doubt showing off your breasts, not quite hidden by the black sweater. Several men stopped what they were doing, glanced in your direction, and ogled those breasts. Even the short red hair added to your allure.

Rising out of the car, I watched as you waited by the front door and strung a couple of cameras around your neck. You were in position, locked and loaded, when the doors opened to a thirtysomething couple. The woman was dressed in an ice-blue dress that skimmed her petite figure, and a white fur jacket warmed her shoulders. The man was wearing black pants, a white shirt, and a sport jacket. Three small yellow roses on his lapel matched the bride's bouquet.

You snapped pictures, followed them down the stairs to a waiting SUV. You said something to the couple I couldn't hear, but they turned back toward you. Both were laughing. You fired off a dozen more images.

I marveled at you and wondered again what it was about you and Clare that wouldn't release me. I'd tried hard to forget. Unhealthy obsessions never end well, as I knew, but even in death, Clare had never been far.

I'd heard identical twins could be hard to distinguish, but I'd never really believed it. There was always something—the shape of a face, the voice, even mannerisms generally varied slightly. But with you two, you were mirror images.

Standing there, I was transported back to a wildly loud New Year's Eve party. Dressed in black, Clare—yes, I definitely knew now it was Clare—tipped her face to the crescent moon. I'd been smitten and glad I'd taken the chance that she'd be there. Seeing Clare on that fateful night had altered the course of all our lives. So many things I'd have done differently.

I could have said the same about you. Thankfully, you'd survived your car accident with only minor lasting effects. The hair, of course, and the lost days. Critical days. And so far, you didn't remember me. Us.

Your lost time was divinely inspired. It had given me the second chance I'd been hoping for as I watched you these last two months.

Maybe Clare was our guardian angel. Our matchmaker.

Lucky for me. Lucky for us.

9

MARISA

The wedding photos went like clockwork. All according to plan. But my client wouldn't have had it any other way.

I tucked the cameras in my carrying case and hoisted it onto my shoulder as my Uber arrived. The drive to the Richmond Police station took less than ten minutes. Normally, it would've been walkable, but with the camera gear, it was a bit of a stretch.

Detective John Richards often worked Saturdays, and I knew my best chance of catching him was before lunch, provided there'd been no homicide to pull him away. I'd told Kurt we had an appointment, but it wasn't exactly official. The time was cemented in my mind, but I just hadn't told Richards.

It was always hit or miss when I called the detective, and more often than not, I landed in his voice mail. He usually returned my calls, but his answers generally were curt and unhelpful. No suspects. No new evidence. No breaks.

But today I was feeling lucky.

I pushed through the front doors of the station and walked up to the front desk. It'd been a different sergeant every time I'd been here, so no chance of camaraderie.

Adjusting the camera bag on my shoulder, I walked up to the woman wearing a black Richmond Police uniform, bars on her collar, dark hair smoothed back, and a grim expression. The brass nameplate read Collier.

The room was full of people, most of whom seemed to be waiting. The smell was stale, and the room painted a grim gray.

"Sergeant Collier," I said.

The woman looked up. "Can I help you?"

"My name is Marisa Stockton. I'm here to see Detective Richards. We have an appointment."

Small lies for the greater good were okay.

The sergeant eyed me as she reached for her phone and punched a few buttons. Her frown suggested my chances of success were low. I expected to hear Richards wasn't in the building or was in a meeting. A face-to-face meeting was a long shot. But faint hearts never win.

"He'll be right out," Sergeant Collier said.

"Really?" I cleared my throat. "Thank you."

Tightening my hand on my camera bag strap, I walked to a wall sporting crime prevention and community outreach posters, the Officer of the Month's picture, and a fire exit floor plan.

A side door opened. "Ms. Stockton."

I turned to see Detective Richards's tall frame move toward me. At age sixty-five he remained as fit as he had been thirteen years earlier. He still wore his hair short, though there was more salt than pepper. Same dark suit, light-blue shirt, tie, badge clipped to his belt. No jacket. His face was long, angled, with cavernous brow lines etched deeper in blue-black skin.

"Detective Richards." I extended my hand and matched his firm grip with one of my own. "I wasn't sure I'd catch you."

His gaze clung to mine. He was judging my sobriety. A fair test. I'd not always been sober when I'd seen him.

"Not many more days," he said, releasing my hand.

"When is retirement official?"

"Two weeks." He nodded toward the door. "Come on up to my office."

If I'd just been subjected to a test, it appeared I'd passed. "Thanks."

"Can I carry your bag?"

"No, thank you," I said. "I've hauled these around so much, they're an extension of me."

Opening the door, he waited for me to pass. "Business is good?"

"Can't complain."

I followed him up two flights of stairs, doing my best not to huff and puff, and then through a familiar maze of cubicles. Like him, the place was more careworn, but not much had changed in the last thirteen years. He led me to the same cubicle I'd sat in as a teenager. The desk was still covered with stacks of files, pink message slips, and large yellow pads covered in notes written in block letters. I glanced at the pictures of his three kids, who'd morphed from young teenagers to late twenties. No wedding band on his ring finger these days.

"Where was the wedding?" he asked.

"At the courthouse. Very casual. Nice to see a couple not focused on all the bells and whistles."

"My first wedding was like that. Big family event, friends on my wife's side I didn't know. Second one was smaller but still had about fifty people. Next time, it's going to be just the two of us."

"Next time?"

"Getting married at the end of the summer. Hoping now that I'm not working unmanageable schedules, I'll have a chance."

"Fingers crossed."

He motioned toward a worn plastic seat next to his desk as he sat in the swivel chair. "Happy belated birthday."

"You remembered."

"I remember a lot about your sister's case. Thirty now, right?"

"That's right. Officially an adult, I suppose."

He leaned back, threaded his fingers together, and rested them on his chest. "I don't have anything new for you, Marisa. No new leads."

"But the case is still open. It's not cold."

"It's active for another two weeks. Then all bets are off."

"So much for my birthday wish."

"Believe me, I don't like leaving the job knowing this case is open. Always stings when a young person like Clare dies."

Whoever killed Clare had stripped her body naked and laid it in the James River. Later, the medical examiner would report she'd been strangled. (It takes at least six minutes to strangle a person to death. Six. Minutes.)

The waters of the James River and a heavy rain had stripped away any DNA on her body except for Kurt's. After the case shifted away from him, it basically stalled. With no additional DNA, if the offender had a record, there was no way to find him. Television crime dramas led most to believe each crime scene had traces of some evidence that would miraculously crack the case. Not true.

Witnesses had seen Clare leave Jo-Jo's house alone, but no one could remember whether she'd walked the five blocks to our home, gotten or been forced into a car, or been pulled into another neighborhood house. One guy thought he'd seen someone approach her, but he'd been too drunk to absorb any details. There'd been an extensive search of the area homes as well as their security cameras. There'd been no trace of Clare.

Some said my sister had been drinking. Others couldn't be sure. A few said she'd looked pissed. Almost everyone, given how she was dressed and her sour mood, assumed she was me.

"Seems after all this time, someone might have said something," I said. "I've heard that can happen when time passes. Relationships break up and an ex spills a secret. Someone's conscience gets the better of them. Even an inmate hears something."

"All possible scenarios but no lucky break like that in this case. Unfortunately, many cases do not get solved."

I rejected the finality of his statement. Someone, somewhere, knew what had happened. Someone had seen *something*. "If you're retiring, could I see your case file?"

"Your sister's case is still open, which means I can't show it to you."

"But you're leaving."

"I'll give the files to another younger cop. He or she will follow up. You'll likely get a call."

It wouldn't be the same. Richards had lived and worked this case for thirteen years. There was no way he could convey all he knew to another detective. "When?"

"In the next year."

Another year. Another year of freedom for a killer. More missed opportunities to collect perishable evidence. "The new cop won't have the history or interest in the case like you did."

He drew in a breath. His chair squeaked as he leaned forward. "I can't give you the files."

I sat silent, perched on the edge of my seat, my fingers still gripping the strap of my camera bag. "What about a copy of your notes? I remember you wrote down everything I said when you interviewed me. You always had that big folio in your hand."

He regarded me but, instead of answering, shifted to another topic. "Tell me about your car accident."

"What's there to say?"

"Paramedics thought you had drugs in your system."

"You're keeping tabs on me?"

"Everyone here knows I care about your sister's case and you'd visited about eighteen months ago. I received a call from the officer who responded to your scene."

I'd thought Clare's case and my visits had dangled at the very end of this department's priority list. It hadn't occurred to me I was on anyone's radar other than Richards's. "I don't know why they made that assessment. I didn't take anything."

He said nothing, didn't arch a brow, smirk, or cock his head. Reading his expressions had always been a challenge. He played his cards very close to the vest.

Still, I felt his disappointment. "You've heard I lost about ten days' worth of memories, right?"

"I didn't know that."

"I still don't know what happened during the days leading up to the accident, but I know I wasn't using. I've been totally clean for a year."

"Slips happen, Marisa. It's fairly common, in fact. No harm, no foul. Looks like you're back on the wagon."

"I never fell off of it," I said clearly.

"Why're you so special?"

"I'm not. But I know right before the missing days, I was committed to my upcoming show. I was excited about work, life. It'd been a long time since I'd felt that good."

"The pictures in your art show focused on the spot where Clare's body was found. That's working shit out in my book. Digging into an old wound."

"I thought taking the pictures would tell me something I'd never seen before. I hoped something would reach out to me or someone else who knew something but hadn't come forward would."

"Have they done that?"

"Not yet."

"The earth generally guards secrets closely."

"Yes, it does."

"Maybe you were playing with fire, and revisiting that time got to be too much for you. You swallowed a pill in a moment of weakness. It happens."

"You sound like Brit. My sister has been walking on eggshells around me since. It's like she's afraid to say Clare's name for fear I'll lose my shit. I'm amazed she hasn't done surprise urine tests."

The corner of his lips tilted in an almost smile. "Are you going to meetings?"

"Last one was three days ago. I'll hit another one in the next few days."

"Good. Keep working the program."

"Yeah. I hear you." I leaned forward, grateful to have one person I could speak candidly to about Clare's death. "It's so wrong, you know? That someone could do what they did and just get away with it. So wrong."

Richards unknitted his fingers and rested them on the chair's armrest. "I know."

He was kind enough not to remind me that the world was full of injustice. Shitty things happened to good people all the time. Clare's death wasn't the only case that was unsolved. He'd once said he had twenty open cases. "Can I meet the new detective on the case? I promise not to hound him or her like you."

His right index finger tapped on the arm of the chair. "You didn't hound me. You care. I can never fault you for that. I'll leave a note in the file for the next detective to contact you."

Brick wall after brick wall. "What about the DNA? Did anyone try to retest her clothes? Technology has changed in thirteen years."

"You know we collected some of Kurt's DNA inside Clare's vagina."

I refused to cringe. "They were dating. That made sense. You'd said once there were three other women found strangled in North Carolina about that time. Were they ever linked to Clare?"

"Manner of death was similar, but none of the samples matched Kurt's DNA. If the cases are connected, I can't prove it."

"You suspected Kurt in those cases, too?"

"I suspect everyone until proven otherwise."

"Including me."

"Yes," he said. "Your alibi was always shaky."

"I told you I was driving that night."

"With a gas receipt to prove it."

I cleared my throat. "I knew my sister so well. I should be able to figure this out."

"None of us know everything about our friends, lovers, siblings. And even if we did, there are always secrets. Lies."

That wasn't true in Clare's and my case. We shared everything. We didn't lie to each other. "Those case notes are your personal property, aren't they? How hard could it be to copy them?"

He stared at me, the frown lines around his mouth deepening. He didn't speak, and I could only guess he was tired of telling me *no* or *I don't know.*

"Or maybe you could just get the report on my car accident. I've not had the nerve to request it, but I'd like to know. I'd like to remember what happened, what went wrong."

"I can get you something on the car accident," he said. "What're you looking for?"

It was my turn to say, "I don't know. I hoped there're pictures and the truth will jump out at me."

"I'll look into it. No promises."

I rose. "Thanks."

He stood. "Take care of yourself, Marisa. And for what it's worth, I'm sorry. I wish I could have given you answers. Clare deserved answers."

In the confined space, I realized how tall he was and how broad his shoulders were. The body of a brawler. "Good luck with the wedding. Call me if you need a photographer. It'll be my gift to you and the bride." I handed him one of my cards.

That half smile appeared again as he flicked the edge. "Will do."

I left the station, grateful to step out in the cold air and feel the sun on my face. I fished my phone from my coat pocket and called for an Uber.

Richards meant well, but in his world, my sister's life and death would always be reduced to a file tucked in a cabinet. Like the headlines splashing the papers thirteen years ago, they'd lose meaning, context, and finally vanish off everyone's radar.

When the car pulled up, I settled in the back seat, watching the city pass as the driver crossed the Mayo Bridge and drove south into the Manchester district. He drove an additional three miles beyond before he pulled into a car dealership.

Out of the vehicle, I walked toward the showroom. No one cared more about this case than I did, and if I wanted to talk to the people who'd been at the New Year's Eve party, I'd need a car to do it. Whatever phobias I might have nursed the last two months had to go.

Last year, when I first learned about the trust fund set up by my mother, I didn't want it, especially when the lawyers told me I had inherited half of Clare's portion in my account. It felt a bit like blood money. But I'd also learned the trust had seen me through three stints in rehab and helped me finally get on my feet. There wasn't a huge fortune left now, but it was still a nice chunk of change, and I'd learned to be grateful for it.

Now that I was more clear eyed, I was more practical, less emotional about the money. Long story short, it made life easier and gave me the freedom to figure out what had happened to Clare.

When I picked out a black SUV and told the salesperson I wanted it, I especially enjoyed watching his skeptical look transform when he verified my bank funds. A raised brow. A second look at me as he sat straighter. I didn't think I'd ever get tired of that expression.

I was in and out of the dealership and sitting behind the wheel of my new SUV in under an hour. It felt so different from my Jeep, the one I'd shared with Clare as teenagers and then totaled.

I gripped the wheel, and my heartbeat kicked harder when I started the engine. I'd been driving since I was fifteen and never once had been afraid.

Not once.

And now, I was.

"Don't be a baby," Clare whispered.

I put the car in drive and pulled out of the lot.

10

Marisa

Saturday, March 12, 2022
4:45 p.m.

The tangerine sun glowed bright over the James River as it hovered above the tree-lined horizon. I stood on the bank, watching the water lap gently against the rocks of the muddy shore. The wind wafted over the trees, fingering the edges of my hair.

Clare's body had been found in this spot four days after she'd gone missing. It had been a jogger, running along the road as the sun was rising, who'd spotted the splash of red floating on the water. But he'd kept running. Then something had prompted the young man to turn around and look closer. He'd told Richards he hadn't realized he was looking at a body until he was within feet of it. Clare had been lying facedown, her red hair splayed on the water.

I'd never see her again. Shit. I'd made so many foolish choices that night.

"Why're you late?" Clare said. "Where are you?"

"I'm still at Jack's." I held the phone to my ear as my head swirled. My body felt like it was melting into the scavenged couch on Jack's front porch.

Jack had dropped out of high school, left his parents' house with no plans of college, trade school, or a job, and now shared a small house with a group of guys in Ashland, an old railroad town twenty minutes north of Richmond. His life was one continuous frat party. The charm that had drawn Brit to him last year was wearing thin, and she was currently not speaking to him. I liked the idea of my older sister on the outs while I had the inside track.

"He has nothing you need," Clare said.

"Last day of the year, and then I'll turn over a new leaf."

"You can't keep doing this, Marisa."

"I'm not. Tomorrow, I'm on the straight and narrow. I want to celebrate the New Year right."

"I have something to show you. You need to come home."

"What? Tell me."

"Not over the phone." Music and laughter blended in the background. "Show-and-tell is more effective."

"I don't like the sound of that." Lights from the front porch glowed brighter.

"Then hurry up and get here."

My head grew fuzzier after the call, and I never made it to the party. By the time I stumbled home the next day, she was missing.

A fresh gust of wind brought me back to today and the shores of the James River, flowing with currents of loneliness and loss. "What did you want to tell me, Clare?"

My last call from Clare had been at 10:02 p.m. How many times had I stared at her name in my call log? I still had a screenshot of it in my photos.

Shaking off the melancholy, I returned to my car and sat behind the wheel, surrounded by the new-car smell that soon would mingle with everyday life—fast food, perfume, sweat after a long day's shoot. A therapist had once told me that the feelings surrounding Clare's death were a little like the smell of a new car: The acuteness would slowly fade and be replaced by a scent that would weave into my life. It would always be there, but it would fade into the background.

I inhaled, wanting to remember this aroma, knowing it would fade in time; however, Clare's loss had sharpened over the years and could still cut through flesh into bone.

"Shit." Driving away from the river, I wound through the neighborhoods up the hill. When I reached a familiar side street, Crowder Lane, I took a left. That last night, Clare had fought with Kurt, stepped outside into the darkness, and vanished.

I didn't drive by my family's old home but went the additional five blocks to the old Mediterranean-style stucco house that had belonged to Jo-Jo's parents. It hadn't changed much in thirteen years. The yard was neatly manicured, and there was a Mercedes parked in the driveway and a collection of boxed delivery packages on the covered front porch. Back when Jo-Jo's family lived there, there'd been several bikes leaning against the side of the house, a trampoline out back, and a basketball hoop at the end of the driveway.

Jo-Jo's parents traveled a great deal for work. Both were often gone during the week and not home until late Friday night. New Year's Eve 2008 they'd been skiing. The size of the house, absence of the parents, New Year's, booze, unsupervised kids—it had been the perfect storm.

When I'd pushed through the front door of my father's home on New Year's Day, a pale Brit was waiting for me.

"Finally," Brit said. "Where is Clare?"

I'd yawned, reached for an aspirin bottle in the cabinet next to the kitchen stove. I tossed two in my mouth, turned on the faucet, and gulped water.

"Get a glass," Brit said.

"Go away."

"Seriously, where's Clare?" Brit's eyes were bloodshot and her hair tousled.

I didn't know the answer but really wasn't worried. "This isn't the first time she slept somewhere else. Call Jo-Jo." I grabbed a soda from the fridge. "What happened to you? You look rough."

"I was sick last night," Brit said.

"Whatever." I'd left Brit in the kitchen, stewing like she did so well, and gone to bed. Dad, still dressed in his tux, had woken me up five hours later, roughly shaking me and shouting, "Your sister isn't home!"

And from that moment on, the next few days and nights had unwound in an uneven, macabre way, first with my father grilling me for answers, then with the calls to Jo-Jo, Kurt, and finally the cops. Then came the uniformed officer who accepted my nonanswers with growing frustration. I'd still thought Clare would show, and I didn't need Brit knowing I'd been with Jack.

Even after the first two days, I'd foolishly expected Clare to walk through the front door, hungover, exhausted, explaining she'd gone on a short trip, and slightly chagrined that so much fuss had been made. I didn't know then that when someone went missing, the first hour was critical. Cops called it the Golden Hour. As time ticked, the chances of rescue diminished, and the operation turned from rescue to recovery.

On the fourth morning, Detective Richards had arrived. He'd never shouted, never raised his voice. And after he told us his grim news, I'd been more fearful than ever to tell anyone what I'd been doing. I'd stuck to my story and told him I'd been on a long drive. I repeated the tale so many times, it felt like the truth.

An opening door pulled my attention forward. A woman came out of the front door of Jo-Jo's old house. She was dressed in jeans, a cable-knit sweater, and white athletic shoes. She must have been watching me through the window, because the more I lingered, the deeper her frown. I'd no idea how long I'd been sitting here, but I knew I'd outstayed my welcome.

When she raised her phone to her ear, I put the car in drive and drove to Forest Hill Avenue, the main artery in the area, took a left, and headed toward the city, winding past businesses and homes toward my apartment.

After I angled my car into the parking space that I'd still been paying for, I hoisted my gear and rose out of the car. My bones ached, and tight back muscles reminded me I was still recovering. After the car accident, I'd had to cancel several bookings. Brit had jumped in, as she did, and found other photographers to pick up the jobs. The lost revenue stung but wasn't crippling. (Thank you again, trust fund.) I'd spent that first week after the accident on Brit's couch, sleeping and often waking with dreams of Clare running through the woods as someone chased her.

Brit had hovered over me. Made sure I had what I needed, including clean clothes and a new phone. When it occurred to me that I was relying on her too much, I'd Ubered back to my apartment.

I punched in the security code on the front door and stepped into the lobby. I crossed to the stairwell and climbed. As I huffed and puffed, I vowed to quit the elevator and maybe start running again. Soon. Today, I could at least take the stairs.

As I pushed into my apartment, my phone rang. It was Jo-Jo.

"Did I catch you at a bad time?" she asked.

"No. Just got back from the shoot."

"That's kind of late. I thought this was a quick morning job."

"I bought a car."

"Did you? That's terrific." A refrigerator door opened and closed, and I imagined Jo-Jo rooting for something sweet to eat. She never could resist a cookie or piece of cake. "What did you get?"

"Black SUV."

"Ugh. Why didn't you replace your yellow Jeep? That was such a fun car. God, how long did you have it?"

"Fifteen years." I'd never buy a Jeep again. I'd shared the one and only with Clare, and when she was gone, I drove it, nursed it, and brought it back from the dead several times. To buy another without her felt like treason. "This one feels more practical."

"Growing up sucks."

I walked to the fridge, pulled out a cold canned seltzer, and pressed it to my temple. "It can."

"After the car, what did you do? The wedding was seven hours ago."

"I drove down to the James River. And then up to your old house."

"Oh, Marisa, not that again."

"What do you mean, not again?"

Silence settled. "The week before your accident, you went down to the river a lot. It was feeling like an obsession."

"How do you know that?"

"You told me when we had lunch."

I hesitated, trying to remember seeing Jo-Jo the week before the accident. I couldn't find a memory of it. "I've taken lots of pictures down there."

"It was never about the pictures." She sighed. "Look, I don't want to rehash that week. It was awful enough."

"No, please serve it up. I still don't remember the week or seeing you and I want to." I walked to the collection of black-and-white photos on my wall.

"We had lunch the Wednesday before. You were asking a lot of questions about Clare."

"Why?"

"You know you go through times when you're desperate to remember every detail."

That was true. There were days and weeks when the particulars of my sister's murder were all I could think about. In the first few years, I drank to shut off the endless questions. Hell, I'd done that for the better part of thirteen years.

I popped the can's top. "What kind of questions was I asking about Clare?"

"You wanted to know if I'd seen her at the party before she vanished. I remember her dancing in my parents' den with a bunch of people. Her arms were waving in the air, but she wasn't smiling. I thought she was you for a second."

"You said she fought with Kurt?"

"He came up to her, said something, and she blew him off. He reached for her, but she held up her hand as if to tell him to stop. I was too far away to hear what they said."

"Kurt said they didn't fight."

"I'm sure he did."

"What happened next?"

"I got distracted with Sam. He was being his charming self."

I knew about succumbing to charm. "And?"

"And then before I realized, it was midnight, a neighbor called the cops, and then there was hell to pay. I spent the rest of the night cleaning up."

"We're still living and breathing," I said, more to myself.

Jo-Jo's parents had been legally liable for the party full of underage drinkers. Both had lost their jobs, and my father had filed a lawsuit seeking $1 million in punitive damages. They'd settled out of court.

Jo-Jo had hated leaving Richmond before her high school junior year. She'd lashed out at me, blaming my family for causing so much trouble for her parents. Yes, I should have been there. Would I have, if not for that pill Jack gave me? It was my fault that Clare had wandered off with a stranger. If I'd been there, she wouldn't have left with him. Ten years would pass before Jo-Jo and I had a civil conversation. By then, I'd forgiven Jo-Jo, her parents, and everyone except the killer and me.

"I'm sorry," I said. "I didn't mean to churn this up."

Jo-Jo sighed. "It was a shitty time. No one came out a winner." Especially Clare.

I shifted my focus back to this year. "You were at my art show, right?"

"Yes."

"Was it crowded?"

"There were about a dozen people there," Jo-Jo said. "It was a respectable showing."

I sipped the soda. "I sold one picture." I didn't remember the sale, but I'd seen my note written in the margins of my datebook: *"FIRST SALE. $400."* "Did I sell it the night of my show?"

"I don't think so."

"According to my calendar, it was a cash sale." There'd been four one-hundred-dollar bills in my purse after the accident.

"That almost never happens anymore."

"I know."

"Did you write down a name?"

I walked to my desk by the window and flipped back to January. The worn bills were still clipped inside the book's back cover. Gently, I ran my fingers over them. "No name. Just the sale. You'd think I'd want to remember the name."

"The sale mattered more. Validation, right?"

"I guess you're right. Officially an artist."

"Why does it matter?" Jo-Jo asked.

"Because it happened during those lost days."

"The Black Hole." Jo-Jo had picked up my pet name for my memory blip.

The details had slipped behind a thick veil and were waiting for me to push back the fabric. Again, why it mattered I couldn't articulate.

"You sound tired," Jo-Jo said.

"I am. Long day."

"Take a hot bath. Go to bed."

"It's five p.m."

"What's your point?" she said lightly. "It's cold, dark, and perfect sleeping weather. You know me—never met a nap or bedtime I couldn't resist."

I chuckled, wishing I could close my eyes and shut my brain off. After the accident, the doctors had given me sedatives. They'd sworn they wouldn't be addictive, but they also didn't know me and how quickly I could latch on to something. Letting go of all substances had been damn near impossible last year.

"Thanks."

"The reason I really called was to tell you I had fun at your birthday party. It was terrific. At least until I made my smart-ass comment about the hats."

"It wouldn't be a party if you . . ."

Jo-Jo chuckled. "I know. Story of my life. Insert foot in mouth. You really are a talented photographer. And it takes someone willing to get lost to make something out of nothing."

"Thanks."

"Find a new subject. Stay away from the river. The answers are long gone. Find solace knowing Clare is at peace."

Countless people had told me that. On rare occasions, that old chestnut defanged the pain, but most days it didn't. "Right."

"What're you going to do with the next thirty years of your life?"

"Good question."

"Well, don't stress about it too much. Go to bed. It'll be brighter tomorrow."

I said my goodbyes, and when I hung up, I drained the last of my seltzer, feeling vaguely disappointed that it didn't have more kick. A few beers would be nice right now. The craving, jacked up by distress, was always there, the proverbial beast lurking in the shadows. I'd gotten better about chasing it away, but tonight, it reached out from the gloom, beckoning me. *Just one. Just one.*

I grabbed my purse, car keys with the dealer's fresh label still dangling from the ring, and left my apartment, locking the door behind me. There was always a meeting to attend, and though I didn't like them, there was some strength in numbers, and right now I felt too alone.

11

Him

THEN
Monday, November 19, 2008
3:00 p.m.

I couldn't say what it was about you—the long red hair; the narrow waist; the full, rounded breasts. All the parts and whole of you are perfect. You're a bolt of lightning and a bomb explosion rolled into one. I can't get you out of my mind. As far as I'm concerned, it's just you and me.

From the flyer, I found out where you planned to be today, so I rose early and drove into town. Now, as I parked on the city side street, I watched you duck into the warehouse space where there was an art exhibit. I hunkered down in my car and waited for a half hour.

Finally, you emerged with a bag and hurried toward the Jeep. So carefree. So perfect. I actually had butterflies in my gut, and the little bastards were gnawing away.

As I got out of my car, your phone rang, and balancing an artist's portfolio case, you fished it from the side pocket of a black leather purse. "Hello? Oh yeah, that's me." You sounded upbeat, but a little distant. "I won't be late. I'll be there in an hour."

When the call ended and you reached for the Jeep's door handle, I sensed it was a now-or-never moment. Sink or swim. "Excuse me." You turned, a smile on your face. There was no hint of suspicion or worry, which was a little troubling to me. A girl can't be too careful in this world. "I'm hoping you can give me directions."

Wide blue eyes brightened. "I'll try."

I could smell your perfume, see the small hoop earrings dangling, and hear your shallow breathing. The only senses missing were touch and taste, but it was too soon for that.

"I'm trying to get to Cary Street," I said. "You'll think I'm a fool because we both know it's directly across the river."

"Of course not! Straight up the street, take the first left and then a right. Follow the road across the bridge, and you'll see the street sign. At that point you can only take a right."

I trailed your line of sight, but as your head was turned, my gaze dropped to the slender line of your neck. "Thanks."

"Sure thing."

"You an artist?" It was such an obvious question it bordered on stupid, but I just needed a few more seconds with you. We'd made a connection, and in this world that was a rare thing.

"That's the dream," you said. "But saying and becoming are two different things."

"I bet you're pretty talented."

You chuckled. It was delightful, self-effacing. "Maybe one day."

"You're showing your work?"

"Not yet."

Talking about your art relaxed you. I'd found a sweet spot. "What kind of art?"

"Photography."

"I bet one day I'll see your name up in bright lights."

You laughed, blushed a little. So darn cute. "We shall see. Look, I've got to go. Been good talking to you."

As you got in the car and drove off, I drew in a deep breath that expanded the tightening muscles in my ribs and chest. I wasn't sure I'd taken a breath since I'd seen you last night.

Obsession wasn't good for me, according to my doctor. He said I took things too far. Crossed boundaries. Maybe I had once or twice, but I'd learned my lesson, and I wouldn't do bad things anymore.

This time nothing bad was going to happen.

12

MARISA

Sunday, March 13, 2022
1:15 a.m.

After sitting in a group meeting for two hours, absorbing stories, excuses, and promises to improve, I made my way home. Still too restless to sleep, I worked for four more hours on editing the photos I'd taken at the courthouse wedding. Normally, I didn't return edited photos for a couple of weeks, but I'd finally caught up on processing the pictures I'd taken before my accident. Though it had been a grueling few weeks on the computer as I'd played catch-up, I couldn't let this time go to waste—I didn't want to box myself in like that ever again. New memo to self: *Don't procrastinate. Sincerely, Marisa-Tomorrow.*

When I finally switched off the computer, it was after one. I grabbed a seltzer from the refrigerator and walked to the large window overlooking the glittering lights of the city. It was a peaceful time of night. Quiet. I'd always been a night owl, savoring the stillness, until the night my car slammed into that utility pole just south of Church Hill two months ago.

After impact, a thick darkness had swallowed me, seeping into my eyes, ears, mouth, and nose. I'd struggled to scream, breathe, and open my eyes, but the weight of the inky shadows had been too heavy.

I'd woken up in the hospital two days later. Brit had been sitting at my bedside, her eyes shadowed by smudges, her hair oily and slicked back, her eyes half-closed.

"Water," I whispered.

Brit had sat up, looked around as if she'd expected to see someone else, and then realized it had been me who'd spoken. She rose, reached for the buzzer, and called the nurse. Nurses and then a doctor had come into the room. My eyelids were raised, and a bright light was soon shining on my irises.

"Marisa, can you hear me?" a man asked.

"Yes," I whispered.

"Do you know where you are?"

"No." Though I was already presuming it was a hospital, I didn't have the words or the energy to articulate the thought. I sensed someone pacing, moving back and forth in an agitated line. Brit. It had to be Brit. Everyone else was operating with clinical precision.

"You're in the hospital," the man said. "You were in a car accident and suffered a head trauma."

"Okay," I whispered. "Water?"

Someone held ice chips to my mouth, and I sucked greedily on the cold moisture, which trickled over my lips but didn't nearly come close to satisfying my thirst. "That's all I can give you for now. Baby steps. You've been through some trauma."

Soft hands took mine in a firm, tight grip. "You scared the hell out of me." Brit. "I thought I was going to be all alone."

"No," I said. "Too tough."

Brit's shaky laughter mingled with sniffles, and when I cracked my eyelids again, I saw the blurred image of my sister swiping away tears.

Poor Brit. Always at my side when I was sick in the months after Mom died. And later cleaning up my self-inflicted messes.

A knock on my apartment door had me turning from the window and the city skyline. I sipped the seltzer, now tasteless and flat, and set the can on the counter. I checked the time, wondered who would come by so late.

I opened the door to Alan. He wore jeans, a worn Georgetown sweatshirt, tattered flip-flops, and tousled hair, all suggesting a long study session.

"I saw your light on," he said. "I've been working and thought I'd take a study break."

"What're you studying?" I asked.

"Decomposition rates," he said ruefully. "Evidence in an upcoming case."

"Attorney?"

"Prosecutor." He scratched the side of his neck. "Thought you might like a beer and some conversation. Tether me back to the living."

His pickup lines were improving. "Sure."

I closed my door, not bothering to lock it because the building was secure, and followed him the ten steps to his apartment. Entering, I found myself facing a wall of unpacked boxes.

"Excuse the mess." He didn't sound terribly upset by the chaos, but he seemed like the kind of guy who knew when to say the polite thing.

"No worries. It took me months to unpack."

I glanced at diplomas leaning against a brick wall. University of Virginia. Georgetown. Smart. Skis leaned against another wall beside a road bike and a half dozen pairs of running shoes. "Tell me about decomposition rates."

Clare had been in the elements four days, and the average daily temperature had been forty degrees. She'd been found lying facedown in the water, which had complicated the decomposition process. The parts of her submerged in water had turned black, but what had faced the air was bloated and breaking down.

He handed me a bottled beer. "You sure? Not a pretty subject."

The icy bottle felt slick against my fingers. I should've handed it back to him. But I wanted to feel normal. Be a regular person. I twisted off the top, telling myself that the smell of the beer would be enough. "I assume it's a murder case you're working on."

"Correct. But can't discuss the details."

"Sure, I get it." Needing to feel normal, I slowly raised the bottle to my mouth, letting the cool glass tease my lips. Hundreds of banked AA meetings should buffer any ill effects of a little beer. I sipped, letting the malty liquid linger in my mouth before I swallowed. I walked to the window overlooking the river. "Your view is better than mine. I see north into the financial district, but you get that plus the lights in Church Hill. And this place is about twice the size of mine."

"I like space." Alan leaned against a pillar planted in the center of the room. He now looked more like the version of Jamie Dornan from *The Fall*. "Still can't picture you wrangling nervous brides."

"They like that I don't get rattled by the inevitable failed plans and mishaps."

"A lot of people are cool under pressure. What makes your work so different?"

I dug my thumbnail into the bottle's label, then took a second sip. "I see the emotion."

"Explain." Head cocked, he appeared genuinely interested.

"I capture the must-do moments. First look, mother slash father of the bride seeing baby girl dressed up, cutting the cake. But I also capture the offbeat moments. They often go unnoticed, and yet they can encapsulate the day."

"But how do you see them coming? Some can be very spontaneous."

"Call it a sixth sense. The energy in the room shifts. I get into the flow."

He took another sip, making me aware I was still holding a nearly full bottle. "Those moments you capture can't all be good."

"Not always pretty but very powerful."

"And the moment from today's wedding?"

"There was a second before they got in the car. They both looked back up at the courthouse steps. I snapped and caught their joy and sadness."

"Sadness?"

"They'd eloped. Decided not to tell the family. Probably felt like a small omission at the time, but they'd just realized how big a decision it had been."

"My ex and I eloped. There was real hell to pay." He took a long sip of beer, then tipped his beer bottle toward me. "How does someone start a business like that?"

"I've always loved photography. So did my sister. We set about teaching ourselves the basics. Fast-forward a few years, I offered to be a second shooter at events for free just to get the experience. Word got around about my photos, and I got my own gigs. I've been at it full time for seven years now." I rarely talked about myself and found it rather unpleasant. "I chase brides, and you chase criminals."

"Technically, they've already been caught by the time I come on scene. My job is to keep them off the street."

"Which brings us back to decomposition rates."

"Last night you ordered two shots of tequila. Why two?"

More talk about me, which I should have avoided, but I heard myself say, "I was born an identical twin. Clare, the sister I just mentioned, died when we were sixteen. I always pour two shots on our birthday."

"But you didn't drink it."

"If Clare can't drink, then neither will I."

"I'm sorry," he said. "About your sister."

"Thanks." Mercifully his follow-up wasn't *She's in a better place* or whatever platitudes made people feel better about my loss.

Alan's direct gaze told me he wasn't afraid of death. He had the good sense not to ask for details, which put points in his column. Too many dug for the minutiae, especially when Clare's case was so public. There was a sense that Clare's death was part of the public domain, entitling everyone to all the facts.

"Okay, now that we've covered death," I said, my lips trying to twist into a smile. "We might want to quit while we're ahead."

"I'm off my game," he said. "Work has dulled my social skills. Normally, I don't lead with death. I begin with the weather, zodiac signs, and favorite wines before launching into the macabre."

"I appreciate the direct approach. I've never been good at small talk, but for the record, Pisces, should be midfifties tomorrow, and loved red wines."

Laughter rumbled in his chest. "Aries, will take a jacket tomorrow, beer man."

I tipped the neck of my bottle toward him, and I carefully and regretfully set it on the kitchen counter next to a bowl of apples and bananas. I wanted to tell him about Clare, press him for details about solving cold cases, but suddenly knew if I didn't get away from that beer, my dance with the devil would not end well.

"Thanks for the beer. I better get going."

"If you come back when the boxes are cleaned out, I promise better conversation."

My idea of good conversation *was* decomp rates, but that sounded weird even to me. "Sounds like a plan."

As I moved to the door, he fell in step behind me, and for a moment, I flashed back to someone watching, walking behind me so close I could smell the scent of his soap and feel a brush of air as his hand reached out toward me.

Agitated nerves tingled as I opened the door and stepped into the hallway. Cool air rushing up the stairwell skimmed my skin.

"Good to know I'm not the only human on the floor now," I said.

"Don't be a stranger."

13

MARISA

Monday, March 14, 2022
10:00 a.m.

I didn't see Alan again on Sunday. A few times I thought I heard him leave his apartment, linger near my door as if he might knock, but he never did. The weather on Sunday had been pleasantly cool, but Monday brought cold, drizzling rain and temperatures in the low thirties. Virginia had four seasons, and they were all in March.

After working all day Sunday on website updates, invoicing, and scheduling, I would have been happy to take Monday off and hibernate. But I had a client coming to the studio for a professional headshot. He had heard of my work through Brit, so I'd spent extra time cleaning my place and setting up the blue-gray backdrop that I'd bought secondhand from a photographer who'd retired two years ago. I pulled the long curtain separating my living and work spaces.

At precisely 10:00, the buzzer at the main entrance shouted out an arrival. I hurried downstairs, saw a man dressed in a suit under the awning, and pushed open the door.

"May I help you?" I'd learned not to volunteer information but to let the customer offer his or her name.

"Paul Jones," he said. His short black hair was slicked back to accent his raw-boned features, tanned skin, and penetrating gray eyes. "Marisa Stockton of MIS Images?"

"You found me. My studio is on the fifth floor."

He followed me up the stairs, which I opted for instead of the elevator. Never a fan of getting in a soundproof metal box with a stranger. I opened my door, stepped inside, and waited for him to pass by. He paused, studied my photographer's studio. His expression remained grim and gave no hint of whether he found the space lacking. Ultimately, what mattered would be the photographs, so I didn't bother to explain.

"How do you know my sister, Brit Stockton?" I asked.

He tugged at the cuff of his coat. "She and I are business associates. We've coordinated several real estate transactions before. She raved about you. And I'm now in need of headshots for a new website I'm launching."

"Great. You mentioned real estate transactions. What business are you in?" Chatting up clients relaxed them and led to better pictures.

"Commercial real estate. I've hired a new office manager, and she's pressing for the headshot. Most of our marketing is done online. Well, you understand. A headshot is worth a thousand words."

"Understood." I guided him toward the drop cloth, studied him a beat, and then reached for an iron-frame barstool with a polished wooden seat. It had an industrial vibe that felt like a nod to the past but was also sleek enough not to feel old-fashioned.

"There's a mirror around the corner, and I've made coffee if you'd like some."

He moved to the mirror, checked his hair as I checked the lights and my camera settings. As he returned, he noticed my pictures of the James River.

"Did you take these?" he asked.

"I did."

"Are they for sale?"

"They are, yes. The prices are still on the back right corner from the art show I had in January."

Paul folded his arms and leaned in toward an image that featured a large oak tree reaching out over the James River with bent, gnarled branches. "I know this spot."

"It's fairly popular."

"I lived nearby and used to run down that road all the time. It always looked just like this in the winter."

A runner had found Clare, and several joggers had run past me when I'd been taking these photos. "It's a popular route."

"I haven't been down there in years."

I motioned for him to sit on the stool. He settled and I adjusted his coat and tie. The advantage to being female was that men would let me fuss over crooked ties and bent collars. "It's not really changed since I was a kid."

"You grew up there?"

"I did. From birth to eighteen."

"Mid-2000s?"

"That's right."

"We likely lived there at the same time."

"Really?"

I issued directions: turn his head left or right, drop his chin, tilt it up. He complied easily, and the entire session took less than a half hour. I ended up with fifty photos, including several I knew would be usable.

I came around and showed him a few images on my viewfinder.

"Good," he said. "You'll email me the digital files?"

"I'll set up a site for you, and you can access the pictures."

He fished his phone from his pocket. "You'll invoice me?"

"Yes."

"And that picture is still for sale?"

"Of the tree? Yes."

He walked to the picture. "May I remove it?"

"Sure."

He glanced at the back. "Can I Venmo you the money for it?"

"Sure." I gave him my username.

He entered the payment. "Sent it."

My phone dinged with a message, and the amount hit my account. Exhilaration buzzed as I carefully took the picture from him, grabbed a paper towel, wiped away the dust, and removed the price tag. I'd sold a piece before, but the memory of that transaction had been lost to the Black Hole. I supposed this was my first-known experience of an artwork sale. The situation felt bittersweet. Gaining at the price of letting go. Did these feelings mirror my January experience? Or were echoes of the really first sale tempering this moment? I would never know. I decided it didn't matter. Feeling good was feeling good.

"You've made my day," I said.

"I could say the same," he said. "This spot stirs a lot of memories for me. This will be a nice addition to my study."

"I don't have paper or a bag to wrap it in." Had I been more organized at my art show?

"No problem." He accepted the framed picture. "Thank you again, Marisa."

I walked him to the door, opened it, and allowed him to pass before I followed him down the stairs to the first floor. I pushed open the security door and stood outside in the chilled air. "I'll have digital files to you in a day or two."

He tucked the picture under his arm and extended his hand to me. I accepted it. His grip was strong. "Look forward to it."

I stepped back into the building, and he slid the picture into the back seat of a Lexus. As he pulled away, he glanced in his rearview mirror and caught my lingering gaze. For a moment, I felt trapped.

As I took a step back, my heart thumped against my ribs. Looking from side to side, I checked the lock on the front door as a memory of distant eyes bored into me from the shadows.

14

Marisa

Back in my apartment, I walked to the row of ten pictures I'd taken of the river. Now two were missing. I raised my hand to the spot where the forgotten first-sale image should have been, as if doing so would summon the buyer and fill the blanks in my memory. Why did it matter who I'd sold the picture to?

I had no real record of the sale, but I still had the negative for the original picture. I slid on my glasses, sat at a light table where I worked with my prints. I opened a notebook filled with negatives tucked in clear sleeves and found the one for the first sale.

This image was different from the others. I'd set my camera up on a tripod the day of this shoot, and I'd walked into the frame. Staring out at the water and using the remote, I'd snapped twenty images. I'd stood still, staring, thinking about Clare, trying to channel her. Part of me hoped my sister was at peace, but my selfish-self wished her spirit were restless, angry, and stalking the earth in search of vengeance.

This picture was the only one in the sequence that had worked. The others on that particular day of shooting either had been out of focus or the lighting was off; however, this image had arrived fully packed with emotion and a shadow echoing my shape that had me wondering if I'd conjured up Clare's spirit.

I moved into my darkroom, which was the apartment's windowless closet. I set up three chemical trays, one for the developer, one for the neutralizer, and finally a water bath. I chose the negative from the sleeve in my binder and centered it on the enlarger. After switching on the red light, I closed the door and shut off the bright light. Centering my photographic paper, I tried to remember how I'd created the first image but knew no matter what I did, this wouldn't be an exact copy. I clicked on the enlarger, burned in the right edge to the count of three, and then clicked the machine off. I slid the paper into the developer and watched the print's twin slowly appear.

The shadow on the right was darker this time, but the effect felt like it worked. Next the neutralizer stopped the development and then the water bath. After I pinned the print to the small clothesline strung over the workbench, I stepped back and studied it. It felt close to the first.

I'd never stopped to consider whether I should limit the number of prints. But now, as I stared at this one, I knew I'd never re-create it again. It was officially retired, and this copy would belong only to me.

This mystery buyer and I now shared a connection. We both owned this print. Our meeting might be forgotten, but the tethers binding us would always exist.

15

Him

THEN
Tuesday, November 20, 2008
10:00 a.m.

I stared at the pictures I'd taken of you in the last forty-eight hours. I marveled at the power your face held over me. You were the first woman I saw when I woke up, and you'd be the last before sleep.

Glancing back at my neatly made bed, I imagined the gray sheets twisted around your naked body as you offered me a satiated smile. I wanted you to want *me*. There needed to be an us.

But the doctor would have said to leave *us* safely tucked away in my brain. Forcing love leads to trouble. Imagining an us could be enough. It was safer.

Still, I couldn't stay away. I needed to see you.

I moved inside and toward a makeshift bar, grabbed a beer, and popped the top. A long pull later, I felt a little steadier, and not as nervous.

The music pulsed, thumping in my head and churning up a primal desire I'd not felt in a long time. I downed the last of my beer as a woman dressed in silver sequins angled toward me. She nodded to the dance floor, and though I wasn't interested, standing and simply staring was a guarantee to get noticed or remembered in the wrong way.

Drink set down, I took her by the hand and pulled her toward me. Emboldened by music and alcohol, she quickly closed the gap between us and pressed her breasts to my body. She smelled of perfume, hair spray, sweat, and booze—nothing like your scent of clean soap and shampoo clinging to freshly washed hair.

When the song ended and a new one started up, she tried to coax me to stay, but I'd had enough. Making a polite excuse drowned out by the music, I left the room and found my way to the parking lot. Leaning against my car, I pulled a cigarette from my jacket pocket, lit the tip, and inhaled. My ears pounded, and I was frustrated that I'd not seen you.

I checked my watch, knowing the event could go on for hours.

And then just like that, you appeared on the front porch, looking a little frazzled and a lot annoyed. Big parties weren't your thing, either, were they? I knew we were kindred spirits.

I considered all the stories I'd rehearsed. The simplest lies were the best. I ground out the cigarette and closed the distance between us. "Hey," I said. "I think I know you."

You looked up, and this close, I could see fatigue had whitewashed your complexion. "Man-who-needed-directions."

I liked the nickname. Couples had nicknames for each other. What should I have called you? *Red* was too obvious. "I thought I saw you in the party. I came out here to get away from the noise."

"You were at Tamara's party?"

"She's a friend of a friend."

You started walking. I fell in step beside you, and we walked down the line of cars toward the Jeep you'd been driving the previous day. Out here, the darkness wrapped around us, cocooning us from the world.

"Want to grab a drink?" I asked. "You can pick the place. I'll meet you there." I grinned, knowing I could be very charming when it suited me.

You glanced back at the house, where the party raged. There was a man on the porch with a blonde. The couple was laughing. You frowned.

"What's with Captain America?" I asked.

"Captain Asshole." You drew in a breath. "A drink would be nice."

I didn't know who the guy was, but I owed him my thanks. "O'Malley's?"

"Sure. I'll follow you."

"Great."

"What's your name?"

You hesitated and then smiled. "Marisa."

"Good to meet you. I'm Jeff." I'd defaulted to a name that wasn't mine because I already suspected how it was going to go between us.

As I drove to the bar, I kept a sharp eye on your headlights, fearful you'd peel off. But you stayed the course. I parked in the restaurant's lot and watched as you pulled in beside me. We were already working as a team.

I was bold enough to press my hand in the small of your back. Your muscles tensed only slightly and then relaxed. I opened the door for you. As we got a booth in the back, you rubbed your cold hands together, using friction to speed up circulation.

You were a good-looking woman, and the dark jeans skimmed your long legs. There was a slight edge to you, but you didn't strike me as the tattoo type. If there were permanent markings on your body, they were discreet and carried the weight of lasting emotion. A significant date, a name, a small heart with a crack in the center. Hell, but you looked young.

You were likely wondering why you were here. You'd already surmised that I wasn't your type, but what the heck, right? I'd already guessed you didn't warm up to people quickly. That was good. Still, you were here now, and that sent a message that you liked me: you wanted to get to know me better.

"Did you take pictures at the party?" I asked. "Any images jump out?"

You pulled a small digital camera from your pocket. "Nothing too fascinating. Everyone was too drunk, and they looked kind of sad."

The waitress arrived. I ordered nachos and a beer, and you ordered a wine. Waitress ID'd you, and you passed the test, though I suspected the card was fake. No way you were twenty-one.

As my head turned, I heard two clicks of the camera. I stayed cool. I'd done nothing wrong, and what's a picture?

While we waited for the drinks, we chatted about the area, and I talked around the details about myself as much as I could. Our conversation was easy, relaxed, as if two old friends had met up after years of being separated. Christ, was it possible to really find a soul mate? The nachos arrived. We ate.

You glanced at the time on your phone. "Almost three hours."

"Time flies."

"I'm going to have to call it a night."

Was work waiting for you, or maybe Captain America? I didn't like the idea of you wedging in a date with me before going to another guy. "Sure, of course." I rose as you did. "I'd like to see you again."

You didn't jump at my offer, which made you cautious and not stuck-up. Selective. Good. Made me want to bend you over a table . . .

"Okay. That would be nice. I'm sure we can work it out."

"How about Wednesday? Unless you're on the hook to help with Thanksgiving."

"No big family gathering for me."

I wanted to kiss you lightly on the cheek. But your body didn't angle toward mine, and there was no moistening of the lips or tucking of a strand behind your ear suggesting you'd like me to be more aggressive. That was okay. Meant there likely wasn't another guy waiting.

"You'll hear from me soon."

"Thanks, Jeff, for rescuing me from a boring party."

A sizzle of desire burned hot in me. The more you held back, the more I wanted you. If I could have taken you in the bathroom then, I'd have put you up against the wall . . .

Slow and steady wins the race, old boy. "Glad to be your knight in shining armor."

Your laugh was quick, genuine, sexy. I stood and watched you walk out of the bar, your shoulders back, your gaze forward. You were good at pretending you knew where you were going. But I could see through the act. You were lost. Needed guidance. But *that* was okay. I was here now.

16

MARISA

Monday, March 14, 2022
6:15 p.m.

Brit texted me midday with an invite for dinner. It would've been so easy to drum up an excuse, but I'd finally typed back **Sounds fun!** The exclamation point was strategic. **What can I bring? Nothing** was her customary reply. Mine was a thumbs-up emoji.

I was late when I pulled into Brit's driveway.

Brit had been as attracted to the zip code as she had to the house, which was a one-story brick rancher painted white. There was a large display window, a red front door, and a carport that never accumulated junk. The yard was manicured with purple and yellow winter pansies nestled under the boxwood hedge.

I grabbed my bouquet, checked the cellophane wrapper for a price tag (peeled off, tucked in pocket), made my way down the herringbone sidewalk to the front door, and rang the bell.

Heels clicked in the stone foyer, and the door snapped open. Was there a little tension behind the smile? Safe bet there was. "Welcome!"

"Thanks for having me." I handed her the flowers, which seemed to lose a little of their glow.

Brit looked past me to the car now parked behind hers. "You got a car?"

"On Saturday."

"That's great."

Inside, I slipped off my ankle boots and followed my sister down the long hallway toward a kitchen. Along the way were small paintings that she had collected on trips to Ireland, Italy, and Greece. The only image that linked to our past was a picture of Brit, Clare, and me. Brit was about five and MC was two. Yellow dresses, white bows, and smiles. Picture perfect. I'd thrown up on the dress after the session.

In the kitchen, David stood at the AGA stove, stirring a pot of tomato sauce. A large bowl of freshly drained pasta swirled in a blue, wide-mouthed bowl to his right, and he wore one of Brit's KISS THE COOK aprons. For a couple who'd met two months ago, the relationship was moving fast.

"Marisa," David said, smiling. He was an attractive man. If I were a casting director, I wouldn't have paired him with Brit, unless I was looking for a sharp contrast. My sister wasn't classically beautiful, but all hard angles and very striking.

"Smells terrific." I smiled but didn't lean in for even a quick hug. We didn't know each other that well.

"My classic Italian grandmother taught me how to make the gravy," David said.

I sipped my water, remembering the beer I'd had at Alan's apartment yesterday. I'd handled it just fine. I'd not gone on a bender as all the AA counselors warned, and I'd thought about it only five or six times since. I wasn't really craving one.

David ladled the sauce onto the pasta, stirring the rich chunky tomato blend into the noodles before topping it all with basil chiffonade.

"I bet you haven't eaten today," Brit said.

"Coffee," I admitted. "Breakfast and lunch of champions."

"I thought that was birthday cake?" David asked as he set the pasta bowl on the table next to a loaf of fresh bread and a salad.

"It was delicious." In truth, I'd only moved it around on my plate at the party, and this morning had tossed the leftovers. Celebrating still felt a little like a betrayal. "Goes great with coffee."

"She didn't eat a bite," Brit said. "I can always tell when she's fibbing."

"Why would you say that?" I asked.

"Please, I've known you all your life. I know when you're telling the truth."

The room grew smaller. Somewhere in the house a grandfather clock ticked. We all sat at the table, Brit at one end, David at the other, and me in the middle. I dished pasta and bread onto my place, convinced the skids of my graceful exit could be greased with a healthy portion of carbs.

"I sold a picture to a client today."

"Really? Which one?" Brit asked.

"One of the river pieces that I showed in January. The client was Paul Jones. He said you suggested me."

"Paul, yes," she said, eyes brightening. "Commercial real estate and destined to own half the city. We've done a few deals together. He lives near our old place."

"He was in my studio for professional headshots," I said. "He saw my pictures on the wall."

"Is that safe?" David asked, turning his attention to me. "I mean, letting strange clients into your home can be dangerous, can't it?"

"Brit recommended him," I said.

"Serial killers can be successful," David said. "They go to college, walk among us."

Brit laughed. "I'm certain Paul is not a serial killer, honey."

David swirled pasta on a fork. "Probably not. But given what happened to Clare . . ."

The room stilled and neither Brit nor I breathed.

"Sorry about that." David coated the words with enough charm to ease my sister's frown. If this exchange had been between Brit and me, we'd be fighting, and I'd be counting seconds to my exit. But David, who'd likely gotten an earful about me from Brit, skated by unscathed.

Brit set her fork down, reached for a wineglass filled with sparkling water. She had to be calculating the minutes until I left and she could crack open a red. Brit loved her reds. So had Clare, for that matter.

I plucked a slice of buttered garlic bread from the platter and tore off a bite-size piece. "I went to see Detective Richards."

Brit picked up her fork and looked at David as if praying for strength. "And?"

"Nothing," I said.

"Who's Detective Richards?" David asked.

"He investigated our sister's murder," Brit said.

I'd heard that word so many times now that it felt more like a bramble brushing my skin than a knife slicing flesh. "There's nothing new to report. And he's retiring in a couple of weeks."

"He's always been good about following up every few years," Brit said.

"Clare died thirteen years ago, right?" David said.

"That's right, babe," Brit said.

"I asked for his case files, but he said he couldn't do it," I said.

"Why?" David asked.

"Formal police records can't be handed out, I suppose, especially in an open case," I said.

"But it's not solved after thirteen years. The cops have had their shot. Now you get yours," David said.

My opinion of David was improving. "Logic and the law don't always mesh."

"What would you do if you had the case files?" Brit's expression teetered between shock and amusement, much like it had when I was nine and she'd caught me tie-dyeing all my clothes purple and white. "Follow up on old leads?"

"That's exactly what I'd do. I'd start making the rounds just like the detective did thirteen years ago."

"If no one knew anything then, they won't now," Brit countered.

"That's not always true. People change over time. Breakups happen, someone dies, priorities shift, and someone is willing to talk. Deathbed confessions. Time can shake things loose."

"You've been listening to too many podcasts." Brit drew in a breath. "Time hasn't changed you that much. Still ready to rush in where angels fear to tread."

I might've been out of control too many times, but now I could throttle the turbulent emotions when they surfaced. "I hope I never change when it comes to Clare." I tore my bread into smaller pieces but didn't eat them.

"It was hard moving on," Brit said quietly, her head inclined toward David. "But I found a way."

And so had our father, in the arms of his second, and then his third, wife. My forward progress had been painfully slow and unsteady, like wheels mired in the mud. Two steps forward, three back. "You didn't lose your other half."

"Clare was your sister, not your other half," Brit said.

Of course we'd been two very different people—I was as moody as Clare had been lighthearted—but we'd been connected since conception, and losing my twin had been akin to a physical loss. "That's not what it felt like."

"She was my sister, too."

"What do you remember of that last night?" I asked. This conversation should have stayed between my sister and me, but I was just annoyed and saddened enough not to care.

Brit drained the water from her wineglass. "I was home sick. You know that."

"You were really looking forward to Jo-Jo's party."

"I wasn't feeling well and not in the mood to stand around with a bunch of high school kids."

"You'd only been out of high school six months."

"Felt like a lifetime," she said.

"You were stoked to go."

Her fingers curled into fists. "And I got one of my stomach pains, like when I was a kid."

"You hadn't had one of those since Mom died."

"I had them but then I finally grew out of them," she said.

"Why didn't you give Clare your car to drive?"

She dabbed her mouth with a white napkin, blotting and leaving a red lipstick impression. "Kurt was picking her up, remember?"

"Did you talk to him?"

"He didn't come in. He was late and honked the horn, and Clare went running. When I made it to the window, they were driving off." She raised a brow, squaring her shoulders. "You never said where you went that night. And don't say driving."

"Buying drugs," I said.

Brit blinked, tossed an embarrassed smile to David. "Refreshing honesty aside, I think we've dug into the past enough."

"Clare called me. She said she had something to show me."

"And I still have no idea what it was," Brit said.

We'd never had a sober conversation about that night, and I could see why now. The long-ignored emotions came with too many sharp edges.

"You both should be proud of yourself," David said. "You've both found a way forward."

"I have," Brit said.

If we were living in a rom-com, this would have been the black moment. I was Brit's quirky, unreliable kid sister who had been holding her back. Now she finally had a chance at happiness, but I was stirring more cauldrons of trouble and blocking her bliss.

Settling into a silence, I took a bite of pasta. Thankfully, David picked up on my mood and began to chat about all things Brit, which seemed to shift my sister's attention toward the positive.

Our dinner limped along for another forty-five minutes. Plates clean, bellies full, we enjoyed strawberry cake and coffee for dessert. Finally, at 7:15, I set my last plate in the sink and announced my departure.

"Thanks for dinner," I said.

Brit handed me a plastic tub full of spaghetti. "Of course."

David was behind me this time, as if the dinner had fused us all as some kind of family. "Don't be a stranger. And keep us posted on your investigation. Who knows, you might unearth something valuable."

"Do my best," I said.

Brit hugged me. David stepped closer, as if judging whether he'd reached the next level, where hugs or maybe a kiss on the cheek were allowed. He wisely opted to hold back.

"Call if you need anything," Brit said. "And don't forget. Tuesday at ten a.m. We go over your books."

She'd told me three times last week. "Got it."

When I stepped into the night, I inhaled the cool air and crossed the sidewalk to my car, my sister's and David's stares trailing me the entire way. Behind the wheel, I started the engine, waved a final good-bye, and then backed out of the driveway.

The need to leave suburbia bordered on desperation, and I didn't take a full, real breath until I reached the interstate. As the lights of the city grew closer, my thoughts turned to Richards. Talking about him had stirred too many unanswered questions, which I knew wouldn't be satisfied by our one conversation or tonight's with Brit.

My phone dinged with a text from Paul Jones as I pulled into my parking lot.

Paul: Looking forward to seeing pictures.

Me: I'll have them soon.

Paul: Spreading the good word about your work.

Me: Thank you.

Paul: You're on my radar. Let's get a drink sometime.

Me: Sure.

I didn't drink, and I didn't date clients, but age had taught me to be more diplomatic. I moved quickly to my front door. Inside, I climbed the stairs, and as I approached my door, I saw a plain manila envelope leaning against it. I picked it up, judged the weight (hefty), and opened my door. Inside, I flipped on the lights, dropped my keys, food container, and bag on the table.

I unfastened the clip on the envelope and pulled out a stack of papers. The first few sheets were my accident report. The pages behind them were not on official forms but handwritten on notebook paper. The date in the top right corner was January 4, 2009. It was the date Richards had opened his investigation into Clare's death.

Shrugging off my jacket, I let it slide off and fall to the floor. Heart beating, I read the first page written in Richards's handwriting:

Sixteen-year-old female. Strangled. Naked. No apparent signs of sexual assault. Found in James River near the Huguenot Bridge.

The past reached out and, in one swipe, hit me hard across the face, forcing me to step back and draw in a breath. Tears welled in my eyes, and I squeezed my lids closed as I struggled to pull in a breath.

I turned from the file, realizing that Richards had done me no favors giving me the notes that he'd taken while investigating Clare's death.

But I wasn't looking for kindness or warm fuzzies. I wanted facts, no matter how brutal.

17

RICHARDS

THEN
Friday, January 4, 2009
9:00 a.m.

Frank Stockton is a big man. Wide shoulders, large hands, a high-top haircut that looked twenty years out of date. He knows his height is an advantage, and he's not afraid to use it. We've met before, and when he looked at me, he remembered.

Beside him stood a daughter in her late teens. That had to be Brit. She was dressed in jeans and an ironed shirt. Her hair was washed, and she was wearing makeup. She was tall and had the bearing of a person who liked to be in control.

However, my gaze settled on the second daughter, the younger one. Her thick red hair was braided, the blended strands dangling over her shoulder like rope. Her face was pale, and her hands trembled slightly. She wasn't anywhere close to pulled together like her sibling.

Staring at the younger sister was unnerving because I'd spent the early morning staring into the dead version of that face. Lifeless, cloudy eyes and skin partly blackened and loosened by the water. I'd known

Clare had an older sister and a twin, but I wasn't really prepared for this mirror image.

"This is my older daughter, Brit, and my second youngest, Marisa." Frank Stockton's face was drawn, but a tan gave him a healthy glow that a distraught father shouldn't have.

I kept staring at Marisa, trying to shake the idea that the dead had risen and followed me here. This was a career first. I cleared my throat. I wanted to lead with questions that I already knew the answers to. They'd show me the person's demeanor when they told the truth. Later I'd have a benchmark when the lies began. "How many daughters do you have?"

"Three," Frank said. "Like I said, Brit is my oldest and then the twins, Marisa and Clare."

"And your wife?" I knew the answer. I'd assisted on her death investigation four years ago, though I doubted the girls remembered.

Under Marisa's brutal honesty was sadness, pain. "Have you found Clare?" she pressed, cutting off my next question to her father. Lack of sleep and crying had stripped her voice raw.

A muscle pulsed in my jaw. Her pain aside, she wasn't running this show. I was. "You and your sister are identical?"

"Yes." She clearly considered the situation grave enough not to punctuate with a teenager's eye roll or sigh.

"When is the last time you saw Clare?" I asked.

"On New Year's Eve. About seven o'clock."

Four days ago, I'd put a clean pad in my folio case, sensing this investigation would require a lot of notes. "Where did you see her?"

"Here at home," she said.

"Where were you the night she went missing?" I asked.

"I was driving," she said, glancing toward her father. "Sometimes I like to just drive. I was supposed to meet her at the party but lost track of time."

I raised a brow. "Just driving?"

"Yeah."

"Why?"

"To clear my head. To settle my nerves."

"Why were your nerves rattled?" I asked.

"It's been that way since Mom died."

Marisa was lying. She might still be reeling from her mother's death, but there was more to be told. I couldn't prove it, but after two decades on the job, I could smell lies and half truths. I also suspected that Marisa was stubborn enough to stick to her story no matter what. The best liars do.

"All I've heard about identical twins is that they tend to stick together. Were you and Clare close?" I asked.

"Sure. Of course. She was my twin. We shared everything."

"Did you two have a falling-out? I have a couple of sisters, and I know how they can fight."

"We weren't fighting."

"And you were out for a drive."

"Yes."

"And Clare, did she like to drive?"

"No," Marisa said.

"What's going on here?" Mr. Stockton interjected. "Do you have news on my daughter Clare?"

"I do." I closed my notebook and studied each member of the Stockton family closely. "The remains of a young woman matching Clare's description were found in the river a few hours ago."

Frank Stockton rubbed the back of his neck with his hand. Brit teared up immediately. Marisa stood stock straight, emotionless.

"You don't look shocked, Marisa," I said.

"I don't know what to say," Marisa said. "Are you sure you didn't make a mistake? Cops aren't perfect."

"No mistake," I said.

Brit began to weep.

Mr. Stockton turned from me, cleared his throat, and braced his shoulders as if readying to pick up a heavy weight. "How?"

"We haven't determined that yet," I said. "I'll know more once I talk to the medical examiner." I refocused my attention on Marisa. "You still insist you were driving?"

"Yes." There seemed barely enough air in her lungs to push the word out.

"Can you prove it?" I asked.

"I have a gas receipt," Marisa said. "I think it's still in my purse."

"I'll want that receipt."

"Sure."

"Whose car were you driving?" I pressed.

"My Jeep. Clare and I share—shared it."

Mr. Stockton's frown deepened, but he didn't press about the infraction.

"Did you have permission to drive the car?" I asked.

"I can drive it anytime I want, but I'm supposed to stay within fifteen miles of the house," Marisa said. "Where did you find Clare?"

"Were you driving in circles, then?"

"No! I broke the rules, okay? Where did you find my sister?"

"We found Clare's body near the Huguenot Bridge," I said. "We haven't determined the time of death."

"She's been there for four days?" Marisa asked.

"I don't know yet."

"What does that mean?" she asked.

"The medical examiner hadn't determined time of death."

Brit let out an anguished cry, pressing her hand to her belly. When Mr. Stockton faced us, his eyes glistened with tears, just as they had when his wife died. He shook his head, as if by denying this information enough times, he could make it go away. It wouldn't. Marisa stood stiff, defiant.

"Do you know where your sister was on New Year's Eve, Brit?" I asked.

"I knew she was going to a party. I was supposed to go, but I got sick. I was here in bed all night."

"The party was at our friend Jo-Jo's." Marisa recited the address.

"You said a boyfriend picked her up?" I asked.

"Kurt Markman. They'd been dating about six months," Brit said. "I saw them drive off."

I asked for and received Kurt's contact number from Marisa.

"Marisa, where did you go after your drive?" I asked.

Already, I'd pegged her as the family troublemaker. If a vase was broken, find Marisa. If a teacher left a message, it was about Marisa. If money was missing . . . The drill was the same every time.

"I ended up parking at the truck stop in Ashland and falling asleep," she said. "I didn't make it home until early the next day."

"You slept at a truck stop?" Mr. Stockton asked.

"Yes," Marisa said.

"What time did you arrive home?" I pressed.

"About six."

"When the ball dropped, you were sleeping in a truck stop?" I pushed.

"What does that have to do with anything?" Marisa challenged.

"Answer the question," her father ordered.

"Yes! I'd had a few drinks," Marisa said.

"How many is a few?" I asked.

"Too many," she said.

She might have been drinking, but she was still holding back. A lie by omission was still a lie.

Her father, to his credit, stepped between Marisa and me. "I don't like the tone you're taking with my daughter."

"I don't enjoy asking the hard questions," I said. "But I'm building a timeline here so I can figure out what happened to Clare."

"I'm calling my attorney," Mr. Stockton said. "If you have any more questions, go through him."

"Why're you asking me all the questions?" Marisa asked.

I studied her face for a long beat. "I'll be asking everyone lots more."

"But you didn't press Brit about being sick," she said.

"What kind of trouble are you trying to stir up, Marisa?" Brit asked.

Marisa's chin jutted, and her jaw pulsed as she gritted her teeth. Her eyes welled with tears. "I'm not. I just don't see why he's asking us these questions."

"I'll talk to everyone." Maybe it wasn't fair to push for answers now, but I was willing to take advantage of their shock. Harder to lie well when you're rattled.

"But you started with me."

Trouble had a stench and Marisa reeked of it. When I'd been in this house four years ago, she and Clare had been only twelve. I'd not spoken to them directly, leaving the questions to the female officer. Unfortunately, I had only vague memories of two girls standing in the backyard. They'd been facing away from the house. One was standing still, and the other was throwing rocks at the back fence.

I was a gambler. I was willing to bet I could fire off one or two more questions before the father shut me down. "You sure you were just sleeping off booze? Maybe you were out with a boy?"

"She's sixteen," Mr. Stockton said.

And fully capable of having sex. But arguing that wasn't a hill I wanted to die on right now. I would circle back around and charge from a different direction later. "Did your sister have anyone who didn't like her? Anyone that might want to hurt her?"

"No," Marisa said.

Brit folded her arms over her chest. "I actually heard Marisa come in around six, if that helps."

"You know for a fact you heard your sister then?" I asked.

"Yes," Brit replied. "She was still a little drunk."

Marisa glanced at her sister, and hints of surprise sparked behind veiled eyes.

Details from the mother's death were coming back. Elizabeth Stockton had a reputation for lying, according to the neighbors. Nothing huge, but dozens of small lies that created her version of the world. Several neighbors insisted Elizabeth could be so convincing because she believed her stories. When she'd accidentally run over a neighbor's flowerpot while backing up the car, she'd said her brakes had failed. When her daughters missed school, they were sick with the flu. The family dog had died of old age, though when one neighbor did the math, she realized the dog was only four years old.

The Stocktons' marriage had not been good, and they'd separated several times, most recently three days before Elizabeth Stockton killed herself with a handful of pills. In the end, there was no evidence of foul play. Only Elizabeth Stockton's prints were on the bottle, and there'd been a very damning suicide note. I'd have to pull the file to refresh my memory, but she had blamed all her unhappiness on her husband's infidelities.

Maybe the girls had learned from their mother to tell the "truth" that suited them best.

"Can I see my daughter?" Mr. Stockton asked.

"The medical examiner is on the scene now." I scrawled the ME's number on the back of my business card. "Call this contact at the medical examiner's office, and they'll arrange for a meeting."

The body would need to be formally identified. The task would have to fall to Mr. Stockton, but Brit was over eighteen and could see her as well. Marisa, at sixteen, wouldn't be allowed. Maybe later, at the funeral home, her father would permit a viewing. The funeral home would find a way to make the girl's blackened skin more natural with makeup. Maybe she'd even look peaceful, at rest, like Snow White or Sleeping Beauty. But the body I'd see forever was frozen in terror.

I wondered what it was like to see yourself lying in a coffin.

18

MARISA

Monday, March 14, 2022
9:00 p.m.

Richards's notes were not the kind of thing I should've read alone in the dark. And for all the resentment I'd harbored toward Richards thirteen years ago, I realized the guy's observations had been spot-on. He'd seen a lot when he'd stepped into our house. A career of summing up people showed.

I hadn't realized he'd worked on my mother's case. In those days, I'd been so blurred by pain that I barely noticed the people coming and going from our house: the cops, a minister who was a friend of a friend, and the neighbors bearing casserole dishes, flowers, and offers to cut the grass.

Richards had not included any pictures with his notes. There was also no autopsy report. He had them but chose not to share. He either was being kind or still didn't trust me. Either way, I gave him props.

He included his own hand-drawn sketches of the crime scene, a general description of the body, and how it had been found. *It.* I had already segregated Clare into two versions of herself: the living girl and the inanimate object. Easier to read, think about all this, if I thought of the body as a thing, not a person. Not Clare.

There were the witness statements from me, Brit, Dad, the jogger who had found Clare (Seth Morgan—I didn't recognize his name), the kids at Jo-Jo's party, including Kurt and even Jack. But he'd not been to the party.

Richards must have logged a hundred hours on the initial investigation. The extensive notes explained the dark circles under the detective's eyes when he attended my sister's funeral a week later. Richards had kept to himself, standing to the side of the packed memorial hall.

As the family filed out, I'd walked out behind Brit and Dad, so numb I could've sworn my feet didn't touch the ground but floated a few inches above the polished wood floors. As my morning pill wore off, my thoughts zeroed in on Richards, and I snapped out of my funk. It was so much easier to be angry than sad, so I tore through the last of the numbness and allowed oxygen to fan the flames of my anger.

It took another half hour for me to get free of the funeral receiving line. I'd stayed as long as I had only because Brit held my hand as Richards prowled around the edges of the crowded room, moving between the groups, comfortable handing out his card and asking questions.

Finally, when I saw him duck out a side door, I couldn't let him escape. He deserved to be punished for intruding on our family's grief.

I pulled my hand from Brit's, said something about needing a bathroom, and left the receiving line. People watched me pass, many doing a double take as if they'd seen the dead come back to life.

I pushed out the side door and jogged toward Richards, who now stood by a tree, smoking a cigarette. I moved up to him, folding my arms to protect myself against the cold and so much more.

"What're you doing here?" I asked.

He inhaled and blew the smoke out slowly. He sniffed, regarded me through the trailing haze. "Paying respects."

"How can you pay respect? You didn't know her."

The end of the cigarette glowed red as he inhaled again. "I might've known her better than anyone in that room right now."

"How could you?"

As he regarded me, I sensed he weighed his words carefully. "Attending a woman's autopsy is pretty damn intimate."

My threaded arms tightened. I had no words to rebut his statement. I'd known my sister since before we were born. We could finish each other's sentences, looked so much alike we could fool our friends and parents, and were privy to dark family secrets. But I'd not been there at that terrible end. None of the details that had defined Clare—the smart one, the sensitive one, and the nice one—mattered now. All anyone cared about was gathering details of her death: Had she known her killer? Was she sexually assaulted? Was she really strangled? I'd seen all these thoughts reflected back in the stares following me since Clare had died.

But I knew nothing about the crime scene or the real, intimate details of her death. Richards did, and in death he was closer to my twin than I was.

"I've had a week to ask around about you," he said.

"Why would you ask about me? What do I have to do with any of this?"

"You were the instigator," he said with certainty. "If you and Clare got into trouble, you always started it."

That was true. "We didn't do anything wrong."

"Depends on who you talk to."

I was a minor, only sixteen, but he stared at me as if I were twice that age. There was no pity, no empathy, just a keen and unsettling interest.

"You were arrested twice for drunk driving last year. Not only too young to drive but loaded. Then you were caught shoplifting. Daddy fixed both issues, and then you and Clare were caught speeding. Oddly,

Clare was behind the wheel. She didn't pass the Breathalyzer test, whereas you, in the passenger seat, did. My guess is you two swapped driver's licenses."

We had. It would have been my third offense, and another DWI would have meant fifty hours of community service. The judge had already stated he'd see to it that every college I applied to would know about my drunk-driving record. Clare hadn't wanted to trade, but she was always looking out for me.

"You don't know that," I said.

"You're right, I can't prove it. But I really don't care about that now. I'm wondering if you didn't swap places the night Clare died. Maybe whoever killed her thought it was you."

"How can you say that?" Anguish wrapped each word.

Richards was unmoved. "We found the clothes Clare had been wearing. They were in a pile a half mile down the road in the bushes. Like someone balled them up and tossed them out a car window before or after they dumped her body."

Picturing my sister being treated as yesterday's garbage hurt.

"Funny thing about the clothes, they didn't strike me as the kind Clare would wear," he said. "I studied a lot of pictures of her this week. Overall impression was pastels and simple jewelry. Nothing like the black torn jeans, boots, and studded leather bracelet we found."

I didn't speak.

The ash on the edge of his cigarette grew. "Clare was the cheerleader, all As, and soccer team, even enjoyed photography like you. She was the whole package. But I've learned to question surface facts. They're only a snapshot and don't always show the whole picture."

"What're you talking about?"

"Come on, Marisa. There had to be more to your sister. What was she hiding?"

"Nothing. She was the best of us."

"Then why was she dressed like you?"

"We wore each other's clothes all the time."

"I never saw a picture of you in pastels, and I've seen plenty in the last few days."

Again, I was silent.

"Why was she at the party dressed like you? And why were you out for a drive? Not many sixteen-year-olds I know go for long drives on I-95 instead of going to a party."

"Driving clears my head."

He dropped the cigarette, ground it with the point of a wingtip shoe. "You said you bought gas in Ashland, twenty-six miles north of the party around eight p.m."

The receipt was legit, and I'd used it to prop up my story. "I told you that. I gave you a receipt."

"Why so far from the party? What else were you doing?"

"I wasn't doing anything." Color flooded my face, and holding his gaze was a struggle now. It felt like he had X-ray eyes.

"Where'd you get the alcohol?"

"I stole it from my father."

"I'm not looking to put you in jail, Marisa. Your family has been through enough. But it's important I know why you were so far from a party that you convinced your pal Jo-Jo to throw."

Allowing one crack in my story would lead to more fractures and then fissures. And then it could all fall apart.

"Clare was passing as you," he went on. "And then she stepped outside and vanished. Just like that she's gone. No one saw a thing."

I'd called Jo-Jo once the news of Clare's death was public. I convinced her to sneak out of her house and talk to me. "Did you see her at all?" I demanded.

Jo-Jo's eyes had been bloodshot. "That party you talked me into having has fucked me seven different ways. The cops are pressing charges against my parents."

"Why?"

"Duh. Underage drinking. They should've been home."

"They chose to leave."

Jo-Jo rolled her eyes. "My father might lose his job."

Richards blew out smoke, snapping me back to the moment.

"I asked all my friends," I said. "No one knows anything."

"Have you ever thought that someone out there thought you deserved a little payback and decided to teach you a lesson?"

The thought had occurred to me. All our friends thought they could tell the Stockton twins apart, but that wasn't true. We'd fooled them before.

"What lesson?" I was careful to keep my voice even, steady.

"I don't know. But I bet there're a few people in that room that don't like you."

"Who?"

"If you sit down and think about it, you could come up with a list," he said.

Jo-Jo and Kurt weren't taking my calls anymore. And there were certainly others. Tamara, my dad's girlfriend's daughter, wasn't a fan, but she had sense enough to keep it to herself.

"Like I said, Marisa, I'm not judging you. Girls like you with brains and too much money get themselves into trouble. What I care about is who you pissed off so badly that they killed you."

Color drained from my face. "Not me. Clare."

"No, kiddo—that killer was after you. I'd bet my reputation on it."

I had shut down after that conversation. That night I swiped a bottle of vodka from the reception, went to my room, and drank until I passed out. I didn't really climb out of that bottle for thirteen years.

In that time, my father sent me to rehab several times. By the time my third stint failed, his third marriage was falling apart, and Brit was in law school. I was on my own.

When I really sobered up, I couldn't look in a mirror without seeing Clare. Even the reflection wasn't buying my own bullshit excuses. To block out that face, I returned to anything that would numb me.

With Richards's words always echoing, I'd never figured out what I had done to kill my sister. *I never meant for you to be hurt. I never, ever . . .*

Now, as I ran my fingers over the copied pages of Richards's notes, I realized I had to make my own list of people who wanted to hurt me. It wasn't a long list, but all it took was one to do the deed.

19

MARISA

Tuesday, March 15, 2022
Midnight

I spent the next few hours rereading Detective Richards's copied notes. My friends' candor, their willingness to throw me under the bus, shouldn't have surprised me, but it did. And it hurt.

"She likes to push the edge," Jo-Jo had said to Richards. "Once we were sunning on top of her father's garage. We did that a lot because it was fun to be above everyone and the rays felt more intense on the roof. Plus, we could take our tops off. Mom keeps saying we're ruining our skin, but we all look better and thinner with a tan, right? Anyway, Marisa rose up out of her chair and walked to the edge of the roof. She dangled a leg over. Clare told her to stop. I didn't because the more you tell Marisa not to do something, the more she's prone to do it. The fall likely wouldn't have killed her, but it would have broken bones or caused a head injury. Clare begged her to stop, and she finally did."

There's a paragraph break, and I imagine Jo-Jo reaching for a can of diet soda and taking a long sip—she drank diet sodas obsessively in high school. "Yes, she uses drugs. Pot before school, coke at parties.

Who knows, maybe someone in her drug world mistook Clare for her. Wouldn't be the first time."

"Where does she get her drugs?"

"I don't know. That's not my world."

"Brit's boyfriend, Jack Dutton, sells drugs," Richards said.

"Like I said, not my world."

"Marisa's been in trouble with the law?" Richards asked.

"Yeah, since her mother died. That really messed her up. Brit tried to play mommy, but it never worked. Marisa resents her, and I think she does half the shit just to piss off Brit and her father."

"Her father is about to be married."

"Yeah, Sandra. Nice, I guess. Marisa said they started seeing each other when Mrs. Stockton's mental health started declining. Brit really hates her. Clare never talks about Sandra."

"What about Clare's relationship with Kurt?" Richards asked.

"What about it? They've been dating about six months."

"But he sees other girls?"

"Not really. I think Tamara was about making Clare jealous."

"What's Kurt like around Clare? Possessive? Easygoing?"

"He's cute but not the brightest. Clare likes him, but she sees other guys. She fought with him at my party."

"About the other guys?"

"Yes."

"Who else was Clare seeing?"

"I'm pretty sure she hooked up with a guy before Thanksgiving. I don't have a name. Maybe Brit would know."

"Did Clare hook up a lot?"

"She got around. She said the sex made her feel less lonely."

"Sleeping with Kurt wasn't enough?"

"She's kind of like Marisa. Trying to fill a bottomless hole, you know."

"And Brit?"

"She tried to hold it all together, but since she went off to college, Clare and Marisa got more out of control."

"The drugs and boys," Richards said, flipping to a clean page on his pad.

"Everything. It was like the twins were asleep and then they woke up."

"Because Brit left."

"Yeah, I guess."

"Why?"

"Who knows?"

"You must have a theory. You and Clare were good friends, right?"

Jo-Jo's answer is not in the notes, but I pictured her nodding. "The twins were sick a lot after their mother died. We all figured it was stress."

"Sick how?"

"Stomachaches, mostly. Tired. They were pretty low key for a couple of years because they just didn't feel well. Mom said given their mother's suicide and their father's affairs, it's no wonder they were a neurotic mess."

I pinched the bridge of my nose. Nothing Jo-Jo had said was a lie, but it hurt to know she'd spilled secrets so easily. Jo-Jo had sworn she'd never tell anyone.

I'd been so angry in those days. My mother had been dead three years and yet the pain cut fresh wounds every day. Brit had left for college, and I started physically feeling better. Which allowed me time to play with my cameras and think about Mom. The loss. I'd shoot pictures until I was exhausted, but when that didn't work, I turned to my father's liquor cabinet.

The first time I drank the vodka, it tasted bitter. But immediately, a warm glow settled over my body, and for the first time since my mother had died, I felt relaxed. The next day, I'd had a raging headache, and I'd thrown up. I'd felt as awful as I had in the first two years after Mom died, and I'd sworn I'd never drink again. But within a couple of days, the flu-like symptoms had vanished, and the sadness and anger roared to life. And so, I drank again.

Within a few months, it took more booze to get the relaxed feeling, but I also didn't get as sick. Even if I did, I didn't mind. Better to barf than to hurt.

"I might have been a bitch, but I didn't hurt my sister," I muttered to myself as I rose and went into the kitchen.

I grabbed a can of seltzer from the fridge and popped the top. Clare had left the party alone, but no one had seen where she'd gone.

Suddenly hideously restless, I set the can down, slipped on a jacket, and grabbed my purse. Jo-Jo was sleeping now, but Jack usually worked at J.J.'s Pub this time of night. Maybe talking to him would shake something loose.

Outside, I welcomed the cold rush as I burrowed my hands into my jacket and braced against the wind as I walked the two blocks to the bar. I pushed inside, greeted by warm air smelling of beer and fried food.

Jack was behind the bar and, when he looked up, smiled as I approached. "What brings you out on a night like this?"

I wouldn't lead with Clare. Whenever I told my friends, they would get that sad, faraway look in their eyes, and even though they pretended to listen, I sensed they were not.

I sidled up to the bar as he set a soda water and lime in front of me. At one time, he'd supplied me with drugs; now he was the most supportive of my sobriety. Jack no longer dealt, and I'd not seen him take a drink in at least a year. If he'd been behind the bar on my birthday, the tequila shots (which I had never intended to drink) would have been water.

"How about a burger and fries?" I asked.

"Sure, kitchen is still up and running." He punched a few keystrokes of the computer. About nine years ago, after my second rehab stint, he'd just bought J.J.'s Pub, and I'd asked him for a job. He'd laughed. Said the last place I should work was in a bar. But I'd needed the money, so he'd agreed as long as I always stayed in the kitchen. Come in through the alley door, leave the way I came in. One step in the bar, and I was fired.

Two weeks in, I was in the kitchen prepping the garnishes for the bar when the cook, Tony, offered me a joint. "Jack says you need to stay sober, but this won't hurt."

Saying no wasn't as easy as it sounded when all the cells in my body cried for a couple of tokes. But I'd held firm. For a while. Jack caught wind of what we were doing, and he fired Tony and me.

"Sorry I was late to your birthday party," Jack said. "Weekends are my busiest time."

"I remember well." In the eight months I worked at J.J.'s Pub, staff came and went routinely. Waitresses and bartenders called in sick, quit without notice, or left early. But I'd always made my shift. Working was my way of proving that this time would be different. Turned out you could work pretty well stoned.

"You worked your share of thirty-hour weekends."

"Who's the manager?" I asked.

"Bill."

The name conjured images of a tall, lean guy with thin hair. "Yeah, I remember him."

"Goes back to the time you worked here. He quit for a while and now he's back." He looked as if he'd say more but then seemed to think differently. "Your party looked fun."

"I wish you'd worn your hat," I teased.

"Never."

"Thanks for the camera bag. Very nice. And I love the instant cameras."

"That was all Jo-Jo."

I shrugged. "The party was nice. Everyone's trying."

Jack and Brit had been together almost the entire summer and fall semester before Clare's death. I used to hear them in Brit's room, going at it. Dad had hated Jack, said he was trouble, but Brit just waited until he was gone before she invited Jack over. She'd gotten everything she wanted, and I was jealous.

When I'd graduated from booze to pot and pills, Jack had hooked me up. The night Clare died, when I was with Jack, I'd gotten so high, my body wasn't my own. After I'd talked to Clare, Jack had kissed me. I'd responded mostly because I felt like I was taking something away from Brit.

We'd ended up in the navy-blue sheets covering his mattress on the floor. He kissed me on the lips, my neck, and then my breasts. I'd been overwhelmed with sensation. I'd known he was undressing me, but I was too lost to care. And then he'd pushed into me.

The invasion had caught me off guard. For all the stupid things, screwing my sister's boyfriend had not made the list until that night. I remembered feeling a little afraid and wishing I'd gone to the party.

After he made his final push and collapsed against me, I had passed out and didn't wake up until 5:00 a.m., when Jack was stepping out of the shower. Towel wrapped around his waist, he was smiling at me.

He kissed me. We had sex again, though this time I was sober and really not into it. After, we agreed never to tell. And I hadn't. Soon after, Brit and Jack broke up. They'd cited distance, different life goals.

"You get your two shots of tequila before I arrived?" Jack asked.

"I did. And I didn't take a sip."

"You got the real stuff, not water?" He frowned and looked worried, as if a demon had been unchained.

"It was no big deal."

"You'd have gotten water if I was behind the bar." He frowned. "Why the tequila? I never understood that."

"Clare loved it. I was the one who hated it. I drank everything else, but not tequila. The shots are always for her."

"I never knew that."

I sipped my soda. "I saw Detective Richards Saturday."

He picked up a rag and wiped down the bar. "Your annual update."

"More or less." I opted not to mention the case notes I'd found at my door. "He's retiring."

"Makes sense," Jack said. "He was in his fifties when he was investigating the case."

"He looks about the same."

"Still has no answers?" Jack asked.

"He interviewed you, right?" I asked.

"Sure. Back in the day." He looked wary, as if mentioning the past would rip open old wounds. "He talked to everyone."

"What did you say?"

"Not much to say. I didn't know anything. I was with you."

I swirled the soda in my glass. "You never told Richards I was with you."

"Didn't seem like a good idea."

"I would've been your alibi."

"I had a few guys come by the house for some business. They all vouched for me."

He'd been dealing out of his house while I slept, which I found oddly comforting. "You didn't try to wake me up?"

"It was better you sleep it off. That way you could drive yourself home. Your car at my place would have sounded alarm bells with Brit."

"Brit's why I never told the cops I was with you. I didn't need to lose another sister."

"She's not an easy woman when crossed."

"Does Jo-Jo ever talk about Clare and the party?"

"From what Jo-Jo said, Clare was dancing and then had a fight with Kurt before she left. Jo-Jo and a few others thought she was you."

"Jo-Jo had to have known it wasn't me. She could always tell us apart."

"Not at first," he said. "According to her, Clare was full-on you that night."

There'd been one picture of Clare that Richards had shown me from that night. Clare was grinning, leaning into Kurt. The dark eye shadow and wild hair always fooled everyone. Once I'd asked for the picture back, but Richards never gave it to me.

Jack twisted the rag between his hands, both covered in tattoos. "Why the questions?"

"Clare's case is running out of time."

"And when the case goes cold, what'll you do?"

"I'm going to walk away and accept that some problems can't be fixed."

"Sounds like an AA spiel," he said.

"Maybe I need to listen more." That was a lie. I'd never accept that Clare's killer hadn't been found.

He tossed the rag in a bucket. "I worry about you."

"Don't. I'm fine."

"I feel responsible for Clare," he said.

"Why?"

"If I'd realized the Oxy was so powerful, you wouldn't have passed out. You could've left and made it to the party on time."

"Why'd you make a move on me?"

He shrugged. "I was eighteen. Thinking with the little head, not the big one. Maybe I wanted to hurt Brit."

The cold glass chilled my fingers. Jack had seemed clear eyed and determined when he'd pulled my shirt off. But no one had forced the drugs on me. "A thousand little fuckups that night. If one had been different, Clare might be alive."

"Never blame yourself," he said. "Never."

20

Marisa

Tuesday, March 15, 2022
4:00 a.m.

When I climbed the stairs to my apartment floor, I noticed immediately that my front door was ajar. I paused, looked toward Alan's. It was closed, and no light leaked from under the door as it did when he was home.

Had I forgotten to throw the lock? I'd never done it before, but since the car accident, I'd lost time, and locating my keys, purse, or cameras always took a little longer.

I fished in my purse for my cell phone and pushed open the door. The apartment was dark and still. Inside, the ice maker in the refrigerator hummed and the radiator hissed. Clutching my phone, I flipped on the light, but feathers of tension rippled up my neck, warning me to be wary even as my mind reasoned I'd simply made a mistake. I'd forgotten a twist of a key. That was the likely answer. And to call the cops over an open door felt like overkill.

I scanned my apartment. Everything was just as I'd left it. The dishes in the sink, the two coffee cups by my large-screen computer, Richards's copied files on the floor by my desk.

I turned on a halogen lamp, which shot light onto the exposed pipes and ducts on the ceiling, and I moved toward my bedroom, still gripping my phone. Mouth dry, heart pumping, my brain said again I was overreacting. *Jesus, Marisa, do you have to get so spun up? You've always been like this.* Overreact *should be your middle name.*

Clare had been my balance when we were kids. Whenever I was frustrated and wanted to break something or cut off a doll's hair, Clare talked me out of it. When Dad gave us the Jeep, I pressed the speed limit past one hundred miles an hour until Clare's screams finally reached me. And when I drove down I-295 drunk, Clare was there to swap IDs.

After Clare's death, I'd been even more out of control. I was an engine with no governor. And then two years ago, I'd overdosed. That had been my wake-up call.

Even now I could remember sitting in that dark alley behind J.J.'s Pub. My eyes had drifted closed, and I'd slid to the ground against the hard, wet brick. My heartbeat had slowed, my breathing was shallower than a teacup, and my hands and feet chilled. In that moment, I knew I'd screwed up. Everyone had said I had a death wish after Clare died, but I hadn't. I'd simply wanted to numb the pain, which was so intense it took my breath away. All I wanted was to feel normal, to keep putting one foot in front of the other.

I'd expected that as Death grew closer, I'd see Clare or my mother. But I hadn't. No bright light. No angels. It had been utter darkness. More loneliness, if that was possible.

Jack had found me. He'd been out dumping the trash, and I must have moaned or done something to catch his attention. He'd cupped my face in his hands and pried open my eyelids with his thumbs.

"What the fuck have you done?" he whispered. "I'm not doing this again."

"I miss Clare," I muttered.

"You and I are too much alike. Loyal to a fault."

He'd called the rescue squad, Narcan was jabbed into my system, and I was dragged back from the brink.

For a couple of months after the overdose, I'd been more measured, but not sober by any stretch. I didn't inflict the self-made errors that had derailed me too many times. Still got buzzed from time to time, but nothing outrageous. And then I'd cleaned up for good last year.

I fumbled for my bedroom light switch, flipped it on, and sent more light spilling over the nightstand and the untouched prescription bottles from the doctor, my reading glasses, a battery-powered alarm clock, and a small pair of Clare's gold hoop earrings I'd jerked from my ears the night of our birthday.

I moved toward the closet, gripped the doorknob, drew in a breath, and yanked it open. Inside were the few clothes I'd bothered to put on hangers, a collection of ankle boots in varying shades of black, and a suitcase I'd not used in years. Next I moved to my darkroom, opened the door, and found only the print I'd developed the day before swaying from the clothesline.

"No one's here," I whispered. "You're alone." Just as it should be.

Back in the living room, I slowly closed my apartment's front door and slid the dead bolt into place. The unsettled feeling chased me to the kitchen, where I slowly lowered my purse onto the counter. I slid my phone into my back pocket and collected Richards's notes from the floor around my desk. I'd already read them twice but was certain I'd missed something. Was this what Richards did with his cases? Did he stare at the files, endlessly revisiting them, even praying over them for the small detail that danced out of reach, like a 1990s sitcom name?

A can of seltzer in hand, I sat on my couch, staring out at the river and the Richmond skyline. I took one sip, found the taste too plain, and set it down. My head dropped back against the couch as I stared at the ceiling. Adrenaline finally crashing, I slowly closed my eyes, surprised my mind was so easily slipping to that euphoric place between awake and asleep. Thinking I should reread Richards's notes, I fought to stay alert, but the soft lure of sleep, now stronger than the notes, guided me toward an edge. One more step, and I fell face forward into sleep.

It wasn't a soft landing like you'd expect. When I hit, my body struck a hard, rocky surface with jagged edges. Moaning, I rolled on my back and stared into the upstairs hallway of my parents' house.

An unidentifiable whisper mingled with the wind as I moved down the long hallway. When I reached Brit's open door, I saw a woman's figure standing by Brit's bed, hovering over her as she nudged my sister's lips open and coaxed her to drink. "This will make you feel better."

When the woman stood and turned, I realized it was Mommy. Her expression was a mixture of surprise and annoyance. And then her features softened, and she smiled. "What're you doing out of bed, pumpkin?"

"I couldn't sleep."

"Poor baby. Let me tuck you back in bed."

"Is Brit sick?"

"Not anymore," Mommy said. "I made her better. Now let's get you back to bed, little miss. Daddy's home, and I'd like to spend a little grown-up time with him."

"Can I see Daddy?" It had been weeks since he'd been home.

"In the morning. Tonight, it's just the two of us."

"Is Daddy mad at us?" I asked.

Mommy smoothed a red strand off my forehead. "Why would you say that?"

"He's always gone."

"He works hard," Mommy said. "And I think he'll be spending more time at home from now on."

I looked back over my shoulder and saw Brit roll on her side and curl into a ball like a contented cat. She did look better. And if Mommy said so, then it must be true.

I startled awake to a doorknob turning. I stood up, half expecting to see my own front door open. But it was closed, still secure as I'd left it. The time on my phone read 6:03 a.m. I'd been asleep for a couple of hours.

Quietly, I moved to the door and stared out the peephole as Alan, wrestling a briefcase and a take-out bag, opened his door. He kicked it closed behind him, and somewhere inside a light clicked on and trickled out under the door.

I should have been comforted that I wasn't alone. But as I stepped back, I folded my arms over my chest and looked around my apartment, struggling with the sense that someone was watching me.

21

BRIT

As I stared out my bedroom window toward the trees lining the property, my thoughts drifted to Marisa, as they often did. The birthday party and the dinner with David had been two odd, disconnected events, but they'd been my way of reaching out to her. I wanted her in my life, but no matter how much I included my sister, our lives never really meshed. Even before Clare died, even before Mommy left us, each time I reached out to my sister, I ended up grabbing nothing but air. Marisa remained out of reach, her true thoughts buried under porcelain features teetering between annoyed and amused.

She'd been like that since she was a baby. Impossible to read. Impossible to satisfy. "An insatiable, excitable child," Mommy had once said. No pleasing her. I'd never understood Mommy's impatience with Marisa until it was my turn to look after her. Clare had been easy enough. A pliable little thing. But Marisa had been headstrong, a bull in a china shop, though I'd found a way to manage her in the end.

"What're you doing?" David asked. "It's cold."

I smoothed my hands over my arms. I'd barely noticed the chill. "Is it?"

Footsteps padded behind me, and he wrapped his arms around my waist and pulled me toward him. The silk of my robe molded against his naked flesh.

"You're worried," he whispered.

A half smile tipped my lips. "That's what I do."

"About your sister."

"Is there any other reason to worry?"

"She's doing fine. She did well at the party and the dinner. What's bothering you?" He rested his chin on my shoulder, and the stubble of his beard rubbed my cheek. We'd been together only a short time, which put us still in the thrilling part of our relationship, but I hoped that never changed. It would, of course. Everything did. But I could dream.

"She's not fine," I said.

"How can you tell?"

"I can." I could recognize the tension building in my sister. The good part about Marisa being a drunk was that she'd been somewhat relaxed. The booze cushioned her reactions. But without it, each sober day sharpened the softness into jagged points.

"She's come so far. She was near death in the hospital. She's lucky to be alive."

I'd met David in the emergency room at the Virginia Commonwealth University hospital. He'd been visiting a friend. I'd been pacing, trying to swallow the dregs of another coffee as I waited for the surgeon to appear and give me an update. David had come up to me with a packet of crackers and a bottle of water.

"You look like you can use this," he said.

The burst of annoyance tempered when I looked up in his eyes. He seemed genuinely worried. "Do I know you?"

"David," he said. "I have one of those faces."

"I never forget a face."

"We can play a guessing game if it'll help," he said.

I'd no energy to solve that little puzzle. "Not much for games tonight."

"Are you waiting for someone?"

"Sister," I said. "She's in surgery."

"I'm here for a friend. He was just brought in for a stroke." He'd coaxed me into a chair, and the two of us had sat in silence. He was a stranger, and yet I felt closer to him than anyone at that moment.

When the doctors told me I could see Marisa, I thanked David and disappeared behind swinging doors. All my annoyance melted when I saw Marisa in her hospital bed. Her face was pale, her hair shorn, and there were endless tubes coming out of her body.

"She can fool you," I said, more to myself, as David now hugged me closer.

"How?"

"She mentioned Detective Richards at last night's dinner. She wasn't going to see him this year, but she did."

"It doesn't hurt for her to talk to him. You said she's been doing it for the last several years. It's her way of feeling less powerless because she knows the case will never be solved."

The windowpane caught his reflection. Our gazes met. "How do you know it won't be solved?"

"It's been thirteen years. You said yourself the river washed away the forensic data. There were no witnesses."

"I've stopped trying to tell her that. She won't listen. Jack called me tonight. She was asking him about Clare."

"What did she ask him?"

"About the night Clare died. No new information, of course. Same old. It's not good for her to stir up the past."

"How so?"

"She's always been obsessed with Clare's death. For most of last year, she was focused on her sobriety. It was all going great. And then last December she started visiting the river. Taking pictures."

"You said she had an art exhibit."

"She did. I tried to talk her out of it. I thought it would be awkward. Embarrassing even. But I was so struck by the power of her images. She's surprisingly very talented."

"Let Marisa ask her questions. Let this run its course," he said. "She'll poke around and realize some puzzles just can't be solved."

I turned and faced him, tracing small circles in the center of his chest covered in a sprinkling of dark hair. "What if she doesn't realize this is unsolvable? What if she spirals out of control?"

"I learned a long time ago not to borrow trouble. Life dishes up plenty without you heaping on extras."

Life had sent more than one person's fair share of suffering my way, and the way I saw it, there was no universal limit. We got what we got. To David's credit he'd never doused me with platitudes. *God won't give you more than you can handle. It'll make you stronger.* All the bullshit that rolled off me like water off a duck.

David kissed me on the forehead, tenderly. He was like that. Gentle, loving. That was how our lovemaking always started. He'd coax me. Woo me. And only when he had me did his kisses and touches grow more urgent. He was passionate to the point of rough, but he never crossed the line.

"You're right," I said, smiling. "No more trouble tonight."

"But you're already worrying about tomorrow's problems." He nibbled my earlobe with his teeth.

"Marisa and I have a ten a.m. meeting tomorrow. I'm going over her books with her."

As if I hadn't spoken, he pushed the robe's silk off my shoulder until the pale skin was exposed. He kissed me first at the base of my neck and then above my breast. Then he suckled my nipple before nibbling with his teeth. Up to the line of too much, before he backed off.

I liked the restrained violence. He could hurt me if he wanted to, but he didn't out of respect. The fear and the worry that always focused my mind faded as my desire grew.

He ran his hand down my belly and to the nest of curls between my legs. When I gasped, looked up at him, he smiled. "Making sure you're paying attention."

"Full and undivided." Times like this, I didn't recognize my own voice.

Fingers slipped between the folds, and I arched as he pressed the nub. Energy shot to my loins, and he reached for the tie binding the robe. Silk slid off my body like a waterfall, pooling around my feet.

"How is it you always know the right thing to say and do?" I asked.

Even white teeth flashed. "Practice."

22

MARISA

Tuesday, March 15, 2022
7:00 a.m.

When I woke, a dull throb pounded behind my ears. I swung my legs over the side of the bed, my bare toes brushing the cool wooden floor. I needed a rug, but all my promises to find one online were always forgotten when my day got started and the computer work sucked me in.

My oversize T-shirt brushed the tops of my knees as I padded into the bathroom, stared at my pale reflection and the bird's nest of hair that greeted me each morning. Oddly, longer hair required less attention. A quick brush and a ponytail had always been enough to make me presentable. But short hair, not so easily tamed, required shampoo and mousse.

It took another thirty minutes to pull myself together. As the coffee machine gurgled, I read through emails and texts, checking for client changes, new business inquiries, complaints, or requests. The usual. As I deleted ads for clothes, shoes, rugs I'd never buy, and teasers for vacations I wouldn't take this year, I came across an email from an unknown address with an empty subject line. Normally, I deleted these immediately, always suspicious of a virus embedded in a link, but it piqued my curiosity. Sort of like a car accident. It wasn't cool to look, but everyone slowed down and peeked. I'd certainly been vaguely aware of the crowd gathering around my wrecked car in January as I'd slipped in and out of consciousness and, of all things, wondered how many social media feeds I'd ended up on.

I sipped my coffee and opened the email. No link to click on but a simple message:

They are all lying.

No signature. And when I clicked on the email address, I didn't recognize the sender. I'd received odd emails before from people who confused MIS Images with all types of health facilities. I'd seen my share of requests for medical scans but never anything odd like this. I glanced toward my front door, still locked and chained as I'd left it last night.

They are all lying.

Who was lying? And about what?

I considered hitting "Reply," but to what end? The sender had not signed their name. I pressed "Delete." Unsettled, I closed my phone. A door opened and closed in the hallway and was followed by the click of a lock sliding into place.

"Have a nice day, Alan," I whispered.

I walked to my desk and thumbed through the interviews that Richards had done thirteen years ago. It wasn't a question of who'd lied, but how many and how often. They'd been teenagers, and fibs, meaning fabrications and untruths, had been par for the course.

But why would they lie to Richards? They'd all known and loved Clare, had stood at her funeral, lost and devastated at the reality of a peer's death.

They are all lying.

I checked the time. There were more edits to be done today, and I'd promised myself to finally clear the backlog that had grown since my accident. Clients had understood I'd been injured, and they also accepted I possessed the digital files to their weddings and holiday events.

Grabbing my leather jacket, purse, and coffee, I shut my apartment door behind me. As I double-checked the lock, I saw a Post-it Note on my door: *"Grab a drink sometime? Alan."*

I looked toward his closed, silent door. I needed to have a talk with him about drinking. The beer had been a one-off. I'd not gotten even slightly buzzed, and in my mind it really didn't qualify as a transgression. Some would say yes, but I wasn't so sure. I hadn't even been freaked out enough to hit an AA meeting.

I fished a pen from my purse, scribbled my response under his bold block lettering, and reposted the note on his door. My scrawl looked chaotic, out of practice. *"Sounds good. M."*

Down the three flights of stairs, I pushed out the front door into the cool air, moist with drizzle. In my car, I drove across the bridge into the city toward the police station. Richards was used to an annual visit, but I'd never doubled back.

I found parking on Grace Street, walked up to the sergeant at the front desk, an African American woman in her late forties. I waited fifteen minutes before Richards appeared. He stood tall, his dark suit pressed, his paisley tie straight and shoes polished.

"Court today?" I asked.

"How'd you guess?"

"You were wearing the same suit when you went to court about three years ago when I stopped by."

"Good memory."

"Wedding photographers notice clothes."

"The trick is not to wear it to a crime scene."

"I've ruined a few pairs of shoes at jobsites," I said. "Mud, rain, splashed wedding cake, even blood—the hazards of nuptials."

His scowl softened as he nodded toward the front door. "I'm on my way to court, so you'll have to walk with me to the parking lot."

I followed him out the front door and down the sidewalk, the cold air tunneling between the buildings on Grace Street. My long legs worked fast to match his pace. "Are you running late?"

"Always." Eyes ahead, he fumbled for the key fob on his ring.

"Why did you give me the copies of your case notes?"

He didn't break stride, and he didn't look distressed. "I didn't."

"Who would've had access to your personal files?"

He clicked the remote, and the lights of a black, unmarked Crown Vic flashed. "I've no idea."

I shook my head. He was the kind of guy who knew more than he let on. "You know."

He opened the door, paused for a moment, and then shook his head. "I don't."

"They were left outside my apartment door along with my accident report."

"Don't know what you're talking about." Calmly, he shrugged off his jacket, opened the back door, and slid it onto a waiting hanger. Slamming the door, he settled behind the wheel, turned on the engine, and rolled down the window.

I glanced around, making sure no one was watching. "Of the people you talked to, who do you think was lying to you?"

A humorless smile lifted the corners of his mouth as he pressed his foot on the brake and started the engine with a push of the button. "Everyone lies to cops. It's a knee-jerk reaction. Even if it's about something small that has nothing to do with the case, they lie."

"You think the people you interviewed about Clare's case were lying."

"Like I said, everyone lies about something. Even you." When I didn't respond, he clicked his seat belt in place. "What were you doing the night Clare died?"

They are all lying.

I could've asked him about the email, but he'd deny it just as he had the files. "It had nothing to do with her death."

"Didn't it?"

"I'm sure of it."

"Then why didn't you tell me the truth?"

"Who's to say I didn't?"

"Right."

I gripped the strap of my purse. "It's always complicated."

"Murder is generally not complicated, Marisa. Revenge. Lust. Greed. When it's all said and done, the underlying motivation is one of those three."

I stepped closer to the car, making it impossible for him to close the door. "Of the three, which one do you think it was?"

"The autopsy proved she'd had sex, but there was no vaginal bruising."

"We know she was sleeping with Kurt. And he had a solid alibi."

"As I've said before, your straight-arrow sister was dressed like you that night. She has sex with Kurt, but what if she ran into someone else who thought she was you? Maybe she resisted and was killed for it."

I drew in a breath. "The killer thought she was me."

"I don't know. But just the possibility is why it's important I know where you were that night."

"I never went to the party. I went to see Jack Dutton. We did drugs and had sex."

He held my gaze. "Brit's boyfriend at the time."

"They were having trouble. I was mad at her and acting like an immature sixteen-year-old."

Interest honed his attention. "Why were you mad at Brit?"

"We'd had a fight that day. I caught her going through my dresser drawers. I hated it when she snooped."

"Could Brit have figured out what you'd done with Jack?"

"That was our first and only night."

"You were together all night?"

"Yes. I think so."

"What does that mean?"

"I passed out right after and didn't wake up until morning. He was in the shower when I came to."

His gaze sharpened. "You can't confirm he was with you all night?"

"No."

He regarded me for a long moment. "Did he ever show interest in you before?"

"I caught him looking a few times, but he never made a move."

"Would his interest have pissed off Brit?"

"Sure."

"Clare was dressed like you. It was dark. Mistakes happen. Even to sisters."

I knew my sister had issues with me, but would she really want to kill me? "Brit was surprised to see me the morning after the New Year's party."

"Really?" he asked. "She didn't know you were out?"

"She said she'd been sick and lost track of time. She asked about Clare. When I told her I didn't know, she got really worried. But she always worried."

"After you passed out, Jack could've left and gone to the party, correct?"

"He said he stayed at the house and did business."

Richards didn't need the blanks filled in. "But he could also have left you."

"I wouldn't have known one way or the other."

Richards gripped the wheel. "Nice guy."

"I know it sounds harsh. But I was a willing participant. And when I spoke to him yesterday, he said he'd given me new, untested pills that were stronger than he thought."

"He gave a sixteen-year-old illegal drugs," Richards pointed out. "And he'd noticed you before. Whose idea was it for you to come by his place?"

"His. He said it would be more private."

Richards shook his head. "You were set up, Marisa."

I'd never felt manipulated. I'd blamed the entire night on my string of bad choices. The idea that Jack had set me up was unsettling enough to pivot the conversation in a new direction. "What about greed?"

"The money Clare was carrying at the time of her death was found in your discarded jeans downriver. But Clare's inheritance from your mother was sizable and was split between you and Brit. You both were set up to inherit at age thirty."

"Brit wouldn't kill either of us for money. Brit was our second mother."

Richards didn't argue. "Your father was cut out of your mother's will."

"He was given use of the house until I turned eighteen; then it was sold, and the proceeds went into the trust." Mom had often joked that Dad married her for her money. I shifted. "I know my parents had marital problems and split up a couple of times when I was in elementary and middle school. But Dad would've had no reason to kill Clare over money he had no claim to."

"Your car accident was in January. Two months before your thirtieth birthday."

"Yes."

"And the paramedics believed there were drugs in your system."

My fingers curled into fists. "I didn't take any drugs. I know for a fact."

Richards cocked his head. "But you don't remember, right?"

"I know I wouldn't have fucked up. I *know* it."

"Okay, then how did the drugs get in your system?"

"I don't know. I don't remember anything around that time." My unease was growing. "The only person who would've inherited my share was Brit."

"And if she died, who got what was left?"

"The church."

"Have you looked at your car accident report?"

"Not yet. Are you saying my accident is connected to Clare's death? That's a big stretch."

"I'm grabbing at straws," he said. "I do that just to shake things up or get a reaction."

What kind of reaction was he looking for in me? "Why haven't we talked this candidly about Clare before?"

"This is the first time that I've seen you truly sober. All the other times I smelled the booze on you. Why waste my time with someone who's out of control?"

I reminded myself he was talking to me now. "I want to know what caused my car accident. My cell phone went missing around that time."

"Maybe it got thrown under the seat of the car or wedged in a tight spot."

"Brit said it was never found."

"Brit said."

"Why do I have faint memories of a man speaking to me and reaching past me?"

"Is that true?"

"My brain got pretty scrambled because of the accident, but it feels true."

Richards drew in a breath, rested a hand on the car's closed laptop. "Watch your back, Marisa. If the accident is connected to Clare, and that's a big *if*, keep your head on a swivel."

"I will." I stepped back.

"I mean it." He pulled out of his space and drove onto the street.

Lust. Revenge. Greed.

They are all lying.

Shit. It could have been any of the three motivations or a combination of the three.

As I turned to my car, my phone rang. Brit. My face felt numb in the cold. "Hey."

"Where are you?"

"Out. Why?"

"Did you forget our appointment?"

"What appointment?"

An annoyed sigh shuddered through the phone. Brit was likely fiddling with one of her favorite gold hoop earrings. "I was going to have a look at your books today, remember? I've been reconciling them since January, and today was the big handover."

I checked the time on my phone. "I'm only ten minutes from my place."

"Doing what?"

"Shooting pictures. The light lured me." Straightening my shoulders released the tension knotting my upper back. "Just let yourself into my apartment. I'll be there in fifteen minutes."

"I already have."

My mind skipped to the Richards files now tucked in my desk drawer. Out of sight, but Brit liked to snoop. "Be right there."

23

MARISA

Tuesday, March 15, 2022
9:45 a.m.

When I pushed through my front door, Brit was casually sitting on a stool at the kitchen island, sipping coffee, reading her phone. I glanced toward my desk. Center drawer was closed.

"Sorry about that," I said.

"No worries. My first client isn't scheduled until noon."

"Late-start Tuesdays." Since Brit had opened her practice five years ago, she'd taken Tuesday mornings and Friday afternoons off. Good for the mental health, which Brit was always mindful of protecting.

"Have you looked at the books?" I asked. The late-winter dampness clung to my coat as I hung it on an iron hook by the front door.

"Waiting for you. Thought it'd be a good test of your memory."

"I've made five business purchases in the last month and posted them all to accounting."

"Always good to check. Plus gives us time."

"We've had a lot of time together the last few months. You've got to be getting sick of me." I walked into the kitchen and poured myself a fresh cup of coffee. One sip, and I knew I'd be wired all afternoon.

"You make that sound like a bad thing." She set her phone down, blue eyes studying me.

"We didn't see much of each other last year."

"And your near-death experience has made me want to change that," Brit said. "The thought of being alone is terrifying."

That tempered some of the annoyance I'd felt since I'd walked into my apartment. Like it or not, we were the only family the other had.

I moved toward my desk, checked the middle drawer, and saw that the copied notes appeared undisturbed. I closed it and reached for my laptop. "The accounts should reconcile easily. There's one new invoice for the Saturday wedding. Again posted."

She slipped on gold-framed glasses and glanced at the spreadsheet on the computer screen. "You're keeping better track of receipts."

"I always have."

She made a face. "You've a very unique system."

"It all made sense to me."

"Tell that to the IRS." She closed the laptop without comment.

"Your little girl is growing up."

"So it seems." She glanced at her left hand and her gold-and-onyx college ring. "What do you think about David?"

"He seems nice."

"We're getting serious," she said. "I think he could be the one."

That was a bit of a shock. I'd never thought Brit would find anyone good enough. But she wanted children, and the clock had to be ticking.

"I guess you can thank me for that," I said.

"I suppose you're right. Though that would've been a terrible swap—you for him. A Faustian bargain."

Would it have been that terrible for Brit? We'd seen each other barely twice last year, and there was the trust money that would go to her. "You have us both."

She grinned. "I know. Speaking of men, I saw Paul Jones yesterday. He's taken with you."

"Is he?"

She chuckled, seeming to enjoy my exasperation. "He's got money."

"No." Anxious to steer the conversation, I asked, "Do you think you and David will get married?"

She twisted the college ring around until all but the gold underside showed. "Who knows."

"You know. You've always known what you want."

A slight smile tipped the left edge of her lips. "Maybe. But wanting and finding are two different things."

They are all lying.

I sipped my coffee. "Did you know Detective Richards investigated Mom's death?"

She frowned as she looked up from the ring. "I did not. So, you've seen him again."

"I have."

"Are you sure he's telling you the truth? I don't remember him."

"He let the female detective do all the interviews, but he was there," I said.

"There couldn't have been much to investigate. It was clear she killed herself."

"That's what he said," I said.

"And then he draws the short straw when Clare died." No missing the suspicion.

"He already had a connection to the family."

"Still, feels a bit incestuous."

I let her comment pass. "When Detective Richards interviewed you after Clare's death, you said you'd been at home that evening."

"That's right. Stomach bug. You saw me the next morning. My eyes were beet red from all the vomiting."

"All I remember is you standing in the kitchen. You looked pissed."

Brit's head tilted. "I was worried about Clare and you. I could never sleep if something was off with either of you two."

That New Year's Day morning, her eyes had been bloodshot. "I guess."

"You guess?" Brit's eyebrows lifted, like when she was exasperated. "Suggesting I lied? That's the pot calling the kettle black. You told him you were just out for a drive."

"I was driving. And then I bought drugs, pulled into a parking lot, used, and fell asleep."

Brit stilled. "You were using?"

Hearing this well-practiced lie breathed life into it. "That's old history."

"I lied for you. I backed up your story to Richards."

"Why did you do that?"

"Family sticks together. You might've been out there doing something stupid, but you wouldn't hurt Clare." Brit traced the handle of her mug with her thumb. "I've asked around about Richards over the years. He comes off as the heavy and then can turn on a dime and be your best friend. His version of bad cop slash good cop. He might have been tough on you back in the day, but it sounds like he's your new friend."

"Why wouldn't he be helpful? I want this case solved as much as he does."

"If he shut you out, then he'll never get the chance to watch you slip up."

I thought about the copies of Richards's notes in my desk. Interesting observations but nothing shocking. Was it just enough to bait the hook?

Brit's backward ring clinked against the stoneware mug. "He's playing you. He's about to retire, and he has one last shot to solve a case that's hung over his head for thirteen years."

"Why didn't you ever tell me about the trust fund before last year?" I asked.

"Because you were high or drunk for most of the last decade. You couldn't touch the money until you were thirty, so why open myself up to you pestering me about the money? I wish I had a nickel for all the hours of energy you sucked out of our family. Marisa broke a vase. Marisa wrecked the car. Marisa overfed the goldfish and killed them. Marisa overdosed . . . again. Every time there was harmony in the house, you found a way to spin everyone up. You weren't ready to hear about the money."

Brit wasn't off base. I'd been high maintenance growing up. If I wasn't sleeping, I was searching for something to help me burn off the excess energy buzzing in my body. It wasn't until the last overdose brought me to the abyss that I stopped.

"I turned it around. I'm sober."

Her gaze softened. "Yes, you did, and I told you about the trust. My little girl, my second-favorite twin, has found her footing, and it's very gratifying."

"Why do you say I'm your second-favorite twin?"

"I was being sarcastic."

"Freudian slip." It felt good to be on the other side of the analyst couch now. "You said the inside part out loud."

"I loved Clare and you equally. Yes, as wicked as you could be, she was just as good. But she was so good, it could be trying. Goody Two-shoes wear thin quickly." Brit shook her head. "You're making me say things I don't mean."

"You thought Clare was perfect."

"She wasn't." She sighed. "Now stop it."

"What did I do?"

"Stirring the pot like you always do."

Richards's comments about my trust fund rattled in my mind as I set my cup down carefully on the counter. "Detective Richards says everyone lies to him. Even if they don't need to, they do."

"It's human nature. People have all kinds of silly secrets they don't want the world to know about, even if the world doesn't care. Protecting those secrets, my dear, is how the best lawyers make their money."

"You're the secret keeper."

Brit shrugged. "I never thought of it that way, but yes, that's what I do. I listen to problems, offer solutions, and then lock the entire encounter into a box. That box only opens when my client and I are alone."

"Who keeps your secrets?"

"Honey, I have none. I'm an open book."

I chuckled. It didn't take a detective to sniff out that lie.

24

Him

THEN
Wednesday, November 21, 2008
6:00 p.m.

You agreed to another dinner. This time you were coming to my apartment. I suggested you might like to see some of the art I'd collected. Nothing nefarious like *Come see my etchings*, but it did sound a little creepy. I thought for a moment you'd reject me, but you said yes. I was still floating.

I'd cleaned the house twice. I wanted it to be perfect. You deserved perfect.

I had wine. A red like you'd ordered at O'Malley's. Just a glass or two for you. No one likes a lush; still, it's nice to loosen up.

As soft music played on the sound system, I studied some of the pictures I'd bought today. They were different types of photography and meant to impress you. I nudged the edge of the frame up a smidge, then coaxed it back down. Needed to be straight. The glass gleamed.

The doorbell rang, and I rolled my shoulders back, glanced toward a mirror hanging in the foyer. Clean, pulled together, but not so obsessive that it looked like I was weird. Which I was not.

Clearing my throat, I moved toward the door at a steady, even pace and then opened it. You looked up, pink faced from the cold, long red hair streaming around your shoulders. God, but I loved your hair. You were wearing a dark faux-fur-trimmed jacket, an olive-green turtleneck, jeans, and lace-up boots. You rocked the artsy vibe, and I was growing hard just looking at you.

You held up a bouquet of yellow daisies. Where you'd found them in the winter was beyond me, but I appreciated you for finding them.

"Flowers?" I asked.

"For you."

"No one's ever brought me flowers before."

You grinned and held them out for me. "Then it's about time."

When I took them, my fingertips brushed your hand, and the skin-to-skin contact rippled electricity through me. You had a power over me. Clearing my throat, I held them up and inhaled. Of course, there was no scent. "Beautiful."

"You said not to bring anything, but I hate to show up empty-handed."

I stepped aside, extended my arm in invitation. As you passed, I caught the faint hint of a perfume I couldn't identify. It was spicy, exotic.

You looked around, curious about the space, likely wondering what it said about me. Clean, organized, with a modern, sleek Scandinavian style. "This place is terrific."

"It's a work in progress." Daisies clutched in my hand, I followed.

"How long have you been here?"

"A few months. I lived in Northern Virginia for a while but then decided it was time for a change. Back to Richmond and my roots." None of that was true, but it sounded better than the truth.

"I don't hear an accent."

"The Richmond accent fades north of Fredericksburg. But I'm picking up a drawl again. I hear it in the vowels."

You took off your jacket, and I noticed your breasts immediately. So beautiful.

Clearing my throat, I turned toward the galley-style kitchen. "Let me put these in water. There's a hook in the entry hallway for your jacket."

"Great." As I searched the cabinet for something to put the flowers in, I was so aware of your movements. The place felt full, right with you here. You were the missing link that I'd been searching for.

I finally found a mason jar, filled it with water, and crammed the daisies inside. They were too tall, and several of them flopped over.

"Do you have scissors?" you asked.

I fished a pair out of the drawer as you came around, stood close to me, and removed the stems from the mason jar. You carefully clipped the ends. Your hair slid forward in a crimson curtain. "I should have brought a potted plant."

You were tall for a woman, but you were still an inch shorter than me. It was hard not to lean in and brush the hair back from your face as you cut the ends of each stem. It was an intimate gesture shared between lovers.

With care, you retucked the flowers in the vase, and they looked perfect in a wild sort of way. "There you go."

"I never could've done that," I said truthfully.

"My mother loved to arrange flowers. When I was little, she would show my sisters and me how to make arrangements."

"She did a good job."

A silence settled, and it was full of unspoken emotions. Mother, sisters, family. What triggered the shift? You gathered up the stems. "Trash?"

I opened a closet door, and you moved past me (so, so close) and dropped the stems in the stainless can. "Even your trash can closet is organized."

"Hazard of the job. Left-brain guys have a tendency to micromanage."

The crimson curtain fell away as she stared up at me. "I'm the opposite. Especially when I'm working."

Your eyes were bright and your lips generous. "Speaking of work, would you like to see a photograph I just bought?"

"Sure."

You followed me into the living room, and I held up my hands toward the black-and-white portrait of the river. "What do you think? I just bought it."

You stood back and stared. A slight frown furrowed your brow, and I sensed you were critiquing the work.

"Does it send you any vibe?" I asked.

"It's sad," you said. "Life goes on despite tragedy. Nothing stops the river, which is why I love it so much."

That coaxed a smile. "I'm glad. Should I hang it somewhere else?"

"It's really perfect here."

"Let me know when you have your first showing. I'll be your number-one fan."

"Thank you."

The idea of sharing you with anyone did not sit well. "Can I get you something to drink? Wine?"

"Terrific."

"Of course." You lingered a beat and then turned your back on the image.

I handed you a glass of red, pleased you were now comfortable enough to drink with me alone.

"What do you do?" you asked.

"Finance." A vanilla description that sounded good but didn't say much.

Your brow cocked, and you gave me your full attention. "You seem kind of young."

I grinned. "Boy genius." That much was true. Always had a brain like a calculator.

"Good for you."

"Some days it feels like 3D chess, and other days it's gambling. It's always changing and keeps me on my toes."

"Nice."

You didn't ask or hint at how much I made. Many women did, and it was an immediate turnoff. "Tell me what you did today?"

"Nothing exciting, I'm afraid. I took pictures for fun. That's always relaxing."

"Is it always relaxing for you?"

"Sometimes it's frustrating. I carve out the time, get ready to go, and then it starts raining. I hate that."

"You look pretty in the candlelight." You looked up, stared at me, silent. "Sorry. I don't want to be rude."

"Sounded like a compliment."

"It was." My throat was tight.

"I think you're attractive."

I knew women didn't mind the look of me. I'd had my share. But it meant more coming from you. I sipped the wine, wondering what you'd taste like.

You set your glass down and closed the space dividing us. I shifted, faced you. At first, I didn't move but stared into your eyes and the red veil curtaining the sides of your face. Finally, I set my glass down and gently kissed you.

Your response was tentative, testing. I wanted to believe that I was your first. I likely was not, but lying, even to myself, came easily. I deepened the kiss and threaded my fingers through your hair. A sigh shuddered through you, and you relaxed into the kiss.

Desire sparked in your eyes. You wanted me. This. After taking you by the hand, I led you to the bedroom. Like the rest of the house, it was pristine, primed and ready for you. I didn't ask if you were sure, or if you wanted this. I'd been waiting for what felt like a lifetime. I wasn't going to let this moment between us get past me.

You backed away, paused as if thinking that this was a mistake, and then pulled your sweater over your head and unhooked your bra.

Jesus, the way the light streamed over your white flesh. I kissed a pink nipple. A moan escaped your lips, and a shudder passed through your body as you kissed me. Whatever embers had been simmering in you had caught on fire. I'd done that. I'd made you want me.

We were naked and under the sheets minutes later as I moved on top of your body, skin to skin. You parted your legs so I could enter. You were so blissfully tight. Just like it should have been for a first time. I wondered if I was hurting you, half hoping that I wasn't and half hoping that I was. I didn't want you to ever forget this moment.

"Tell me you love me," you whispered.

"I love you."

25

MARISA

Tuesday, March 15, 2022
8:00 p.m.

The afternoon quickly turned to evening as I sat at my computer, working. By eight o'clock, I'd finished the last of the backlogged files and emailed albums off to my clients. As I stared at the last image of my last January couple, taken on the snowy grounds of the Tuckahoe estate, I thought about what Richards had said. *Everyone lies.*

My work at this January wedding conveyed a happy couple, ready to spend a life together. The truth was that the bride was deeply in debt and had had to use six different credit cards to pay my fee. She hadn't told her husband-to-be about all her pending bills because she was sure he'd understand when she told him after the wedding. The groom, who'd gotten really drunk at the rehearsal dinner, had said to me in passing that he'd slept with one of the bridesmaids last year. I was not sure why he'd told me. Maybe, all dressed in black as I was, I looked like a confessor.

They are all lying.

Still, it felt good to be caught up. My brain was clear, and the weight riding on my shoulders post-accident had eased.

I lay on the couch, rolled on my side, and stared out the large window toward the city. What lies had my friends told Richards? I'd lied about Jack and the drugs. Jack had lied about being in bed with me all night. What about Jo-Jo, Kurt, Brit, and even Clare? What else still lurked in the shadows?

The walls of my apartment felt smaller, tighter. The beast inside remembered the two sips of beer. Why hadn't I had a few more sips? If two were fine, four would've been all right. No one would have known.

The beast was back, whispering sweet temptations.

I reached for my phone and texted Kurt.

Me: What are you doing?

Kurt: What do you have in mind?

Me: Dinner at J.J.'s Pub. Headed there now.

Kurt: Great minds . . . already here.

I was mildly surprised he'd chosen J.J.'s Pub. This wasn't his neck of the woods. But maybe he'd liked it. Wanted to give it another go.

It took only a few minutes to pull on cold-weather clothes and hurry out my front door. I checked the lock, three times, and then I was down the stairs and out the building's main door. Cold air channeled by the buildings whipped across my face. Ducking, I shoved my hands in my pockets and hustled down the two-block walk to J.J.'s.

The first person I saw inside was Kurt. We'd not seen each other since my birthday party, and again it struck me as odd that he was here.

He looked up as I entered. His smile was slow to warm up, like a bulb flickering, but then he beamed out full wattage. He rose. I moved toward him easily, as I'd seen Clare do a million times while they were dating.

I leaned in, kissed him lightly on the lips. It wasn't a sexual kiss, but a peck shared by friends. "What brings you back here?"

"Other than you? The fries. The beer. I like the place," Kurt said. "Why'd you reach out?"

"I've been digging out from a backlog of files and realized I need to see other humans. I thought about you."

He pulled out a chair, glanced toward the door. "Have a seat?"

I rested my hand on the back of the chair and noticed two menus on the table. "Are you expecting someone else?"

"I may have been stood up," he said easily.

"You don't sound too torn up about it." I sat, placed my purse in the chair beside me.

"The ego is bruised, but I'll survive." When a waitress came to the table, he ordered another beer and a club soda for me. There's an advantage to having a history with someone. They know where all the bodies are buried, so to speak.

"Who was the lucky girl?" I removed my jacket and felt his gaze drop to my breasts. Men always noticed them.

"A work associate," he said. "But it looks like she had a better offer. Already a half hour late."

"And if we'd both showed up at the same time?"

He grinned. "I'd have picked you."

I laughed. "Good to know."

"You're never boring, Marisa. And maybe I subconsciously picked this place hoping I'd run into you. It was good seeing you on Friday."

"It was nice." Also, odd and kind of disturbing.

The waitress brought our drinks. I sipped and found the soda lacking. My nerves could have used a little calming. Beer would have been so nice. "Now that I have you, mind if I dig up the past?"

He stared at me over the rim of his iced mug, took a long drink, and then finally nodded. "Sure."

"Richards."

He winced. "Ouch. Not the blast from the past I was hoping for."

"I've seen him a couple of times this week."

He picked up his beer mug and paused. "Okay."

"Nothing new to report on Clare's death. It's a semiactive case headed for the freezer. He's retiring."

"Sorry to hear that." He took a long drink.

"Are you?"

"No."

"He interviewed you, right?"

"He certainly did. Many times. Don't be fooled by his easy style. That one's a hawk."

"Do you remember what he asked you?" I asked.

"Anything and everything. Once my DNA was found on Clare, it sounded alarm bells. Exactly when did I see Clare last? Did we fight? Did you or Clare piss me or anyone else off so much to kill? And then when Dad hired an attorney, the questions shifted, and the cops backed off. Did I know of anyone who might have wanted to hurt Clare or you? Did I see anyone follow her out of the party?"

Clare or you. It was always coming back to me. "And what did you say?"

"That I had picked Clare up for the party at your house. I thought it was you at first. She walked straight up to the car, leaned over, and kissed me on the lips. I'd never fallen for the MC-dog-and-pony-show switch before, but I did at first."

"What was the tip-off?"

"Her breasts. They're smaller than yours." He'd the good sense to keep his gaze on my eyes.

"Were you mad?"

"No. Turned on. We drove to the party and went to the pool house. Had sex on the deflated floats."

"Did she say why she wanted to be me?" I'd never asked because I'd been in too big a rush to see Jack.

"She said being you was more fun." A half smile tugged his lips. "She'd walked on the wild side once or twice and found she really liked it. Said she felt less pressured when she pretended to be you."

"Less pressure?"

"To get the good grades, follow the rules, do Brit's bidding."

"I didn't realize she felt that way."

"I know you two liked to switch things up, pretend to be the other. Didn't she take your PSATs for you?"

I cleared my throat. "No comment."

"I thought so."

"She hated it when I needed her to be me."

"Maybe at first. Then she liked it. She'd started drinking, you know."

I tried to picture my twin embracing the role of the bad sister. "What happened at the party?"

"When we actually got to Jo-Jo's house, she said she wanted to dance, but I didn't. My teammates were there, and I wanted to hang out. She was annoyed, then said okay and got lost in the crowd. That's when Tamara appeared. Maybe if I had danced with Clare, she'd still be alive."

"Have you seen Tamara recently?"

"No. I've done my best to distance myself from all that."

"Did Brit tell you my birthday party would be filled with all the suspects?"

"No, but I'd have come either way. I wanted to see you. Tell you I was sorry."

The years peeled away, and I was looking into the eyes of a wounded eighteen-year-old boy. He still carried the weight of Clare's death.

"Did you tell Richards that you'd gotten us mixed up?" I asked.

"No. It didn't seem relevant. I'd enough to explain when the DNA tests came back. I had to tell him we'd had sex the night she'd died. That's when I became Suspect #1."

"You two were dating. Sex would have been understandable."

"What mattered was that I didn't tell Richards until he had the DNA in hand."

"And when Clare left the party, you were talking to Tamara, right?"

"Yeah. That's the beauty of being an eighteen-year-old. Erections were easy to come by." He held up his beer. "Those were the days."

Kurt's dad had been diagnosed with ALS a month before Clare died. Kurt had told Clare how much he feared watching his father go downhill so fast. He'd felt helpless against a random, ugly disease. It didn't have motive or intent. It simply struck as a wild animal might. And Clare's murder, the police, and media scrutiny had made his father's disease progress faster.

Kurt had left Richmond and come back a year later when his father was dying. He had skipped college, taken over the family business by the age of twenty, and all his dreams of playing college or pro ball had vanished.

"Did Clare mention that she'd had a fight with Brit right before she came to the party?" he asked.

"What was the fight about?" Brit had said nothing about a fight.

"She never said, but she was stewing about it in the car. I think that's why she was in such a mood that night. I told Richards, but if he asked Brit about it, she came up with something that turned it all back on me."

I'd read Kurt's statement, and he'd said nothing to Richards about a fight between Brit and Clare. Maybe there were other files Richards hadn't shared. Maybe Kurt wasn't being truthful. *Everyone lies.*

"Where were you that night?" Kurt asked.

"I was with Jack. We were high." Richards knew the truth, and he wouldn't be shy about telling anyone if it got him his arrest. Sooner or later I'd have to also tell Brit.

"Jack?" He cocked a brow. "Weed, coke, or pills?"

The lemon floated in my club soda. "Pills."

"You were having trouble with drugs then, weren't you?" he asked.

"I didn't think so, but yes."

He sipped his drink. "Is there any reason to keep churning up Clare's case? Some problems don't have a fix. I know that better than anyone."

"I think I'll always keep trying," I said. "I owe that to her."

"Why don't we get out of here?" Kurt asked.

"And?"

"Go back to your place. For new times' sake. Weird on your birthday, I get it. But we really could be good for each other."

The drinking Marisa likely would have said yes. But sober, I was different, or at least wanted to be. "We tried that the other night."

"No one likes a quitter." He winked.

I glimpsed the high school boy who'd once had the world by the tail. I half expected to hear Clare pipe in her two cents, but she was quiet. "Don't think so."

He drank. "Can't blame a guy for trying."

"I don't," I said. "But our ship isn't meant to sail."

Suddenly, the bar was too loud and the room too full. Had it changed that quickly since I'd arrived? "I've got to go."

"I thought you came in for dinner?"

"I'm not hungry anymore, and I think what I really wanted was fresh air." I kissed him quickly on the lips. "Take care."

Shrugging on my coat, I left the bar. Outside I took one step and glanced back through the window. Kurt rose from his chair and walked to the bar. He took a seat next to a blonde, smiled at her.

The past was lightning in a bottle, as Kurt had said. Impossible to recapture.

26

HIM

THEN
Wednesday, December 5, 2008
9:00 a.m.

I'd thought we had a real connection. Two souls meeting. But you'd not responded to any of my texts or phone calls for two weeks. I'd been furious after the third unanswered text, and then I became worried. What if something had happened to you? Maybe you'd fallen or been attacked outside your home. When I parked outside your place, I waited nearly an hour before you appeared, juggling an overloaded, worn backpack.

I was relieved to see you and then just as quickly annoyed. You'd been busy. But how much effort did it take to return a text?

I followed you and kept a safe distance, trailing you along the interstate into the city, and finally to Main Street Station. The historic building still remained an active train station, with a collection of people dragging suitcases for the Amtrak slowly pulling into the station from the south. Were you leaving town? Running away? What could you be doing here?

Out of the car, I turned up my collar and trailed behind you, mingling into everyone hustling to catch the train as it slowed.

I found you on the second floor, kneeling by a small table where you had set down your backpack. You frowned slightly, just as you had when I'd entered you. Concentration, pleasure, and maybe some pain all blended together.

I held back, watching as you raised a camera to your face, checked the lighting (I assumed), and then walked to the long glass-paneled room called the Shed. You didn't wait for the passengers to leave but started snapping as they hugged, stood alone checking tickets, and walked to their train car.

Was this your artist's way? You were a bit of a voyeur, like me.

There'd been no distance between us when we'd been in bed. You'd enjoyed our lovemaking. I knew when a woman was having fun and when she was not. And you'd come. I'd felt the orgasm ripple through your body as you'd clung to me.

After it was over, we'd both dozed. I'd gotten up to go to the bathroom about 2:00 a.m., but when I returned, I discovered you'd left. Had you been pretending to sleep when I'd kissed you on the cheek? Were you just waiting for your chance to escape?

Frustration simmered. You owed me some kind of explanation. You don't just fall into a man's bed, make him feel things he'd not felt in too long, and leave. It wasn't right. Cruel even.

You kept shooting pictures for another half hour, catching the light as the clouds outside parted and the sun shone through the open glass.

I could confront you here. Seeing me face-to-face would make it impossible for you to dismiss me. But that felt too public. Too dangerous. There had to be a way to get you alone. We needed privacy so I could prove to you how much I loved you.

27

Marisa

Tuesday, March 15, 2022
9:15 p.m.

When I arrived back at my apartment, I paused by the door and tried the knob. It was locked. Good. Because I knew damn well that I had thrown the dead bolt when I'd left. I twisted the key, and inside the apartment I switched on the light. As I lingered in the entryway, an odd sense that something was wrong washed over me. Everything was as I'd left it. The half pot of coffee rested on a cold burner. My computer screen was off. Dishes stacked in the sink. Shit, not again.

I moved to my desk drawer and opened it. The file Richards had given me remained as it was. So why was the air charged with a strangeness that was unsettling? Had Brit returned?

A cool breeze rustled over my skin, causing me to turn to the window facing the river. It was ajar. Open only a few inches, but I knew for a fact I'd not opened it. Maybe in the late spring or fall, but today had been too cold, even for the radiator heat.

Gripping the handle, I pulled the window closed and searched around the sill and floor. Nothing was out of place. Maintenance rarely came through, and when they did, they left a note on my front door. They could've forgotten.

My purse still on my shoulder and keys in hand, I walked slowly into my bedroom, where I discovered my neatly made bed. A chill inched up my spine. I could count on one hand the number of times I'd made my bed. It'd never seemed practical, considering it would be undone by nighttime. I hadn't made it this morning.

Making the bed would have been a Brit move. And maybe she left the window open to let in fresh air. I could imagine her just popping by, doing her mommy thing, and then going on her merry way.

I'd tolerated my sister's comings and goings since the accident. I'd needed the help for the first few weeks. And it had been moderately okay, but now I didn't need her. And she was crossing a line.

When I was fourteen, Brit often came in Clare's and my room to search drawers, under beds, and inside closets. She'd said it was what Mom would've done. She was just looking out for us and making sure we didn't get in real trouble. I'd resented it then, and we'd had terrible fights that often led to another bout of whatever plagued me when I was stressed. The night Clare died we'd fought over her snooping.

I fished my phone from my pocket, dialing Brit's number.

The phone rang three times and went to voice mail. As I readied to quiz Brit, I thought questions about trespassing (because that was what it was) would trigger unwelcome attention. She'd get defensive. Act hurt. And I wasn't up for that kind of drama tonight.

As I stared at the made bed, I said, "It's me. Call me when you can."

I slid the phone in my pocket and walked to the bed.

Carefully, I skimmed my fingers over the smooth comforter. The nerves in my back tightened. I'd once woken on a neatly made bed in a dorm room at Brit's college. I'd risen, looked back at the bed. My mind muddled by drink, I didn't remember how I'd gotten there, or what had happened the prior night. I'd felt dirty. Imagined hands roaming my body.

I now curled my fingers into a fist and stepped back from my bed. My skin tingled, and I turned as if I expected someone to be standing behind me.

I was alone, of course. Still . . .

I backed out of the room and moved into the kitchen. Opening the fridge, I stared at the collection of seltzer cans. The beast howled. If I closed my eyes, I could conjure the malty flavor of the beer I'd had at Alan's. I'd not gone on a binge or bender. A few sips and I was done. Maybe I'd changed. Maybe I could handle it.

Glancing over my shoulder at the bed, I wondered whether a beer or two would really be that bad.

Crossing to the bed, I grabbed the blankets and yanked them all off the mattress. Tossing them all on the floor, I plucked out the sheets, balled them up, and carried them to the small washer and dryer that barely accommodated the set. The blanket and comforter would require a trip to the Laundromat, something I wasn't willing to do tonight.

Pouring in extra soap, I switched the dial to hot water, closed the lid, and pressed the "Start" button. The lid locked, water rushed inside the machine, swirling around dirty memories I didn't want to remember.

28

MARISA

Thursday, March 17, 2022
8:00 a.m.

I sat in the waiting room for Dr. Brenda Webster, the neurosurgeon who'd operated on me after the accident. Today was my sixty-day follow-up, give or take a few days. I always chose the earliest appointment, hoping to avoid the crowds of people like me recovering from a brain injury. Some fared far worse than I had, and seeing them reminded me of how close I'd come to losing it all.

It had been easy to wake early. My couch was not the most comfortable, but for some reason, even after I'd pulled the warm sheets from the dryer, I had been unable to sleep in my bed.

I glanced at a two-month-old copy of *Newsweek*, barely scanning the headlines as I flipped the worn pages that had likely never really been read. No one came here for current or old news.

"Marisa Stockton." The heavyset nurse was dressed in scrubs. She was in her late forties and wore dark-rimmed glasses.

I set down the magazine, shouldered my purse, and rose. "That's me."

The nurse smelled faintly of clean soap and antiseptic. "Follow me."

I trailed behind her, not daring to glance toward the open exam rooms. When we reached my room, I gratefully ducked inside and sat on the exam table. The nurse took my temperature and blood pressure, then checked my pulse and vision. "Have you been drinking?"

"I thought I wasn't supposed to."

A brow arched. "Have you?"

"No."

"Smoking?"

"No."

"Daily exercise?"

"My work is pretty active. I've always counted it as exercise."

The nurse glanced at my chart. "Photographer."

"Right."

"The nurse tells me your vision checked out. Has it been consistently good?"

"None."

"Sleep?"

"On and off. But that's always been normal for me."

"Okay, the doctor will be right in." The nurse left me alone, and as I shifted to get comfortable, the thin paper topping the exam table crinkled. Seconds later, the door opened.

Dr. Webster was in her early sixties, wore her gray hair short, and never used makeup to brighten her pale skin. She extended her hand. "Marisa."

I was always surprised by her strong grip. "Dr. Webster."

"Is your sister Brit here today with you?"

"I've graduated to solo trips. Just bought a new car, so I'm mobile."

"Good to hear that. Step in the right direction." Dr. Webster glanced at her pad. "Not sleeping well?"

"Like I told the nurse, that's normal for me."

"How many hours a night?"

"Three. Maybe four."

She frowned. "What about dreams?"

"Always."

"Anything from around the time of the accident?"

"One," I said. "I'm driving with my foot pressing hard on the accelerator, and I'm confused, having trouble focusing."

"So the same dream."

"Yes."

"Any memories?"

I thought about the smoothed bed comforter. If that had been a memory, I didn't want to share it. "No."

"And no alcohol, correct?"

"That's right." Two sips of beer still weren't enough to check the *yes* box.

The doctor removed a small penlight, clicked it on, and moved in front of me. She flashed the light back and forth, turned my head from side to side, and then inspected the spot on the side of my head where she'd made her incision two months ago. "How do you like the short hair?"

"Okay once I had a hairdresser even it out and the bald spots filled in. I keep thinking more hair should be there."

"I wish I could've saved it."

"Better my brain," I said.

"When you were first brought in, you were terrified. Do you remember that?"

"A car accident will do that, won't it?"

"This was different. You thought someone was chasing you."

Chasing me. My mind flipped back to sitting in a booth. There was a nearly full cola in front of me. My head was heavy, my vision blurring.

"You okay?" Dr. Webster asked. "Got a far-off look."

"Hazard of being an artist," I joked. "Our minds drift."

"Where'd it go?"

"What does it matter?"

"I want to make sure you can articulate your thoughts."

"Thinking back to a time when I was in a bar. I felt drunk, confused." Hearing the words made it all feel uglier and dirtier. And then more hopefully: "Not a first for me."

"Do you think it happened prior to the accident?"

"I don't know. Past and present memories mingle these days."

Dr. Webster's gaze softened as she clicked off the penlight and pushed it in her pocket. "Something trigger this thought?"

"I don't know."

"Do you remember the incident?"

Incident. Made it sound like a line item in a report. "No."

"When did this happen?"

"Like I said, the details are fuzzy. It could've been years ago." I sighed. "Brit says the paramedics thought I was on drugs."

"Toxicology screens weren't run until after your surgery. They found nothing."

"I wasn't using."

The doctor nodded slowly. "The last memory you had was your art show."

"I was nervous. I remember pacing back and forth in front of the pictures I'd just hung at J.J.'s Pub. Suddenly I wasn't really ready to show my work. I wanted it to be perfect, and it didn't feel perfect. Jack, the bar owner, told me to stop worrying. The last thing I remember was kissing Jack on the cheek, thanking him, and leaving. That was about two o'clock in the afternoon."

"And then waking up in the hospital?"

"That's right." And yet between the bookended memories were a drink in a bar and faint images of a frantic drive. "Is there anything you can do to bring back my lost memory?" With Brit in the room, I'd never have been as candid.

"As I've said, nothing but maybe time will fix it. Brains take time to heal."

"Time doesn't heal all wounds." No missing my bitter tone.

"Not always, but it can help. Keep a diary of your memories. Write down immediately what comes to you, no matter how random or silly. Do this for a week and then go back and read your notes. There might be a pattern."

"Okay."

"I'd like to see you back next month. Just a standard follow-up. Otherwise, I'd say you're almost back to where you were."

"I'll make an appointment."

"Good."

When the doctor left, I rose and glanced toward the stainless towel dispenser and caught my reflection. I looked almost the same. Felt almost the same. But something inside me had changed since the accident. I was jumpier. Nervous to be alone. Paranoid. The subconscious knew more than me, and so far, it wasn't talking. But that was going to change.

***

On the way home, I stopped at the electronics store and found a young guy with green hair and a nose ring who wore the company's trademark blue pullover shirt. Asking about surveillance cameras sounded quirky to me, but when I finally spit out the words, he didn't seem to care. His indifference said something about either him or the state of the world. Everyone watching everyone.

I left a half hour later, a few hundred dollars lighter and with three mini cameras in a plastic shopping bag. Back at my apartment, I spent the next hour setting up the cameras, finding the most traveled angles in my apartment and tucking them beside potted plants, between books, and in my camera case (hide in plain sight). Next, I synced up all the screens to Wi-Fi and a freshly downloaded app on my phone.

I opened the app, stared at me standing in the center of my apartment. Watching the phone, I walked toward the front door until I was out of range and then toward my bedroom. Each camera caught a version of me, and the red lights signaled they were recording. The recording lasted only twenty-four hours, but that should've been enough time if I ever had a moment like the one I'd had last night.

Was I expecting to catch someone breaking into my apartment? No, not really. I hoped I was wrong and that it was my overactive imagination playing tricks on me. But a niggling feeling deep in my core whispered otherwise. Whatever had happened in the moments leading up to the accident meant something. The neatly made bed and open window meant something. *I know where you live. I can get to you.*

"Whoever you are, I'm now watching you," I said softly.

29

BRIT

I stared at the picture of the twin girls. They were wearing green dresses, bows in their red hair, and big grins. They'd been five when the picture was taken, and I remembered the day as if it were yesterday. Neither one of them had liked the bows, and Mommy had worked hard, smiling, waving favorite dolls, and promising ice cream if they'd smile. None of it had worked, until I had stood behind the photographer and started making funny faces. Clare had been the first to smile. Marisa, always the stubborn one, had finally given in and grinned. To this day I could tell them apart in the picture based on Clare's bright grin and Marisa's begrudging smile. Anyone else looking at the picture couldn't have told who was who, but I could. I'd rarely been fooled by my girls.

A knock on my office door had me turning, squaring my shoulders, and smiling as my secretary poked her head in through the crack. "Jack Dutton is here to see you."

A warmth still spread through me when I heard his name. Whatever we'd had a long time ago was gone, but he'd been my first, and that reserved a special place for him. "Send him in."

Jack entered my office, grinning, standing tall in his navy sport jacket, white button-down, and khakis. At thirty-three he remained as fit as any teenage boy. In high school, he'd done time in juvenile detention, and when he returned to the outside world, the kids had been as fascinated as they were scared of him. The boys wanted that rough edge, and the girls were drawn to his dangerous good looks.

Now the dark-blond hair was shorter, but it was still thick, and the bangs were ready to slip over his forehead.

I'd been surprised when Jack had started flirting with me in my senior year. Though he had his pick of the blond freshmen, he'd gone for me, the brown-haired geek. I'd been studying my ass off so I could get a scholarship and get out of my house. But after that first look he'd shot my way, I forgot all about the twins, Dad's plans to remarry, and my academic future. When Jack was in the room, life just felt better.

It'd taken little effort for him to coax me into the back seat of his car. I'd been lonely, afraid, and feeling so overwhelmed by life I could barely breathe. He had taken my virginity in his Wrangler on a hot June night. We'd dated on and off through my senior year, and when I left for college, he'd visited once. But by then my workload had grown, and away from home and high school, his allure had faded for me. I couldn't see a future with a guy who had a record and dim prospects. After Clare died, the breakup came easily. When I told him, he said he understood. He was cool and calm, and I'd been disappointed he wasn't more torn up.

"Hey, Brit." He crossed the room, kissed me on the cheek. He still smelled of the same expensive aftershave. "You look fantastic."

"And so do you." His charm had been what had won me. "Have a seat." I gestured to the two walnut chairs. The desk behind the chairs was expensive and had cost a good chunk of my inheritance, but it was worth it. "So, you want to talk about buying more real estate?"

"I do. I've come into some extra cash, and I've never been a fan of playing the stock market. Like I told you, I want to invest in more property."

"I might have just the building for you," I said.

"I'm all ears."

"The buildings around the corner from J.J.'s Pub. Real estate in the area is reasonable now, and there're a couple of apartment buildings that might be ripe for purchase."

He crossed his legs, brushed imaginary lint away. "I own an apartment building in that area. It's not super popular."

"Which makes it a good investment. Especially since you've also bought the Church Hill building for the next restaurant."

"Assuming the bottom doesn't fall out of the real estate market," he said, smiling.

I wasn't stupid. I'd been in love with Jack, but I wasn't blind to what he did. In high school he'd dealt drugs, and later he had become a serious dealer. When he finally got caught, he was over eighteen, so his juvenile record couldn't be held against him. But he'd still done three years in state prison. Once out, he was up on his feet very quickly. There'd been no whiff of trouble, but that kind of swift recovery was rarely legal.

"There's always risk, but you've never been afraid of that. And you've always had a head for numbers," I said.

He grinned. "I do."

"I can broker this deal, but I'll warn you my rates have gone up." Risk required higher fees, and I never apologized for being good or ruthless when it came to work.

"I don't want cheap. I want the best. Plus, I don't see this as my only deal, and I'd like to work with someone I know and trust."

"You trust me?"

His gaze settled on mine. There were no hints of humor. All business. "We've had our ups and downs. Most of the downs were my fault. But you handled the last sale well."

"I don't trade in illegal deals." It had to be said at least once, out loud.

His expression would've given a choir boy a run for his money. "This is a straight-up real estate transaction."

It wasn't. But again, it all had to be spoken for the record, just in case.

"What property do you have in mind?" he asked.

"It's the building next to Marisa's. Since you own her building, it makes sense to acquire the one next door."

"And the tenants?" he asked.

"You can raise the rent or renovate and turn it into condos. Either way, you make money."

"How many tenants are in the building?"

"Fifteen. Like Marisa's building, the units are super large and can be broken up into more apartments or condos or office suites."

"I don't have to wait out their leases?" Jack asked.

"I wouldn't have suggested the property if I thought that would be a problem. The job of breaking leases is mine."

"Okay. Send me the paperwork for the apartment building, and I'll look at it."

"Do you have the same plans for Marisa's building?" I asked.

"For now, I'm keeping it as is."

"I'd think you'd want to convert both at the same time. More efficient."

"No, for now Marisa's building stays as is."

"Okay."

Business settled, he relaxed back in his chair. "Speaking of Marisa, how's she doing? She looks good."

"She's getting stronger every day. She was always the toughest of our lot."

"What about her memory?"

"Other than the missing days, fine."

"Still no idea how she had the car accident?"

"I think she had a slip," I said. "She says she wasn't using, but I don't believe her. Even a little can make her paranoid. The problem is she'll never be totally well until she admits her mistakes."

"Good luck with that. She never acknowledges it when she's wrong."

"I'm not pressing. She's still fragile." Marisa had insisted on going to the doctor alone today, and I hadn't liked the idea at all. She needed a second set of ears. But I knew my sister well enough to know direct assaults weren't effective.

"You like her best this way, don't you?" Jack asked.

"What way?"

"Fragile. You two always butted heads when she was firing on all cylinders."

"That might've been true, but I want to see my sister healthy, whole, and thriving."

"I remember how you fussed over her and Clare in high school. They were both sick a lot, and you were always coming to their rescue."

"All the doctors said it was stress. They needed me."

"You were their real mom."

That was why I'd never been in a rush to have children. I'd already raised two. "I loved them both."

He eyed me. "We all knew how obsessed you were with your sisters. Didn't think you'd ever find the time for a man in your life. How'd you meet David?" Jack asked.

"In the hospital after Marisa's accident."

"An odd place to find love. But even flowers grow up through the rocks, right?"

Jack's curiosity over David was puzzling. He wasn't the jealous type, and he didn't get that attached to anyone. "That's what I say."

"What's David's deal? What does he do for a living?"

It felt odd to be talking about my love life with an ex. But better than more endless talk of Jo-Jo and how much he loved her. "Stock trader. Lived in New York, came down here last year. Originally from California."

"Bring him by the bar. I'll treat you two to dinner. I didn't have time to talk to him at Marisa's party, and I'd like to get to know the guy who has captured your heart. We can double-date with Jo-Jo."

"Sure."

Grinning, he rose. "Good, text me dates."

"Will do."

As he turned to leave, he hesitated. "Marisa is still chasing Clare's case. She was asking me questions. I think she feels guilty that she wasn't at the party that night. Feels like if she had been there, she would have saved Clare."

"We all carry guilt," I said. "If I hadn't been sick, I'd have gone."

"We all wonder if." The lines in his face deepened. "I'd like to see Marisa find some peace."

"She'll be fine as soon as she lets this case go," I said. "Nothing has ever come of Marisa's questions during her short periods of clarity and sobriety. This time might seem different, but I'm realistic enough to know she'll have another characteristic stumble."

"You really think she's that fragile?"

"Yes." I didn't mention it, but Marisa's kind of failure kept men like Jack in business.

"What do you think? Richards is a pit bull."

"I've made my own inquiries in the police department, and the case will turn cold the moment Richards retires. Nothing to worry about. The clock will run out on him." I didn't like talking about

Clare's case for obvious reasons. I smiled. "I'll send you my specs on the building."

He leaned forward, kissed me on the cheek. He was a tempting creature. Being with him was akin to dancing on the knife's edge. But I wasn't going down that garden path again. "I'm looking forward to our next deal."

"Me too."

30

Jo-Jo

Thursday, March 17, 2022
1:00 p.m.

Fear rattled my nerves as I stared at the test strip that I'd peed on twenty minutes ago. I should've done this test when I first woke up this morning, but I'd been too nervous. Jack had lingered for a second cup of coffee, and I'd wanted to be alone when the results revealed themselves.

Jack and I had been trying to have a baby for a year now, and so far, no luck. He'd brought up the idea of us getting tested for fertility issues, but I wouldn't hear of it. We'd only just started, I'd said. Didn't want to turn sex into a chore. What was the rush?

Now as I sat in the bathroom and watched the test strip closely for a double set of blue lines, I panicked a little. He'd been the one who'd really wanted the baby. I'd been fine with just the two of us, but he was certain a baby would make us stronger. It might make *us* stronger, but *I* would be weaker. I'd be more vulnerable if he fell back to his old ways. Which, of course, he would not. He liked being legitimate, and he'd sworn he didn't want to go back.

The bedroom door opened, footsteps crossed the room, and then a knock on the bathroom door startled me out of my trance. "Yes?"

"Let me in," Jack said. "I know what you're doing."

"What am I doing?" I considered hiding the stick in the trash so that he wouldn't think I was silly. This was my third test this week.

"Babe. I saw the tests in your purse, and I'll see it when I take out the trash."

Rising, I opened the door, held the test behind my back. He stared down at me, a half grin on his face. He was supposed to be in a meeting with his attorney. Now he was home, and I felt as if I'd been caught doing something I shouldn't.

His hair was neatly combed, and he wore a collared shirt and sport jacket, which for him was formal wear. "What's the verdict?"

I glanced at the test and saw the single line. Not pregnant. Relief washed over me. "It's negative."

His brows knotted. "Are you sure?"

I handed him the test. He glanced down, frowned, before he smiled again. "It could be wrong."

"It's supposed to be ninety-nine percent accurate."

"One percent is one percent."

"A long shot."

"My life is a long shot." He studied the test. "Aren't you supposed to do these in the morning?"

"I suppose."

He tossed the test in the trash and took my hands in his. "Don't look so stressed. It'll happen."

Yes, it would. So why was I so fearful of it? "I know."

"I know how to fix that frown," he said softly.

In his world, sex solved everything.

"Do you?"

He took me by the hand and guided me away from the bathroom. "Look at it this way, we'll increase the odds. Insurance, just in case."

"I have to leave in an hour. I'm meeting Marisa."

"Marisa? What for?"

"She wants to get coffee. I don't have to teach today, so why not?"

Marisa's call had thrown me off my game. I didn't want to see her, see Clare, today of all days. The last thing I wanted was a reminder of secrets I had never told. But saying no looked worse.

The mention of Marisa's name brightened his gaze as he ran his hand up my side under the oversize T-shirt and squeezed the tender flesh of my breasts. Jack had always had a thing for Marisa and once had asked me to dye my hair red. That idea had flown like a lead balloon.

Now he pushed me toward the bed with enough force to send me tumbling backward. I was annoyed at his callousness. And a little turned on. If I were pregnant, there wouldn't be many more days of wild sex for the foreseeable future.

"Are you pretending again?" I asked.

He pushed off his pants, tugged my cover-up off, and opened my legs. "How so?"

Games. Always playing games. "Who am I today? Marisa? I saw the way your eyes lit up when I mentioned her name."

He hesitated for an instant and then pushed inside me, rougher than usual. "Does it matter?"

Jack had dated Brit, but I believed he really wanted Marisa. He'd gone out of his way to give Marisa work after rehab, helped her stay sober, even bought her damn apartment building. I'd once asked about her, but he'd just laughed and reminded me he'd picked me.

That victory had been thrilling at first, but I wasn't so sure who'd really won. Jack had secrets, which hadn't bothered me when it was just us. The pregnancy scare had shifted everything. I might not be pregnant now, but I soon could be. "No, it doesn't matter."

31

MARISA

I arrived at the coffee shop five minutes late and wasn't surprised to see that I'd beaten Jo-Jo. The woman never met a schedule she could keep. I glanced at my phone. There was another text from Paul. I wasn't feeling diplomatic and deleted the message. Sooner or later, he'd get the hint.

I ordered a cappuccino and was sipping mine when Jo-Jo rushed in fifteen minutes later. Her cheeks were flushed, her gaze flighty. She'd the look of a woman who'd just had great sex. I sipped my drink, hoping to hide my smile and envy. Not for Jack, but for an ideal of love and marriage I wasn't sure existed.

Jo-Jo sat quickly in the chair across from me. "Am I that late?"

"Twenty minutes. Basically, right on time."

"Better late than never." She smiled, didn't seem to care about the time, as if it were already forgotten. Had to give Brit credit. The Scarecrow hat had been on point.

"You look relaxed. How's Jack?"

A slight hesitation and then a grin. "He's fine. But you didn't ask me here to talk about Jack."

"Can't friends just visit?" Foamed milk swarmed around my mug's interior.

"They can, but we rarely do. We haven't really spoken in years, and now we're becoming a regular thing."

"Can I get you a coffee?"

"I'll grab it." She fished a wallet from her purse and dashed to the counter. Back in less than a minute with a steaming latte in her hand, she moved very quickly when she put her mind to it.

I waited until she had her first sip. "Richards."

Jo-Jo made a face. "He must be a thousand years old now."

"Sixty-five. Ready to retire. I saw him on Tuesday."

She brushed back a brown curl off her forehead. "And?"

"Tell me about the night you last saw Clare?"

Jo-Jo's face paled a fraction as she grimaced. "Why would you want to bring that up? Christ, I don't want to go there today."

"I don't wake up ready to revisit my sister's death. It sucks for me. But not talking about it doesn't solve anything."

She held up a hand. "Right, right. It's just that talking about Clare hurts."

I traced the stoneware rim of my mug. "Like opening a festering wound that's never healed."

She sighed, sat back. "Did you know he was waiting outside my school last year? He wanted to go over the case. We spent a half hour going over the same old questions."

I'd assumed my yearly visits were what had been enough to keep the case active. "He didn't tell me."

"He's been lurking around all of us—Jack, Kurt, Brit, and me—for thirteen years. I know he spoke to Jack two years ago, and I'm sure he found a way to cross paths with Brit and Kurt. I compared notes with Jack, and he asks a variation of the same old questions. I suppose he's hoping time will make us forget what we originally told him, or some-one will spill the beans on someone else."

"Time changes people. What did Richards want to talk to you about?"

Jo-Jo sighed. "This is the last time, M. I want to let that time go. I know it's hard for you, but we all have to move on with our lives."

Bitterness soured my next sip of coffee. "Time is eating away at the case, and one day there won't be any crumbs left. I don't want my sister forgotten."

Jo-Jo closed her eyes, pinched the bridge of her nose before she looked at me again. "He had questions about the party at my house."

"And?"

"Like I've told him a half dozen times, I was at the party with Sam. We were upstairs in my bedroom and, well, you know. That always was our thing. When I came downstairs, I saw you . . . or rather Clare. She was dressed just like you, and she was drinking a beer. I called to her—you—but she turned and left the house."

"How did she seem?"

"She looked pissed, and I heard she'd fought with Kurt."

"You didn't hear them fight?"

"I know they did."

"How do you know?"

"I just do. Kurt started to follow her out of the party, but then Tamara called out to him, and they started dancing."

"That wasn't the statement you gave Richards."

She paused, her cup near her lips. "How do you know what I said to Richards?"

I ignored her question. "Kurt said he didn't fight with her. He said she was upset about something. Very emotional."

Jo-Jo set her cup down. "Why weren't you at the party? And don't lie this time."

"I was with a guy. I got really high and passed out."

"Who was the guy? You weren't dating anyone then."

I'd kept this to myself for thirteen years. But one way or another, it would get back to Jo-Jo. The weight of all the secrets was growing too heavy for me to bear. I knew I should keep my mouth shut, but I couldn't stay silent. "Jack."

"Jack? *My* Jack?"

Maybe sobriety would really stick if I cleared the decks. "I'm not proud of it. I was at his place to score drugs, but when I got there, he suggested I try a sample for free, and then the next thing I know, we were in bed. I was kind of out of it."

She sat back, folding her arms over her chest. "You had sex with Jack?"

"For what it's worth, I don't remember much."

Jo-Jo shook her head as she regarded me. "You never told Richards about the drugs or Jack, did you?"

"It didn't seem that important at the time. But I came clean with Richards on Tuesday."

"Why didn't you tell Richards about Jack from the beginning?"

"I'd lost one sister. I didn't want to lose the other one," I said. It sounded feeble now. I wouldn't have lost Brit over sex with Jack; at least, I didn't think I would have. "Did Jack come to the party?"

"You said he was with you."

"I don't remember most of the night."

"I didn't see him," Jo-Jo said.

If she had, would she have told me or Richards? She'd already lied about Clare's argument with Kurt. "See anyone lingering around Clare?"

"No, no, no. Thirteen years has not changed my answers. Look, I don't want to go back there."

"You were Clare's best friend," I said. "She told you things that she didn't even tell me."

"She didn't tell me everything." Jo-Jo's face flushed. "You know she and I weren't that close all fall."

"But she came to you with something. Your face looks like it did when the store clerk accused you of shoplifting and you denied it."

"What look?"

I cocked a brow. "Never mind about that. What matters is that I don't believe you now."

The rosy hues of her cheeks deepened. "I can't help that."

I wasn't going to apologize. If stirring trouble, making her feel stressed, and ruining her day were what it took, I'd do it to catch Clare's killer. For the first time, I actually understood Richards's frustration with liars. Knowing and proving were two different beasts.

"I really can't help you," Jo-Jo said. "I can't tell you what I don't know. I'm really sorry."

Drawing in a deep breath, I dialed down my frustration. "Sorry doesn't do me any good, Jo-Jo. I've had a bellyful of sorry."

"I want to help."

"Clare told you everything important. Why was she upset enough to leave the party?"

"If I did know, I wouldn't tell even now."

"I suppose I should be grateful that Clare had such a loyal friend."

"What's that mean, Marisa?"

"You're willing to keep her secrets after all that's happened and all this time. Takes a strong person to hold in a secret that long."

"Stop pressing me, Marisa. I can't help you."

What had Clare told Jo-Jo? I could keep pushing but knew right now she wasn't going to tell me. I hoisted my purse onto my shoulder and stood. "Clare loved you."

Jo-Jo's breath was quick and ragged. "I know. I loved her. I was willing to do *anything* for her."

"Secrets don't help anyone."

32

Marisa

Thursday, March 17, 2022
5:00 p.m.

I removed the file Richards had given me and shuffled through the interviews until I reached the report on my accident. There were several pictures and notes on my estimated speed, my apparent head injury, and an interview with Jenny Taylor, the witness. Photos of my Jeep twisted and mangled were haunting. It was a miracle I'd made it out alive.

The accident was as lost as the night I woke up on the neatly made bed and my night with Jack. But since January, not a few days went by without me feeling fragmented moments of panic.

My first real memory after the accident featured Brit. My sister had been in my hospital room. She'd been talking with authority to someone about me. Brit had always been in charge of Clare and me. Even when Mom was alive, she'd run the show. Disaster struck, and it was Brit to the rescue.

"Will she remember the accident?" An unknown man's voice felt vaguely familiar, but I couldn't place him. Maybe one of my doctors or a nurse.

"The doctors are hopeful she'll remember," Brit said.

"Have you been here the entire time?" the man asked.

"Almost nonstop. I don't want her to be alone."

Knowing Brit, she'd been hovering over me, watching me sleep, calculating therapies, treatments, doctors' appointments. Brit liked logistics. Taking care of people gave her purpose.

In the hospital bed, my eyelids felt heavy, and it took effort to pry them open just halfway. The light in the room was dim, but I could see the muted television playing a game show. I wanted to call out to Brit, a blurry mash of soft mauves, but the tube down my throat made it impossible. Brit's back was to me, her attention on the man just out of my field of vision. Finally, unable to sustain even this silent communication, I closed my eyes.

Now as I clung to the memory, I replayed the man's voice. *Have you been here the entire time? Have you been here the entire time?* What had been unfamiliar then was familiar now. It was David. They'd met at the hospital, but it never occurred to me he'd been in my room.

I rubbed the back of my neck, working out the tension, angry that he'd seen me like that. I'd been utterly helpless in the hospital. I'd hated the feeling. Felt trapped by the weight of my injuries. And David, a man I barely knew, had been there and seen me at my worst.

All that I'd struggled to remember and what had come to me was David. Maybe this was the beginning of recalling those lost days. Maybe there finally was a little light in the darkness.

I closed my eyes, replaying the moment, but I must've drifted off, because when I woke, the sun was rising over the river. I rose, walked to the bathroom, and splashed cold water on my face. Glancing up into my shadowed eyes, I thought for an instant Clare was staring back at me. *Do something. Figure this out.*

I grabbed my purse and headed out. In my car, I sat for a minute, looking up at the stars in the clear night sky.

I started the engine, pulled out of my parking lot, and crossed the Mayo Bridge toward the city. I wound up on Fourteenth Street and then turned right onto East Broad Street, weaving through the centuries-old buildings of Shockoe Bottom and back up toward Church Hill. It was after six when I stopped in front of Libby Hill Park.

I stared down the hill. According to the accident report, my Jeep had been spotted speeding down Broad Street. At the bottom of the hill, I'd taken a sharp right and almost immediately hit a utility pole with enough force that my Jeep's engine block cracked, and the vehicle's front end crumpled like paper.

The investigating officer had asked me several times about my phone. I'd assumed it was in my purse, but he'd assured me it hadn't been found in or near the car. Brit had always wanted me to install Find My Friends, but I'd never been comfortable with my big sister tracking me.

I surveyed the area, wondering what would have brought me up to Church Hill. I loved it up here, loved the vistas of the river. I'd shot a wedding at St. John's Church about two years ago but to my knowledge had not returned since. But I had.

The police estimated that I'd been going at least forty miles an hour based on my short skid marks. An aggressive speed on these narrow city streets had to mean something. What had spooked me?

Back out on the road, I drove down Broad Street and turned onto the side street where I'd crashed. As I drove the darkened street, passing rows of parked cars to my left and right, I searched for something familiar.

Nothing about the historic wooden townhomes sparked a memory. I slowed as I approached the accident site. It wasn't hard to miss. The utility pole, once darkened by weather and time and covered in flyers, had been cut down after the accident, for fear it would collapse.

It'd been replaced by a new pole, telegraphing a freshness out of place among the hundred-year-old townhomes.

I found an empty spot, parallel parked, and then shut off the engine. Keys and mace in hand and out of my car, I crossed the street to the spot. Running my fingers over the pole's smooth new wood, I closed my eyes, trying to remember.

Panic. Fear. Desperation.

Whispers of them all drifted through me. It would be logical to be afraid after the trauma of an accident. But I'd been terrified before.

I drew my fingers away from the pole as if they'd been scorched. Why had I been afraid before? Forty miles an hour in this area was insane. Only someone running for help or away from danger would be so foolish.

There'd been no one who had needed my help. This I knew from Brit, who had asked me over and over why I'd been driving so fast. Brit had chalked it up to the drugs she and the paramedics assumed had been in my system. *There goes Marisa again. High, drunk, or loaded.*

But I had been riding high in early January. I'd been busy printing and mounting my photographs for my show. I'd had several weddings, and I'd been diligent about following my AA program. My life was on track. There'd been no depression or sense of loss, my usual past triggers.

I wasn't using. I'd no memory at my disposal to back this up, but I knew I'd been sober.

Someone must have drugged me. Richards said it happened more often than anyone wanted to admit. The realization was as clear to me as the street in front of me now.

The doctors had been more focused on saving my life, so there'd been no examination to determine whether I'd been sexually active or assaulted. The bruises on my body had been explained away by the accident, so if someone had hurt me right before, then the crash would've hidden their deeds.

Hand to my chest, my heartbeat drummed as fast as my fingers. Someone had drugged me.

"I'd been in bars since I'd sobered up, but I never drank booze."

The memories were there, but they danced just out of reach. *We're here. We're here. Shine a light on us.*

"I want to. Come closer. Just a little."

When moved toward the truth, my steps became mired in quicksand. Redirecting, I shifted back to my last real memory. Hanging pictures in J.J.'s Pub. Jack had been on-site that day and had helped me carry the two dozen framed black-and-whites into the banquet room.

"We've never had an art show before." He laid the stacks of wrapped frames on a large cocktail round.

"Thank you for allowing me to be your first."

Jack's grin had a self-deprecating quality that was so charming. "Not exactly the big time."

"It is for me," I said. "It's the first time I've showed anything outside of my apartment."

"Fingers crossed you sell out."

"Doubtful, but thanks." I'd not been keen on showing my work, but a few in my AA group had insisted. I'd reached out to Jack, and he'd immediately agreed. Showing these pictures felt a bit like stripping down in a crowd of people.

He nodded toward the wrapped collection. "Should I unwrap these?"

I drew in a breath. "That would be great."

"I have a hammer in the back room."

"Not necessary." I reached in my backpack and pulled out a hammer and packet of nails. "I didn't want to start driving holes in your walls."

He studied the reclaimed barnwood that he'd hired a contractor to put up a couple of years ago when he'd bought O'Malley's, renamed it, and renovated it. "Doubt it'll make a difference to this old wood. It's seen its share of history."

"Then if you don't mind, I'll arrange the pictures around the center of each wall. Like wrapping the room in pictures."

"Sure."

He pulled brown paper off the first image and held it up. As he studied the print, his amusement vanished. "Brit said they were powerful."

I watched him, seeing sadness and anger play across his features. "You could say I'm working shit out."

Absently, he traced the edges of the frame with his thumb. "I'm surprised you went back to this place. I've never been able to."

"It was a first for me. I've avoided it all these years until last fall. Then I couldn't stay away. I've been back at least twenty times."

He set the picture on the empty banquet table. "You need to let this go."

"So I keep telling myself. But I can't. Maybe if we ever find out who did this to her, I will."

"What good will knowing do? She'll still be dead."

"At least her killer won't be running around free." The idea that a person could have taken Clare's life and then gotten on with their own life was intolerable.

"Who says he's free? Whoever did something like that has got to have demons." His scowl deepened.

"That's very specific."

He raised a brow, shook his head. "It's common sense."

"Is it?"

"Maybe I listen to too many crime podcasts." The muscles in his face had tightened and deepened the lines in his forehead.

"Are you okay?"

"I miss her, too. I liked her a lot."

"The nice twin. The gentler one."

"I always liked your grit," he said.

"Brit thinks I'm nuts. Again," I said.

"Great attorney, but she doesn't know everything," he said. "Did you ever tell Brit about what we did the night Clare died?"

Us. The one-night stand, laced with revenge sex aimed at my sister, had remained my secret. And after Clare died, it seemed trivial. "No."

"I thought you had. She broke up with me right after Clare died. Brit never brought your name up when she cut me loose. But I figured if she knew, her pride wouldn't let on. Brit needs control."

"I never told her. We were all shell-shocked after Clare. I don't think either of us has sustained a relationship since."

"It wasn't a genius move on my part."

"Maybe it's a stupid question to ask, but why me? I thought you and Brit were happy?"

"We'd drifted apart. The long-distance thing between us was getting old." A ghost of a smile tugged his lips. "And I always thought you were— and still are—hot."

"Thanks?"

He chuckled. "Don't tell Jo-Jo."

I nodded. "Are you coming to my opening?"

"No. I've got to be at the other restaurant, and I'm checking in on the construction of our new restaurant location. But you'll have my top staff here."

"To handle the hordes of people?" I almost hoped no one showed. I'd had to talk myself into this and would've talked myself out if quitting weren't equal to losing face.

"Either way, you'll do great. I bet you make a sale."

"I'll take that bet."

He held out his hand. "I'm willing to put a dollar on the table."

I accepted his hand, grateful whatever moody vibe I'd just gotten from him had gone away. He was back to being Jack, my friend. "It's a deal. If I sell a painting, I'll pay you a dollar."

"Consider it my commission."

He refused any money for the space rental or a real commission on sales. Kept saying to remember him when I hit the big time.

A car's front end squeaked, and I turned to see a woman dressed in scrubs behind the wheel of a small red car angling into a parking spot. The woman raised a coffee cup to her lips, and for a moment our gazes met. I must've looked insane standing here.

The woman got out of the car. "Are you okay?"

"Yes, I'm fine."

"It's early." The woman sensed something was off and couldn't let it go.

"I was in a car accident here in January. I came to see the spot."

"That was you?"

"It was."

"My roommate saw it happen. She said the crash made a horrific noise."

"I was going too fast." I wanted to add that I wasn't drunk, that I didn't use drugs, but spilling random explanations to a stranger didn't make much sense.

"Are you really okay?" she asked.

"Just trying to remember the accident. It's all a blank. Did your roommate tell you anything about it?"

"She said she saw you hit. As she ran out of our apartment toward your car, another man came up to help. He stayed with you while she called 9-1-1."

"A man?" Carving through the inky blackness, I sensed the faint memory of a man's hands gently touching my forehead. The report hadn't mentioned a man. "Who?"

"I don't know. He was gone when she got back."

Had he been the one who'd comforted me? Had he taken my phone? I couldn't back the feeling with facts or memories, but I knew this guy wasn't random. "Anyone catch his name? I'd like to thank him."

"No."

I looked up at the apartment building and noted the numbers. "You and your roommate live here?"

"I'm Roberta Paulson, and my roommate is Jenny Taylor. I can give her your number. She'll call you when she has a moment."

"Thanks. If I could call her, that would be great." Roberta gave me her number, and I texted her a note explaining the situation.

"Look, I've got to get a shower and take a quick nap. Working a double," Roberta said.

"Thanks for stopping. This has been helpful."

"I didn't tell you much."

"Any and all pieces are welcome." The early-morning chill had seeped into my bones.

Everyone lies.

I'd lied about using drugs and sleeping with Jack.

Jack had lied about spending the night with me.

Brit had omitted she'd fought with Clare that last night.

Kurt, who'd been scrutinized the most, might have been the most honest of us all.

And Jo-Jo was lying, too. Maybe she'd not fabricated a story, but she wasn't telling everything she knew. Her lies were ones of omission.

33

MARISA

Friday, March 18, 2022
6:30 a.m.

As I climbed the stairs to my apartment, Alan's door opened. His voice mingled with a woman's. I couldn't make out whatever they were saying, but I picked up an awkward strain that ran under the words.

I reached the top landing as Alan kissed the woman, who wore a cocktail dress and heels that looked painful. They both turned toward me.

"Morning," I said.

"Morning," the woman said.

Alan's demeanor was casual, as it always was when we passed each other in the hallway. He seemed a little chagrined and also curious about my sudden appearance. Likely wondering where I'd been this early as he questioned his own timing. Maybe he assumed I was coming home after a night like the one he'd had.

"Have a good day," I said as I fumbled with my keys.

As I twisted the lock, the woman's heels clicked on the stone stairs as she vanished down the stairwell.

"You're up early," Alan said.

I paused in the doorway and faced him. "Couldn't sleep. Out for a drive."

Alan's hair was tousled, and his T-shirt was on inside out. Roguish, charming even. "I've a fresh pot of coffee on. Should be finished brewing now."

"You didn't offer her coffee?" I asked.

"I'm tired. She's a tea drinker."

I shook my head. "She and I can never be friends."

He chuckled. "A deal breaker for me, too."

"Was there a deal to be broken between you two?"

"No." He jabbed his thumb over his shoulder. "I make a mean cup."

"I can't say no to that."

As I passed by, I caught the whiff of his scent mingling with the faint perfume of his guest. My post-sobriety celibacy kick left me a little jealous of this woman who had a sex life. A little sex would be nice occasionally, but with me it seemed everything was either all or nothing.

"How do you like the place?" I asked.

"It's great. I love the privacy, the view, and the rent."

"It's a real find."

"How long did you say you've lived here?"

"Three years." In the sink were two wineglasses. One had red lipstick on the rim.

He opened the cabinet and pulled out two mugs. "Milk?"

"Yes. And sugar if you have it."

"A woman after my own heart." He set a sugar container in front of me and a half-full milk carton.

I dressed my coffee, sipped, savored the jolt and flavor.

"You were out driving?" As he stared at me over the rim of his cup, I imagined this was how he looked at a defendant on the witness stand. He allowed the silence to wheedle my story loose.

"I was in a car accident in January. I cracked up the car and my head. I've lost about a week or so of time before the accident, and I thought seeing the site would help me remember."

"Did you remember anything?"

"Bits and pieces, but I can't figure them out. It's as if someone dropped a thousand tiny puzzle pieces on a table and I've been given three and told to guess the picture on the box."

"Missing time can't be easy."

"It's only ten days, but I know it was important."

"I keep meticulous records in my calendar. I can tell you what I did on this date ten years ago. I couldn't imagine not knowing."

"I've never been good at keeping track, beyond work appointments. I had an art show on the Friday before, a wedding on Saturday night, a new-bride meeting on Tuesday—and several digital files show I'd done a good bit of editing that week. Those are my only concrete markers."

"When was the accident?"

"The following Friday."

"What about your phone? GPS history? Texts. Emails."

"My phone was missing after the accident." I stared into the creamy depths of my coffee. "My sister insists I'm making something out of nothing. But it's important, and I can't tell you why."

"I saw your sister here. Brit Stockton, right?"

"Yeah. How did you know?"

"I know a lot of the attorneys in the city. She's tough."

I couldn't tell if it was a compliment or a complaint. "After our mother died, she was the primary caregiver for my sister and me. She had to grow up fast."

He sipped his coffee. "What caused the accident?"

"The report said I was intoxicated. But I don't drink or use drugs."

"You took two sips of the beer I gave you." He did have an eye for detail.

"Big mistake," I said. "I did it without thinking and should always be thinking."

"Maybe on the day of the accident, you weren't thinking, either. Maybe someone offered you something, and you took it before you realized. It just got ahead of you as you were rushing to get home."

"It's a good theory."

"But . . ."

"I don't think I screwed up."

He frowned. "Could you have been drugged? It happens too often."

"I don't remember."

"Did the hospital test your blood?"

"They were too busy getting me into surgery. Later they did test, but the tests were inconclusive. But even if they found a substance, I didn't willingly take it."

"Who're you trying to convince?"

"I didn't screw up." I wasn't afraid of myself, but of someone else. I sipped my coffee and carefully set the mug down. "Here you're offering me coffee, and I start spilling my guts. You have a way, Mr. Bernard."

He studied me, clearly recognizing my deflection. "The *Mr.* makes me sound too old."

I smiled. "You're not." Suddenly a little too aware of him, I stood. "And I've got a mountain of editing today, and you've got to get to work."

"Are you working a wedding tonight?"

"No."

"I never followed up on my sticky-note invitation."

"Maybe another time."

Unfazed, he walked me to the door. "I'm going to hold you to that. See you around."

"Will do." As I crossed the hallway, I felt him watching me, but when I turned back to smile or wave or something, he'd vanished into his apartment.

As I closed the door, my phone began ringing. I glanced at the number and didn't recognize it. Still, with new clients reaching out all the time, I accepted the call. "Marisa Stockton."

The line crackled with silence on the other end.

"Hello?"

Nothing.

I glanced at the number. "This is Marisa Stockton."

The line went dead.

My first thought was Alan. He'd tried to call, maybe even dialed the wrong number. I walked to my computer and typed in the number. There was no listing.

Hang-ups and wrong numbers weren't unheard of. Still, they always left me restless, unsettled.

I was being ridiculous. Overreacting, like I did so well. I closed my eyes, took deep breaths, and shifted my attention to my daily schedule. Routine kept me grounded and focused. Today, there was some editing I could do, emails to read and respond to, but it was only a few hours of work, and I was ahead of schedule. Time enough for that later tonight.

Morning sunlight streamed through my window, drawing me to the view. It was going to be a beautiful day. One that would be wasted if I stayed inside. Without thinking, I moved to my old camera bag, thought very briefly about swapping it for the new one Jack and Jo-Jo had given me. It was fancy, upscale, something I would've dreamed about owning once. I checked my equipment, made sure my batteries were charged, and shouldered the old, familiar bag. Locking the door, I heard Alan moving about. It was nice to have another human on the floor.

Down the stairs and out the front door to my car, I fired up the engine, grateful that the early-morning chill had softened.

The route was new for this car, but all too familiar to me. I headed south and wove through the suburban side of the city toward Riverside

Drive. As I turned down the winding road, tension rippled through my body.

When I'd been shooting in December, I'd driven myself to the point of exhaustion, splitting my time between here and whatever function I was hired to shoot. The mountain of work had gobbled up any extra time I might've had to brood. Each night I had fallen into bed completely drained. Finally, when I'd shot this place from every angle, I turned my back on it. I'd hoped I'd expelled the demons. What I realized now was that they'd not gone anywhere. They'd simply gone silent.

I parked in the public parking space and grabbed my camera bag. Locking the car, I headed toward the shore's edge. When I'd been here last, the trees had lost their leaves and the landscape was stark and barren.

Now there was some greenery budding and blossoming on the naked branches, signaling the land was returning to life. It struck me as unfair. My sister was dead, but the shoreline that had hidden her body was getting yet another renewal on life.

I raised my camera and snapped pictures.

When Richards had told my family about the discovery of Clare's body, I'd excused myself and then sneaked out of the house and driven to the crime scene. When I'd arrived, the area was taped off, so I'd parked a half mile away and walked in. The riverfront land was roped off with yellow crime-scene tape, and a team of forensic technicians and uniformed officers were searching the brush and shoreline for evidence. I stood back, praying that whatever they found would somehow prove that they'd made a mistake. The body on the rocks was not Clare.

At the crime scene, I'd lingered in the cold, huddling in my jacket, when an officer had made a discovery. He'd found a black blouse with a deep-V neckline. My shirt.

I'd bought the shirt five days before Clare died. I'd taken my father's credit card from his wallet and treated myself to a few post-Christmas treats. Dad didn't like when he saw all the bags in my room, but as long as I wasn't bothering him, that gave him time with Sandra.

The night of the New Year's Eve party, I'd come into our room to find Clare looking at the top. Since she'd started dating Kurt, she'd been dressing more and more like me. I'd told her to go for it.

What if she'd not worn that blouse? What if she'd dressed as Clare and not me?

After Clare died, I was a mess and Dad could no longer ignore me. He needed to prove to himself and the world that his absentee parenting had not led to Clare's death. The police and the neighbors were watching now, he'd said many times. I needed to be on my best behavior.

Brit had offered to drop out of college, but he wouldn't hear of it. No sense pissing away both their lives because of Clare and me. His solution had been to ship me off to Catholic boarding school. The change of scenery didn't help—demons do travel—and if there was trouble to be found, I located it. By summer break, I'd been expelled.

So it was just me and Mother Brit, who fell back into her role as the fussy surrogate parent. She drowned me with enough attention for two. I'd gotten pretty sick that summer, and again the doctors theorized it was grief. I'd suffered two major losses in three years, and it was no wonder my body was breaking down.

Frankly, I thought the experts were all correct. It made sense that I was shutting down. Grief was a powerful enemy that sucked not only energy but the will to live. I was ready to die and unwilling to fight death off anymore.

But by August, Brit was in DC interning for a congressperson. I was feeling better and smart enough to know if I pressed too hard, Dad would ship me off again. I begged to stay home. Swore I would be good. Dad reenrolled me in my old high school, and though I was still using, I kept it at manageable levels. As long as I kept trouble behind closed doors, I was free to do what I wished.

Our lives had been splintered by that New Year's Eve party, too many innocent lies, and a damn black blouse I'd bought with a stolen credit card.

My phone rang, startling me from my thoughts. Detective Richards. The man had radar. "Hello."

"Can you meet me at the coffee shop on Grace Street?" His voice was gruff with hints of annoyance.

"Why?"

"There's something I want to tell you about your sister that I never did before."

"What?"

"Not over the phone."

"I can be there in a half hour."

"See you then."

34

RICHARDS

Friday, March 18, 2022
9:30 a.m.

When Marisa entered the coffee shop, I was relieved to see her eyes were bright, and there was a warm glow in her cheeks. She was a far cry from the thin, pale teenager with charcoal-smudged blue eyes. In my career, I'd seen few real happy endings, and I wanted to believe Marisa was going to be one of them. She deserved to be happy.

She grabbed a cup of coffee and came toward me with a plate sporting two doughnuts with green sprinkles. She sat, settled her camera bag by her chair. "I remember you eating doughnuts once when I came by the station."

"No more."

"Just one?"

"Tell it to my blood pressure. Doc says limit the sugar, fat, and cigarettes."

She slid off her jacket and then sipped her coffee. "If you don't mind then?"

"Have at it. Enjoy that youthful metabolism while you can."

"Hit the big three-oh. Not so young."

"Baby," I growled. "What I wouldn't give."

"I heard a lifetime's worth of aging jokes last Friday," she said. "But I'm not complaining." Bracelets on her wrist jangled as she popped a piece of doughnut into her mouth and then wiped green sprinkles from her fingers.

"Any luck remembering your car accident?"

"No, none. But I visited the site early this morning. Met a woman whose roommate saw the accident happen. She said there was a man on the scene who stayed with me while she called 9-1-1, but he was gone when the cops and rescue squad arrived."

"Her name is Jenny Taylor."

"Good memory."

"I made a point to read up on your accident. Ms. Taylor couldn't remember much. Said your guardian was a white guy. Thirties to maybe late forties. Not fat or thin."

"Could be half the city."

"Exactly. In high-adrenaline situations, our brains don't process details as well."

"My phone went missing after the accident. I think that guy might have taken it."

"Why do you say that?"

"I have a faint memory of someone reaching into the car, and it goes missing. I don't suppose you could ping it or something? Find the phone, find the man."

"I can try. But if he took it, it's long been traded or sold."

She picked up another hefty doughnut fragment. "Still."

"I'll see what I can do."

"Thanks." She took a couple of big bites, making me pine for my youth and the cartons of ice cream I could eat. "Did you bring me here to talk about the accident or my sister?"

"Your sister." I sat back in my chair and met her unwavering stare. "I told this to your father, but he never wanted me to tell you or your sister. I promised I would keep it private as long as I didn't think it stood in the way of solving the case."

"Maybe you should have told me."

"I thought about it. But I wasn't interested in piling more onto your shoulders. You were already in a bad place, and by the looks of it, you'd been there for a while."

"I looked that terrible?"

When she'd overdosed two years ago, I'd known if she kept up her pace, she'd be dead within the year. And here she was. "I know troubled when I see it."

"That obvious? I thought I was better at hiding it."

Her sunken eyes and hollow cheeks still came back to me from time to time. She'd needed a lifeline. And I had wanted to help but knew there wasn't much I could do other than keep tabs on her.

"What do you have to tell me?" she asked.

Bad news was best delivered swiftly with no drama. "Clare was pregnant."

She stared at me, her eyes reflecting a jumble of shock, confusion, distrust, and then anger. "That can't be right. She would have told me."

"She wasn't that far along."

"How do you know this?" Anger tightened her tone.

I cleared my throat. "The autopsy."

Pale features grew a little whiter as she sat back, her mouth opening slightly. She'd always been so consumed with anger it was hard to tell what else was going on in her head. "Are you sure she was pregnant?"

I listened for signs of deception in her words and searched for more in her body language. I wanted to find anything that hinted that she'd known Clare was pregnant. Marisa would've been the logical person for Clare to talk to. But I saw only pure confusion and then sadness. "Yes."

She cleared her throat. "How far along?"

"Five or six weeks, according to the medical examiner. She might not have known herself. Did she appear different to you?"

"Over the holidays I was sick. My stomach always got worse at the holidays. If Clare had been off, it would have been easy for me to miss."

"Was she dating anyone?" I asked.

"Kurt. They'd been together about six months. And you know they were sexually active."

"Anyone else?"

She shook her head. "Everyone assumed I'd be the one to get pregnant, but I didn't sleep around. The idea of physical contact was always unsettling to me. But Clare craved it. She needed to hear she was loved. And as you and I both know, young males will trade sweet words for sex. I could tell when she'd been with a guy, but I never asked with who."

Finding love in dangerous places. "I can't believe you didn't know something, Marisa. You were twins, you shared a room."

"There was nothing. She was her regular self. But clearly she kept more secrets than I realized." She traced the rim of her cup. "She used to carry that stupid point-and-shoot camera with her. After she died, I looked everywhere for it but could never find it."

"Other people mentioned the camera."

"You said everyone lies. I guess that included Clare, too." A slight tremor rumbled in her tone. "Clare called me that last night about ten."

"I remember the call from your phone records."

"She said she had something to tell me. I lost count of the nights I replayed those words in my head. I'm not even sure if those worn words are even accurate or a blend of truth, time, and that pill I'd taken. Jack was sitting in front of me when she called, so I didn't say much. I thought I'd see Clare in less than an hour."

"You said you weren't feeling well at Christmas."

"Yes. Stomach pains came on suddenly. 'My tummy hurts' was a constant complaint. I had a battery of tests, but none of the doctors could figure it out."

"And Clare?"

"She never got as sick as I did."

"Were there times when it cleared up?" I asked.

"It was really bad after Mom died, and it came on and off until Brit left for college. It vanished that fall."

"But came back at Christmas."

"Yes." She frowned. "When I moved out of the house for boarding school, all my symptoms went away."

"When's the last time you got sick like that?"

"Beyond a common cold or a raging hangover? Not at all. What're you getting at?"

"You've said yourself you've always been a handful. Clare was the quiet one."

Absently, she tapped a ringed finger against the mug. "What're you getting at?"

I sighed, pissed that I'd not pressed this theory harder seventeen years ago. "I can't prove anything, Marisa. I've seen similar cases, but they're always hard to prove."

"What cases?"

"A caregiver makes his or her charge sick. Usually it's a mother-and-child scenario. Baby gets sick, Mom gets attention for herself while caring for the child. Child improves, attention goes away, and then the child gets sick again. It's called Munchausen syndrome by proxy."

She glared at me, clearly annoyed I'd brought up the idea. "Mom made me sick on purpose? Why?"

"You were likely easier to handle if you were sick and in bed. And I remember your parents had marriage problems. When one of the kids became ill, your father came home."

She shook her head. "But I kept getting sick after Mom died."

"You said it yourself: Brit stepped into the mother's role."

That prompted a startled, nervous laugh. "Brit was sick as a kid. The doctors all thought it was something genetic, but they never could figure it out. They said we'd outgrow it."

"When did you outgrow it?"

She drew in a breath. "After Brit left for college." She squeezed the bridge of her nose.

"Think back to all the times you were feeling good. Where was Brit?"

She closed her eyes. "She went to computer camp each summer. Clare and I always felt really good within a day or two. I thought it was the summer sun and heat that made me feel good." She met my gaze. "We were both sick within days of her return. Why would she do that to Clare and me?"

"She learned from your mother. Your father said how much he admired how well she took care of his girls."

She pressed fingertips against her right temple. "Daddy always appreciated Brit and how well she took care of Clare and me. He said it so often, I resented her. So did Clare." She shook her head, a frown furrowing her brow. "I think back to the nights I'd wake up feeling ill, and she'd be there. *See, I told you that you needed me.* When I overdosed, she was there. After my car accident, she was a rock."

"How was Brit after you sobered up?" I asked.

"We barely spoke." She grabbed a bead on her bracelet and absently moved it back and forth on the chain. "Why would Mom and Brit poison me? That's a hell of an accusation."

"I'm not making any allegations. I'm just spitballing. Telling you what I think I saw."

"What would this have to do with Clare's death?"

"You said Clare resented Brit as well. Did you ever talk about those feelings?"

"The summer before Clare died, Clare was so happy to see Brit leave. And when Brit came back, she started refusing any food or drink. She kept saying she was trying to lose weight."

"And she felt better?"

"Yes."

"Maybe she was putting the pieces together."

"But she never said a word to me."

"It's a hell of a thing to accuse someone of."

"I caught Clare snooping in Brit's room after Brit left for college. She brushed it off and said she was looking for lipstick or earrings."

"And then Brit came home for the holiday break."

"And I got sick."

"Was Clare still snooping in Brit's room?"

"Yes."

"Brit got sick the night of the party?"

"That's right."

"Maybe Clare was putting the pieces together. Maybe she gave Brit a dose of her own medicine and wanted you both to see the results."

"That's a lot."

"Brit controls you via medications. Brit leaves for college, and then all the emotions you and Clare didn't deal with come alive. Clare gets pregnant. Clare discovers Brit's lies. Clare is murdered. Three things can happen and not be related, but I find that's rarely the case."

"Did you run DNA on Clare's baby?" Her voice was hoarse, soaked with emotion.

"Yes. I tested the fetus's DNA against Kurt's, Sam's, Jack's, and every male at that party. I even tested your father's."

"Daddy? Jesus."

I was doing my best to give her the G-rated version of the world's dark side. "None matched. And the DNA never appeared in any criminal DNA databases, so without someone to compare it to, it's not helpful."

"You said you think Clare could have been killed because people thought she was me."

"That could still be true." He sipped his coffee. "But women who are murdered are more often than not killed by someone who knows them. And when a woman is pregnant, it drastically increases her chances of being killed by the father."

"Seriously?"

He shrugged. "I move in an ugly world."

"You said five or six weeks pregnant?"

"Yes."

"Six weeks before she died would have been mid-November. I visited Brit at college about that time. Clare stayed home. Brit and I spent an extra two days in Charlottesville shopping. We got home on Sunday."

"Clare was on her own for two or three days."

"Yes. I thought she'd be spending her time with Kurt. Have you asked Jo-Jo? Clare might've spoken to Jo-Jo about someone new or secret. At times those two were pretty close."

"Jo-Jo never mentioned another guy. And I asked several times."

"Why wouldn't Jo-Jo tell you everything?" she asked, more to herself.

"You tell me." I leaned back.

"Do you think Jo-Jo knew about the baby?"

"She never told me about it," I said.

"But you said everyone lies, right?"

"Yes, they do. Jo-Jo seems like an airhead, but she married an ex-con who's made lots of money in the last five years. That suggests to me she's more comfortable with trouble than you'd think."

Marisa shook her head as these realizations sank in. "You don't appear affected by these facts. Just another day on the job."

"Don't be fooled."

Her eyes were filled with a bottomless sadness that had touched a soft spot in my heart, even when I'd known she was lying. I'd always found a reason to excuse her.

"What do you do to deal with all this nastiness?" she asked.

"There was a time when I drank, picked fights with my wife, and isolated myself. That led to two divorces and a damaged liver. Now I'm retiring before all this eats me alive."

"We should start our own club." Her lips lifted into a half smile that held no mirth.

"Right."

"Not knowing who killed her is eating me alive," she said. "I can't let it go."

"We might not ever get our answers. And if we don't, you have to find a way to make peace."

She understood the pain of loss. Her mother, her sister—the one-two punch would've sent anyone spiraling. And a sister poisoning her took it to another level.

If there was a blessing, Marisa had never stood over her sister's lifeless body; nor had she been a firsthand witness to the violence inflicted on Clare by the killer and then the medical examiner. I wasn't so lucky.

"You make it sound easy," she said.

I shook my head. "I can lie to anyone, including myself, and say that a change of scenery or a wife will fix all my problems. It helps, but it never really heals the mark left by a homicide."

"You must be covered in scars."

"Not as bad as you might think."

Marisa arched a brow. "You're a good liar, aren't you?"

"One of the best."

35

Jo-Jo

Friday, March 18, 2022
2:00 p.m.

My hand trembled a little as I stared at this morning's test strip, which sported double stripes. It represented a hard-fought battle of temperatures, fertility tests, and timed sex to optimize potency. Touchdown. Score one for the team. Odd, but I'd stopped really trying to get pregnant a few months ago and hadn't bothered with the charts, graphs, and data streams.

But the longer I sat and stared at the dual lines, elation over the win calmed to the cold realization that this baby would bind me to Jack forever. Not that he wasn't a good guy. He was. He'd made mistakes, but that was the past, right? I'd seen the shift in him five years ago, when I'd walked into J.J.'s Pub. Jack had been standing behind the bar, moving with purpose and precision, like a captain in command of his ship. I'd always thought he was hot, but this newfound confidence in him was far sexier.

And I'd known I could leave at any time, even after the *I do*s gave me the freedom to enjoy our life. Men could be left, communication limited to divorce attorneys, and finally locked in the past. But a baby couldn't be easily left behind.

My hand slid over tender breasts to my still-flat stomach. The bigger tits were nice now, but what would become of my body after the kid? All the sit-ups, ab crunches, and planks to get into shape. Jack appreciated a tight body, but how would he feel about me growing wide and pear-shaped? Of course he'd still love me—he'd said he'd meant "for better or worse." But the baby would change my body—my life—and I wondered if he would still want me sexually. I'd heard enough of the teachers at school complaining in the lounge about how dull their lives had gotten since their babies.

Jack liked dancing close to the edge. He was always looking for the next rush, even if he now found it in business instead of a back-alley deal. Beyond the thrill of this test's positive result and the baby's birth, I wondered what would happen in the endless months and years of parenthood. He wasn't the type to drive a van or cheer at a soccer practice. Would he stick around for the mundane moments? Would our commingled blood in the baby be enough to keep him with me?

"Of course he will," I whispered. "He wants this baby as much as me." And we weren't kids in high school. We were in our thirties. Mature adults.

I'd stared at a similar positive pregnancy test in high school. It had been Clare's.

She'd gripped it in her hand the afternoon of my New Year's Eve party, her young, pale face drawn tight with panic. "What am I going to do?"

I had felt myself shrinking inward at the idea of having to face such a choice. At sixteen, I'd heard of other girls at school who'd thought they were pregnant, but I'd never had a front-row seat to this kind of moment.

"I don't know," I said honestly. "Should we tell Brit or Marisa?"

"God no," she said. "I don't need Brit hovering and shaking her head in disapproval. I can almost hear her now: 'I'd expect this from Marisa, not you.'"

"I'll always stick with you," I said. "I've got your back."

Tears rolled down Clare's cheeks. "They'll hate me. They'll think I'm such a loser."

"Look, you aren't the first to have this problem," I said. "And you won't be the last. This can be fixed." The minute the comment came out of my mouth, I regretted it. I sounded like my own mother. *Your problems aren't that special.*

Clare looked at me, her cheeks flushed from vomiting. "Great."

"I'm sorry. I don't know what I'm supposed to say."

Clare smiled and shrugged. "Nothing to say."

"When did this happen?"

"About six weeks ago," she said.

"Who's the father? Kurt?"

"I don't know," she whispered.

My mind ticked back through the days and weeks. We'd both been here, home for the fall break. I mentally profiled the boys at school, trying to replay who'd shown interest in Clare. Her flaming-red hair made her impossible to miss.

"You have to have an idea?" I asked.

"His name is Jeff. But beyond that I don't know much."

"I know everyone in the school," I insisted.

"Not this guy." She squared her shoulders. "It doesn't matter."

"And you don't want to tell this Jeff guy? He should at least pay for the clinic visit."

"I doubt I'll ever see him again."

"I can talk to him."

"No. Don't do that." Clare carefully wrapped the test strip in toilet paper and set it in the trash can.

"I'm glad you came to me with this. Reminds me of the days we shared everything."

"Me too."

I hugged her, holding her close, knowing I'd never tell a soul. This was our secret. "You still coming to the party tonight?"

Clare drew back. "I need to talk to Marisa. I've got to tell her something important anyway. After that, if all hell doesn't break loose, I'll come."

"What do you have to tell Marisa?" I asked.

"It's between us right now."

"We're sisters, too," I insisted.

"I know. But I have to tell Marisa first."

I hid my disappointment with a smile. In friend groupings of three, someone is always left out. "Sure."

Clare stood, smoothed her hands over her jeans. "I'm going home to change. I'll be back in a couple of hours."

"Are you telling Marisa about the baby, too?"

"Later. Maybe tomorrow."

I pushed down another tide of jealousy. Clare was my friend. I'd do anything for her. And still she always defaulted to Marisa. Blood was thicker than water.

"You sure you're okay?" I pressed.

Clare's smile was only half-hearted this time as she moved to the door. "Seriously, I'll be fine. We'll talk about this next week. Nothing to be done about it now."

"I'll be waiting for you."

"Thanks." Clare sniffed, raised her chin. "Okay. See you soon."

Clare had been in such a state, she'd forgotten her coat. Though I'd been tempted to take it to her, I decided she could get it when she came back. If she wasn't going to really open up to me, then she could wait for her coat.

Shaking off the memory, I rose and moved into Jack's and my bedroom and then the walk-in closet. Rising on tiptoes, I grabbed an old shoebox and sat on the closet floor. Carefully I removed the top and dug through the random keepsakes until I found the small point-and-shoot camera.

The battery had gone dead a long time ago, but when I'd discovered Clare had left it tucked in her coat pocket, I'd opened the viewfinder and looked at the pictures. I'd scrolled back to the November dates and looked at the images. Marisa sitting on her unmade bed. Jack with Brit. The morning sky. An art show in the city. And the partly turned face of a guy I didn't remember. Was he the guy?

The camera had also proved that Jack had been around Clare about the time she got pregnant. I had always thought Clare told me everything, including anything to do with Jack. But maybe Clare and Marisa were more alike. Marisa sure had kept her night with Jack a secret for thirteen years.

I'd never told anyone about Clare's baby or the camera, not even the police detective who stared at me with the wary eyes of a predator. I'd never told Brit or Marisa. The baby was a secret that I alone had shared with Clare and the camera my only tangible souvenir of her. Besides, telling would've broken the bond between us, and I couldn't let that last tentative connection break.

The cops must have figured out about the baby. There'd been an autopsy that had delayed the funeral by a week. And Kurt had told me the cops had taken cheek swabs from all the boys who'd been at the party. There'd been no public announcement about the pregnancy, and Marisa never mentioned it. I figured the baby was one of those details they were keeping secret. Their ace in the hole to catch the killer.

Once I'd seen an autopsy on YouTube. It was gross, and I'd been thinking about Clare as the doctor's knife sliced around the breasts and down the belly, creating a Y shape. Imagining Clare getting cut up made me cry.

I shoved aside the old memories as my stomach rolled. I stood and filled a glass with tap water and sipped slowly.

And now I was pregnant and feeling just as nervous as Clare had looked that day. Of course, our situations weren't even comparable, but fear, nerves, and uncertainty didn't care about age or job description.

The front door opened, and I quickly put the camera back in the box and tucked it behind sweaters on the top shelf.

I recognized Jack's steady steps, which reminded me of marching soldiers going into battle. He said he'd picked up the purposeful footsteps in prison. "Get from point A to B as quick as you can," he'd said. "Staying alive was the single goal." He still approached every day like he was fighting to stay free.

"Hey," I said, smiling. "I thought you had meetings all day."

Something in my voice (nerves maybe) must have caught his attention. He missed very little. "I thought you'd be at school."

"I called in sick."

"What's wrong?" Feeling his strong arms always calmed me, and I should've been thrilled to tell Jack about the baby. This child was what we both wanted. What we'd dreamed about for the last three years. And yet I drew in a deep breath before I said, "I'm pregnant."

He laid his hands on my shoulders, studied my face closely. "What? You said it was negative yesterday."

"The test this morning popped with double lines."

He stood still as stone, and I thought he might be annoyed. He always looked like a statue right before he exploded. But he broke the stillness with a slow, steady smile. "Jo-Jo, that's fantastic. Are you happy?"

"Shocked. Scared. Happy. I'd given up thinking this was going to happen."

He hugged me close, wrapping me in the strength of his arms. He smelled of restaurant-renovation sawdust, fresh cold air, and the Irish soap I bought him. "You're going to be a great mom."

"You mean it?" I asked against his flannel shirt.

"Of course I do. I always thought that, even back in high school."

I drew back, looked up at his face. His square jaw was covered in stubble, but there was a rare softening in his gaze. Sudden tears burned in my eyes. I wiped one away. "Sorry."

He smoothed a tear off my face. "What's gotten you so upset?"

"I was thinking about Clare."

Stiffness rippled through his muscles. "That was a long time ago."

"I just keep thinking about that last night. I know I need to put it behind me, and I have for the most part. But it comes back when I least expect it."

"Because of her pregnancy?" he asked softly.

I'd lied to Marisa when I said I'd not told anyone about Clare's pregnancy. I'd told Jack last year. It was New Year's, another time of year rife with triggers, and I'd had too much to drink. I'd whispered my secret and immediately regretted it. Time and booze had given me the permission to betray Clare.

Jack had not said much, frowned as if he were working this bit of information into a bigger puzzle. He'd held me close, asked about the baby's father. I didn't know. He'd kissed me and taken me back to our home. As we'd made love, I could've sworn Clare was standing in the corner, staring at me, her gaze filled with pain.

Now he tipped my face back with his crooked index finger. "Did you ever tell anyone?"

I couldn't look him in the eye. "No. Only you. I told Clare I wouldn't tell anyone, and I shouldn't have told you."

He nestled his chin on the top of my head, and he wrapped his arms tighter around me. "No, it's good you did. I'm not a fan of secrets. Especially between us."

But it hadn't been his secret or mine; it had been Clare's. And I'd betrayed Clare when I'd told him. "Should I tell Marisa?"

"Don't tell anyone. The cops don't take kindly to witnesses who held back information. Clare is the past. You've got to let her go."

Jack was right. Clare had dominated the past. And our baby would rule the future. "What if Marisa doesn't let this go?"

"She will," he said. "She's never chased after this case for more than a week or two before she loses interest."

I looked up at him, realized he was staring at me. "You think so?"

"I know so. It's not good for her or her sobriety." He tightened his hold.

"You're right. I need to stop worrying."

Soon Marisa would give up her yearly quest for whatever truth she thought was out there, and we'd all get back to our lives.

I'd never told Jack about the camera. Maybe blabbing about the baby had shocked me into silence. There were plenty of reasons to keep the camera secret now. It would bring the cops and reporters swarming back into my life, and Marisa would be pissed. This was a secret worth keeping. I'd the baby to consider now. Blood was thicker than water.

36

Him

Memories were my worst enemy. The one that now played over and over was seeing you hit that utility pole. I could hear the brief squeal of tires, the impact, the crunch of metal, the shattering of glass, and the hiss of the cracked engine block.

I'd lingered as long as I could, spoken to the other woman, who said she had called 9-1-1, and when we were alone, I'd spotted your cell phone lying on the floor. The calls and texts I'd made to you were on its memory card. I'd been careful to use a prepaid phone, but cops had a way of tracing the point of sale and, if motivated, digging through endless hours of video footage. I'd have been fucked if they found me on one of those recordings. So I'd reached in the car and grabbed your phone, tucking it in my pocket.

Now, as I poured a stiff drink, I fished your phone out of a drawer. I'd seen you type in the passcode once: 2009. The year your sister had died. Not genius, but personal and memorable for both of us, just like the print you'd made that reminded me of you both.

I scrolled through the last week before your accident to the night of your show. You'd taken several selfies, with friends and fans, I suppose. I recognized a few of the faces, including Brit, who was sexy in a buttoned-up kind of way. Your sister's smile was brighter, but given the subject of your photography, I could understand the darkness in you. Death had left a deeper mark on you and me.

A few pictures of you at the opening looked posed. You were standing in front of your collection, smiling, but it was not joyous. It was sheepish, as if you'd felt like an impostor and didn't belong there at all.

In all the photos, you were standing in front of the picture that I'd bought. As I scrolled back further, I searched for hints of any man in your life. Thankfully, I didn't see anyone who gave off a romantic vibe. The men you were pictured with at various weddings were totally into you. How could they not have been? But you stared at the camera, clearly not noticing them like a lover would. That was good. I liked the idea that we had something special.

As I scrolled back in time, I could see your health decline. You got thinner. Your eyes grew hollower. Your skin got pastier with each new year. It was a descent into drug and alcohol addiction. It was not a pretty journey, and I was happy to return to your present healthy, whole self.

I gulped down the whiskey, closed the phone, removed the battery, and tucked it in my dresser drawer. The last thing I needed was for someone to trace the phone and find me. That would have required some explaining.

Restless and unsettled, I couldn't relax. I'd killed you once and had nearly done it a second time. Christ. How could I have hurt someone I loved so much? Someone I'd do anything to protect.

Unable to calm down, I grabbed my keys and coat and headed out to my car. I knew where you lived. And I'd been there before so many times since your accident. I was not stalking but doing my best to look out for you. Your guardian in the shadows.

After a short drive I parked in your building's lot. I stared up at the corner apartment and noticed your office light was on. Working late. You really needed to take better care of yourself.

Your slim frame passed in front of the window. You stared out into the darkness, and it felt like you sensed me. You must have felt our connection. It had never been broken and never would be.

37

Jack

Seeing Brit several times over the last week had brought back a lot of memories. Some were good, and some not so terrific. Many on the outside of our relationship tagged us as complicated, but what we'd shared had been really simple. I'd shown her the dangerous side of life, while she'd shown me the respectable version. We'd opened each other's eyes to what we could be. Once we'd taken what we needed, the relationship had run its course.

Now I was so close to having it all, and I didn't want to take even one step back.

I'd been sitting in my car in front of David's townhome for an hour when he finally pulled up. Out of my car, I tossed my cigarette to the pavement and ground out the embers. This was my third trip to his house and the first time I'd caught him. For a guy who worked at home, he wasn't around much.

I'd not seen David since we were teenagers, and to see him sitting in J.J.'s Pub celebrating Marisa's birthday had caught me off guard. I'd not said anything, but the more I thought about him living in my town, the more doubts I had.

When David saw me moving toward him now, he momentarily froze, just as he'd done at the birthday party. I'd first met him years ago at a juvenile-detention camp. I was sixteen and in for breaking into homes and stealing. He'd been eighteen and working at the camp as a church volunteer.

David grinned. But I knew better than anyone that a smart man smiled no matter how nasty the shit sandwich. *Never let them see you sweat.*

"Jack, it's good to see you." Survival Rule #1: sound genuine, even if you aren't feeling it. "What brings you here?"

"I was in the neighborhood checking out my new restaurant location. It's two blocks from here. Want to get a drink?"

"I didn't know you were opening up here."

"Bought the property in December. Renovations started in January. Drink?"

David could always smell a lie, which was why I led with the truth. Another smile. "Sure, why not? There's a bar down the street. A bit of a hole-in-the-wall, but the beer is cold."

I huddled deeper into my jacket. "Singing my song."

David had never been an athlete, but he'd been leaner the summer we crossed paths. He'd been everyone's best friend, and that trait had earned him points with the boys at camp as well as the counselors and guards. However, a bad diet and too much desk time had softened him. I never wanted to lose my lean body, my edge.

"I remember Brit saying at the birthday party that you lived in the area, so I gave it a try," I said.

He didn't question how I'd found his address. Back in the day, I'd been the kid who traded in information. "Glad you did. We didn't have much time to talk at Marisa's birthday party."

"Brit went all out, didn't she?"

"That's how she rolls. No half measures for that woman." David slowed as we approached a pub located in the basement of a four-story brick row house. He walked down the three steps, opened the door next to the red **OPEN** sign, and held the door for me. "Gets better, I promise."

I followed him into the dimly lit bar. The faint scent of smoke drifted from the shadows, mingling with a blues song played over an unseen sound system. As I strolled toward the bar, I glanced at the black-and-white, framed posters of old blues-guitar players. I'd been here several times to check out the competition. What I had planned for my new establishment would smoke this place.

"If memory serves, you were into beach music," I said.

He chuckled. "'Myrtle Beach Days' is my theme song."

"Let me get this." I ordered two beers.

"Thanks."

When the bartender served two bottled beers, I handed one to David, and we found an empty booth. Jackets off and hung on pegs, we sat.

David held up his beer. "Thanks again."

I tipped my bottle toward him and took a long pull. I'd tried the sober route for almost a year, but lately had a drink or two. I knew now how to keep it in check, so I wasn't worried. "What did you think of Marisa's birthday party?"

"Like I said, Brit never goes halfway. She put a lot of thought into it. Wanted to make it a blast from the past. The *Wizard of Oz* hats were definitely icebreakers."

"That's for certain."

I'd been assigned the Lion hat, a.k.a. the coward. If I were a betting man, and I was, I'd say Brit was sending us all a message with those damn hats.

"Are you and Brit serious?" I asked.

"Yeah. I'm going to ask her to marry me."

"Seriously? You just met her two months ago."

"That's right. We met in the hospital after Marisa's accident."

"I met Jo-Jo when she was in high school, but when we met again five years ago, it took me weeks to get her to go out on a date with me. She knew I had a record and didn't want any part of it. Does Brit know that you know me from before?"

"I didn't see the point in bringing it up."

"I don't like remembering the camp. But I told Jo-Jo about my time there and in prison. Better she see me for who I am. For better or worse, right?"

"Right."

"Don't worry, I won't say a word. You saved my ass in camp, and I don't forget my friends." I had been dealing in camp and was expecting a shipment through the kitchen. It'd been stolen by one of the kids, and my ass would've been in a sling if I didn't sell and repay my supplier. David had told me at the meal break who'd taken the drugs. It didn't take much to steal them back or beat the hell out of the thief. From then on, David saw to it that my stuff was protected. He always refused a cut. His payback would come later, in the form of one hell of a favor.

David drank his beer. "Good to know. Thanks."

I grinned. "When are you going to do the deed—ask Brit to marry you?"

A hesitant smile tugged at his lips. "Later tonight, actually. I'm meeting her for drinks in a couple of hours."

"Best of luck to you. She's a great gal. She's been through hell and back. Mother died, then her sister. Father split, then died. A lot of tragedy in one family. But you know that."

"What's bringing all this up, Jack?" David asked. "You don't do anything without a reason."

"Neither do you."

David shrugged.

"Like you, I'm protecting what's mine. Jo-Jo just told me she's expecting."

He tipped his beer bottle toward me. "Congratulations."

"A lot on the line now. Not just a wife but a family to protect."

David traced his finger along the moist exterior of the glass. "This is an odd conversation, Jack. Not one I wanted to have tonight."

"You're right, man. Not appropriate. But we need to make sure we understand each other. I can't afford to clean up any more of your fuckups."

David slipped back behind his silence.

I sipped my beer. "We both care about Brit, and we want her to be happy. She and I are going to be doing big business together."

"What're you getting at?"

I offered my best grin, the one I saved for unruly patrons and squirrelly drug dealers. "Keep the past in the past. Don't do anything to screw it up like before."

"I've no intention of screwing anything up."

"Nobody ever plans to fuck up." The beer tasted weak, too watery for my tastes. "I know how hard atonement can be. Everyone wants to judge you for your past."

"This is friendly advice?" he asked.

"You know me better than that." I laughed. "It's a promise. I'll fuck you up bad if you mess with Brit or share the old days during some pillow-talk session."

"It's in both our interests if I don't."

"That's right." I rose, tossed two twenties on the table. "Best of luck tonight. She's a fine woman but a real ballbuster."

38

MARISA

Friday, March 18, 2022
7:15 p.m.

"Did you know Clare was pregnant?" I asked Brit the instant she opened her front door.

Brit was taken aback by me and my question. I'd not called because I knew she'd put me off. She was fine with showing up at my place unannounced, but that shoe never fit well on the other foot.

"Yes, I knew. Dad told me when he was sick two years ago." Brit averted her gaze and opened her door wider, already tensing at the idea a neighbor might hear. "Come in. I'd rather not have this conversation on my front porch. Neighbors are nosy."

I stood my ground, not caring whether the whole damn neighborhood heard me. She wasn't telling me the entire truth. "Why was I left out of the loop?"

"Inside or we don't talk."

I stepped into the foyer, and she closed the door behind me. "Dad only told me because he was sick," she said softly. "Dying churned up a lot of regrets for him. Though that man had many reasons for remorse, that one rose to the top. And as I remember, two years ago, you were drinking heavily."

"I've been sober a year."

"And learning your dead sister was pregnant would've helped you how?"

"I had a right to know."

"I didn't want to challenge your delicate hold on sobriety."

"I had a *right* to know. She was my sister. My twin."

"You don't get the rights of an adult when you're high." Her sharp words lingered between us before she drew in a breath. "Look, I feared if you knew there was a baby, it would be too much."

"The baby could have been the reason she was killed," I said.

Without a word, Brit turned and walked down the hallway to her kitchen. From the fridge she pulled out a seltzer for me and set it on the counter before moving to a wine bar and uncorking a bottle of red. She poured a generous serving. "Dad said Richards was worried that the baby's father could have killed her. But Kurt's DNA didn't match. Who was the father?"

Mama Brit didn't have all the answers.

"Clare was with several guys, some she might not have remembered. I'm not judging. We all dealt with Mom's death differently. For me it was booze, for her it was sex, and you control."

"Control? I didn't want the control. Dad *needed* me to look after you two. We were all in over our heads after Mom died. The last thing I wanted was to play mommy at age fifteen."

"You're right. It wasn't fair. Dad wanted to forget about all three of us," I said. "Our home was his physical address, but he checked out months before Mom died. All three of us felt orphaned. The lush, the slut, and the control freak. We were quite the trio."

Brit's lips thinned into a grim line. "You make us sound like monsters. We were kids, doing the best we could."

"Did Mom poison us?"

"What?"

Richards's theory still felt so far-fetched, but I hoped saying it out loud to Brit would give it credibility. "It's called Munchausen syndrome by proxy. In our case, poison a kid to get Daddy's attention."

"Did you get that idea from Richards, too?"

"Is it true?"

"How would I know?"

"Because we kept getting sick after Mom died. Did you continue the tradition?"

"Richards is filling your head with shit. None of that is true. I took you to doctors. They all agreed the stomach pains were stress!"

As much as I wanted to press, that didn't matter right now. Clare's death topped all our family's demented emotional problems. "Did you know seventy percent of women are murdered by someone they know and that the incidence of a woman being killed rises when she's pregnant?"

"That factoid from one of your internet searches or Richards?"

"Does it matter?" I asked.

She took several sips of wine. I smelled the fruity aroma and felt old cravings kicking in. I popped the seltzer, found the manufactured lemon flavor bland.

"It'll always matter. Richards is filling your head with lies."

"Why would he lie?"

She laughed. "Honey, he's desperate to make an arrest in this case. Not solving Clare's murder ruined his career. He's lucky they let him ride a desk the last thirteen years."

"I believe him."

Brit shook her head. "I can't do this right now. I'm supposed to meet David for drinks."

"This is more important, don't you think?"

"I can't fix the past. But I can try to build a decent future. You should do the same."

"You're building a future with David?"

"Maybe. Why not? He's good marriage material."

He'd shown up out of nowhere at the hospital after my accident. Happenstance was possible, but not likely. "He doesn't seem your type."

"We all grow up, Marisa. The bad boys are all fun and games when we're young, but you can't make a life with them. You should try to find a normal guy instead of your latest addiction."

"What's that mean?"

"You're swapping one addiction for another. Staying off the booze and drugs and now obsessing about Clare. You always take it too far."

"I'm not obsessing. I want to find Clare's killer. I thought you'd want the same."

"Thirteen years! It's been *thirteen years*. It'll take a miracle to find her killer now." When I readied a rebuttal, Brit held up her hand. "Save it. I'm too tired. And I'm not going to ruin this bit of happiness coming my way, so I can't indulge you right now. We'll talk in a few days. You know your way out."

Brit set her half-full glass of wine on the counter and walked past me to the back staircase leading from the kitchen to the second floor.

The cold shoulder and smothering, heavy silences were her specialties. I should have been immune to both by now, but the isolation stung. We were the last of our family, but that still wasn't enough.

My gaze settled on the glass of wine. Of course Brit would just leave it out at a time like this. It was a test. Brit liked her little tests.

I raised the glass, held it up to the light. She knew I'd look at it, swirl it in the glass, wonder how much I'd actually taste as I slugged it down. I sniffed the wine, inhaled the scent, and then lowered it back to the counter, ready to prove to Brit I was a different person.

I carried the bottle and wineglass to the sink, studied the vintage. Expensive. I poured the bottle down the sink. As I reached for the glass of wine, an irresistible urge overcame me. It wasn't a craving or longing but a powerful force that devoured all my good intentions, common sense, and a year's worth of sobriety mantras. As I readied to dump the glass's contents down the drain, I stopped.

I raised it to my lips and gulped it down in two sips. "Fuck you, Brit."

39

MARISA

Friday, March 18, 2022
7:45 p.m.

My mind was still buzzing from the wine and the anger boiling in my veins when I parked in my spot at my apartment building. I reached for the plastic bag filled with three bottles of grocery-store merlot.

Bottles clinking in the bag, I hurried up to my apartment, glanced toward Alan's door, and was grateful there was no sign of life. Any contact with a familiar human might have derailed this headlong journey to destruction, and I didn't want to be stopped. Inside my place, I closed and locked the door behind me before I removed each bottle from the bag and lined them up like soldiers ready for battle. My purse slid off my shoulder to the kitchen floor, and I reached in the cabinet for a glass. No fancy wineglasses to be found, only regular tumblers. Grabbing one, I twisted the top off and filled the glass nearly to the brim. I held it up to the light just as Brit had. Back in the day, I didn't even bother with a glass. It was straight out of the bottle, emphasis on buzz, not taste.

Even as anger scorched through reason, I had enough presence of mind to pause as I raised the glass to my lips. "This is what I am. The family lush."

Clare's own self-destructive path had likely led to her death, and now as far as I was concerned, mine could lead me to the same dark ending.

Closing my eyes, I drank the wine. It was cheap, too sweet and fruity, but like Brit's expensive blend, I barely tasted it as I guzzled the liquid until I saw the bottom of the glass. Drawing in a deep breath, I swiped my hand over my mouth and then refilled the tumbler. My head spun a little. My system wasn't used to the booze, and the alcohol hit my system and empty stomach like bricks.

I refilled the glass, and I walked to the window and stared out at the river now drifting over the rocks as if it had all the time in the world. Why had I chosen this apartment with this view? Any sane person would've stayed away from the river that had cleaned all the evidence off Clare's body and hidden her killer's identity. But I'd chosen this daily reminder that rubbed salt into a wound, ensuring it never healed.

My vision blurred, forcing me to sit on the couch. I closed my eyes, pressing the glass to my temple as Clare's voice whispered in my head.

"Guess what Brit's been doing," Clare said.

*I was darkening the shadow around her eyes. I liked the smoky Daryl Hannah–in–*Blade Runner *look, and since she wanted to be me tonight for the New Year's Eve party, I was going all out. Maybe over the top, but Clare deserved to be noticed. "What? Did mini-Mom iron our jeans again?"*

Clare stared at me. "Bigger than that."

"What?" I loved stories of Brit's screwups, which were few and far between.

"Wait and see."

"What're you talking about?" Her double talk annoyed me.

Clare fiddled with a tube of lip gloss. "Taste of her own medicine."

I darkened her pale eyebrows. "Speak English, Clare."

"It's better to show, not tell. But it's going to take a couple of hours."

"Okay. Puzzles." I tossed the pencil on my makeup table. "I've got to go to Jack's house." I blended her blush and stepped back. She could be me.

"Why are you going to see him?"

"Same as everyone else. Getting a little something to help celebrate the New Year."

Clare's gaze met mine in the mirror. I could have been looking at myself. "That's not the way to do it. He's got a weird vibe."

Her critique hit a nerve. "You screw everything with a heartbeat, Clare. At least I haven't crossed that bridge yet."

Clare stood, stepped back. "The shit he sells could kill you!"

"So could one of your boy toys."

Her face paled. "I'm not doing that anymore. Just Kurt now."

I pulled on a leather jacket. "What's changed?"

"It doesn't matter." Clare stared at me as if ready to say something, but then she seemed to think better of it. "Just get home as soon as you can. Like I said, I have something to show you."

"You're being very mysterious tonight. Are you okay?"

She smiled. "Of course."

I was too jumpy to press. "Can Kurt pick you up so I can use the Jeep?"

Clare frowned. "I don't think you should go. I don't like the way Jack looks at us."

Her real concern smoothed my ruffled feathers. "It won't take long. I'll be back before you know it. And we'll ring in the New Year at Jo-Jo's party."

Clare's brow furrowed as she stared into the mirror. "Everyone's going to think I'm you."

"Isn't that the point? You've been dressing up like me a lot lately."

"How do you know?"

"I can tell when my stuff has been worn. No big deal," I said. "However, if you show up to the party on time and sober, they'll know you're not me."

Clare smiled. "I guess."

"The eye makeup goes perfectly with the blouse."

I moved to my closet and chose the jeans I'd bought a few weeks ago. They'd cost over three hundred dollars, and I'd taken a morbid pleasure when the clerk swiped my father's credit card. "But wear these with it."

"You haven't even worn them." Clare moistened her lips, and for the first time, I noticed she looked pale. "Great."

"You okay? You look like you don't feel well."

"I'm fine. Drank too much beer last night."

"You? Drank too much?"

"Kurt can be a bad boy," she said, offhandedly.

I'd caught Kurt staring at me before and now wondered if he was the reason she'd been dressing up as me so much lately. Kind of weird to think my twin and her boyfriend channeled me when they got it on. But who was I to lecture? He made her smile, and we'd done precious little of that since Mom died.

"You know, you can tell me anything," I said.

"I know. And I will, but for tonight let's have fun. It's the New Year, and I want to ring it in in style. I need to have a really good time tonight."

Something in her voice caught my attention. "I can drop you off at Jo-Jo's."

"No, take the Jeep. Kurt will pick me up. Just be careful, okay?"

Now, as I stared at the river, I wondered for the millionth time whether, if I'd changed one little thing that night (the makeup, the jeans, leaving her to ride with Kurt), Clare would have lived.

My head spun and churned up all the emotions buried deep. "I barely hugged her that last time."

Tears fell down my cheeks. My stomach tumbled. There'd been a time when two glasses weren't even a warm-up. But tonight, it hit me between the eyes. Drawing in a breath, I rose off the couch and stumbled. Lightweight. Out of training.

I moved to the kitchen and grabbed the bottle by the slim neck. I took a long drink. "Any job worth doing is worth doing well."

40

Brit

I sat in the back of the Uber staring out the window, watching the lights of the city pass. I should've been happy. Should've been excited to see David, who, if I'd read his body language correctly, was going to ask me an important question. I'd also added Find My Friends to his phone when he'd been in the shower last week, justifying the move because he needed looking after just like Marisa. When he'd been late last week, that little app had told me he had been at a jeweler's in the West End. Didn't take higher math to add up that equation.

I should have been thrilled, over the moon, but Marisa's visit now shadowed all those thoughts.

Marisa could ruin the best, most perfect day. She was the dark, angry cloud that had hung over our family since the day she'd been born. And after Mom's death and most especially after Clare's, she'd never once considered that we were all hurting in our own ways, and none of us had time for her anger issues.

And now she was doing it all over again. If her stupid, drunken car accident wasn't enough, she was now using our *dead sister* to drain the fragile happiness from my life.

Before I'd left the house, I'd noticed the glass of wine and the bottle, which I'd accidentally left behind, had been emptied. That bottle had cost me fifty bucks, and I hated the idea of it going down the sink . . . and of Marisa gulping it like it was MD 20/20.

It would have been too bad if Marisa had drunk any of the wine. It would have been another nick in her fragile sobriety, which, let's face it, wouldn't stand the test of time. Marisa didn't have that kind of discipline. She was a loose cannon. A tragedy better suited for the stage.

Another stint in rehab was all we needed, but I'd rise to the occasion as I always did.

"We're here," the driver said.

I realized then that the Uber had rolled up in front of the historic restaurant in the city's Northside. "Thank you."

Climbing out, I muscled away the tension with a shoulder roll and allowed the cool air to temper the anger that had left my face warm and flushed.

My smile was forced, but as I held it, *and* held it, it felt more natural. Like my mother, I used the same damn smile to get through the worst of life. And I'd keep it plastered on all evening even if it killed me.

I pushed through the doors of the restaurant, annoyed by the blast of heat. There'd been something comforting about the shivering air. Discomfort kept me on my toes, made me think more clearly. Comfort, however, was dangerous. Easy to let one's guard down if too lax.

The hostess was a young woman in her twenties with ice-blond hair, bright expressive eyes, and the scripted word *Fearless* tattooed on her wrist.

"I'm meeting David Welbourne."

Ms. Fearless checked her list and smiled. "He's here. Right this way."

"Thank you."

I followed the woman's swaying hips clad in too-tight black pants. Aware of white tablecloths, soft music, and the hum of subdued conversation, we moved around tables and rounded a column. David was sitting at a corner table, and when he spotted me, he rose, looking a little nervous. It was charming to see and made me feel better. His eyes slid over me, and I noted appreciation mingling with curiosity. He'd better like what he saw. I'd put enough thought into the outfit this morning.

Leaning in, I kissed him on the lips. He tasted of wine and nerves. "What's got you so worked up?"

He touched his tie—an item I'd never seen him wear—and smiled. "You. Always you."

I smiled. Once I'd been the center of attention in my parents' lives, and then the twins had come along and my parents had become buried under a mountain of diapers, screams, and feeding schedules. Mommy and Daddy barely noticed me much after that.

But not tonight. Tonight, I had David. And I was his center. "I love you."

His cheeks blushed in the most adorable way. "I love you."

He held the back of my chair as I settled in my seat and placed a small beaded handbag in my lap. Carefully, I unfolded my napkin as he filled my wineglass with the open bottle on the table. He knew I liked a bottle best when it had time to breathe, time to soften. As I raised the glass, he sat and then clinked his against mine.

I sipped, trying to imagine Marisa staring at the open bottle in my kitchen. Of course, it'd been thoughtless of me to leave it behind. Not the kind of thing one does around an alcoholic. But Marisa had upset me. She'd thrown me off guard when she'd told me Clare had been pregnant. Dad had never told me she was expecting, but for some reason I couldn't admit that to Marisa. I'd not been thinking when I lied.

"That was a far-off look," David said.

I set my glass down carefully. "No far-off looks tonight. Just you."

"You don't have to do that with me."

"What?"

"Hide what's bothering you. I knew you were upset when you entered the room."

"How could you know?"

"You purse your lips." He puckered.

I laughed and sipped my wine again. I'd not known David in college, but since the day he'd walked into my life, he'd always been easy to be around. "My expression wasn't that bad."

"Maybe not for everyone else, but I'm getting to know you pretty well."

Yes, he was. I wasn't sure if that was a good thing or a bad thing.

"Tell me," he said.

"The usual. Fight with the sister."

"Marisa?" He leaned in a fraction, concern deepening his frown lines. "What happened?"

"She won't let Clare go. She won't just accept that some problems, no matter how terrible, just don't have fixes. The best anyone can do is manage their feelings and keep putting one foot in front of the other."

"That's worked for you."

"It can work for anyone." The wine was delicious, but the bottle Marisa had either drunk or poured down the sink was better.

"But not for Marisa."

"I don't want to talk about her," I said carefully. "I want to talk about you. How did your day go?"

"Sold millions of dollars' worth of stocks and bonds." It was his standard line when I asked him about work. He rarely said much about his days, and when I pressed him for stock tips, he laughed and said, "Buy low, sell high."

"Really, *only* millions? These days, darling, if it doesn't start with a *B* or *T*, people don't think much of it."

He chuckled as he reached in his pocket and set a small black box on the table. "I stand corrected."

I set my wine down. A nervous thrill shot through my body. "What do we have here?"

"Open it and find out."

My satisfied smile was as close to genuine as it came for me. Red manicured nails glistened in the soft light as I reached for the box, held it in the palm of my hand, and then slowly opened it.

Inside was a solitaire diamond set in white gold. It was a decent size, but the setting was plain to the point of old-fashioned. I wondered if he'd put a lot of thought into choosing the ring. Or if it had been recycled from a mother or grandmother. If he knew anything about me, he'd know I preferred yellow gold. Bigger diamonds. And nothing that any other woman had ever worn. "It's lovely."

"It belonged to my mother."

Ah, a family heirloom that meant something to him. Great, more past invading the future. He took the box and removed the ring. Automatically, I held out my hand and watched as he slid it on my ring finger.

It sparkled in the light as if hoping it could dazzle me into acceptance. "And is there a question that goes along with this ring?"

He held my hand. "Brit, will you marry me?"

Of course I would. He fit nicely into my life, and even though this ring didn't exactly suit my tastes, I could work with it. "Yes."

He leaned forward and kissed me. "Really?"

Arching a brow, I touched his face. "Have you ever known me not to speak my mind?"

He grinned and kissed me on the lips again. "No, I've not."

I rolled the words *engaged* and *fiancé* over in my mind. Neither felt right, like a new pair of shoes that pinched, but in time, the words would stretch and mold to fit.

Marisa likely wouldn't care one way or the other about this momentous moment. I'd ask her to be my maid of honor, seeing as she was the lone surviving sister. Given a choice, I'd have chosen Clare, who'd always been my favorite. If the universe had ever really screwed up, it was taking the wrong twin.

"Those lips are pursing again." His eyes were hawkish. "Doubts?"

"Just working through the logistics of a wedding. You know me." I smiled. "Have to have all my ducks in a row."

"I'm sure Marisa will help. She's been to enough weddings to know what works and doesn't. Who knows, she might be willing to take our engagement pictures. Of course, we couldn't ask her to do the wedding. She'll be in it."

Like it or not, I was stuck with Marisa.

41

MARISA

Saturday, March 19, 2022
7:00 a.m.

Jackhammer. There was a jackhammer pounding against the sides of my skull. My mouth was dry, and my stomach lurched. I rushed to the bathroom and threw up. When the heaves finally stopped, sweat soaked my body and clothes. Rising, I looked in the mirror and found bloodshot eyes staring back. My mascara had wept down my cheeks, and my jacked hair stood up.

It had been more than a year since I'd looked at my face after a binge. That face, *this face*, was so familiar. And now here I was, right back at square one.

I hated this face. It personified failure, weakness, and a lack of impulse control. I turned away, closed my eyes.

Immediately, I swayed and found myself back on my knees, vomiting again. This time when I rose, my body shook. I wanted to crawl back in bed and pull the covers over my head. Shut out the world until I could deal with it again. But that was what the old Marisa would've done. She'd have surrendered to the illness, just as she did as a child.

Instead, I turned on the shower taps, and as steam filled the room, I stripped off clothes reeking of sweat and vomit and carried them directly to the unit's small washing machine. With the washer chugging, I returned to the bathroom, stepped under the shower's hot spray, and let the warmth spread over my chilled skin and ease the tension banding my muscles.

Past experience told me that I'd feel like crap for the rest of the day. A cold cola and a couple of aspirin would help, but there was nothing else to be done other than suffer through this.

Served me right. I'd let Brit push my buttons. I'd fallen for one of a thousand traps she'd been setting for me for years. The pleasure-and-pain seesaw I'd been balancing for a year had dipped toward pain with just a few words from Brit. Instead of taking it on the chin, I'd done what I'd always done. I numbed it.

Through bleary eyes, I realized Brit was happiest when she was driving me to rehab, holding my hand through another detox, sitting at my side after the car accident. So smug. My weakness gave her strength.

I tipped my face toward the water, and hot spray pulsed against my skin. "You're too old to let this happen. Too smart."

I shut off the water and toweled off. In my room I dressed in jeans and a gray sweater. For the sake of morale, I put on makeup, dried and styled my hair. As I'd said to a woman at a meeting a few weeks ago, "Get back on track, old girl. The future can still be bright."

Meetings. The idea of facing my peers and turning in my one-year chip sucked. We didn't like to call it the walk of shame, but that was exactly what it was. But disgrace, and the desire to avoid it, was a powerful motivator.

After setting up my coffeepot, I grabbed a large trash bag and collected the three empty wine bottles, which I stowed under the kitchen sink. For the secret drinker, cleanup was a key step. Couldn't have the empties lying about.

As the fresh pot of coffee gurgled, the front doorbell rang. The list of people who could make it past the security door was short. I wasn't interested in seeing anyone and was tempted to just wait them out.

The bell rang again.

"I know you're in there," Brit said. "I can smell the coffee."

Shit. The woman had radar. No doubt, Brit had been thinking about that glass of wine she'd left out on the counter, like bait in a trapper's snare.

Drawing back my shoulders, I moved to the door. A quick glance in the side mirror told me I didn't look like a complete dumpster fire. Not my best, but presentable.

I opened the door to Brit and David. A doubleheader. How lucky could a girl get?

Brit eyed me closely, taking in my face, hair, and clothes. Narrowing eyes scrubbed off my makeup to see the woman behind the mask. "Good morning!"

"Good morning." My voice sounded like rough gravel, forcing me to clear my throat. "Sorry. I was up late editing." Lying also came naturally to a secret drinker. I'd often joked at meetings that if I were Wonder Woman, I'd have a Lasso of Lies.

"Morning, Marisa," David said.

"Hey, David. How're you two this morning?" I stepped aside and let them in. The sooner they said their piece, the faster they'd leave.

Brit's gaze swept the apartment, searching for the bottles. She looked a tad disappointed when she didn't see any. If David hadn't been here, she'd have searched under the kitchen sink in the trash can, but with him, appearances trumped validation.

"We have news for you," Brit said.

"Oh?"

"We wanted you to be our first," David said.

"First?"

Brit held up her hand, displaying a white-gold ring with a solitaire diamond. "We're engaged. David popped the question last night."

I had to admit I was shocked. My sister, who thought out every move carefully, had accepted a marriage proposal from a man she'd known eight weeks. "Wow, that's amazing."

"We know it's a bit fast," Brit said.

"But the heart wants what the heart wants," David said.

I studied the ring. Not Brit's style, and I wondered how long it would be before she had the diamond reset. "It's lovely."

David took Brit's hand in his. "I hope you're happy for us."

"Of course I am."

"David thought it would be fun if you took our engagement pictures. Not the wedding, of course," Brit said. "You'll be in the wedding party and can't very well be running around with a camera."

I pictured myself in an eggplant or fuchsia dress with flowers in my hair, standing beside three of Brit's friends dressed exactly the same. "I'd love to do your engagement pictures."

David smiled. "That's great. I know whatever pictures you take will be fantastic. Brit tells me how talented you are."

"Thank you." My stomach tumbled a little. How many brides and grooms had I photographed who'd been hungover from the rehearsal dinner and rallied to project the image of the perfect couple? How many families had used the wedding stage to prove they weren't dysfunctional?

I missed Clare in times like this. We'd commiserated when Dad had announced he was marrying Sandra. All the side-eye and suppressed giggles when that happy couple fawned over each other. There was no one else now who would understand the true meaning of one of my eye rolls or smirks.

"I don't have much of a family," David said. "And you two only have each other. I feel honored that Brit is allowing me into your inner circle."

Our inner circle. Brit, Clare, and I had been an oddly tight little, disjointed unit bound by our mother's death, our father's abdication, and our own destructive habits that kept us looking out for each other. And now the remaining Stockton sisters had David, leaving me to wonder what was wrong with him.

42

HIM

It took me three days to get up the nerve to visit Marisa in the hospital. I spent too many hours figuring out how to get inside unnoticed. I'd finally resolved to dress in an orderly's scrubs. These individuals moved about the hospital easily and often went unnoticed. Credentials were an issue, but that turned out to be easier than I thought as I lingered in a coffee shop near the medical center. An older man who went to pay his bill at the register left his lanyard and identification at his table. As his head was turned, I swiped them and slipped outside to the busy sidewalk.

It took some asking around to find Marisa's floor after she'd been moved from the surgical unit, but again motivation was a powerful tool. I was soon stepping into her room with an armload of clean sheets I'd swiped from a cart.

The room was dimly lit, and the television mounted on the wall was muted. Marisa was lying in her bed, her eyes closed. Her head was wrapped in a large bandage, and I could see the surgeon had cut her hair on the right side of her head. Long hair on the left and shorn on the right, the lopsidedness was almost comical.

Machines beeped as I set my linens down and walked to the bed. Her face looked pale, drawn, and without her expressive eyes staring back at me, rather plain.

"Marisa," I said softly.

Her chest rose and fell in a steady, even pattern. She was going to live. That much I could see for myself, but what would she remember?

I took her hand in mine as I'd done so many years ago. It was cold, limp. I squeezed it gently at first, but when she didn't respond, I tightened my grip, knowing I was crushing her knuckles against each other. Finally, her forehead furrowed. Relief surged. Knowing I was hurting her didn't bother me. She was alive through no fault of her own. She'd been a naughty girl who had put me through a lot of worry during the last twenty-four hours. It seemed only fair she got a little back.

I leaned closer to the bed until my lips brushed her ear. "Marisa, wake up. I need to know you're in there, Marisa."

She didn't react until I folded her wrist back on itself. A self-defense move I'd learned years ago when it had been done to me a few times, and it hurt like hell. No different from what a doctor did with the pins and needles they stuck in a patient.

The frown deepened, the heart rate monitor sped up, and then her eyes fluttered open. I eased off the pressure, knowing a real spike in her heart rate would summon a nurse.

At first her gaze was vacant, and I assumed that she was swimming up toward consciousness. "Marisa, can you see me?"

Her head shifted toward me and those eyes focused. She stared into my face a long moment. I tensed, fearing she'd scream or call for help. But there was no flicker of recognition.

"Can you see me?" I asked.

She nodded.

No sign of panic or worry. No ugly realization that I was not the man she'd once thought I was. I was glad of that. It had been crushing to see the horror and anger in those eyes. I wanted back the dewy, hazy eyes I'd looked into so many years ago as I'd come inside her when she was someone else.

"Can you move your fingers?" I asked.

Fingers painted with chipped red nail polish wiggled.

"That's good."

"Where am I?" she whispered.

"You were in a car accident," I said. "But you're all right now. You're going to be fine."

She swallowed and moistened her lips. I went to the sink, dampened a washcloth, and pressed it to her lips. "The nurse will give you liquids soon. This will have to do for now."

She sucked on the cloth, drawing in as much moisture as she could.

"Go back to sleep," I said gently as I touched the side of her face. "I'll be around, and you'll see me soon. You're safe now."

Her eyes closed, and I carefully draped the damp cloth over the sink. As much as I wanted to linger, the longer I stayed, the more I invited trouble. It wouldn't be good to be found here. I'd be forced to explain my presence and then perhaps the stolen credentials of a man thirty years my senior.

Out of the room, I ducked my head and headed toward the service elevator. I pressed the button as an orderly rolled a cart past. A phone rang at the nurses' station. The doors opened and I hurried inside, grateful when they closed. Head still tucked because there were cameras on the elevator, I did my best not to fidget.

When the doors slid apart, I crossed the lobby and moved out into the bright sunshine. Euphoria rushed my system. Marisa was alive. And she didn't seem to remember me. Her confusion could be a one-off from the drugs, but her heart rate had not spiked, and there'd been no panic or fear registering in her features.

I thought I might have another chance with Clare and Marisa, who in my mind now were one and the same. Two spirits in one body. We had another chance to get it right. To start anew.

43

Jo-Jo

Saturday, March 19, 2022
11:00 a.m.

I'd blocked out anything to do with Clare for years, but now that I was pregnant, I couldn't stop thinking about her. In fact, Marisa's text felt like a sign from Clare, who had to be watching me again. Judging me. She wasn't happy with my silence.

The baby would soon grow and fill my body, and I realized there was no more space inside me for secrets. If this baby was going to thrive, I had to break ties with the past. Maybe that was why I'd slipped the camera into my bag before I'd come here today.

However, the instant I saw Marisa's face, I saw only one thing. She'd been drinking. It'd been a long time since I'd seen the puffy, pale version of her face, and I'd begun to think I'd never see it again. I was sorry to see it. "You got drunk."

Marisa sat down at the café table, drawing in the slow, steady breath of someone who was nauseated. I knew the look. I'd seen it on my own face enough times in the mirror lately.

"I did," she said. "I screwed up."

"Are you going to a meeting?" I asked.

"Right after this lunch," she said. "Ready to turn in my one-year chip and start over."

There was a surety in her tone that took some of the sting out of my disappointment. I wanted to believe she was on the right path. "At least you're not making excuses."

"Lying is a waste of time. I never did handle a hangover well, and to pretend otherwise is stupid."

"You and me both." A waitress came to the table. We both ordered colas and french fries. "Brit called me. She said she and David are getting married."

"The happy couple came by my place this morning and told me."

"So Brit saw you like this?"

Marisa grimaced. "Up close and personal. No lecture, though. I can thank David for that one. She'll wait until we're alone before she really lays into me about something."

"Has she already started the wedding planning? Knowing Brit, she's picked a venue, chosen the church, and roughed in a seating chart for the reception."

"Aren't all brides ready to jump into the planning with both feet?"

I hadn't been excited about planning my wedding. Facing all the choices and decisions had been overwhelming. I'd asked Jack a few times to elope, but he'd been determined to give me a formal, proper memory. I understood he needed the validation, the public showing that he was back on track. I supposed the baby was going to be another notch in his respectability belt. "Do you like David?"

"I don't know him."

"Not the dashing sort I'd have put Brit with."

"Love is blind," Marisa quipped.

I laughed. "Your sister is not. Is he rich?"

"I think he's got resources. He does something with money, so that's got to be a plus in his column."

"David seems nice enough," I said.

"I don't know him that well, really."

"Maybe she'll mellow after she gets married."

The sodas arrived and Marisa sipped hers carefully. "Right. Did Jack change much after you married?"

"Well, he's slowed down a bit." Considering he'd been living at a breakneck speed, a more relaxed pace for him was still full steam ahead for most people.

"That's a good thing. But . . ."

"He's still the same guy under all the success. He's always hurtling after the next deal. Needs the rush of a make-or-break deal."

"Legitimate deals, right?"

"Yes, yes, of course." That couldn't have been totally true. The restaurants hadn't done great business last year, and still he'd bought me several nice pieces of jewelry in the last few months, and this morning he had been talking about buying a bigger home.

Marisa raised a brow. "You don't sound convinced."

I was afraid now more than ever that Jack would land back in jail, or one of his business associates would turn on him. No matter how many times I said the past did not matter, it did. "I am. Really."

She was silent for a moment, looking at me like Clare used to. *I hear your words, but I see behind them.* Marisa had known Jack as long as I had, and if she was telling the truth, she'd been too high to really offer consent when they had sex. But that was the old Jack. Not the man I'd married.

I took a sip. "What did you want to talk about? I can't believe you're pumped about Brit's wedding."

"Richards told me Clare was pregnant."

I drew in a breath, surprised she'd not known this. "Yes."

Marisa leaned in. "So, you did know?"

"I found out the night she died."

"You never told me."

"You were mourning Clare's death. I didn't see the reason to grieve over her baby."

Marisa stabbed her fingers through her hair. "How far along was she?"

"She was two weeks late."

"She would have gotten pregnant around the time of the city art show."

"That's right."

"I canceled on her at the last minute. Brit wasn't in a rush to get home, and she wanted to take me shopping."

Clare had been annoyed and hurt when we'd spoken about Marisa's last-minute change of plans. "I remember."

"Did she meet anyone at the show?" Marisa asked.

"I don't know. She and I weren't as close around that time. You both had grown distant."

"It didn't have anything to do with you," Marisa said. "We were feeling good for the first time in a long time and were just thrilled to be getting out. We didn't mean to leave you behind."

"We were all quite the trio."

"Yes, we were," Marisa said. "I don't know how we'd have gotten through the sickest days without you."

We'd been the Three Musketeers. All for one. My hand slid into my bag, and my fingers ran over the camera's smooth finish. Telling Marisa about the camera might blow back on me, but I'd be finished with all the secrets. And I had Jack now. He would protect me.

Marisa watched as I removed the small pink camera from my purse. Her eyes softened as recognition flared. "That was Clare's. I looked everywhere for it."

"That last time I saw her, she was wearing that blue coat. She forgot to take it. I didn't bother to return it because I thought I'd see her again. And when I heard she was dead, I wore it to be close to her. The camera was in the pocket."

"You never told Richards about it," Marisa said.

"I didn't."

She ran her fingertips over the smooth casing covered in small flower stickers. "The police went through all my cameras."

"When everyone started demonizing my parents, I didn't want more cops breathing down my neck or another reporter crawling farther up my ass." I sighed.

Marisa pressed the silver power button, but the camera didn't turn on. "How long has the battery been dead?"

"At least a decade. I never bothered to replace the batteries."

"I can get batteries at the drugstore or a photo shop."

"She carried this everywhere. Always snapping pictures when no one was looking."

"Did you ever look at the pictures?"

"I did years ago. But I didn't recognize anyone. Whatever faces I'd seen have long been blurred by time."

Marisa traced a faded daisy sticker. "I don't know what I'm looking for, but just having this piece of Clare means a lot."

"I hope you see a face you recognize." I smiled. "Now go to your meeting."

44

MARISA

Saturday, March 19, 2022
8:00 p.m.

I had kept my promise to Jo-Jo and attended my AA meeting. I sat in the circle, quiet, sipping my coffee, wanting the meeting to pass without me saying anything. I was really more concerned about scoring batteries for Clare's camera than sharing feelings. But I couldn't afford another screwup, and if this show-and-tell helped, then so be it.

The group leader, Mark, quickly zeroed in on me. He'd read a version of my story so many times, the pages were tattered and torn. He'd been waiting for an opening to say my name.

"Marisa, I sense you'd like to share," Mark said.

I dug from my pocket the one-year chip that he'd placed in my hand last month. I cleared my throat. "I had a bad night. Drank three bottles of wine."

I forced myself to look around the room and meet the gazes of everyone. Refusing to cower, I saw some disappointment, sadness, but mostly understanding.

"Was there a trigger?" Mark asked.

"Family stuff," I said. "I should've seen it coming a mile away."

"And the next time?"

I couldn't promise there wasn't going to be another Brit land mine. "I'll call my sponsor."

"I thought you didn't have one," Mark said.

He was right. I'd refused the help. "I'll get one."

Mark nodded. "Keep the chip. We'll celebrate next year with it."

"I'd rather you take it. I'm starting over, and next year I'll want a new one. Eyes forward, right?" I intentionally used one of Brit's bullshit sayings to remind myself that she could set all the traps she wanted, but I could maneuver around them.

I laid the chip in Mark's palm. Releasing this stupid piece of plastic was sad, but with it went the guilt weighing me down since this morning.

"Keep up the good work," he said.

"Good work?"

"You're here, aren't you?"

"Right. I'm here and still standing."

When I stepped out of the meeting room, Mark followed. "I'm proud of you."

"Mine is an old story."

"But no less poignant." He handed me a folded slip of paper with a phone number on it. "I know you don't want a sponsor, but you should have backup. If you have a bad patch, call me, okay? Friend to friend."

I creased the paper with my fingers and then hugged him. "Sure. Fair enough."

Walking down the church's concrete stairs, I looked up at the night sky. Clear, it was made bright by stars and a full moon. Tonight was no different from last night or the night before. I still remained a drink away from oblivion, which likely explained the uneasiness churning in my belly.

I searched the darkness, half expecting to see someone lurking, watching me. But the shadowed alleys were still and quiet. I shook off the feeling, chalking it up to withdrawal from the booze.

Twenty minutes later, I'd swung by three different drugstores until I found the right batteries. At home, I dropped my purse by the front door, clicked on the lights, and sat on the couch, more exhausted than most days.

As moonlight streamed through my window, I opened the camera's battery compartment and dumped the old two out. The connection points were a little corroded, so I spent another few minutes cleaning them. New batteries loaded, I sealed the case. Crossing my fingers, I pressed the power button, praying it still worked. After a moment's hesitation, the white power light turned on and the screen sparked to life.

Holding my breath, I looked at the last picture Clare had taken. It was of me, sitting on my bed in our room. My long red hair hung around my face, which was still youthful enough to hide the drinking. I'd never noticed her taking the picture. Five minutes later I left the house and never saw her again.

My throat tightened and tears welled in my eyes. I wondered if there was any wine left in the bottles stowed in my trash can. Shit. This was why I'd gone to the meeting.

The next two images took me back in time an hour to the version of Brit I remembered best. She was smiling, dressed in her blue silk robe, and her clean, softly rolled hair was piled on top of her head. She was wearing makeup. She looked as if she felt fine and was still in New Year's party mode. Sometime between those moments and two hours later, she'd become too sick to leave the house.

The next few images were candids of the family. Dad off to the side. The Stockton girls sitting by the half-decorated Christmas tree. (It had been my job to finish it.) There was random garland and holly in the background, and the date stamps—December 26, 25, 24—slipped back in time with the images. There was a picture of Dad, his girlfriend

Sandra, and her daughter, Tamara. Tamara's arm was still in a sling from a fall down the stairs, and she was frowning as she talked to Dad and Sandra. That kid was always either talking, complaining, or flirting with Kurt. But she'd done us all a favor when she'd broken that arm and delayed the wedding.

I kept pressing buttons until I hit the first of December and then worked my way back in time. There were a few of me, but I was always looking off to the side. Clare could be quick with the camera, and a distracted person could miss the soft *click*.

There were two images of Kurt. In one, he was wearing his football jacket. He'd been more muscular, leaner in those days. His hair was short, and his face bore the same grim expression his teammates shared. Reminded me of children mimicking adults who really understood the world. Next there was a shot of Jack and Brit, standing arm in arm, smiling.

I scrolled back to late November, when Clare would have gotten pregnant. The first was a wide shot of an art studio in the city that had long ago closed. That was the show I was supposed to have attended.

The next image was of a young man. Tall, broad shouldered, dark hair, and facing away from the camera. I couldn't make out his face.

In the next frame, he was turned slightly to the side, and his profile was in full view. Dark eyes, rounded face. My first thought was David. It couldn't be David, could it? He'd had no ties to the city or us then.

Suddenly restless, I rose from the couch and walked into the kitchen and made myself a cup of coffee. The coffee dripped into the carafe as I rested my elbows on the counter and placed my head in my hands.

As I stared at this much younger version of David, a name called out to me from the Black Hole. Jeff. I didn't know any Jeffs but was suddenly certain that, during the lost week and a half, I'd met a Jeff.

When the coffeepot was full, I filled a mug and stirred in extra teaspoons of sugar and a splash of milk. The sugar would soothe my nerve endings' cravings that I always had after a drinking binge, and the caffeine would chase away the fatigue creeping up my spine.

The longer I stared at the photo, the more convinced I was that the guy was David. Clare could never have met David. He was five years older than us. He'd gone to the same college as Brit, but he'd been a junior her freshman year, and she'd never mentioned they'd known each other in college.

At my computer, I typed in David Welbourne's name. His profile appeared on a few financial sites, which all linked to his website. His professional headshot looked outdated by a half dozen years. He'd gained weight since and his hair was grayer. This version of David looked more like Clare's photo.

David's website didn't list a physical address, just an email address and a PO box. Brit had said he worked from home.

Brit and he had met at the hospital after my accident. He'd appeared, explaining he'd arrived to visit a neighbor who'd suffered a stroke. He'd started making conversation, and they'd learned they'd gone to the same college. Brit had said how helpful he'd been. He'd taken her mind off me. He'd shown up a couple of times, and when I was out of the woods, he'd called Brit, asked her out on a date. The rest was history.

Two college alumni who'd reconnected in an emergency room after my accident. And now he was going to be a permanent part of Brit's life. I sipped my coffee, found it had grown cold.

I rose, placed the mug in the microwave, and hit one minute. I hadn't been introduced to him until the night of my birthday party. He'd seemed nice. Easygoing. As the wheel spun in the microwave, I couldn't summon too many more details about David.

"Who the hell are you?" I muttered.

Without thinking, I reached for my coat and purse and headed out the door. I double-checked the lock and then hurried down the stairs and out the front entrance to my car. Behind the wheel, I quickly locked the doors and started the engine. I didn't know where David lived, but

I'd bet he was at Brit's tonight. Knowing my sister and her rigid schedule, she'd ask him to leave at some point. She didn't like waking up with a man in her bed, a quirk Jack had complained about back in the day.

Finding him wasn't a given, but I drove west and then took the off-ramp that led me along Cary Street and the side roads leading to Brit's house. As I drove onto my sister's block, I spotted the second car in her driveway.

After driving past, I circled the block and, cutting my lights, parked at the end of Brit's street and nestled low in the car. With the heater off, the air chilled quickly, forcing me to huddle deeper into my coat.

As I tipped back against the headrest and closed my eyes, I drifted back to the night of the accident, navigating the shadows shrouding it.

I sank deeper into myself and imagined moving through the darkness, hoping I'd spot a memory that would light up a portion of my path. I reached for the steering wheel, gripped it as I pretended the car was moving down the street toward the utility pole. There would've been a hard strike when the car impacted. My body, untethered by a seat belt, would've jolted forward as the airbag deployed. I'd nearly hit the steering wheel with my head, but the airbag had violently shoved me back.

These were the facts I'd read in the report. None were supported by memories. There was nothing.

Jeff. Who are you?

Suddenly, I pictured a man standing at a bar with two sodas. He laughed at something the bartender said. It was a rich, infectious sound. And then he began to turn toward me.

My eyes popped open. Like kindling trying to catch fire in a strong wind, the flames went out. Damn.

I looked up to see David leaving Brit's house. My sister stood by the front picture window, wearing a black silk robe cinched at her waist. She was waving. Smiling as she pushed back sex-tousled hair.

David got in his car, started the engine, and backed out of the driveway. Brit watched and then turned as his car passed mine. I dipped low in the seat, looking down, fearing just my stare would draw his attention.

When he passed me, I started my car but didn't turn on the headlights as I shifted the gear to drive and moved forward slowly. There was only one way out of the neighborhood, so I didn't have to guess his direction. My headlights still out, I followed as he rounded the corner. Red taillights blinked at a stop sign, and he turned onto Cary Street.

Turning on my lights, I followed, careful to keep enough distance. There were some people on the road this time of night, but not enough to give me real cover.

David continued onto the interstate and headed east. As I trailed behind him, I watched as he made his way around the city and then took the final exit toward the lighted buildings of the financial district. This was also the exit I took when coming back from Brit's.

To my surprise, he took the southbound exit away from Church Hill, drove toward my apartment building, and pulled into my building's parking lot. I kept driving, stopping at the next corner and parking. In my rearview mirror, I watched him drive by my empty space. He paused only briefly before pulling back out on the road and retracing his steps. I did a quick U-turn, trailed behind, watched him turn east down Main Street toward Church Hill. Why had he stopped at my building? Had Brit given him something to drop off for me?

As a light caught him at a cross street, I turned right, circled the block, and picked him up on the other side of the light. Minutes later, he parked in front of a historic townhome that wasn't particularly remarkable. The front porch required repair, and the building needed the siding replaced. He climbed the front steps and vanished through the front door. Lights flipped on, their glow streaming through original windows made of handblown glass.

I studied the house, searching for any sense of familiarity. I imagined my hand trailing over the weather-beaten wood railing, wondering if splinters or gray paint had clung to my skin. Rubbing my smooth palm, all I felt was the small ridge of calluses trailing under my fingers.

David passed in front of a window and then pulled the shade down. As he reached the next window, he paused and stared out into the darkness as if he could feel my gaze. I sank into my seat but did not look away.

Had I caught him staring at me before? Memories from the darkness whispered, but the sound was so faint I could barely make out the impressions. I was certain now I'd been in the bar, sipping a cold Coke. It had tasted slightly bitter, but I'd been thirsty, so I had kept drinking. On the table in front of me was the print I'd sold.

One by one the lights went off in David's house.

I noted the address, started my car, and as I drove back down the hill toward my crash site, I spotted the bar on my right. It was closed for the night, but I parked and walked to the window. Cupping my hands around my eyes, I peered inside to darkened tables. Nothing triggered my memory, and when a car passed by, slowed down, I hurried back to my vehicle.

Down the side street, I glanced toward the utility pole. If I'd been going forty, even thirty, miles an hour, it was no wonder I'd missed the turn and swerved into the pole.

I'd never been able to explain why I'd been headed in this direction. Now I realized I'd been in Church Hill selling my first print. But who had I sold it to?

"Come on, just tell me what happened?" I whispered. "Just a few more clues. I'm good at puzzles."

But the silence grew mutinous, so I gave up, turned the car around, and headed home.

Ten minutes later, I parked in my spot and crossed the lot. As I pressed the keys of my security pad, my phone rang. The unexpected shrill startled me, and I forgot where I was in the sequence. When I pressed "Enter," the system denied me. My phone kept ringing. I didn't recognize the number.

Hands trembling, I entered the security code again, and the door opened this time. Inside, I glanced around the darkened parking lot, half expecting to see David staring back at me. *I see you. I know you've been following me.*

A chill oozed over my muscles as I gripped the phone and stared at the number. Finally, the ringing stopped, and I waited for a voice mail message to pop up. Nothing appeared. Wrong number. Maybe.

Back up on my floor, I glanced toward Alan's door and saw the light trickling out. Footsteps echoed inside his apartment. The man never slept. Pot calling the kettle black.

Inside my apartment, I flipped on a light and went straight to my computer, where I searched the phone number of the call. There was no listing for a business or person. Wrong number. Spam. A drunk dialer.

Or had David crossed paths with Clare at the art exhibit or me at Brit's university? I'd been drunk my one night at Brit's school and passed out. When I'd woken up, I'd been in a dorm room by myself. I'd been fully dressed, and the bed was neatly made, but nothing about how I'd gotten there felt right.

Random dots could be connected a thousand different wrong ways.

Playing devil's advocate, maybe David really had driven through my parking lot tonight because Brit had given him something to pass on to me. Maybe he didn't see my car, so he kept going.

It happened. All logical. Made sense.

Don't borrow trouble.

But my identical twin had been murdered. I could've died in a car accident two months ago minutes from David's townhome.

I dialed Detective Richards's number. The call went to voice mail, and I could almost imagine him rolling over, glancing at my name on his phone, and cursing as he turned away.

"This is Detective Richards." In the recorded message, his enunciation was clear, concise. "Leave a message at the tone."

"Detective Richards, I just wanted to run something by you. A person no one's ever thought about. Call me when you can."

I hung up, walked into the kitchen, and grabbed a seltzer from the fridge. It cut through the dryness in my mouth and was far more hydrating than the coffee. It didn't have the kick of wine, and right now, I'd kill for a bottle or two, but the seltzer was what I could have.

Reaching in my pocket, I pulled out the shiny new First Meeting coin and did something I'd never done before. I called my sponsor, Mark.

45

Him

NOW
Saturday, March 19, 2022
10:00 p.m.

Outside your apartment building, I stared up at the light from your corner unit. You'd not been home tonight. Where had you been? You went to your meeting on Seminary Avenue today and stayed longer than you normally did. Most times when you made a meeting, you were late, rushing in five minutes after the start time. But today, you'd been early, waiting at the door when the meeting coordinator, a tall, lean guy in his midthirties, got there to unlock the door. You'd helped him with one of the bags in his hand, you'd shared a joke, and you'd vanished inside. You'd stayed past the regular end time and walked out with the same coordinator. He'd hugged you, held you close.

The longer your body lingered close—too close—to his, the more my anger grew. Whatever was going on between you two looked like it was far beyond the realm of professional, and I didn't like it one bit. Many men who went into counseling weren't the most mentally healthy individuals. They carried their own demons that they struggled to control. Someone like that would think nothing of taking advantage of a pretty woman who'd had a rough couple of months. It wasn't right.

I should've been the one taking care of you. I should've been the one to take you home from the hospital and nurse you back to health. The accident had been just that. An accident. I'd not meant to hurt you. I would never have done that.

But your sister had been a guard dog at your hospital room, keeping a watchful eye on anyone who came and went. And when you were discharged, your sister took you to her own home and kept you there for a week.

When you finally returned to your apartment, I'd kept a close eye on you, but I'd not approached. I wanted to make sure your amnesia was indeed permanent. And if your memory loss was the real deal, I needed to plan for our second chance.

I'd screwed up the first time. Been too anxious. Too ready to show you how much I loved you. And you'd freaked.

Just like Clare had panicked all those years ago. I'd not wanted to hurt her, either. I'd loved her. Loved you both.

No, this time, I was going to be very careful. I'd stay close to you and, when the time was right, find a way for us to be truly alone.

46

RICHARDS

Sunday, March 20, 2022
10:00 a.m.

As I stood in front of Marisa's apartment building, I wondered if I'd lost my fucking mind. I'd let her call go to voice mail, telling myself I didn't want to deal with her or be reminded of a high-profile case that I'd never been able to solve. I'd less than a week to go. I would leave the job, and my life would move on. Time for fishing off Florida's Gulf Coast. Let the younger guys take a crack at Clare's case.

But Marisa's words played over and over in my head, and concentrating on anything else was a shit show. Out of the car, I lit a cigarette. I'd promised myself I'd quit the smoking as soon as I retired, and technically, I still had six days and five remaining packs to finish.

I inhaled, letting the smoke trail up as I stared at Marisa's window. The lights were on. She was up and about.

Every fucking time I looked at her face, I saw her mirror image lying on the medical examiner's table. Pale, drawn, slack jawed. I remembered how the pathologist's blade had slid over Clare's chest and around her breasts as the doctor made his Y-incision. I'd felt such rage and sadness and to this day still carried some of it.

Both Clare and Marisa looked so much like their mother. Elizabeth Stockton had been found by the family's housekeeper while the girls were at school and the husband on a business trip. Elizabeth had been lying in a bathroom, naked in a tub filled with cool water. Her body was cold and still. The housekeeper had called the cops, and I'd arrived within an hour of the first responder.

I'd been aware that young children lived in the house, so I'd sent the housekeeper to intercept the girls at school while we tried to track down the father. The housekeeper had taken the girls for ice cream or a trip to the mall. I don't remember, but she bought us enough time to clear out the body and for the father to finally arrive home that night.

From all accounts, the Stocktons hadn't had a good marriage. Neighbors reported verbal fights and slamming doors. A few were surprised that Elizabeth had killed herself. She'd sworn she'd keep her marriage together for the sake of the children, whom I believed she was slowly poisoning. And then, just like that, she took a handful of pills and died.

My sights had turned to Mr. Stockton immediately. He was having an affair with an office associate and was often gone for days at a time. A dead wife, especially a rich one, would solve a lot of his problems. Another alarm bell had been the death of the neighbor's dog, Rex, who came by the Stocktons' house often for treats that the girls gave him. Rex, healthy and young, had been found dead in his owner's driveway of an apparent poisoning two weeks before Elizabeth's death. It wasn't uncommon for a killer intending to use poison to practice on an easily accessible animal.

And then four years later, Clare had died, and I had two dead females in the same family. One via suicide and the other strangulation. I'd looked hard again at Mr. Stockton. If anything happened to the girls, he could make a reasonable claim that he should inherit their portions of the trust. But Elizabeth, days before she died, had amended her will, declaring that if a child should die, her portion would be split between the survivors. If all three girls should die before their father, the money would be given to the American Cancer Society.

Maybe the Stocktons were just one of those rich, privileged families stalked by tragedy. Maybe some folks just got extra helpings of shit sandwiches. Maybe.

I tossed the cigarette to the asphalt and ground it out with the tip of my polished loafers. I walked up to the front entrance, found it propped open with a rock. The security door was for the residents' protection, but it could be inconvenient when carrying in a load, and this kind of rigged setup happened a lot. Stupid.

I opened the door, kicked the rock aside, and waited until it closed tightly behind me. Striding toward the elevator, I pressed the button for the top floor. Inside, the floor felt sticky under my feet and smelled of beer. I rode the elevator to the fifth floor.

Two units on this level. Marisa's was apartment A, the one on the left. But it was the door to B that opened with a quick snap, and my hand slid immediately to my Glock. The habit was so ingrained, I doubted it would ever go away.

The man who appeared was tall, lean, with mahogany-brown hair cut short and combed back. He wore a dark suit, light-blue shirt, and gray tie. He was the kind of corporate guy who lived in this area, only this man looked vaguely familiar. Dressed up on a Sunday, but he didn't strike me as the churchgoing type.

The man closed and locked his door. "Can I help you?"

"No." I'd learned long ago that explaining myself only wasted time.

"Are you lost?" The man lingered, looked toward Marisa's door as if he didn't like that I was close to it.

"Nope." I knocked on the door.

"I'm Alan Bernard."

I reached for my badge. "Detective Richards. What do you do, Alan?"

A brow arched more out of curiosity than alarm. This guy was accustomed to seeing cops. "I'm with the Commonwealth's Attorney's Office."

And I knew him from somewhere. We'd crossed paths at some point. "Richmond Homicide."

"There a problem?"

"It's an old one that goes back a long time."

Marisa's door opened, and her gaze darted between the two of us. She wore jeans, a simple T-shirt, and no shoes. Dressed like this, she looked a decade younger, and I was again reminded of the body on the medical examiner's table.

"Detective Richards?" Marisa said. "Looks like you've met my neighbor, Alan Bernard."

"We just made introductions," I said.

Alan stepped forward. "He's with Homicide."

Marisa's expression softened. "I know. We go way back. I can explain later."

"I'm holding you to that," Alan said.

Her smile warmed another degree. "Knock on my door when you get in tonight."

"I'll be home late."

"I don't sleep much."

Another hesitation, another sideways glance, and Alan headed down the stairs. Both Marisa and I waited until we heard the security door close.

"You got my message," she said.

"I did."

"Coffee?"

"Sure." She turned into her apartment, and I followed, closing the door behind me.

I'd been to her father's home multiple times, first for her mother and then later for Clare. I'd spent time in the twins' bedroom, sitting on Clare's neatly made bed and staring across to Marisa's tangled sheets and comforter and scattered clothes on the floor.

The difference in the twins' personalities was evident immediately. From levels of cleanliness to wall posters, to their choice of clothes, Clare and Marisa were opposites. Maybe the internal differences were a reaction to the physical similarities. Each girl needed to be her own person, and they'd expressed their differences any way they could.

This apartment was a far cry from the sixteen-year-old version of Marisa's side of the bedroom. There were no frills, a couple of sweaters puddled on the floor, and the images on the walls were stark. As she moved toward the open galley kitchen and reached for two cups from open shelving, I was drawn to the series of black-and-white framed prints that ran along the wall. I recognized the location immediately. God knew I'd walked those shores enough times.

"I guess you think it's odd of me to focus on that place." She poured two cups.

"It clearly left an impression." Accepting a mug, I sipped, found the flavor good, really good. One thing I wouldn't miss about the work was the shit coffee.

She stood beside me, her cup cradled in her hands. She smelled of rose soap, which hit me as strange. She didn't strike me as the flowery type. When the mother had died, I'd asked around about all three girls. Oddly, I'd always felt paternalistic toward Marisa, whose demeanor had appeared to be a coping mechanism. Unlike Marisa, Clare couldn't release her rage but balled it up inside, and Brit, well, she was just plain sneaky.

As I turned from the photo, I caught the curve of Marisa's breast in my peripheral vision. I was old, not dead. Creepy maybe, though she was no longer a kid but a thirty-year-old woman. "You said there was someone else."

"David Welbourne."

"Who's that?"

"My sister Brit's fiancé. He's a money manager who works out of his home."

"Are you drinking again?" I had a nose for alcoholics. Took one to know one. And I sensed she'd had a tussle with sobriety.

"Hear me out." Her gaze didn't waver. Either her worries were fueled by boozy paranoia, or she was batshit crazy.

"Are you drinking again?" It surprised me how much I was rooting for her sobriety.

She drew in a breath. "I had a slipup the other night. I drank a couple of bottles of wine. But I went to a meeting last night and today, I called my sponsor once, and I'll hit another meeting tomorrow."

I muttered, "Shit," as I stared at her. No sense in asking how something like that had happened. Sometimes it just did. That was what made a lush so hard to love. But that didn't temper my disappointment.

"Jo-Jo had Clare's camera."

"I thought we looked at all your cameras."

"You looked at mine. Clare had a small one that was hers. Clare visited Jo-Jo hours before the party. She left her coat, and in the pocket was the camera."

"And Jo-Jo didn't tell me this why?"

"It was her private connection to Clare. She liked having a piece of Clare no one else did. The three of us were pretty tight at one point. Some called us the Three Musketeers."

"She might also have let her killer go free." The words tasted bitter as I ground them out.

"I know. And you can deal with her on that score later. For now, let's deal with the bigger issue." She had the focus of a dog with a bone.

"Which is?"

"You said the DNA of Clare's baby did not match any of the males in her life. Around the time she got pregnant, I went to visit Brit at college and Clare stayed behind to attend an art show. I was supposed to go as well, but Brit talked me into staying in Charlottesville and shopping."

"I remember something from the notes that I took at our interviews. Didn't you get drunk while you were at your sister's school and passed out?"

"That's right."

"Okay."

"Clare used to like to take pictures. She always had this camera with her. I clicked through them and saw an image in mid-November of a guy who looked like David."

"David? Did he live in the area about that time?"

"He was in college with Brit, which is an hour's drive away. He said his family is from California, so he must have been visiting friends in the area over the Thanksgiving holiday." She handed me the camera.

I clicked through the images. "You know that for a fact?"

"A theory."

"Has David ever indicated that he saw Clare or you before her death?"

"He's never said anything to me."

I studied the rounded face of a man with dark hair. He was looking away from the camera, and the image was slightly out of focus, as if he were intentionally turning away as Clare clicked. I wanted to be excited but had been disappointed too many times. "This is all you have?"

"David met Brit at the hospital right after my accident. I'm in surgery, and he just happened to show up."

"Random connections happen."

Her eyes still turned a vivid shade of blue when she was angry. She ran long fingers over her shorn hair. "You once said that when facts appear connected, they generally are."

"You're correct. But coincidences do happen." I walked to the kitchen counter and carefully set down my cup. "This picture is not enough for a warrant."

She moved toward me, standing within a couple of feet. "I followed him last night."

"What?"

"I drove to Brit's house, thinking he'd be there. He was, so I followed him home because I wanted to see where he lived. On the way back downtown, he circled through my parking lot before heading home."

"And?"

"Nothing. He drove home to his place in Church Hill. There's a bar down the block from his townhome, and I could swear I was there. *And* his residence is only minutes from where I had my car accident."

The flukes were piling up. "It's not smart to follow him."

"Maybe, but this is the first lead I've had in thirteen years."

"Why did Jo-Jo give you the camera now?"

"She's pregnant. And she has been thinking about Clare a lot. She knew Clare was pregnant."

"She never told me that." I'd never bought Jo-Jo's innocent look and vague answers, but sensing and proving were two different beasts. "Was that omission also because of her special bond with Clare, too?"

"They were best friends," she said.

"She's also married to a former con who's done very well for himself recently."

"What's that mean?"

"Most restaurant owners I know have struggled the last few years. And yet Jack is sitting on a pile of cash."

"When did you become so attuned to Jack?"

"He dated your sister at the time of Clare's death. I looked into him and found he'd served time in juvenile detention for breaking and entering and theft. If he'd been a couple of years older, he'd have done serious time. And then a few years later he did real time in state prison."

"He might be sketchy, but he's Jo-Jo's problem. I'm focused on who killed Clare."

"Why now?"

"I've been half-assing my life for the last thirteen years. Young, drunk, fill in the blank, but I was out of touch. Now I'm dialed in, and I won't let this lead go."

That prompted a laugh. "You haven't been half-assing it. You struggle, but who doesn't?"

She shoved out a sigh. "You busted my chops enough times when I came to see you."

"Tough love," I said. "Holding your hand and telling you it'll be okay wasn't going to get you on the right path."

"It might have," she said.

I arched a brow. "You believe that?"

"No."

"And through it all, you've been the one that's continued to ask me about Clare. Not your father when he was alive or your sister."

She twisted a ring on her pinkie. "I kept hoping you'd solve this."

"So did I."

"The police know how to do this kind of thing and have more resources than me. But maybe it takes someone on the outside to figure this out."

"Okay, Nancy Drew, what do you think happened?"

She glanced down into the milky depths of her coffee, swirled it. "Like you said, I got drunk while I was visiting Brit at college. David, by the way, was a junior at the same school. I wake up in a dorm room, lying fully dressed on a perfectly made bed. I stagger back to Brit, and we go shopping. We don't get back to Richmond until late Saturday. I remember being annoyed because I missed the art show."

"Did Clare know about it?"

"We were supposed to meet there."

"How would David know about it?"

"I'd had the art show flyer in my pocket but couldn't find it the next day."

"You're saying he took it?"

"Maybe."

"It's a stretch."

"I know. But I do know Clare went to the show. She raved about it. Maybe he went, too, thinking he'd see me. They meet, she ends up sleeping with him and gets pregnant. David circles back on New Year's, and he finds her at Jo-Jo's party. They fight. You said you only found Kurt's DNA in her. Maybe this time she refused to have sex with David. She'd told me that night she'd decided she was only going to be seeing Kurt going forward. Maybe David got pissed over the rejection. Whatever happened, David lost his temper and strangled her."

"You're describing a crime of passion. Strangulation is very intimate and personal. But to strip her down and dump her body miles from where she vanished is calculating."

"He cools off and realizes what he's done. He might have lost it, but he's not stupid. He doesn't want to go to jail for this."

"Reasonable. DNA can prove if David impregnated your sister, but it doesn't prove he killed her."

"It, along with the picture, puts you one step closer."

"All valid, but again not enough to get a warrant."

She set her cup down next to mine, sloshing coffee on her hand, which she wiped away on her jeans. "But don't you want to know if David was the baby's father?"

"Sure, I want to know." I could pull strings and get a discarded cup or bottle from David. Then a few more strings later, I'd have the DNA checked. "Ask your buddy Alan how a defense attorney would spin this in court. Two young adults have consensual sex, she gets pregnant, he never knows about the baby, and she tragically dies."

"You know Alan?"

It had taken me a moment, but I had finally placed Alan. "He worked for a defense firm before joining the Commonwealth's Attorney's Office. We went head to head on a case three years ago, and ol' Alan raised enough questions to plant a crop of reasonable doubt in the jury's mind. And FYI, that was a rape and murder case."

She sighed.

"Look, he's a lawyer and was doing his job," I said. "He's on the Commonwealth's dime now, but that doesn't change the fact that all lawyers think alike."

"Okay. He's a lawyer. Not a crime."

I scratched the side of my head, swallowing a favorite jab at lawyers. (If there's a hell below . . .) "We'd have to prove David came to Richmond at least twice, found Clare at the party, and killed her. That's hard to do in current cases. And don't forget that Clare was dressed like you, and many at the party thought she was you. Her pregnancy might be irrelevant."

"If you had to bet the farm, where would you put your money?"

I hesitated, put aside all my doubts, and went with my gut. "On the baby daddy."

She grinned. "Look, if David happened to discard a coffee cup in a public place, and we could pull DNA, test it, and *if* it matched the DNA of Clare's baby, then you'd have a reason to talk to him."

"The backlog of DNA tests on cold cases is at least a year, and I only got a week left."

"What if I had it tested at a private lab?" she offered. "I can work fast. I don't want to lose this opportunity."

"Are you going to rifle through his trash?"

"Maybe. Or have a coffee with him and keep the cup. He's engaged to my sister, and he's already mentioned me doing the engagement pictures."

Whenever I landed on the trail of a killer, excitement ran high, much like making a basket from center court or catching a fifty-yard pass. "Don't do something like this alone."

"I'm a big girl."

"If I had a nickel for all the times I'd heard that one, I'd be able to pay for that new boat I had my eye on. Don't."

"When you're gone, Richards, the next guy isn't going to care as much about Clare's case as you. The next guy didn't walk the crime scene, talk to everyone when their stories were fresh, or watch the pathologist cut open my sister. You've skin in this game. If you didn't, you'd have ignored my call."

"Let me ask around about David Welbourne. I'll make calls today. But until I know more, stay away from him."

Marisa shook her head. "How long do I have to wait?"

And now I was negotiating with her. "Give me twenty-four hours."

"And then you've five days before you're gone?"

"I don't turn into a pumpkin, Marisa. I'll still be in the city for a little while longer. And last I heard, phones and computers are fairly efficient."

A grin tugged her lips. "Okay."

I jabbed a finger at her. "If you don't stay sober, the deal is off."

"That was a one-time thing."

"I said the same to myself more times than I could count."

"Believe me, that's all I hear at the meetings. *It won't happen again. It won't.*" She mimicked a child's whiny tone. "I'm not prepared to make a lifetime guarantee, but there won't be a slip until you retire."

Six whole days of sobriety. I knew she meant it. All the best alcoholics repented well. And I wasn't going to judge, because the demon lived in me, and he was always hungry. "I'll call you."

"Fair enough."

I met her gaze, holding it, hoping I could burn sense into her. "Give me twenty-four hours."

"Deal."

47

Marisa

Sunday, March 20, 2022
1:00 p.m.

My intention was to honor my bargain with Richards. I'd made the promise with honor in my heart. I wanted to give him his twenty-four hours, but when he left my apartment, that restless energy that always buzzed in my system tilted to a new level when Paul texted again, still looking for that drink. I deleted the message, but suddenly computer work would not satisfy me, cleaning the place felt like a waste of time, and the apartment walls shrank closer together as the seconds ticked.

I heard Alan's door across the hallway open and close. He'd said to come over anytime. And now, at least he'd keep me from rushing down to David's. I grabbed my keys, locked my door behind me, and crossed to his door. I knocked.

Determined footsteps moved to the door before it opened to Alan. He was wearing his dark suit pants, jacket, and tie. "Marisa."

"You said to stop by."

He regarded me with unveiled curiosity.

I shifted. "You been to church?"

"Deposed a cop. How did your visit with Richards go?"

"He told me you two know each other."

"We crossed paths in a case a few years ago. For the record, I was representing the man he was trying to put away."

"You going to invite me in and tell me about the case?"

"I was representing a rapist and murderer."

Best policy or not, honesty wasn't easy. "You'll have to tell me more than that to chase me away."

He stepped aside, but his frown suggested he expected I might not stick around too long. He closed the door but remained near it as he faced me. "Do you remember the Lee case?"

"Vaguely." A woman had been raped and beaten to death, I thought. I didn't remember the details. Stood to reason barely anyone remembered Clare.

"My client was high on meth when he arrived home, found his girl-friend asleep on the couch, and after he raped her, he beat her to death. My client's father had money, he hired my firm, and I was assigned the case. I got his sentence reduced to five years."

"So he's back to his old life now." I couldn't hide the bitterness.

"He still has one year, sixty-five days to serve."

"Why'd you represent him?"

"Everyone deserves a defense in this country."

"And you made a few dollars."

"Yes."

"Why'd you join the Commonwealth's Attorney's Office?"

"Maybe righting some karma."

"Richards investigated my sister's death. She was strangled to death thirteen years ago." I was amazed how I recited the facts as if they didn't belong to me.

He drew in a breath, but to his credit he didn't say he was sorry. Maybe he'd figured out that the families of victims hated that word. "Clare Stockton."

That was a surprise. "You know the case?"

"I was in law school when she died. My professor spent a week discussing the case."

"Why?"

"It was a criminal-defense class. Our job was to come up with a viable defense for the killer if found."

"Did you have any suspects?"

"Do you really want to do this?"

"I do."

He undid his tie and pulled it free of his shirt. Carefully, as he rolled the tie up, he said, "We all believed the killer was male given the extensive bruising on her neck. Clare Stockton had a history of sexual activity, which put her in contact with at least five males we were able to identify. All had alibis and none of their DNA matched her fetus."

Annoyance flared. "How'd you know about the DNA? My sister Brit and I didn't know. I thought that wasn't public."

"I was curious about the case. Called a buddy who had access to the autopsy files."

"Were you always that diligent in school?"

"I could be. Still can be."

"You have a good memory for details."

He reached for the door handle. "When I first saw you in J.J.'s Pub, I was a little taken aback. Then I saw the two shot glasses and remembered Clare had an identical twin."

"You knew my history all along."

"Yes. Ready to leave yet?"

"Maybe in a minute."

"Okay." He passed by and moved to the kitchen, silently setting a pot to brew. "Why was Richards here today?"

"I've been put on this planet to irritate the man until my sister's case is solved or until he retires."

"He's not warm and fuzzy, but a good cop."

"I've come to appreciate each of those traits."

He filled a mug and pushed it toward me. "No cream, but sugar."

"I'll take it."

He pulled a box of sugar from the cabinet and handed it and a spoon to me. I poured in a liberal amount. When I caught him staring, I simply said, "Lunch of champions."

"So why did you knock on my door?"

"I don't know." The spoon clinked against the mug as I stirred. "Trying to stay out of trouble."

A slight grin tugged at his lips. "I've never been described as someone's safe space."

"Talking to you is keeping me from seeing someone I shouldn't."

His interest sharpened. "Why shouldn't you be talking to this person?"

I shrugged like an unruly teenager. "I think he might have known my sister but so far has flown under everyone's radar."

He didn't rush to fill the silence. "Who?"

"I probably shouldn't say until I have proof."

He raised his cup, stared at me over the rim, again letting the silence fill the air.

"That's a cop trick, isn't it?"

"What?"

"The silence."

He arched a brow, but he didn't respond.

Now I was smiling, feeling oddly good. It had been years since I'd believed I had the right to speak freely about Clare or had even a faint

hope this case might get solved. And the fact that Alan had remembered her didn't upset me. It was vaguely comforting. Not everyone
had forgotten.

This newfound lightness made me want to have a drink. I set my
cup down and rose slowly. He didn't speak as he watched me come
around the counter.

Human contact might distract me, and I didn't think I'd ever had
sex totally sober. All my interactions had been lost in a haze of booze
and drugs. Sure, there'd been physical pleasure, but never truly an inten-
tional connection.

Leaning in, I kissed him gently on the lips. "Stop me if you think
I'm overstepping."

His hand rested gently on my hip. "Are you sure?"

I kissed him again. "Yes. That a problem?"

"Not yet. Try again."

I moistened my lips. My heart beat wildly, and my skin tingled. I
kissed him again, and this time pressed my breasts against the smooth
cotton of his dress shirt. His hand came to the small of my back and
pulled me toward him. Not insistent or sloppy, but careful and testing.

When his hand slipped under my T-shirt and slid up my side, I
sucked in a breath.

"That okay?" he asked.

"It is." My voice sounded raspy. "Been a while."

"I'm in no rush."

I cleared my throat. "I assume you have a bed."

"I do."

***

It was after three when I woke beside Alan. My body felt liquid and
boneless, and I could've spent the afternoon here. I was considering

round two when it suddenly occurred to me that Jenny Taylor, the nurse who'd called 9-1-1 after my car accident, might recognize David's picture. If he'd been the man at my accident, that would be more reason for Richards's warrant.

I kissed Alan on the lips. "Can I see you again?"

He cupped his hand on the back of my neck. "Why not stay for a while?"

I kissed him again. "I can't. But rain check?"

"Not going to play junior detective, are you?" He held my face in place.

"Nothing crazy."

I kissed him again, felt his hand slide to the side of my face as I reluctantly pulled away. I dressed quickly, aware he was watching. "See you soon."

He sat up, stood, and crossed to me. "Counting on it."

Across the hallway and then in my apartment, I grabbed my purse and coat. The police had never been able to identify the Good Samaritan who'd been at my accident, but Jenny might. I pulled up Brit's social media page and found a picture of my sister and David. His face was partly turned while she stared boldly at the camera. Avoiding cameras seemed to be a talent he'd perfected. I took a screenshot.

I drove to my accident site, now clogged with parked cars from all the Alans and Marisas in the world who'd the good sense to stay at home and linger in bed on this cloudy Sunday afternoon.

I circled the area twice before finding a spot and then hurried back the extra half block up to Jenny's town house. I glanced at my phone and David's smiling face. Not the best likeness, but short of stalking him and taking his picture, it was the best I could do for now.

After hurrying up the stairs, I knocked on the front door. Music mingled with a news station and the yap-yap of a barking dog. Footsteps sounded in the hallway, and whoever was inside was asking the dog to stop barking.

The door opened, and the woman standing there was freshly showered and dressed in green scrubs. She wore no makeup, and her dark hair was pulled back into a sleek ponytail. She was holding an old terrier, who was growling at me. "Yes?"

"I'm Marisa Stockton," I said. "I was in the car accident by your house in January. Are you Jenny Taylor?"

"Yes."

"I spoke to your roommate."

"Yeah. She said you'd come by. How's it going for you?"

"Good. I'm lucky."

Like so many of the nurses in the hospital, she studied me as if judging my ability to focus and speak clearly. "That's nice to hear."

"A week's worth of missing time and a shorter haircut, but in the grand scheme, lucky."

"If that's all, you're *very* lucky. You hit that pole hard."

I gripped my phone a little tighter. "Did you see the accident?"

"I'd just gotten back from walking Cody. He's old and has to go out often." Cody glanced up at me, and I carefully held up my hand, allowing him to sniff. "After I heard your car hit the utility pole, I put Cody back inside and hurried to the site."

"Your roommate said there was another man on the scene."

"Yes. He was right there. Initially, it was just me and him at the crash site."

"I appreciate all you did for me. I don't know what would have happened if you hadn't called 9-1-1 so quickly. I'm here to thank you and this other man if I can find him."

"I didn't get his name, but he must have been driving behind you. By the time I put Cody inside and returned, he was gone."

"No one else saw him?"

"I told the police officer about him, and when the officer asked around, no one said they'd seen him. But like I said, he vanished before the crowds showed up."

I pulled up the picture from Brit's social media page and then David's professional headshot. "Could it be this guy?"

The woman stared at me, a quizzical look on her face before she dropped her gaze. "It's hard to tell. This guy's face is turned, and the other guy looks younger. And it was dark that night."

I enlarged the picture with a swipe of my fingers. "Can you have a second look?"

Again, she studied the picture. "It could be him, but I can't be sure." Jenny rubbed Cody's head. "Did he just happen by, or is this about something else?"

"Like I said, I don't remember the accident or the week leading up to it. I'm not sure of much at this point."

Jenny's brows furrowed. "Was he trying to hurt you?"

I considered lying. Then decided I'd had enough of that. "I don't know."

"Let me take another look." Eyes narrowing, Jenny studied the picture.

My heart beat faster, and I couldn't decide whether I wanted David to be identified. It would have been just like me to stir up another shit-storm in Brit Stockton's life.

The woman shook her head. "I can't say for certain if it's him or not. I'm sorry."

"Anything you remember about the guy?"

"He was pretty upset. He was clearly worried about you. He reached in the car, shut off the engine, and told me to call for the rescue squad."

"How long were you gone?"

"Two or three minutes. Maybe a little more. Time really slows at moments like that."

"Okay, thank you." I glanced at David's face one last time and tucked the phone in my back pocket. Maybe I was overreaching. Maybe I wanted to find Clare's killer so badly I saw connections that didn't exist.

"Sorry I couldn't be more help."

I turned and was on the bottom step when the woman called out. "Do you know Clare?"

"What?"

"I thought he called you Clare."

48

Brit

I fiddled with the ring on my finger, twirling it round and round. The ring was a lovely gesture, but it wouldn't work. I'd already made an appointment with my jeweler, who was a genius at redoing gems and gold. He'd redone a good bit of Mom's and Clare's pieces for me. Annoying to take this extra step, but necessary because I wouldn't spend the rest of my life bothered by a ring that should carry such meaning. The ring might not have been right, but I would fix that. Just like I fixed everything.

Marisa entered the restaurant only a minute late, and I was pleasantly surprised. My sister was chronically tardy because she liked disrupting everyone's world. She was so afraid of boredom that she created chaos for entertainment value. Likely that was what had prompted this little invite.

But that was the old Marisa, I reminded myself. Marisa 2.0 wasn't perfect but was an improvement, thanks in large part to all the effort I'd put into her. I rose, laying my napkin beside my place setting.

Marisa was dressed in dark pressed pants, a light cowl-neck sweater, and boots. She'd styled her hair and was wearing makeup. A far cry from the woman exhibiting all the hallmarks of a binge. *Miracles do happen.*

She kissed me on my cheek. "I'm so glad you could join me. Last-minute invites always feel presumptuous. And I wanted to see you in person to apologize."

The apology was an unexpected pleasure. "Sisters fight. Emotions run high. I get it."

"I thought a dinner with just the two of us was in order."

"Agreed." We'd come here as kids with our father and mother to celebrate the holidays. The decorations were festive (Mom wasn't a decorator), and more importantly, the food was delicious (Mom wasn't a cook).

Marisa smiled. "Seemed only right we celebrate your engagement. This is a big deal."

Our argument had rolled off her back so easily. She'd accused me of poisoning her. I'd never poisoned anyone. I'd dispensed medicine. This mood shift of hers triggered my suspicions, but I was skeptical by nature, which was what made me such a good attorney. But I had to let whatever conspiracy theories go. "Thank you."

"We need to spend more time together. We're all that remains of the family."

I reached for my water glass, which was slick with condensation. "Soon we'll have David."

Marisa's smile widened. "He seems very nice."

"He is. I never thought I could be so happy."

"You deserve this," Marisa said.

The waitress came, I ordered a white wine, and Marisa stuck with seltzer. I considered not ordering wine but decided responsible drinking was a part of my life, and Marisa needed to adjust.

"David mentioned engagement pictures. I'd love to take them," Marisa said.

"I'll need to lose five pounds before we do that, but yes, I would love you to do the pictures. And I promise, I won't be choosing any over-the-top bridesmaids' outfits for you and the others. No ruffles or puffed sleeves."

"Thank you. Who're you thinking about in the wedding party?" Marisa asked.

"You, of course, the natural maid of honor. There's Karen from the office; Robin, my college roommate; and Carol from the workout group."

"Four is a good number. Who's David choosing?"

"He has a brother."

Her water glass stilled by her lips. "Have you met the brother?"

"Not yet, but we're planning on meeting soon. Beyond him, I'm not sure. That's the nature of a whirlwind engagement."

"Have you set a date?"

"Next on my list of must dos. All the planning centers around it."

"What about his mom and dad?"

"They've passed. It's just David and Jeff."

"Like you and me."

"A small family can still be a strong unit."

Marisa absently adjusted the spoon on her right to the outside of the knife. "David went to the same college as you, right?"

"He did. We didn't know each other then."

"That's surprising that you wouldn't have crossed paths at college."

"It was a big school."

"And his family is from California?"

"Yes. He and his brother, Jeff, grew up in Sacramento. Then after college David moved to New York, the world's financial capital."

"Why did he leave New York for Richmond?"

"Why not?"

Marisa grinned. "Sorry to be so nosy. I'm just trying to catch up. How old is he?"

"Two years older than me. He said he spent most of his college years in the library and was able to graduate a year early, at the top of his class, even after doing a year of mission work."

"Nice."

Marisa's interest was a welcome relief. I'd worried that she'd have no interest in my marriage, but to my delight, this was a bonding moment. David, Marisa, and I were going to be a happy family.

49

MARISA

Sunday, March 20, 2022
6:00 p.m.

My early dinner with Brit had accomplished less than I'd hoped. All I'd really learned was that David had a brother named Jeff. Jeff. The name that again reached out from the Black Hole. I could hear Richards now: "Millions of Jeffs in the world."

David would have been twenty-one when he could've crossed paths with Clare or me in November 2008. Clare's photo suggested she'd seen him in town six weeks before she'd died. She wouldn't have snapped such a close-up image of a random stranger.

David might have been from California, but he'd gone to college less than an hour's drive from Richmond, and this alleged time in town had been over the fall and winter breaks. It was all doable. I had no idea who he'd stayed with, but the answer was there.

I dialed my phone. Jo-Jo picked up on the third ring. "M. What's up?"

"I'm standing across from David's house."

"David. As in Brit's David?"

"Yes. Do me a favor and call me in fifteen minutes."

"Why?"

"Just in case."

"Case of what? Should I call Jack and have him come over there?"

"No, no. It's fine. Just call me in fifteen."

"Not a second longer."

"Thanks." I looked down at the image Clare had taken of David. Richards had as much as told me, without saying it, he needed a DNA sample from David, and to have it tested before he could move forward. If it was a match to Clare's baby, then Richards had reason to talk to David. Too many ifs . . .

I crossed the street to David's townhome. As I climbed the steps, I ran my hand up the painted wooden railing. My fingertips brushed a section where the paint had chipped and someone had painted over it. I paused and looked at the railing. Carefully, I ran my hand back and forth over uneven wood, again trying to conjure any memory. Had I been here before?

I closed my eyes, coaxing any image or momentary flash from the shadows. But nothing presented itself to me. No memory whispered a lost truth.

Irritated by the nothingness, I climbed the remaining stairs to the front door. I rang the bell, adjusted my stance as I willed my shoulders to relax.

When the door opened to David, panic surged. It ran bone deep and went far beyond collecting a discarded cup or strand of hair. Suddenly, I was spooked and couldn't give a logical reason why.

"Marisa?" Annoyance morphed into curiosity and then what felt like pleasure. "What're you doing here?"

"I just had an early dinner with Brit. We were talking about the wedding."

His head tipped a fraction, and his grin was pleasingly warm. "Girl talk."

"Don't let Brit hear you say 'girl talk.' She'd correct you and say 'woman's discussion.'"

He laughed. "Right. My very independent Brit."

Hackles rose, but I smoothed them down. "I was hoping we could talk about the engagement pictures. I thought if we could put our minds together, we could brainstorm ideas. To surprise Brit, which is no easy feat. Is this a good time?"

"Right. That's a great idea." He nodded to the foyer behind him. "Come on in."

"Great."

Stepping inside, I gripped my purse strap. Tension rippled over my muscles and breath tightened in my throat. As I moved down the hallway, no sense of déjà vu set off any alarm bells.

"How did you know where I lived?" he asked as he closed the door with a firm click.

"Brit told me. I mentioned I'd like to talk to you about the pictures."

"Right. She should know. She's been here enough." He walked past me and crossed the open-concept room that adjoined a kitchen outfitted with a large island. "You look great today," he said.

"Well, when I have dinner with Brit, it's always wise to bring my A game. Trying to be a good sister."

"You're a good sister, Marisa. And I know Brit loves you very much. I can't tell you how many times I've caught her fretting over you."

"I'm a work in progress."

"Making fine growth. Can I get you coffee?"

"Sure. That would be great." I'd had a gallon today, but that wasn't the point.

My gaze wandered the room. Neat, midcentury modern with a long, low couch in front of a fireplace surrounded by marble. Above the mantel was a black-and-white photograph of the Sierra Nevada during a fire that wrapped gray smoke around the jagged peaks. It was a stunning piece.

"Like it?" He set up the coffee maker and hit "Brew."

"Very nice," I said. "Where did you get it?"

"I was traveling out west. Saw it in a gallery and couldn't pass it up. Some images come chock-full of emotion. But you understand that, don't you?"

"I do." Silence was broken only by the gurgling coffee maker.

"I'd love to see your work. Brit says it's very good."

I arched a brow. "Brit said that?"

"She speaks highly of you."

That I doubted. Worrying questions and comments were Brit's way of reminding herself and me that I'd failed many times. She was a better person when I was screwing up. "Nice to know."

He ran long fingers through thick bangs that made him look younger than his thirty-five years. He was an attractive man. Perhaps his face was a bit full for my tastes, but his brown eyes had a way of looking at me without making me feel stalked or targeted. Still, they missed little.

"You take cream and sugar, right? Not the calorie counter like Brit."

"Correct."

I moved toward the kitchen, watching him pull two navy-blue mugs from a new set of walnut cabinets. He poured coffee in each and from the refrigerator removed a carton of creamer. My brand. He set it on the counter beside the cups and a small sugar bowl. "I know this must be bittersweet for Brit and you. I mean, not having Clare."

Every time he said Clare's name, it felt off, as if he were trespassing. "Not a day goes by that I don't think of her."

He frowned. "Her death is very painful for Brit."

I didn't want to dwell on Clare's ending. I was more interested in the days leading up to her death. "You know she liked to take pictures, too?"

"Really? Brit didn't mention that."

"She wasn't as into it as me, but she liked it. Who knows if she would have stuck with it, but I remember her always snapping pictures with her point-and-shoot camera. Dad gave us matching ones for our last birthday together."

"Do you have any of her pictures?" David asked.

"She never got any developed. All her important pictures were on her camera."

"What happened to the camera? Do you have it?"

"I think my father threw it out with all her things."

His expression looked pained. "He threw her belongings away?"

"While I was at boarding school. He thought the memories would upset me." What had deeply troubled me was coming home to the too-clean room. Her sketchbooks, clothes, books, and makeup had vanished. The twin beds were gone, and in their place sat a double. Room for one.

"That's a shame for you."

"Yes."

He pushed the creamer and sugar bowl toward me. "I'll let you dress it," he said as he raised his cup to his lips.

I splashed a generous amount of creamer in my cup and then followed with two heaping teaspoons of sugar. My spoon clinked against the inside of the mug as I stirred. He watched me as I raised the cup to my lips. I hesitated, pretended it was too hot. "Need to let it cool off."

"Your sister likes it hot." He actually blushed. "The coffee, I mean."

"Just her style." I set the mug on the counter.

He cradled his cup, took a sip. "Where do you envision taking our engagement pictures? I went on your website, and your portfolio is impressive. Pictures are unique, unforgettable."

"Thank you. Do you and Brit have a favorite place?"

He set his cup down next to mine. His DNA now rimmed the mug's lip, but was it enough? How much would Richards need?

"You'll have to ask Brit. I want her to be happy with the pictures. I'm afraid I disappointed her with the engagement ring." Below the utter calmness churned something.

"Why do you say that?"

"She doesn't hide her emotions well." He sipped his coffee again. "From me anyway."

"Brit's usually a straight shooter. She'd tell you if she didn't like it." That wasn't exactly true. My sister could circumvent anything to get what she wanted. She'd drug or poison her younger sisters for peace and harmony in the house. Jesus, who did that to their children or sisters? Monsters.

"She's like you in many ways," David said.

The surprise comparison didn't sit well. "How so?"

"You're not a good liar," he said. "You might think you can hide your feelings, but you can't from me."

I stilled. "What do I have to lie about? I came here to talk to you about engagement pictures."

"No, you didn't."

I set my cup down. "Okay, why am I here?"

He smiled, sipped his coffee. "You tell me."

Had I stood here before, talking to him? I still had no specific memory, but I *had* been in this area before my car accident. I was more certain than ever. My mind raced back toward the Black Hole, but instead of penetrating it, I slammed against it. I tried to reach inside and grope for any kind of memory or hint. But there was nothing. No clue. Just a feeling I was on the right track.

"I don't have an agenda, David," I said.

"Seriously, why did you come here? And don't say the engagement pictures. Did Brit send you here? Did she want you to tell me something?"

"Brit's never used me to do her bidding. And even if she did, I wouldn't."

"Why not? You two are sisters. The last of the surviving Stocktons. Blood is thicker than water." His smile waned and he tapped his index finger against the side of the mug.

"Brit didn't send me."

"She doesn't like the ring. We've established that," he said. "What else is bothering her?"

"I never said she didn't like the ring. Your words, not mine."

"Maybe she doesn't like me as much as she thought." He leaned toward me, his eyes darkening a shade. "Maybe the ring is just the beginning of the end." That easy smile tightened around his lips.

"This is not a conversation you should be having with me. Seriously, I was just asking about the pictures."

He held up his hands. "I'm sorry. I'm getting all worked up over nothing. I get that way sometimes. Worst case–scenario kind of guy."

"I wouldn't say that. You just got engaged. Makes sense you'd be nervous."

"I suppose I am nervous, aren't I? I was in love once, but she died. I'm just afraid of losing again."

Jenny had said my Good Samaritan had called me Clare. Could he be talking about Clare? "I'm sorry."

"It's okay. I mean, we're going to be family."

"Right."

He picked up his mug, dumped the coffee in the sink, and set the cup on the counter. "Coffee this late will keep me up all night."

"Look, I'm sorry I showed up unannounced. You and I can schedule a meeting with Brit about the pictures later." Whatever idea I'd had about DNA collection suddenly didn't warrant being alone with this man. "I'll just take off."

"Have you ever been in love, Marisa?"

"What? No."

"Maybe when Brit settles down with me, you'll find someone to take care of you."

"I don't need taking care of," I said.

"We all do." His smile returned to its former brilliance. "I don't want to chase you off."

"You're not. Really." I rose and shouldered my purse.

"I feel like I'm rushing you off."

"Not at all." I thought about the mug sitting inside the sink. But there was no way I could just reach around him and pocket it.

Still, to leave could end my one chance to learn more about him and Clare. I could push this a little further. "Do you mind if I use your restroom before I go?"

"Sure, second door on the right."

"Thanks."

Down the narrow hallway, I let myself into the bathroom, closed and locked the door. Towels folded neatly on a small shelf above the toilet, soap in a dispenser, and black-and-white checkered floors scrubbed so clean even the grout glistened. I moved toward the small medicine chest, hoping he kept a comb or extra toothbrush here. I'd no way of proving it was his, but I didn't need proof for a private DNA test. I just needed a sample, and then when I had the sequencing, I'd have a chance of Richards and his forensic department comparing it to what was on file.

I set my purse beside the sink on the floor and raised the soap dispenser to my nose, inhaling the clean, neutral scent. The sense of smell was supposed to be a good conductor of memory, but there wasn't even a vague feeling of having been here before. Maybe we'd never met here, but in the bar down the block.

I opened the medicine chest and studied the collection of bottles bearing the names of several tranquilizers. I reached for a bottle and twisted off the top and poured the blue pills into my hand. Carefully, I moved them around with my finger.

A memory flashed, but it hadn't happened here. It was at the home where I'd grown up. Brit had dropped blue pills into a mortar and was grinding them with a pestle. "What're you doing?" I'd asked.

Brit had turned, her expression a mixture of shock and annoyance. "Grinding up vitamins for Clare and you. You've both been feeling poorly, and I thought this would help."

"I don't like pills."

"That's why I'm putting these in a milkshake. Chocolate for you and strawberry for Clare."

I hadn't argued, but I'd poured most of my shake down the kitchen sink when Brit turned to answer a phone call. Had David ground one of these pills and put it in my drink at the bar? It made sense if I were selling him a print, I'd have met him in a public place.

I now replaced David's pills, keeping one for myself, and then pulled on a drawer handle. It stuck. I yanked harder. When it popped open, I glanced toward the door, hoping the sound hadn't echoed. Inside were a bottle of aspirin and a small comb and brush. I lifted the comb out of the bristles and studied the teeth. Almost clean except for a few single strands of hair. That should be enough, assuming they were David's.

From my purse I pulled out a zip-top bag I'd loaded at home and carefully put the hair inside.

"Marisa, everything all right in there?"

I shut off the tap and grabbed my bag. "Fine!"

Running my fingers through my hair, I practiced a smile, decided it looked a bit demented, so I ditched the attempt. I'd gotten what I came for, and I now had to get out of here.

When I stepped into the hallway, David was waiting for me at the end, blocking my path to the door. "Are you all right? You look pale."

"Talking about Clare always upsets me," I said honestly. "I had a memory, and it caught me off guard."

His hand slid into his pocket as if he were totally relaxed and had all the time in the world. "I didn't mean to upset you."

"It's okay. It's just been a long time since I talked about her to anyone."

"Doesn't Brit talk about her?" His tone was casual, as if we were long-standing friends.

There was no getting around him in the hallway. Left or right, he could block me. "She doesn't like to."

"Still, looking at you must be a constant reminder. I don't know what I'd do if I lost my brother and had to stare at his twin every day."

"Jeff?"

"That's right. How did you know?"

"Brit." I reached for my phone, gripped it in my hand, and stepped toward him.

"Brit. She connects us now."

"That's right." The hallway door behind him was open now, and I could see just enough to realize it was a bedroom.

He cocked his head. "Clare was strangled, right?"

That stopped me midstride. "Yes."

His brows drew together. "That's so awful."

I couldn't say Clare's death had broken my family. It had already been in pieces. But Clare dying had shattered any hope that those pieces would ever be mended. "It was. Is."

"I didn't mean to be so pushy back there. I overstepped. I love Brit so much. I just want you and her to be happy."

"She is. We are." The best lies were short.

"Can we start over?"

"Of course, but I really have to be going," I said. "I've a client meeting this evening."

"With who?"

"An executive. He might want me to shoot his corporate brochure."

"Branching out?"

"Keeping busy." I moved to step around him, but he shifted toward my path.

"I'd like you to stay a little longer."

"I can't, David."

As if I hadn't spoken, he said, "From the pictures Brit showed me, I can see that you and Clare aren't totally identical. I'd have to look closely, but when I do, I see your eyes are slightly wider. Your lips are fuller."

"David, you need to move." I sidestepped to the left, but he blocked me with his arm.

"I want to show you something."

"I really have to go."

"It'll just take a second." He backed up until he reached the open bedroom door.

I didn't move at first. Yes, I was closer to the front door, but also closer to his bedroom.

"Come on," he coaxed. "I don't bite."

I inched close enough to see the neatly made bed and above it the print I'd sold from my art show. My stomach tumbled. Blood drained from my head. "You bought my print."

"I did." He sounded proud, pleased with himself.

"We met at the bar," I said.

"That's right." He rubbed the back of his neck with his hand. "I haven't told Brit this, but you were drinking when I arrived. Well on your way to drunk."

"That's not true."

"I'm afraid it is. After the sale, I was worried about you. I followed you. I told you not to drive, but you wouldn't listen."

"No."

"I followed. You hit the pole."

I scrambled through my memory, gathering all the fragments I'd remembered. What he was saying could fit. I could have had a slip. But I shook my head. "I don't believe you."

"Don't worry—I'll never tell Brit."

My phone rang, startling us both. I stepped back and answered, "Yes, hello?"

"It's Jo-Jo." She sounded breathless.

"Jo-Jo. What can I do for you?"

"I'm calling," she said.

"Of course I can meet you at my apartment." I cupped my hand over the phone. "It's Jo-Jo, Jack's wife."

David frowned, took a step to the right, freeing more of a path for me.

"Sure," I said quickly. "I'm just visiting with David Welbourne at his home. Where're you?"

"I'm driving to your place," she said.

David's eyes sharpened. The outside world had pierced this little bubble of ours, stunning him briefly. I dashed through the narrow space separating David and the wall and hurried across the living room to the front door. "Jo-Jo, I'm ten minutes away."

I yanked open the front door, savoring the cool air sweeping across my flushed cheeks. I hurried down the stairs, the uneven paint skimming under my palms as I took the steps two at a time. I heard his footsteps behind me, not running but moving with quick, determined strides.

"Marisa, wait," he said. "We need to talk."

I didn't turn back but hurried across the street. "Jo-Jo, if I'm not there in ten minutes, call the cops."

"What's going on? Are you really with David?"

"Yes. I got batteries for Clare's camera. I'm certain one picture is of a younger David."

"David? That doesn't make sense."

"I'll explain it all when I see you." I fumbled in my purse for car keys, my fingers skimming over sunglasses, tissues, gum, change, and wallet until they brushed the metal remote. I opened the door with a click. Heart pulsing, I slid behind the wheel, locked the door, and started the engine.

"Does Richards know you're there?" Jo-Jo asked.

"I'm calling him now."

"Be careful."

"Right." As I put the car in gear, David hurried across the street toward me. He held up his hand, reached for the door handle, but I shoved my foot on the accelerator and raced down the street.

The roar of the engine combined with adrenaline as I glanced in the rearview mirror and saw David staring after me. He was hurrying to his car. It all felt like a replay.

I drove down Broad Street quickly, but this time I was clearheaded as the sun's red light glowed over parked cars, a handful of pedestrians, and then the side street I'd turned recklessly down months ago.

Through the city center, I turned left and crossed the Mayo Bridge into the Manchester district. I drove past J.J.'s Pub and then straight toward my apartment. As I parked, I fumbled for my phone and dialed. "Richards. Just saw David. I have hair and a pill sample. They need to be tested. Call me."

I punched the security keypad, and the door clicked. I opened it; ran into my building and up the stairwell, keys in hand; and opened my front door. Closing it quickly behind me, I locked the door and slid the chain into place.

As I turned, I closed my eyes, willing my heartbeat to slow. *I'm home. Safe.*

When I opened my eyes and moved toward the kitchen, I saw two shot glasses sitting on the counter. Beside them was a bottle of tequila. I didn't own shot glasses, and I sure as hell didn't keep tequila in the house.

50

Marisa

Sunday, March 20, 2022
6:30 p.m.

The apartment was quiet. But it felt wrong, off, just as it had been when I'd found the door ajar. My hand in my purse, I fished for my cell, which had found its way into a corner. My fingers slid over the bag's contents until it glossed over the phone's smooth surface. "Is anyone here?"

I opened my security app and discovered the cameras had been pulled off-line. I turned to leave, willing to dial 9-1-1 and be seen as a fool for calling in a false alarm. My hand was on the chain when footsteps sounded in the back hallway. I whirled around.

In the shadows, I could see the outline of a man. It couldn't be David. There was no way he could have beaten me here. Kurt didn't have a key. Maintenance wasn't scheduled. And then the man stepped closer into the light.

"Jack." I was as confused as I was startled and also relieved. "What's going on? If Jo-Jo called you, I'm fine."

His face was calm, but even when he'd been breaking up barroom fights at J.J.'s Pub, he'd never gotten upset. "She told me you went to see David."

"Just a visit. To talk about engagement pictures." I wanted to keep my theories about David between Richards and me for now.

He moved toward the counter, so sure of himself, as if he belonged here. But that was Jack. I'd never seen him endure an uncomfortable moment. "Marisa. You okay? You look rattled."

"I'm fine. How did you get into my apartment? Where's Jo-Jo?"

"She called me and told me you were upset. I told her not to worry about you. And I own this building. Having a master key is one of the perks."

"You bought the entire building? When?"

His grin broadened. "Last year. Business has been good."

I knew him well enough to show my anger. Friends didn't have the right to waltz in here. "That doesn't give you the right to come in here."

"But we're old friends, and we never get a chance to catch up. Besides, we've a few things to talk about."

It was as if I hadn't spoken. "You broke into my apartment."

His casual, easy smile added menace, not charm. "So much for dashing to a lady's rescue."

"Why would I need rescue? Is it because I went to see David?"

"Let's sit down. Have a drink. There are a few things we need to discuss."

"I don't drink."

"That's not true. Jo-Jo told me about your fall from grace."

"That booze is not mine."

He removed the bottle's top. "I must say I was disappointed at first, but then decided it's okay if you do drink. Booze always calmed you down." He carefully filled each shot glass.

"Did you learn that trick from Brit?" I asked. "Keep her drugged so she's easier to handle?"

"She told me you could get agitated when you were a child. She learned how to calm you down from your mother."

"My mother? Richards thinks my mother might have been drugging me." I thought back to all the lazy afternoons in middle school when all I could do was lie in my bed and stare at the ceiling. Or the nights when my belly had hurt so bad. Images of the blue pills clutched in Clare's hand flashed. "Did Brit continue this sick practice? Did she get the pills she gave me from you?"

His jaw tightened, drawing the cords in his neck tighter and flexing the tail end of a snake tattoo. "Brit and I always helped each other out."

"I'll just bet. It was no accident that you gave me a strong dose the night we had sex."

He raised a brow. "You wanted it. I didn't have to ask twice. Besides, I thought if you relaxed, you'd have more fun."

I'd been so out of it that I had never questioned his sexual advances. "Does Jo-Jo know you're here?"

"I told her I'd take care of you. I told her not to worry. She knows I'm good at taking care of everything. She doesn't ask too many questions. That's why we get along so well."

Had Jo-Jo shown me the camera because she wanted to help or because she knew I'd suspect David? What did she know about Jack that she'd failed to disclose? Jack's DNA didn't match Clare's baby. But as Richards said, the baby daddy might not have killed Clare.

"You look upset. You don't need to be," Jack said. "We're old friends, right?"

"Did you kill Clare?" I pressed.

"No. I didn't hurt Clare." He traced the wet rim of a shot glass. "I was with you the night she died, remember?"

"No, I don't remember. You gave me enough to knock me out all night."

His brow furrowed. "That was a mistake. I just wanted you to relax."

"There were at least six unaccounted hours. Plenty of time for you to drive to Jo-Jo's party and kill Clare."

"I didn't go to the party. And I didn't kill Clare."

"Where did you go while I was passed out?" I calculated the distance to the door behind me. Or if I screamed, would someone on the floor below hear me? The cameras in my apartment weren't recording, and there was no alarm system to trigger. "What aren't you telling me?"

"First, I need us both to take a shot for Clare."

He might have lured me with drugs once, but not again. I wasn't that stupid, desperate kid anymore. "I'm not fucking drinking it."

His eyes darkening, he held up a glass and gently swirled it. "You want to drink it. I know that beast inside of you is growling with thirst."

I took a step back. I had a lock and chain on the door. How fast could I unscramble them? "You strangled Clare, didn't you?"

The lines around his eyes and mouth deepened. "I really didn't. I liked Clare. I had nothing to do with her death."

"Then why're you here? Why do you want me to drink? You know I went to see David, and you've clearly put pieces of the puzzle together."

"I'll admit I wasn't happy to hear you went to see David."

"Why not? He's engaged to my sister. We could have been talking about engagement pictures."

"Come on, Marisa, you didn't see him about pictures. Jo-Jo told me she gave you Clare's camera. You looked at the pictures and figured it out."

"You know about the camera?"

He searched my face intently. "Jo-Jo told me about it when she called me in a panic ten minutes ago. She's really worried about you. Jo-Jo can be an airhead, but she was always so loyal to you and Clare."

My stomach tumbled, and I wanted to throw up. "Jo-Jo told you I was going to see David, didn't she?"

"She did."

"And now you're here. Why would you care about me seeing David unless you know that David killed Clare?"

He drained one of the shot glasses and refilled it.

My heart hammered against my chest. "Did David kill my sister?"

"Yes, he did."

His words triggered a horrific but very fleeting sense of relief. A truth that had eluded me for thirteen years had been told, but the knot always balled in my belly wouldn't release. "Because of the baby."

"That's right. He saw you first at college when you were visiting Brit. When you passed out at the party, he took you back to his dorm room and, like the good gentleman he is, let you sleep it off. He found the flyer in your pants pocket when you were passed out. You left while he was out getting breakfast for you both. He didn't have your name but wanted to see you again. He went to the art show in Richmond. He saw you coming out of the art show."

"I never made it to the show. I drove with Brit to Charlottesville to shop. He saw Clare coming out of the show."

"David didn't realize you were a twin. Common mistake. You two were always one of a kind."

"What happened?"

"He struck up a conversation with her. Found his attraction growing. And David, being David, started following her. They ran into each other again, and he coaxed her into bed. He was certain he was in love."

"He told you this?"

"Later. After it all fell apart."

My stomach tumbled. "After he killed Clare."

"That's right."

I'd never have put Jack and David together. They ran in very different circles then and now. "How do you know David?"

"I met him in juvie. During his gap year . . ." He grinned. "Only a rich boy can afford a gap year. Anyway, during that year, he interned with the chaplain at the boys' home. He and I became good friends.

Helped me out of a few tight spots, and I offered to repay the favor if I could."

"He followed Clare to the New Year's Eve party." I imagined David arguing with Clare and him wrapping his hands around her neck. When he killed her, he must have panicked. "He called you for help."

He appeared pleased, but he didn't answer.

All these years of wondering and praying for answers and Jack had known all along. While he'd hidden the truth, he'd also pretended to be my friend. Did he get a rush watching me struggle? Emotion tightened my throat. "What happened after she told him about the baby?"

"He offered to marry her, but she laughed at him. She told him she never wanted to see him again. David's number-one problem is that he gets too attached, and if he hates anything, it's rejection. He lost his shit, as he's done before. At least the time before, the girl survived."

"What girl?"

"That doesn't really matter." He leaned a little closer, as if sharing a secret. "Turns out his daddy is rich and sent him to the juvenile facility as a volunteer for a reason. Tried to scare the boy straight."

Bitterness soured my stomach as tears welled behind my eyes. "It didn't work."

"That place rarely spit out a better version of any boy." His expression grew pensive. "For what it's worth, he said that Clare's death was an accident."

"Accident? How does a man accidentally wrap his fingers around a woman's throat and squeeze the breath out of her for over five minutes! That's hardly an accident."

"When David's pissed, he forgets himself."

How many times had David's parents excused away his violence? Often enough that David clearly had become accustomed to having his messes cleaned up. "You took her body and did what?" Richards had said the body's removal had a calculated feel to it.

"While you slept like a baby, I told him where to drive to, and I met him there. I stripped her, tossed her in the river, and dumped her clothes downstream. He called her Marisa, and that's when I told him he'd killed Clare."

All along he'd thought he was dealing with me. Clare's game of pretend had been too good. "Did he care?"

"Not so much upset as confused. He even argued the point, said she'd told him she was Marisa."

Even in death, Clare and I had been interchangeable. "Did you tell him she had a twin?"

"No. I didn't want him coming after you."

And in the end, he'd found me. Had that been karma or just my great luck? I refused to dwell as I searched his gaze for any sign of remorse. I saw none. If anything, he seemed relieved to share the grim details he'd carried for thirteen years. "Where's David been all this time?"

"New York. Had the good sense to stay away. But then there was a bit of trouble in the Big Apple, and he came down here, thinking if he were near me, I'd keep him out of trouble like a good brother would. He was looking me up at J.J.'s Pub when he saw your flyer. I didn't know he was here until I saw him at your birthday party."

"Brit said David had a brother."

He grinned. "He was talking about me. We used to joke at juvie that we should have been related by blood."

My brain was a computer on information overload. "Did he cause my accident?"

"He did. Your memory loss bought me some time, but I knew eventually he was going to lose control again, or you'd figure it out. You're too sharp, too focused, these days to be ignored. And those pictures you took of the river. Those are the images of a woman on a mission."

"Did you break into my apartment?"

"No. But that sounds like classic David. Bet he got a copy of your key from Brit." The chill behind the smile was frightening.

"That's why David let me leave," I said. "He heard Jo-Jo's name and knew you had to be near."

He shrugged. "I'm the fixer."

"I told Richards about David."

"Exactly," he said. "Richards will have to look into David after today."

"David will tell the cops you helped him dispose of Clare's body."

"Even if he does, he can't prove anything. Sure, we were in juvie for a couple of months years ago, but that interaction doesn't equal murder." He looked toward my bookshelf, where I'd hidden a camera. "Have you figured out that I cut the Wi-Fi to the apartment? No surveillance cameras are working, so again it's your word against mine now."

I was amazed how calm we both sounded. No tears. No shouting. Just a reasonable conversation. It was unreal. As I glanced at the shot glasses, I knew this wasn't going to end well. Had he also spiked the tequila?

Before I lost my nerve, I turned to leave and ran toward the door. Quick footsteps closed the distance between us as I frantically fumbled with the locks. He grabbed my arm, whirled me around, and pushed me back into the kitchen. He clamped on the back of my neck and picked up the first glass.

I glared up at him, my lips pursed. He shoved the glass against my mouth. Tequila trickled over my lips, down my chin, and to my chest. When the glass was emptied all over me, he shoved me down on the floor with such force, my right shoulder hit hard and knocked the breath out of me. I sucked in air as pain rocketed through my system. He dumped the second glass in my mouth and then held my lips and my nose closed until I swallowed.

The fire burned down my throat, hitting my stomach like cement. I tried to spit it out, but it was too late. The poison was in my system.

"Seems fitting your last drinks should be tequila. No one will argue that you finally decided to end it all with a tribute to Clare. We all know how you go off the rails this time of year."

"Why are you doing this now?" I asked. "It's been thirteen years. At best, all I've done is prove that David fathered Clare's baby."

"Jo-Jo is pregnant. I'd do anything to protect that kid. And I can't risk David folding and telling the cops about me."

"He can still do that."

"Not if you're dead."

"Your DNA will be all over my apartment."

"I'll have time to clean up after you pass out. You won't die right away. It'll take time for you to slip away. And then I'll clean up."

"And then you and Jo-Jo will ride off into the sunset and be a happy family."

"That's the idea." He pulled me up to my feet and yanked me toward the bottle, poured a second glass, and held it out to me.

"She'll tell the cops she called you about David and me."

"She won't tell. Drink. Once you drink, you'll calm down."

"I don't want it." I pursed my lips.

"Drink."

"Or you'll strangle me?"

He balled his hands into fists, drew back, and punched me in the gut. My midsection convulsed, and for a moment I almost blacked out. As I gasped for air, he poured the shot into my mouth. I coughed, nearly choking.

Pain radiated through my body. I looked toward the bottle, craving more and hating myself for it.

"You want it, don't you?"

I moistened my lips. I did want it. The craving was so strong, it threatened to overtake me.

He filled both glasses. "Like I said, your art show was proof—you were more fired up than you had been in years. And you were clear-headed. That was a dangerous combination."

"David bought my picture. I saw it at his place." My head spun and my vision blurred.

"They're very compelling pieces, especially for him."

"Did he drug me when I sold him the print?"

"Yes."

Though I'd sensed David's lies about my drinking, it felt good to hear I hadn't. "I must have stumbled out of the bar and made it to my car."

"Again, you're a survivor."

"He followed. He was there at the accident."

"Yes."

"He took my phone."

He handed me the next shot glass. "For once, he was thinking ahead."

I raised the glass to my lips, glanced into the liquid depths, and then downed the shot. The booze did what it always did after the first or second drink. It made me believe all things were possible. I poured another shot. "There's ice in the refrigerator. My head is hurting. Can you get me some ice?"

He studied me a beat. "Of course."

He crossed the kitchen, grabbed a dish towel hanging over the sink. Draping the terry cloth over his palm, he opened the freezer and filled it with ice. He carefully twisted the end, forming a loose ball of ice.

"I'm sorry," he said, handing me the ice pack. "I don't like to hurt people. I'm really a gentle soul. But blood is thicker than water. You sided with your family after Clare died and sold out Jo-Jo. Christ, your father sued her parents."

I pressed the ice to my jaw, flinched as the cold touched the bruised skin. "It was a shitty thing."

"So, you get it?"

"I do." I downed the shot and licked my lips. Even though the booze promised I could do anything, I knew it lied. Soon, my mind would fog. But for now, I was calm but still in control. I had to make the best of this very fleeting sweet spot if I was going to get out of here alive. "Can I have more?"

"Of course."

As he turned to get the bottle, I twisted the towel tightly around the ice. He looked up at me just as I swung the ice ball and struck him hard against the side of his head. He staggered as I reached for the bottle of tequila.

"No, no, no!" he shouted.

He reached for me as I gripped the bottle's neck and swung it with my full weight behind it. Tequila sloshed over us both as the hard glass hit him on the side of the head, breaking into pieces that cut into his skin.

He grimaced, slackened his grip, giving me time to break free and scramble out of the kitchen. As I neared the front door, his footsteps thundered behind me. I ripped one of my river pictures off the wall and swung it around, striking him hard on the side of the face. Glass shattered into shards, cutting deep into his skin. He fell back as I threw the framed picture at him, wrestled the chain and locks open before reaching for the doorknob. I gripped the cold metal and twisted.

As I ran for the stairwell, I pulled in a breath, trying to shove out a scream. I stumbled down the stairs, gripping the rail. Cool metal slid under my palm as I struggled to even out my breathing. Upstairs, Jack's footsteps thundered out of my apartment.

Down to the fourth floor, I turned the corner and kept running. My legs were weak, and I felt sick to my stomach.

"Marisa," Jack said. "Don't do this!"

Third floor, I heard the front door to the apartment building open and close. Someone was there. I kept running, and when I hit the second-floor landing, I stumbled but caught myself after an exaggerated step.

Jack was getting closer. He was now only one floor behind me.

On the first floor, a couple stood by the elevator. They were holding hands, staring blissfully at each other as I burst around the corner smelling of tequila and fear. "Call 9-1-1, please!"

They stared at me shocked, confused. It was one of those moments when we all think we know how we'll react, but in the end, we're stunned into silence by the unexpected.

I ran toward the woman, staggering. "Call 9-1-1!"

Jack burst out of the stairwell door behind me. He saw the couple. Tried to smile as blood dripped from a jagged cut on his cheekbone. "It's okay, she's just upset. We had a fight."

"He's trying to kill me!" My belly ached from the blow, and my blouse was doused in tequila. I raced toward the couple, grabbing the woman's sleeve.

The woman snatched her arm away.

"She gets this way when she's drunk." Jack's voice was almost calm now, and I was shocked he had recovered so quickly. "She has mental problems. My wife called and asked me to check in on her. I caught her drinking and she lost it."

Had he been this calm when he'd stripped Clare's dead body and laid her in the river?

The man frowned, but it was the woman who reached for her phone. As she readied to dial, Jack hurried toward her. "Please, she's sick, and we don't want the police involved. With her record, they'll put her back in the mental hospital."

"He's lying," I rasped.

The doors to the building opened with a sudden rush of energy. David, breathless and pale, looked at me and then at Jack. "Jack."

"She's sick," Jack said. "Tell them she's sick. She needs help. We're here to help her. I'm an old friend, and David is to be her brother-in-law."

"That's not true!" I shouted. "They aren't trying to help me."

The woman lowered her phone. "Are you sure?"

"Yes," Jack said. "She needs help."

"We can help her," David said.

"No!" I shouted. My head spun, and as I ran to the door, David grabbed my arm.

His face was oddly calm. "It's okay, Marisa. I'm here now. I've got you."

I tried to snatch my arm free, but his grip was stronger than I'd ever imagined. My heart rammed against my ribs, and I thought back to the moment he had confronted Clare on New Year's Eve. She must have been terrified when he wrapped these same hands around her neck.

"Let me help you, Marisa."

I twisted my arm, straining against his iron grip. "Is that what you said to Clare?"

Mentioning her name caught him off guard for just an instant.

"Did she beg you to stop?" I shouted. "Did you even care that you were hurting her?"

"I never hurt your sister." David glanced toward Jack, and I imagined them rehearsing the words over and over. His fingers bit deeper into my arm.

"Let's get her to the hospital," Jack said.

"Yes, the hospital," David repeated.

I knew in my bones if we left this lobby, I would die. "I'm not going!"

Jack took my other arm, and when he glanced back at the couple, he was actually smiling, as if he were dealing with an angry toddler. "She'll be fine. She needs a doctor."

They pulled me toward the door as I tensed every muscle in my body. I wasn't going to die without a fight.

Blue lights flashed on the walls, and when I turned, I saw the blue lights of two cop cars. Richards was taking the steps two at a time. He punched in the security code, gun drawn, and entered the lobby.

I screamed his name, never more grateful to see anyone in my life.

"On your knees, Dutton and Welbourne. Now!"

Jack shook his head. "She's sick, Richards. She's had a breakdown. We were trying to help her."

"He's right," David parroted. "We're here to help."

"No!" I shouted.

"On your fucking knees!" Richards yelled.

Jack seemed to consider his options and then raised his hands and knelt. David's grip slackened. I jerked my arm free and staggered away. He knelt and put his arms behind his head.

Uniformed officers approached the lobby as lights flashed in the parking lot and Richards reached for the handcuffs hooked on his belt.

"How did you know?" I asked.

He clinked the handcuffs on Jack's left and right wrists. "Jo-Jo called me. She was worried about David hurting Jack."

I stumbled back, my head spiraling. "Jo-Jo called you?"

"That's right," Richards said. "That little lady was worried about your safety and her husband's. She was really worried David would hurt you both."

Crashing adrenaline and the booze sent my head spinning. I leaned against the wall. The muscles in my legs turned slack, and I lowered to the floor. My vision blurred and went black.

51

MARISA

Monday, March 21, 2022
4:05 a.m.

When I woke up in the hospital emergency room, my head was pounding, all the muscles in my body ached, and my mouth was as dry as cotton. A nurse stood by my bed, taking notes as she checked monitors.

"I want to get out of here," I said.

The nurse looked down at me and smiled. "Good, you're awake. We were worried about you, given your recent head injury."

"I'm fine." I didn't know that, but it was more important to me to get out of here. In a hospital, I was vulnerable to David.

"The doctors ordered an MRI and a full exam, and they didn't find any trauma."

"Terrific." I tried to sit up, but my head spun. "I need to go home."

"Detective Richards is outside. He wants to talk to you."

"Richards?"

"He's been sitting outside your room since you arrived. Stay put so I can get him. I can't have you falling."

I sank back into the pillows and closed my eyes. "Fine."

The nurse moved around the curtain and out a door. Seconds later footsteps approached my bed. The smell of Richards's brand of cigarettes reached me before he did. Oddly, the damn scent was comforting.

"Marisa," he said. A chair slid across the floor to my bed.

I opened my eyes, blinked to clear my vision, and stared into a face etched with fatigue. "Richards. Where are David and Jack?"

"We arrested them both. David and Jack are lawyering up, and both are insisting that you got drunk and went crazy."

"I'm not crazy. David spiked my drink in January and caused my car accident. And Jack made me drink. I didn't want it."

"I know. I know. I had a conversation with Jo-Jo. She's been guarded but she said enough. She's got a few legal challenges of her own to handle."

I shook my head, not caring right now about Jo-Jo's lies of omission. "Jack said David killed Clare because she didn't want him." Tears I'd been unable to shed for thirteen years burned in my eyes, welling until they spilled down my cheeks. "He strangled her, and Jack dumped her body like trash."

Richards laid a calloused hand over mine. "We're digging into it all."

"David worked at Jack's juvenile facility." I had to tell him everything I knew.

"Let us do our job," he said. "I'll see it through this time."

More tears welled in my eyes. "You never gave up on Clare. Everyone else did, but not you."

"And neither did you."

Brit entered the room, her eyes red-rimmed and her hair tangled. She had the look of a woman who'd not slept last night. "Marisa."

I swiped away a tear and turned slowly. All I could think about were the little blue pills that she'd fed Clare and me.

All the times I'd been so ill. She'd learned from my mother how to control me, but both had pushed me on the path of substance abuse.

Staying on that trail was my own damn fault, but maybe, just maybe, I'd never have gone down that road but for them.

"Brit."

"I'm so sorry." She moved toward me as Richards stood, though he didn't step away from the bed. "I had no idea."

I shifted away from her. "I can't do this right now."

She looked stricken. "The police told me what Jack and David did to you. If I'd had any idea . . ."

"Leave me alone, Brit."

"Marisa, let me take care of you, like I always have."

I stared at her stricken face. "Why do I always end up feeling worse when you're close?"

"What are you talking about?" Brit asked.

"I didn't really feel good until you left for college. That fall you were gone was the first time in my life I felt great."

Brit didn't respond.

"Is that what Clare figured out?" I challenged. "Did she realize the pills she'd found were the ones making us either zombies or sick?"

Her expression telegraphed pity, as if I'd lost my mind. "That's ridiculous."

I shook my head. "But me being me, I was passing out by then."

Brit glanced at Richards and then at me, just like Jack had. Her face morphed from sister to lawyer. "I didn't give you anything. Whatever Clare thought she knew was wrong."

"Your mother died of a strychnine overdose," Richards said. "In small doses it would make a person ill."

"What are you saying?" Brit challenged.

"It's an odd drug of choice," Richards said. "Most suicides don't use it. But it's very effective if you want to make someone appear chronically sick. You were fifteen when she died?"

"You know I was," Brit said.

"Maybe you figured out what your mother had been doing."

Brit held up her hand and took a step back. "If you ever repeat that again, I'll sue you and anyone associated with you into poverty. I would never have hurt my mother."

"Or sisters?" I asked.

"Of course not!" Brit shouted.

Richards shrugged. "Don't get all twisted up. There's no way of proving anything. I'm just tossing out ideas."

I'd always assumed our mother had killed herself. It hadn't occurred to me that Brit could've given her the pills. Mom poisoned her children, Brit continued the tradition with her sisters, and Clare closed the loop. We were a sick, toxic family, and I realized it would never change.

"Get out, Brit," I said. "Maybe one day I'll be able to deal with you, but not now."

Brit reached out for my hand. "Marisa, this is ridiculous. I need to take care of you. David is in jail. We need each other."

Richards moved between Brit and me. "I suggest you go now."

Brit stared at me, her eyes pleading. "Marisa, I'm your sister. I've always been there for you."

"Leave," I said.

Richards took Brit by the arm. "Now."

Brit snatched her arm away. "This is ridiculous. I'm leaving now, but this is not the end of it."

When Brit vanished around the curtain, I listened for her clipped heels moving down the hallway. When the sound finally vanished, I released my breath. "Richards, get me out of here."

"You need to stay a couple more hours."

"No. I'm leaving with or without your help."

He studied me a long beat. "Stay put. Let me scrounge you some clothes."

***

Four hours later, I rose out of Richards's car as he hurried around to my side to help me stand. He'd pulled a few strings and found me clothes from the lost and found. The sweatshirt was two sizes too big and the jeans had to be held up with a belt, but the athletic shoes fit. They all smelled of hospital. My gut ached, but at least the hangover wasn't so bad.

"Jack owns this building," I said.

He walked me to the front door, punched in the code, and guided me to the elevator. He hit the button. "A buddy of mine reprogrammed the keypad and changed your locks." He reached in his pocket and handed me two keys. "New set. No other copies."

As I looked at the lobby, residual panic tightened my chest. I didn't want to return to Jack's building or my apartment. But for now, it was all I had. "Thanks."

We made our way to the elevator, past a forgotten strip of crime-scene tape and fingerprint-dusting powder. As the elevator doors opened and we stepped inside, he handed me a slip of paper. "The new security code."

I crumpled the paper in my fist. "Florida's got to be looking pretty good now."

He tugged the cuff of his jacket. "I've asked if I can stick around for a few months."

I understood. He'd chased this case for thirteen years and wanted to see it to the end. "How does that square with your fiancée?"

"She gets it. All my wives understood, they just got tired of being second. My gal knows this really is short term."

I'd carried the weight of Clare's death for so long. Having the answers hadn't eased the burden, but I sensed in time, it would fade. The doors opened, and we stepped onto my floor. "I owe you wedding pictures."

"You don't have to do that."

"I'll be offended if you don't let me."

An almost smile tugged his lips. "Sure. That would be nice."

I stepped into the apartment to see the crime-scene powder dusting many of the hard surfaces in the kitchen. Thankfully the glass had been cleaned and the tequila wiped up.

"I had the team in while you were in the hospital. It's a bitch to clean up, but we found Jack's prints on the counter and on one of the glasses. Give me time. I'm interviewing David this morning. I'll build a case against them both."

"Can they get away with this?" The fear had been stalking me for hours.

"No. The evidence is growing."

"You said yourself a good defense lawyer can get around what you have so far."

"We've come too far, Marisa. They won't get away."

"Let me talk to David. If he talks to me about Clare, you can use that, right?"

"This isn't my first rodeo, Marisa."

"I know. But you might need me. I can talk to him."

"We'll see." He looked around the apartment as if satisfying himself it was clear. "Can you manage alone?"

I looked back at the door and the bright shiny brass locks. "I can. Thanks."

"Lock the door behind me."

I jangled the keys in my hand. "Will do, boss."

When he left, I turned each lock and chain, and only when the last was thrown did his steps echo down the stairs.

I walked up to one of the remaining pictures and stared at the misty landscape. "We did it, Clare. We did it."

52

MARISA

Tuesday, March 22, 2022
10:00 a.m.

I arrived at the Richmond City Jail the next morning to find Richards waiting for me in the lobby. He was dressed in his going-to-court suit, and he'd polished his shoes. "Marisa. Did you sleep well last night?"

"All things considered, I did." I hadn't gotten a full eight hours, but the sleep I did get was more restful. "Where's David?"

"He's in holding now. Already has a lawyer. You were right. He's not talking, and Jack is sticking to his story. Unless I can get him to talk, I won't be able to hold him for more than twelve more hours."

"But you're testing his DNA."

"It'll take more than a positive DNA test and the picture he bought from you to hold him. Neither is a crime."

"She was underage."

"Statute of limitations on statutory rape has run out. I've interviewed him twice since he was brought in, and he's denying everything. Says he doesn't know Jack that well. His lawyer is about a half hour away from arriving and has instructed David not to talk to the cops."

"And Jack?"

"He's still in holding but will be released in a couple of hours. He insists he found you drinking, and you attacked him."

My blood alcohol had registered 0.1. "And the bruises on my body?"

"All a part of his attempt to keep you from hurting yourself and him. He's claiming you attacked him first." He dropped his voice. "This isn't the first time for these two. They likely had a story locked down thirteen years ago. And they're sticking to it."

"Where's Brit and Jo-Jo?"

"They've not been allowed to visit yet."

"I'll talk to David." Richards had made his request when he'd called this morning. He now hoped seeing me would shake up David.

His face was grim when he nodded. "Follow me."

I presented my ID to the officer at the front desk, and Richards swiped his badge, which allowed us access through double doors, where he checked his gun in a locker as I checked my purse. We made our way down a nondescript hallway, and he opened the last door on the right for me. Inside was a large table with two chairs. On the other side of a thick piece of plexiglass was another table with a setup that mirrored this one.

"I can stay with you," he said.

"It might be more effective if I'm alone with him. Assuming you have cameras."

"Several," he said. "We don't want to miss a word. He'll also be handcuffed."

"All the better."

"Have a seat," he said. "We'll be right back."

I sat in a chair, shifting my weight until the hard back didn't press against my darkening bruises. I was going to be six shades of blue for the next few weeks.

Two minutes later the door opened and David, now dressed in an orange jumpsuit, was escorted into the adjoining room. His hands and feet were shackled. Richards walked him to a seat on the other side of the partition. When David saw me, his expression softened, and his gaze ran over me as if taking inventory of all my injuries. I waited until Richards left the room and closed the door behind him. We weren't in a private room, but maybe David would forget if I played it well.

"What happened?" David asked.

I shifted, didn't suppress a wince. "Jack."

His brow knotted. "I'm sorry."

In his world he really was sorry. "I don't blame you. He's more than either one of us bargained for. Have you seen Brit?"

"We spoke on the phone. She's gotten legal counsel for me. He's on his way."

Brit was helping David. The idea soured my stomach, and it took a moment before I could speak without anger sharpening my tone. "She's a great advocate to have in your corner. She'll get you the best."

"She's one of a kind."

He looked so calm, so normal. Another surge of rage cut through me, and it took all my control to ease back in the chair and appear relaxed. I remembered Richards's tone, always even and calm. Yelling wasn't going to get David to talk.

"I've been thinking back to the last time I spoke to Clare," I said. "She'd had a couple of drinks and I was high. No surprise there, right?"

"You're sober now."

I was the proud owner of another newly minted first-day chip to prove it. "Doing my best."

"You should be proud," he said.

"Thanks. I don't always feel proud. Especially when I think back to Clare. She had something she wanted to show me, but we never met up."

"What did she want to show you?"

"I think she wanted me to see Brit sick. That night Brit became ill like Clare and I did as kids."

"She said she had a sensitive stomach."

"It was more than that. See, Richards thinks our mother was poisoning us. When we were sick, the doctors were nice to her, and Daddy hung around more."

His handcuffs clinked as he leaned forward. "Oh, Marisa, I'm so sorry."

"It's a mental illness. It's demented, and I don't want to believe it, but it all makes sense." I flexed my fingers, trying to relax the stiffness and the urge to grip the chair's arms. "After Mom died, Brit didn't get sick anymore, but Clare and I did. We also went through phases where we were kind of out of it. I can't prove it, but I think Brit was drugging us and Clare figured it out." It felt so strange to be telling this terrible secret to the man who'd killed my sister. But I had to give a little to get a little. "That's what Clare and Brit fought about before the party. Poor Clare wasn't in her right mind when she went to that party. She was devastated by what she'd found out."

He stared at me, saying nothing, and I didn't rush to fill the silence. Let him chew on that information nugget for a while.

"She went to the party dressed like me," I said finally. "She was looking for trouble, I think."

He didn't speak, but he was listening.

"She'd found out she was pregnant. She was freaking out on all levels."

"Where were you?"

"Jack drugged me. Had sex with me."

"He raped you?" His voice hardened.

"Intoxicated consent isn't really consent, is it?"

"No, it's not."

"When I went to see Brit before the fall break, someone found me. I was really drunk. God knows what they could've done to me, but that person, my guardian angel, laid me on a bed and let me sleep it off. That's an act of kindness I'll never forget." I'd not mention he'd drugged me in the bar.

His shoulders relaxed a fraction.

"Thank you," I said. "Thank you for saving me that night."

"Why do you think it was me?" David asked.

"I don't know for certain. But I've had a chance to get to know you. You're an upstanding guy. You wouldn't force or take a girl that's too drunk."

"No, I would not."

"I'm pretty sure when the DNA tests come back, they'll prove you were the baby's father." As he leaned back, I held up my hand. "I'm not blaming you. Rather, I want to thank you. You were nice to Clare when she needed it most. She and I both were pretty lost in those days." I wasn't sure how many more thank-yous I could toss this guy's way before I lost total grip on my control.

When he again didn't respond, I said, "And then you came back for me. You were my first sale, weren't you?"

"I liked the print. That's not a crime."

"You've done nothing that's a crime. You loved my sister, you supported my art, and you've been nothing but kind to Brit."

He drew in a breath, exhaled it slowly.

"What's worrying me is Jack. He's going to walk in a couple of hours. And he scares me more than anyone. He's saying you killed Clare, but I think it was him. I think he left me while I was passed out and came to the party. I don't know if he confused her with me or if he was just trying to hurt another Stockton girl." I paused, realizing my heart rate was kicking up. "When he gets out, and he will, he's going to come after me again."

"He won't do that."

"I think he will. I don't know what I'm going to do."

"He won't hurt you. That I promise. When I get out of here, and I will, I'll keep an eye on you."

"I think he's setting you up," I said.

"Why would he do that?"

I dropped my voice and leaned toward the plexiglass. "He's smart. Really smart. And we both know he's a survivor."

"He tried to hurt you. That's not smart. He'll go to jail for that."

"Assault is a world away from accessory to murder."

David's frown deepened.

I allowed real tears to fill my eyes and spill down my cheeks. "I wish you'd been there for Clare. The idea of Jack strangling her in the bitter cold and then stripping her naked breaks my heart. I hated the idea that her last moments were filled with such fear."

His eyes glistened.

I pushed up my sleeve, knowing he'd see the darkening bruises on my forearm, and held my hand up to the glass. "I'm scared."

"He's not going to hurt you." He raised his hands to mine. "I swear. I'll always be watching you."

I smiled, brushed aside a tear. "Like Clare."

"No matter what Jack says, I loved her. She loved me."

I wanted to reach through the glass and smash his forlorn face. "I know. And I know she was so emotional then. She said things to me I know she regretted."

"I understood she didn't want to hurt me."

"There were times when she'd start screaming at me. When she did that, I always thought I'd lose my mind. She could be so dramatic."

His eyes grew a little distant, and when he looked at me, I wasn't sure who he was seeing. "I just wanted you to be quiet and listen to me."

He was mixing us up, so I played along. "I couldn't control myself. I'm sorry."

"I thought you'd gone to sleep. I thought you'd wake up and we'd talk and work it all out."

"Having a baby scared me."

"Not me. Never me. I asked you to marry me."

"Why did I go to sleep?"

He dropped his hand. "I put my hands around your neck to silence you. I just wanted you to be quiet. Then you went to sleep and you didn't wake up."

Tears glistened in my eyes. "You didn't mean to squeeze so long. I know that."

"I didn't mean it. I didn't."

Rage charged me, but I pushed it aside. "And you called Jack."

"I didn't want to. But I didn't know what else to do," David said. "He could fix anything."

"Where did she die, David?" I asked.

"In my car. We were in the back seat. She changed her mind and wanted to leave. I just wanted to talk."

I still kept my fingers pressed to the glass. "It's no one's fault."

He looked up at me. "I'm so sorry."

"Jack stripped her, didn't he? A fixer would have thought about DNA."

"I could barely watch. I was crying. And a mess."

More tears sprang from my eyes, but they were prompted by rage. "Did you carry her to the river and leave her there?"

He shook his head and dropped his gaze. "No. I couldn't do it. I couldn't leave her. Jack did it."

The door to my room opened and Richards appeared. "That's good, Marisa."

I rose. My legs were shaky, and my hands were trembling.

David looked up at me. "I'm sorry. Forgive me."

He would spend the rest of his life suffering. He would rot in hell. I wanted to rail. Tell him I hated him.

"Let it go," Clare whispered. *"Don't carry this anymore."*

My shoulders slumped. "I'll never forgive you, David. Never."

53

MARISA

Tuesday, March 22, 2022
Noon

After a long hot shower, I dressed in old sweats and a T-shirt and spent an hour scrubbing all the surfaces covered in fingerprint powder before my body gave out and I had to lie down on the couch for a nap. I wasn't sure how long I slept, but when I woke, the sun was setting over the river.

A knock at my door had me rising carefully. My body was still stiff, and my gut tender to the touch. At least the hangover from the tequila was fading. I moved to the door and looked out the peephole. Alan.

I undid the locks and opened the door. "Hey."

His gaze swept over me. "I heard what happened. I know you probably need time, but I had to see you."

The concern in his voice touched me, and it took a moment before I could speak. "What can I say? Never a dull moment."

"Are you okay?"

"No, but I will be."

He held up a bag of burgers and french fries. "Want to come by for dinner? You don't have to talk if you don't want to."

"I won't be great company now."

"You're many things, Marisa Stockton, but one of them is not boring."

I laughed and quickly paid for it with a jab of pain. "Sure, burgers sound great."

Tomorrow, I'd find another meeting, talk about what had happened, and get back to my work and art. My life would go on. There'd be no Clare or Brit. And Jo-Jo, no doubt, would be consumed with Jack's trial and the baby. She'd saved me, but she'd also lied. If I never saw her again, that would suit me just fine.

I'd cut these people out of my life. I would be okay. I should've felt lost and lonely, but I didn't.

"You did it," Clare whispered.

No, we did. We did.

54

BRIT

Six Months Later
Tuesday, October 18, 2022
Noon

I'd accepted Jo-Jo's invitation to meet because I was curious. I didn't really want to know how she was doing. I didn't care if she and Jack were dreading his trial. I didn't care if she was ready to deliver or if she was afraid of the future.

All I wanted to know was whether she'd heard from Marisa. I'd not spoken to my sister in seven months and was very curious. In fact, not knowing how she was doing was a little maddening. Was Marisa sober or was she drinking again? My money was on the booze. All this pressure from the police and media was a recipe for disaster. If the booze hadn't gotten her yet, it would soon. It always did.

I'd insisted Jo-Jo and I meet at a neutral, discreet location. With Jack's impending trial, the last thing I needed was to be seen with his wife. I should've said no to her request, but curiosity is deadly powerful.

My phone led me to the address she'd given me. It was in Hanover County on a rural stretch of road. Off the beaten path, as requested.

Dust kicked up around my car as I rolled down the long gravel driveway. I parked at the top portion in front of a two-story, newly constructed craftsman-style home. I checked my phone and switched on the recording app. (Never can be too careful.)

This place was well crafted, and I wondered if Jack had taken some of that cash he'd had tucked away and built this house. He always wanted a large home filled with children.

Climbing the stairs, I rang the bell and was quickly rewarded with the steady *thud* of lumbering feet. When the door opened, my gaze was immediately drawn to Jo-Jo's round face and her very full belly. She looked bloated and pale, and there was no sign of the glow women in her state professed to have.

"Brit, thanks for coming." Her voice echoed in the empty foyer.

"You look well."

"I'm a beached whale." She stepped aside, and I entered quickly. This was the country, but prying eyes existed in the sticks as well.

"As I told you on the phone, I can't give you any legal advice."

Jo-Jo closed the door. "I know. I just wanted to talk. I have coffee in the kitchen."

"Where is Jack?" I asked. "Is he here?" He could have been lurking in the shadows, as he had been when Marisa had come home to her apartment.

She turned, slowly and carefully. "He's meeting with his attorney today. He goes to trial next week."

Jack was a smart man and knew the only real pieces of evidence against him were the assault and battery charges from his attack on Marisa. His attorney had already pressed for a dismissal, citing Marisa's drug and alcohol use, but the judge had refused. If Jack had not punched Marisa, he could've skated free entirely because David—my lovable, manipulative David—hadn't produced any evidence backing his claims that Jack had helped him dispose of Clare's body.

The only DNA linked to Clare belonged to David. Tests proved he had fathered her unborn child. When I'd learned that detail, it had stung deeply. I thought about all the nights we'd talked about making a baby of our own one day. Bastard.

David had hired a top-notch attorney, who was already arguing that fathering a child was not a criminal offense. His case would go to trial in the new year.

"How are you holding up?" Jo-Jo asked.

"Well enough," I said. That wasn't true. There'd been some terrible, lonely nights filled with tears and anger. But in the end, I pulled myself together. Putting one foot in front of the other wasn't always easy, but it was the only way to get out of hell.

The scent of new construction hung in the air as I followed her down a hallway painted a light gray. There were no pictures on the walls, and the rooms to my left and right were empty. The hallway ended in a bright kitchen with a massive island covered in white marble. The only splash of color was a wooden bowl of apples by the farmhouse sink. There were two coffee cups from a local shop.

"Is this your new home?" I asked.

"We're considering it. I convinced the Realtor to let me visit alone."

"Aren't you the clever one."

Jo-Jo set one of the cups in front of me. I pried off the top and confirmed there was no cream. Had she asked Jack what I liked? The coffee smelled good, and the cup warmed my fingers, but I hesitated to drink. To this day, I hated to accept a drink I hadn't poured myself.

A frown furrowed Jo-Jo's forehead. "Have you spoken to David?"

I set the cup down carefully. "I have not. There's nothing for us to talk about."

"I thought you'd want to see him and get some kind of closure. Marisa talked to him."

"Closure is for the weak. And my sister was helping the police." I was a little amazed how well Marisa had handled herself.

"After all these years, she solved Clare's murder."

"With a little help from you."

"I just gave her Clare's camera."

"After all these years, why give it to her now?" I asked.

"It seemed the right thing to do." She raised her chin, as if she'd stepped up onto the moral high ground.

"It wasn't the right thing to do five, ten, or thirteen years ago?" I pressed. I could smell evasion.

"I was young. Scared. And I didn't want to drag my parents back into the limelight."

"Your timing couldn't have been more perfect," I said. "I mean, with David in town."

Jo-Jo didn't take the bait but angled in a new direction. "Jack's attorney has seen the footage of Marisa and David's conversation in jail. David said some terrible things about Jack."

"Did he? I wouldn't know." That wasn't true. I still had sources in the department, and they kept me posted. David had happily told how Jack helped him dispose of my sister's body. Even now, when I thought about David squeezing the life out of Clare, I remembered how he could be rough in bed, and how I'd actually enjoyed it.

"He thought Clare was Marisa," Jo-Jo said. "Clare had been pretending she was Marisa the night they met. And for whatever reason, she kept the charade going whenever they were together."

I shouldn't blame Marisa for Clare's foolish game, but for some reason I did. All trouble led back to Marisa. "Doesn't really matter which sister he killed, does it?" It did, but I'd never say that out loud. "Have you seen Marisa?"

"I called Marisa several times, but she's shut me out. I do know she moved out of her apartment and found a new place in the Fan. She's still seeing Alan."

"Good for her." Marisa always came out on top for a little while.

"It's her word against Jack's," Jo-Jo said. "At least that's what Jack's attorney said."

I'd have made the same argument. Perhaps that was why my practice had actually seen a bump since all the news about David and Jack broke. My clientele was less reputable these days, but a thief was a thief regardless of the cost of their suit. "I still don't understand why you called me."

"Jack wants to talk to you."

"Why?"

"He wants to tell you he didn't help David."

"David's testimony is compelling."

"I don't believe David. I think he's sick, and he threw Jack's name into the mix because they'd known each other at camp."

"Aren't you bothered that your husband tried to kill Marisa?"

"She was drunk. Out of control. I think seeing David did a number on her. She was far more fragile than I realized."

Part of me wanted to rise to Marisa's defense. Old habits, I supposed. However, her credibility wouldn't have been in question now if she'd made better choices. Which was a shame, because the pressure of the trial would eventually get to her, and she'd start drinking again. I was tired of cleaning up after my baby sister, but I would rise to the occasion if she called and asked.

"I'm not going to speak to Jack or on his behalf. And I will never forgive him," I said.

"He's a good man who's made mistakes in the past."

Could she really be this clueless? "Honey, he did more than make mistakes. And for the record, I hope they lock his ass up for years."

Jo-Jo's face contorted with shock. "You two were friends."

"Not very good ones, it seems."

"Can't you talk to Marisa and get her to testify on his behalf?"

And I thought I had a big set of brass ones. "No."

Tears welled in her eyes. "If not for Jack or me, do it for the baby."

339

"Clare's baby or yours?" I shook my head, amazed at the pure bitterness lacing the words.

She paled, and her hand went to her belly. "Jack needs another chance."

There weren't enough chances in a lifetime for Jack. No matter how many times he was saved, he would find a new way to break the rules. "I'm surprised you haven't run for the hills, Jo-Jo. Why haven't you put as much space between you and Jack as possible?"

"I won't run. He's my husband and I love him."

"Jack won't do much jail time, and he will be back in your life."

She swiped away a tear. "That's a good thing. He loves me."

Love. I could write a book on it. I started toward the door. My hand on the knob, I turned and looked back at Jo-Jo. "Be careful of Jack, darling. He's a sweet talker, but he's a scorpion. And sooner or later, they do bite." I grinned. "Takes one to know one."

EPILOGUE

MARISA

Tuesday, October 25, 2022
5:00 p.m.

When I arrived at the small rental house in the historic Bon Air district, I smiled at the fresh cluster of pumpkins on the front porch steps. Alan. He'd done little things like this since we moved into the space three months ago.

On my best days, I dreamed of a future with him, but I was smart enough to know that all any of us really had was now. And today was really good. And I was willing to bet tomorrow would be, too.

Alan opened the front door. He was smiling, clearly pleased with the pumpkins. "How'd it go?"

"It's all over but the crying," I joked.

He crossed the porch, took the bags from my shoulder, and kissed me. "Did Richards look nervous?"

"He was beaming." I'd never seen Richards truly happy, and it gave me hope. "And so was his bride. They leave for Florida tomorrow."

He lingered close. I knew he was worried about me. "The office will need him back in January for Jack's trial."

Jack's trial would be in February, and David's case would be heard in March. "Do you think they'll get away with it?" I asked.

He pulled me into his arms, and I allowed my body to relax into him. "They'll both do time. Practically speaking, I'll bet money Jack cops a plea because he wants to be out for his kid. David will do serious time."

"All these years I thought Jack was my friend, but he was just keeping me close. I guess it was a kind of thrill to him, seeing me tipping out of balance."

He rested his chin on my head. "You knew the killer was out there. You kept pressing when everyone gave up." He kissed me. "That takes stones, Stockton."

Pressing and pushing came naturally to me. "It was harder living with the unknown."

"No more unknowns."

I kissed him, grateful for his optimism. Life was full of unknowns. But these days the emotions weren't so jagged. I wasn't perfect; nor was I ever free and clear of the booze. Never would be. But 219 days of sobriety was no small feat. And today, right now, I was willing to call my life a win.

ABOUT THE AUTHOR

Photo © 2015 StudioFBJ

New York Times and *USA Today* bestselling novelist Mary Burton is the popular author of more than thirty-five romance and suspense novels, including *Don't Look Now, Near You, Burn You Twice*, and *Never Look Back*, as well as five novellas. She currently lives in North Carolina with her husband and three miniature dachshunds. Visit her at www.maryburton.com.